In
DEEP

In DEEP

a novel

Bruce Jones

CROWN PUBLISHERS, INC.
NEW YORK

Published by Crown Publishers, Inc.,
201 East 50th Street,
New York, New York 10022.
Member of the Crown Publishing Group.

CROWN is a trademark of Crown Publishers, Inc.

Manufactured in the United States of America

Library of Congress Cataloging-in-Publication Data

Jones, Bruce.
  In deep / Bruce Jones.
    p. cm.
  I. Title.
PS3560.04585I5 1991
813'.54—dc20   91-7599
                                                    CIP

ISBN 0-517-58205-8

Book Design by Shari deMiskey

10 9 8 7 6 5 4 3 2 1

FIRST EDITION

To my mother and father

In
DEEP

PROLOGUE

*T*HE TWO BOYS CAME DOWN TO THE SEA BRINGING noise and fumes to Sunday morning fog.

It was cold, even for Southern California, even for June, and the boys, not yet twenty, bearing little fat along their tanned, muscular torsos, felt the chilly air and far chillier water. If they resented this, they apparently resented more a life without surfing. It was what they did.

They arrived in a rusty Volvo owned by Todd, who parked it along an empty, early Sunday morning curb, unlatched the tailgate, and withdrew his shiny, freshly waxed board from atop Gerome's. They each pulled on the upper halves of black neoprene wet suits. Bottom halves were for sissies. They zipped up, hoisted their boards, faced a fog-shrouded shore, sun-bleached hair iridescent under undulant clouds of moisture. They didn't attempt conversation over the booming surf; they'd done this before.

Todd locked the car, hid the keys in the sand beneath

a gray stone, and lurched with Gerome toward the brac-
ing freedom of swells the weatherman had promised
would be high today.

Gerome pulled ahead, straight into the gray horizon
and slapping foam; Todd hesitated at the shoreline to
dislodge a metallic sliver. The beach was becoming ever
more debris-stewn, an occupational hazard. The sliver
had not provoked bleeding, to Todd's eminent relief, his
fear of sharks already being disproportionate to the facts.
The movement allowed him to pause long enough to spot
the woman.

She lay supine against a red-and-white towel some
sixty yards or so down beach, just beneath the ivory rise
and greenish crest of the palisades. She seemed to be
quite naked. Todd lingered long enough to satisfy his
adolescent curiosity about her breasts, which, from
where he stood, appeared commendable, then dashed
unperturbed into the surf after his companion. There was
nothing unusual about nude bathing on this stretch of
Santa Barbara coast; the boys had seen it often, grown
happily inured. They had come to surf.

They did so for half an hour, moving apace with the
biggest swells, which coincidentally broke larger down
beach near the sunbathing woman—if there had been,
indeed, sun to bathe in.

Todd was finally thinking about this when he paused
in thigh-deep foam to stare again. The woman lay
silently on her bright red-and-white towel, face to the
filtered sky, arms at her sides, legs slightly parted. He
could just detect the dark tuft of pubic hair, the generous
loll of pink-tinged bosom beyond. She wore sunglasses.

"You're getting a hard-on, asshole." Gerome grinned
somewhere behind him.

It was partially true; he'd had to urinate for some
time now; that and the woman's ubiquitous presence had
stirred him.

Gerome always peed in the water, but Todd didn't
like that. His chosen spot—out of sight from prying
eyes—was a small cleft of rock not far from the woman.

There, back to the sea, face to stone, he could get the urethra muscles to relax. He'd have to walk past her to get to it, though.

Shivering, Todd laid his board on the sand.

"Ask her if she likes it two at a time!" Gerome snickered, and flopped on his board, knifing a comber as his comrade advanced on the cliff.

Gerome paddled out and over the next lazy swell, feeling the chill across his rubber-encased back, aware of his aloneness, of tales he'd heard of vanished swimmers, of what might be down there; thoughts always close, dancing at the periphery, tax-paid, like the rock scrapes and the cold, for the privilege of the sport.

He stroked farther, turned and straddled the board for the next wave, saw Todd signaling from beside the woman. A good swell was building and he caught the crest to carry him to shore, trying to believe his abruptly thudding heart was the result of exertion alone.

Laying his board beside Todd's, trudging toward the palisades, instinct told him otherwise. Todd was staring at him, not at the woman, his body rigid, spasming at intervals. Face gray.

A few more yards through truculent sand, and Gerome could see why the red-and-white towel was mostly red. . . .

TULLY

*T*HEY HAD THE YELLOW POLICE TAPE UP BY THE TIME
Detective Sergeant Eustes Tully reached that section of
Laredo Beach.

Mostly the tape provided a comforting declaration of
professionalism; there weren't many people on the beach
besides the two boys, it was still too chilly. The tape
helped devulgarize the contrast between death and sce-
nic oceanscape—this kind of thing didn't happen in
Santa Barbara.

Detective Sergeant Brumeister was waiting with his
snide smile, just this side of the tape. Detective Tully had
never cared for Brumeister; Brumeister was the only
man on the force who called him Eustes.

"Morning, Eustes, come to view our floater?"

Detective Tully had not yet had his coffee. "No, William, I thought I'd come down here on my day off and
see if I could catch a few waves, hang ten. Who told you
she was a floater? Billings said she's dry."

"Dry's the word, Eustes, could have used a few quarts of the old petro gel."

You would say that, asshole, thought Tully.

"See the fight last night?"

"No, William."

"The nigger won. You have any money down?"

"No, William."

"Should have come to me." Then, when Tully shouldered past indignantly: "Always nice to see you, Eustes."

Asshole.

Tully straddled the tape, nodded at the forensic crew. "Top of the morning, Ted, what have we got?"

Ted Sears was sealing the sunglasses into a plastic evidence bag. He looked wan and bloated in the morning light, like everyone else. "Two smudged whorls on the left lens, probably hers. No skin under the nails. Nothing on the toenails. She didn't die here. Towel, standard white beach towel, one of a million. Oh, yeah, a black one-piece swimsuit was lying beside her, but it was dry. That's all. Fred wants a word. How's the arthritis?"

"Intermittent."

"Did you try the Icy Hot?"

"I will, thanks."

Fred Wanamaker, county coroner, moved his back out of the way and Tully could see the corpus delicti. She shone, even against the sand. But it was hard to ignore the mess between her legs.

"Did she float, Fred?"

Wanamaker turned, smiled faintly in Tully's presence, took off his wire-rimmed glasses with a circular motion. In the harsh light, Tully thought he looked old. Certainly jaded. "Hi, Tully. No, didn't Billings tell you?"

"Brumeister got it mixed up."

"Asshole. No, she's ours. Ten to twelve hours ours. You can kiss the Coast Guard good-bye."

"Shit."

"Always on Sunday, eh? I'll need her in the lab, but the vaginal assault alone would have done it."

"Yeah?"

"Both labia shredded, vaginal walls destroyed. We'll find a punctured uterus, mark my word. No other marks."

"Semen?"

"Not externally. Need the autopsy, find the hubby quick."

"Who says she has one?"

Wanamaker, who had a reputation for psychic prognosis, turned and viewed the body. "Just a feeling."

They watched her a moment.

"Pretty, huh, Tully?" Then, almost unprofessionally wistful: "But she won't tan today."

Both men were silent for a time.

"How old do you think, Fred?"

"Thirty-two, -three. Dancer. Or athlete, look at the legs."

Tully was gazing at the surrounding sand. It wasn't bloody and it wasn't mussed except for two approaching rows of barefoot impressions.

"Those belong to the boys," Wanamaker confirmed.

Tully glanced at the black-and-white down the beach, the two blond heads huddled within. Brumeister was doubtlessly grilling them. But they didn't do it, and the killer's tracks had been swept clean by anything from the tide to the wind to a small whisk broom. Too bad it didn't take some of this garbage with it.

Ted Sears walked up. "I had a great day at the zoo planned for the kids. They love that train."

"Ted, the Parks and Beach Department comes through here every morning and picks up, smooths over the sand with a grader; make sure you've got all your pictures before they come."

"Right."

Tully stooped to the sand on impulse, poked aside a rubbery helix of kelp with his index finger, uncovering a smooth glass sphere the size of a half dollar. "What's this look like to you guys?"

"Flashbulb," Wanamaker said.

Tully blew sand off it. "I thought cameras had these things built in nowadays." He squinted over his shoulder at Sears.

Sears shrugged.

Tully turned and extended a hand. "Gimme a bag, Ted."

Sears found one and Tully dropped the object inside with his handkerchief, sealed it. He straightened and held the bulb to the murky sun.

"It's been fired," Sears commented.

"My old lady used to have one of those cameras," Wanamaker mused.

Tully handed the bag to Sears. "Dust it. But I want it back even if it's clean."

"You got it."

He turned then and looked out at the ocean horizon, dark blue meeting lighter blue now that the fog was burning off.

"Going to be a nice day after all," Sears said.

Tully felt the dead woman behind him, pressing invisibly at his back. Not for everyone, he thought.

"All right," he commanded the air about him, "let's finish up and get her out of the sun."

He walked down the beach to tell Brumeister to let the two boys go.

Detective Tully sat in the McDonald's regarding the pay phone on the opposite wall with baleful eyes.

It was time for another of those calls.

There was still a good bite-and-a-half of Big Mac left. And two or three fries at the bottom of the greasy paper sack. And a good three sips of Coke if there was a drop. No point in calling until he'd finished eating. A man had to eat, after all.

He looked at his watch for no particular reason. He sighed. He stared at the legs on the teenager sitting with her boyfriend across from him. Her boyfriend had orange spiked hair. What would a good-looking pair of gams like that want with a geek like him? Kids.

Now the Big Mac was gone and so were the fries and only one sip of Coke was left.

This is bullshit, get it over with.

He resolutely stashed his paper leftovers in a louvered trash container and picked up the receiver, shoving in dimes.

He dialed a familiar number.

"Hello."

"Hi, it's me."

"What's the matter, Eustes?"

He pinched back a sigh, steeling himself. "Why do you automatically assume something's wrong?"

"Why else would you call?"

"Because I like to talk to you, maybe?"

"You're canceling."

Shit. She always knew. Always. "Something came up, Mae."

Silence.

"Are you there?"

"Something always does."

He felt his stomach tighten despite himself. "It's serious, or I wouldn't break our lunch date."

"I'm sure." Patronizing.

A woman's been murdered, he thought, but didn't say it. Instead he said: "It's my job, I'm a cop. You know that."

"What about dinner—"

"I'd like to. I'll phone you."

"—that is, unless it's an inconvenience."

"It's not."

"If you're too busy—"

"It's not a goddamn inconvenience!"

"I don't see the need for profanity."

"Look—"

"You know I don't care for it."

"I'm sorry. I'll phone you, okay?"

"Can I count on that?"

"Yes."

"Eustes—?"

Grinding his teeth, knowing what was coming.

"Eustes—promise me?"

"All right, yes. I promise."

"I don't think it's too much to ask. Is it too much to ask?"

"No."

"If it is, just—"

"It isn't too much to ask."

"I love you, darling."

"I love you, too, Mae. I have to go now."

"Until tonight, then."

He hung up without saying good-bye, his only way of getting the last word.

CHAPTER 2

MOTHER

MOTHER CAME TOPSIDE TO THE FOREDECK TO AVOID the smell of chemicals. Mother disliked the chemical odors, especially the hypo fixer.

She stood in the cool Pacific breeze, florid muumuu gathered about her, gazing out across the dark waters to the silhouetted lump of the Channel Islands and the winking lights of the oil platforms. Behind her, Santa Barbara's "Riviera" hills winked with diamond lights, sequestering executives and movie stars and a million hopes and dreams. Mother's own dark dreams lay unfulfilled still, but she was getting close, she was getting close, and there was time.

She gazed into the dark waters below the yacht's scuppers and thought about money and thought about Sonny and thought about women and thought about death. To port, a flying fish broke the surface with iridescent terror, pursued by another kind of death, flashed across the moonless surface, and rejoined its own world. Mother contemplated all the fish in the sea and all the work ahead and allowed herself a long, deserved sigh. It was a nice night, though, especially with the crew gone ashore. A night to be alone with Sonny.

She descended to him.

He already had the screen and projector set up, the newly mounted slides lined up in the carousel tray, ready to begin tonight's show.

Mother eased into the tan leather couch before the screen, looking up with a proud smile as Sonny came through the cabin door with the silvery tray, fresh from the galley: sardines in mustard sauce with soda crackers, and General Foods International Coffees' Café Mocha. Her favorite evening snack.

"Thank you, Sonny." She reached for the coffee and took a delicious, chocolatey sip: no caffeine, no sugar—Nutrasweet. Mother did not use products with saccharin. Saccharin had been found to cause cancer in laboratory rats; it said so on the label. She couldn't imagine how the American government—a government she'd always respected—allowed the sale of such products. Or why they still allowed the sale of things like cigarettes. Didn't they care about people's health? It was shameful.

There were many things wrong with the world, she supposed, the result of wicked men doing wicked things. Far too many to count, really, to ever realistically do anything about, though God knows one must try. Wicked men. Grown from wicked little boys. And this the sad result of one great, heart-wrenching truth—the real root of all evil—bad mothers.

How many bad mothers were there? How many had there been throughout history, throughout the world?

The statistics were dizzying, and it was probably best not to think of such things. Thinking of such things led to confusion, and it was vitally important to remained unconfused at all times. You must—above all else—know who you are.

Still . . . one could hardly not think of them, could one?

The best thing, perhaps, was simply to try to be a

good mother oneself, to set a precedent through example. To do what one could in one's own little way. To protect one's offspring from all the worldly evils one could.

That's what she had always tried to do with Sonny.

Even though, of course, she'd failed.

Even though it was, in all probability, too late for Sonny.

Still, she must not stop trying.

She sighed heavily again and closed her eyes for a weary moment as Sonny started the projector. It was very tiring being a good mother.

The first slide showed the bright, sunny beach.

Sonny always started things this way, just some simple, idyllic shot, focusing on nothing particular—perhaps an umbrella here, a wheeling gull there. The bright blue expanse of white-crested Pacific.

Now the child. Cavorting in the sand, usually, or the edge of the shore, or just sitting quietly perhaps, with plastic pail and shovel. This one had a Day-Glo beach ball, was balancing it on his middle finger like a basketball player. Smiling. Mother smiled, too. They were all so sweet. So innocent. Even as Sonny had once been . . .

The next shot showed the boy's mother.

Young. Pretty. Athletic.

She wore a dark suit, dark glasses, dark glossy hair.

She was lying in the sand on her blanket in this shot, oblivious to the boy, to the ocean, to everything but the warm, bronzing rays, her own private thoughts. Her own private thoughts . . .

Now here was a slide of her sitting up, taking a picture of the boy with one of those new throwaway cameras. Mother didn't like those cameras. Mother didn't like the whole idea of throwaway. It was a throwaway society now. Not the way it had been when she was young. Someday, she thought, we will be throwing away the people themselves. Not that we wouldn't be better off without some of them. . . .

Here was a slide of the young mother talking to a man on the beach. A tall, attractive man. Who was the man, Mother wondered. What were they talking about? Were they talking about the little boy? The slide didn't answer.

And here, at last, was the final picture.

Sonny had done a good job with it. He always did.

It was dark now, so of course he'd had to use the flash. But the old camera still did a pretty good job.

The little boy was gone now, safe at last ... gone away somewhere like the setting sun, like the fleeting promise of youth. The beach looked alone and quiet, desolate. You couldn't see much of it, only the dark edges just beyond the woman where the probing flash had reached. The rest was scalloped blackness. As black as the woman's hair. As black as the black swimsuit crumpled beside her pale, naked body. As black as the dark crust of blood drying there between her legs. . . .

CHAPTER 3

MITCH

*I*T WAS HOTTER HERE THAN HE WOULD HAVE
expected.

Stillman rowed them to a shallow spot amid senti-
nels of dead spruce stumps where the big bass were
reported to lurk. He let Mitch borrow one of his best
lures, one he'd had good luck with. They fished for an
hour, getting mostly snags and bluegill. They were running sweat by the time noon approached.

Mitch was debating suggesting a shaded area, not
wanting to push, when, to his surprise, the other man
offered him a leather-encased chrome flask. The dinghy
was loaded with beer. A sixth sense persuaded Mitch to
accept the drink.

Stillman took two short pulls, fiddled with the cap,
reconsidered, and took another one. He screwed on the
cap and put the flask away.

"What's up, John?" Mitch finally broached.

Still avoiding his eyes, Stillman watched the lake.

Mitch shifted on the plank seat.

14

At length, Stillman sighed, began to reel in. "This isn't going to work."

For a brief moment, Mitch allowed himself to believe the other man meant their present location, knowing that wasn't it. That it was something far worse.

Stillman settled, letting the bourbon blossom.

"I have some bad news, Mitch."

Mitch's mind raced everywhere, always just behind the true dread. Was someone in John's family sick? No, or he wouldn't have invited Mitch fishing. Mitch felt a familiar chill, suddenly knowing what was coming.

"We lost Classic Oil."

Four words that left Mitch's mouth abruptly dry, made the dinghy bottom evaporate, plunging him into icy water.

"When . . . ?"

"Carlson found out Thursday while he was in New York. They weren't satisfied with our investigation of that plant that blew up in Arkansas. They're going to go with another insurance agency." He let it sink in. "That's a fifty million dollar account."

"That's bullshit. We had to pay off on that one. They were in the wrong and they knew it!"

"Of course they were. That isn't the point. They felt someone more experienced at insurance investigation could have turned our case around."

"You mean my case—"

"Our case, Mitch. When the agency handles a client, it's the agency's responsibility. We're all responsible for the failures—the successes, too."

He was coming on too consoling-apologetic. Mitch would have felt better if Stillman were really mad. "Did Carlson talk with them?"

Stillman was nodding patiently. "He talked. They want out. They're going with Brewster/McCallan Under-writers."

Something officiously final about his tone. Mitch let it rest a moment, still denying what was coming, then said, heart pumping: "Where do we go from here?"

Stillman's hand flinched toward the flask.

He made himself look at Mitch, eyes hooded. "I'm sorry, Mitch. I thought I could make this last until Sunday, at least have a nice weekend, catch some fish—"

"Carlson's letting me go."

Stillman swallowed. "And it has nothing to do with your ability, or Carlson's faith in it. He thinks you're one of the best, he told me that personally. But an account that big . . . they need someone's head on a pike. And, well . . . it was your case."

You bastard! You just said it was the company's case!

And he could see now that Stillman was secretly glad. Not just because it wasn't he who was getting the ax, but because of who was. He had never liked Mitch. Mitch had always suspected it, tried to press a friendship that wasn't there.

Stillman was nervous because he was afraid of Mitch, not because he felt for him.

"Carlson's really just sick about this, he told me that himself."

"But he's doing it anyway." Mitch had nothing left to lose now.

"For the company. He's sure the Brewster thing will fall apart, that Standard will come running back. But not at the cost of losing face; they need their scapegoat. You know how it is. I wish you could have seen the look on Carlson's face."

"I wish I could have, too—why the hell didn't he tell me himself?"

"I know you're upset, Mitch. Carlson thought you'd take it better out here, away from the others."

"Well, he was wrong!"

"Please, Mitch, this is hard enough—"

"Yeah, I can see you're all busted up. Do you know what this means, John?"

"You'll find work—"

"In a pig's eye! No reputable agency will touch me when this leaks!"

Stillman patted the air between them with a sooth-

16

ing motion. "Carlson gave implicit instructions to ensure the termination of your employment be kept in the strictest confid—"

"Bullshit! It's already in half the watering holes in Westwood! Good Christ, John, what the hell am I supposed to do? I'm in debt to my ass, I just bought a house!"

"Naturally there's severance pay—"

"Good! Six month's worth? 'Cause that's what it will take! I've got four hundred dollars in the bank!"

"Savings?"

"Bonds I can't touch for ten years!"

Stillman stared at him.

There really wasn't anything the other man could do and Mitch knew it, but he needed to hurt something, someone, and now. It helped a little that most of the gloat had dissolved in Stillman's eyes. Even the vengeful recognize the bottom, and this was the very bottom. Dear God, he could be on the street, literally.

For one awful second he thought he was passing out.

Stillman caught the signs and pushed the flask at him. Mitch pushed it away angrily. Regretting he had, wanting another drink.

They sat listening to distant outboard wakes slap the shore.

"Jesus . . . Jesus . . ."

The sound of his own soft whimpering terrified him.

"What can I do, Mitch?" Stillman sounded sincere.

Mitch dragged his eyes open to look at a tear-blurred distant horizon. It had been years since his eyes had been even close to watering. It stung. "Nothing."

There was nothing anyone could do.

He was back to square one again. Back to failure.

No one could help him now.

The hollowed-out feeling would not leave, had become what felt like an ongoing, permanent part of him.

They returned to the cabin, all thoughts of fishing and fun as distant as yesterday. Mitch felt he was walking on foam rubber, moving through a separate plane at once familiar and alien, eyes searching frantically for a remembered security now strangely elusive. A new landscape had been defined, and he didn't know the way. He was aware that Stillman was still there, somewhere at the periphery of Mitch's sight and hearing, but he kept catching only fragments of sentences, nodding to accommodate without real acknowledgment. Gradually he came to understand that Stillman was anxious to leave. It seemed a reasonable request.

Then he remembered that they had previously arranged something he'd somehow forgotten: Stillman was going back, Mitch was staying on for a few days here at the lake. He couldn't conceive of why, just now, he'd agreed to that.

Stillman was carrying his luggage to his car. A Mercedes. Mitch had considered buying one of those. In another life.

"Are you sure there's nothing I can do, nothing you need?"

"Like what?" Mitch was not being sarcastic, naïvely clinging to the desperate notion that some power outside himself could actually save him. Stillman was still trying to supply an answer he hadn't expected to have to make when Mitch slapped his arm and told him not to worry, thanked him and guided him into the Mercedes. He was aware of the wonderful sound the German car's door made as it shut, was aware of the rich leather upholstery smell. He suddenly hated the woods and the cabin, as if they were somehow the cause of this misery—this is where it had begun. It hadn't, though. It had begun weeks ago. Maybe years ago. Maybe this was all his life was ever meant to be. A failure. A good-for-nothing, washed-up—

"Sure you're okay?"

"I'll phone you in a few days." Mitch smiled, not meaning it but thinking it sounded somehow right, hoping it would sooth Stillman's concerned look, not because he cared about Stillman but because he was sick of the look. Strangely, he felt sorry for Stillman now. He has to go back to it. I'm free. Dead, but free.

"Look, Mitch—"

"Don't start dragging the lake yet, my family's got plenty of money." It was a lie that seemed to work. He extended a hand to Stillman. "Thanks, John, I'm sorry I lost my cool down there. I'll be fine. And now without you banging around in the boat, maybe I'll catch some fish."

"I want to do this again, Mitch."

"I know. Soon. Thanks again, drive safe."

"So long."

He went back inside the cabin before the Mercedes was even out of sight, hoping that now that he was alone he could cry. Thirty-nine years old and out of work again. It was inconceivable. He couldn't see a way out this time. He could only see himself in the mud at the bottom of the lake. And maybe the fact that this didn't frighten him is what frightened him most of all.

He sat in the boat in the middle of the lake staring desultorily at the plastic float, trying to remember if he'd baited the hook. The sun was setting and lights twinkled across the surface of the water, glowing off the larger boats that had appeared magically at the end of the day, party boats, filled with happy drunken people, rich people. He realized that there were no lights on his dingy and that sooner or later he stood in danger of being hit, but he couldn't let the prospect of anything so mundane concern him just now.

He was thinking about the Classic Oil case.

There had been a lot of pressure on the agency. Classic Oil had had one of their refineries blow because of substandard construction. Classic was being sued by the families of those who died in the explosion and wanted to prove that the construction firm hired to build the plant was at fault. Unfortunately, Mitch learned that the work had been approved and passed by an incompetent upper-level executive at Classic and was unable to keep the press from getting hold of the facts. Classic lost, and All-American paid only part of its losses, arguing that Classic had been unduly negligent. Classic ended up paying the rest of the damages out of its profit margin, and the stockholders had not been happy.

Classic blamed Mitch for uncovering the facts. For doing his job *right!* For not covering up like some cheap crook.

That's why it was so hard to understand his dismissal.

But there it was. And here he was. In the middle of a lake. Broke. Out of work after a year of unbelievable success. Ruined.

Okay, it sounded overly dramatic, but it amounted to the same thing. No one in his right mind would hire him now.

Joanne. Nellie. The money he'd spent. Sweet Jesus.

Nobody made you spend it.

The house was lost, that was foregone. The car, too. Effectively killing Joanne and himself in that order. Especially Jo. She'd wanted to start classes at UCLA this fall, earn her PhD. At least Nellie wasn't old enough for school yet.

Where would they go? *Where?* They owed, they owed. After all his years of stumbling through career after career, he'd thought he was entitled to some luxuries.

Obviously he'd been wrong.

Jo would find out now, find out the truth about him at last. That he was a failure.

All right, stop with the self-pity campaign. Think, *think!*

He could go back to freelancing, but he'd worn out his welcome with most of the private agencies in town. Besides, he wasn't that good at it anyway, trying to make it from week to week, never knowing where the next dime was coming from. All-American, that was what he was good at. Two more years with the company and they wouldn't have let him go no matter what. Two more years and he'd have been promoted to just under

Carlson. But wishing things were different wasn't going to change it.

He dully shook his head in the bobbing boat. He hadn't been this close to real poverty in twenty years. He didn't know if he could face it again, he honestly didn't. He wasn't a kid anymore, didn't have the knack for failure he used to have. He'd gotten spoiled by All-American with its fancy offices and its health plan. Now he realized he had lucked into the whole thing. He wasn't really any good. At anything.

Thank God Dad was dead, didn't have to see this.

He didn't know if he could face Jo, though.

He didn't know if he could do that.

More and more the muddy bottom seemed the correct option, the only option. He knew that because of how dispassionately he considered the idea, how calmly. At least there was the life insurance; All-American had seen to that. He was loaded with it. And boating accidents do happen.

Was he really considering this? He almost smiled. Yesterday his world had made complete sense. Not perfect, maybe, but logical. Now, mere hours later—

God, why did you do this to me?

Had he said that out loud? He couldn't remember.

C H A P T E R   4

TULLY

*D*ETECTIVE TULLY GOT THE PAGER CALL THAT AFTER-
noon at Taco Bell.

He ate there a lot. He liked it. He liked junk food in
general.

Once, years ago, when he was still in Narcotics, a
towering, whippet-thin black pimp named Slydell Wash-
ington had offered to buy him a fancy meal at Chez
Rourke in exchange for keeping his trap shut about a
glove compartment full of coke. "Be glad to escort you
to the station, my man, but have not yet dined this evening! Could I induce you to be my guest?"

Tully, as it turned out, hadn't dined that evening
either, so he went along, allowed Slydell to stuff him
with lobster bisque, fresh steamed vegetables, the house
wine, and a towering chocolate parfait, belched gratefully, hauled Slydell's ass downtown anyway, and stopped
off later for a Big Mac, infinitely preferring the latter to
the earlier rich cuisine. Junk food, to a bona fide gourmet
like Tully, could be an art in itself.

And you couldn't beat the Burrito Supremes at Taco Bell at State and Fifth. Or the blonde at the cash register. The girls in fast-food joints all wore those tight red or blue tee-shirts and those silly hats. It was fun, you could flirt with them. They knew they looked silly, and they ate up the compliments. Tully didn't know how to flirt with the waitresses in fancy restaurants. Maybe that's not why you were supposed to go there. Whatever the case, it wasn't as much fun. Eating was supposed to be fun.

He let the pager beep loudly until he had finished his Cinnamon Crispas and washed them down with Coke; it was always bad news and bad news could wait until he'd been fed. He found the pay phone in the back.

"Detective Tully here."

"Let me guess . . . the enchildada with beef."

"Hello, Brumeister, just thinking about you."

"Yeah? Having a foot-long hot dog, are we?"

"At Taco Bell? No, I'm having the Tuesday special— Turds-on-a-Stick."

Brumeister's piggy chuckle. "You always had a shit-eating grin, Eustes. We got a make on your floater. Wanamaker got a match on her prints. Worked for the VA."

"I'm waiting." This had to be bad or Brumeister wouldn't have volunteered to call him.

"Mrs. Charlotte Cunningham, 1748 Anacapa Street. Say, that's right near the Taco Bell, isn't it?" Voice venomous with sarcasm.

Christ, he hadn't made a house call in a year. He could see Brumeister's smug grin. "Any children?"

"One little boy. Seven."

"I don't suppose you or Christi would like to do this?"

"I don't suppose we would. Enjoy your spic food."

The Cunninghams had a nice home, by Southern California standards. Tucked away in the leafy hills of midtown, it boasted the requisite tile and stucco of the thirties while retaining the quaint singularity of design not yet leavened by the postwar boom. One was reminded of Hollywood's golden years; indeed, some of those faded stars still inhabited the mansions that seemed to spring up with the irregularity of unfrocked palms. Prices were stiff here, inexcusable by Midwestern standards. Santa Barbara's beaches and college community kept the nearby downtown streets lively and viably touristic. A nice place to live if you bought early, though even paradise had its shadows: transients filled the palm-lined city parks, encouraging rats, encouraging resentment; of late, someone had been distributing arsenic-laced wine bottles near the Amtrak station in an effort to discourage the vermin, human and otherwise. Smog crept up from L.A., and Route 101, which bisected a main street, was becoming increasingly overloaded.

Still defiantly lovely, tawny beaches under bloody sunsets, the Gold Coast basked in its last hurrah.

John Cunningham wasn't cheering.

He watched Detective Tully with a face drained of all expression.

"Dead . . . ?"

"Perhaps you'd like to sit down, Mr. Cunningham."

"No . . . no, thank you . . ."

It was unreal, it was always unreal. There's no way to tell a man his wife is gone without sharing his unreality. It pervades the air, a white vacuum to insulate the mind from insanity. Here was Mr. Cunningham in his own living room, telling Detective Tully, a stranger, "no, thank you." It was nuts.

It would get worse: Cunningham had to deal with murder as well, a concept he'd probably never truly contemplated in his life.

Unless, of course, he'd committed it himself.

Detective Tully, standing at the door, was watching for signs of that.

Cunningham wasn't asking when or where, just staring at Tully's breast pocket.

That might mean something, might not. Some of

them were psychic, unsurprised by sudden tragedy. Some of them dreamt it the night before. Some of them just went right into shock.

Cunningham looked poised for something. Paralysis or evasion? Tully would have to walk lightly to find out.

He explained to Mr. Cunningham where his wife was found and her condition. He did it gently but without holding back. He watched the man's face without appearing to. Cunningham kept staring at his pocket.

"I'm awful sorry, Mr. Cunningham. May I get you a drink?"

"A drink? No."

"Would you like to sit down now?"

Mr. Cunningham would not.

Finally Tully took a seat himself, on a handsome burgundy sofa near the door, watching the other man, hands folded in his lap.

A minute passed.

Time to see if it was shock.

"She's at the city morgue, sir. I'm afraid we'll need you for identification."

Cunningham nodded. "Of course. That makes sense."

He looked trapped.

Tully waited.

In a moment, he was rewarded.

Cunningham turned, seemed to see the detective for the first time. "Would you like something to drink, Mr. Tully?"

"No, thank you."

Cunningham nodded, moved sleeplike to the picture window. It fronted a neatly trimmed lawn, inset sprinklers, fat, handsome palms, immaculate neighboring abodes across the street.

The house smelled vaguely of wood oil and something else. The something else was the people who lived here. No two houses smelled alike.

"Are you married, Mr. Tully?"

Detective Tully, but that was okay. "No."

Cunningham turned to stare at him. "Why not?"

It was an honest question. "Never found the right girl."

Cunningham watched the window.

"I did."

"I'm very sorry, sir."

Cunningham shook his head slowly. "No. Not my wife. Someone else. I'm having an affair, Mr. Tully. Charlotte knew. She and I filed for divorce last week . . ."

That was it, then.

Tully groaned inwardly. The husband didn't do it; you don't divulge information like that even if you're very, very clever, and Cunningham wasn't. Shit. Now the legwork began. Now there was a real reason to feel for this poor slob. Cunningham wasn't feeling trapped, he was feeling guilty.

"Did either you or Mrs. Cunningham have any enemies, sir? Anyone you have reason to suspect might hold a grudge, even an old one?"

"No. Of course not."

"No one's threatened you recently, no heated arguments?"

"No."

"Where were you last Sunday night, Mr. Cunningham?"

"I didn't kill her, Mr. Tully."

"I know that."

"With Sue."

"Does Sue have another boyfriend, a husband?"

"No."

"And your wife was here at home?"

Cunningham frowned. "No. She took Jason to the beach in the morning. Then she brought him back here and told me she was going to her mother's house in Carmel."

"Jason?"

"Our son . . ." Cunningham's eyes brimmed with fresh pain. "My sister was going to watch him while Charlotte was away. She lives down the street."

"Was your wife driving or flying?"

"Flying. I dropped her at the airport myself."

"Do you have your mother-in-law's number?"

Cunningham was already heading for the phone.

He dialed Northern California. Charlotte's mother hadn't seen her daughter all weekend, she assumed they'd all decided to drive up and surprise her. Tully could hear her cry come from the receiver when Cunningham told her the bad news.

When the husband hung up, Tully asked for a recent photograph of Charlotte and a list of their closest friends and relatives. It wasn't a long list. But it didn't matter. This wasn't a crime of passion. Not coherent passion, anyway. It was the crime of a psycho. There was a lot of that going around these days.

Tully gave Cunningham a card and told him to call the station when he felt up to viewing the remains. He made Cunningham promise he'd call his sister to come over and spend the rest of the day with him. Cunningham thanked the detective and closed the door. Detective Tully walked to his car past a kid on a skateboard. The kid looked at him blankly; the look was familiar. Then he remembered where he'd seen that look before.

On Cunningham's face.

Tully reached out a hand and ruffled the kid's hair. "Maybe you'd better go inside, Jason."

The kid stared at him, then picked up the skateboard and headed for the house.

Cunningham would be all right. He had Sue. And Jason had his father, didn't he?

Charlotte had nobody.

On the way back to the office he remembered and called Mae from his car phone.

"Hi, Mae, it's me."

"Well, the stranger."

"Please don't start, at least wait until midway through the conversation."

"Did you call to cancel dinner as well as lunch?"

"I called to ask you where you'd like to eat tonight."

"You pick."

He suddenly felt very tired. "I was thinking," he began without thinking, "maybe we could stay in this evening, just the two of us, you know . . ."

"You want me to cook?"

The tightening. "No, I could order out, pizza or something."

"You know what that stuff does to my stomach."

Fried chicken, then, or whatever you want."

"You don't want me to cook, is that what you're saying?"

He sucked in a breath, trying to keep his voice steady. Don't lose it. Don't. "Whatever you like, Mae! Would you like to cook or not?"

"Whatever pleases you, Eustes." Distant. Hurt. Reminding him he'd raised his voice in spite of himself.

He gripped the wheel, trying to find control.

"Look . . . why don't we go to that little Italian place you like, the one on State Street."

"Fine. If that's what you want."

"Mae, what do *you* want?"

"I said fine. Why do you insist on shouting? I'm not deaf yet."

Tully winced back a headache begging to knock through. "Fine. Is seven all right?"

"Seven's fine."

"I'll see you then."

"If you're going to cancel, please give me at least an hour's warning."

"I'm not"—he lowered his voice—"I am not going to cancel. Can't you ever give me the benefit of the doubt?"

Silence.

"Mae? Are you there?"

"Until seven, then."

"See you then."

"Drive carefully, Eustes. It looks like rain."

"I will."

"And you know those tires of yours, practically bald."

"I *will!*"

"I only want what's best for you, son."

"I know," he whispered against the headache. "See you tonight, Mother."

CHAPTER 5

CLAIRE

CLAIRE GREELY, UP TO HER NECK AGAIN, STRUGGLED
valiantly.

This time it was in Big Piney Lake water, above
which she was desperately trying to keep her chin while
simultaneously wrestling with the flat, cumbersome
expanse of water skis, the unwieldy life jacket riding up
painfully under her armpits, and the simple act of taking
a breath. All this while attempting a game smile in the
general direction of her empathetic host, Santiago Dias,
waving to her, with his blinding smile, from the wheel
of his motorboat some twenty yards away.

How had she ever let him talk her into this?

Waterskiing in the morning light had been one thing,
but the sun was on the horizon now, night closing rapidly, the lake choppy with the wake of other boats heading for shore and the big dinner cruisers patroling the
evening waters. It was not, to Claire's mind, a time for
skiing. "Oh, but you'll love it!" Dias had exclaimed infec-
tiously. "There's nothing to equal the thrill of skimming

the darkened surface of a great lake as the shore lights twinkle on one by one about you! *Fantastico!"*

Right. He'd mentioned nothing about its legality—or lack of it.

Claire inadvertently gulped lake water, gagged, spit, and tried not to lose her grip on the tow handle, which had a habit of pulling just beyond the reach of her frantic fingers. Dias's ChrisCraft idled lazily in the water, drifting forward slightly, guiding her gently through the warm waves. She wondered if he were aware of this. He often seemed lost in his own boyish enthusiasm—his greatest appeal. At other times, she felt he was more aware of others than he let on, that he was secretly teasing, testing her, seeing if she lived up to some private standard. To her dismay—and irritation—she felt compelled to oblige him in this, to live up to that standard, resentful though it made her. She didn't like being coerced, winningly or otherwise. Yet there was something undeniably disarming about that smile of his. And he never pushed, not outwardly. Why did she sense Dias was smarter than he appeared? Or was cunning the word? Or was dangerous the word?

And what was there about that possibility that attracted her so?

Was it because she had known him for two weeks now and he hadn't tried to fuck her yet?

She surprised herself with the unbidden slang. But that's what it would be with Dias: he wouldn't make love to a woman, he would fuck her. Hard. Long.

And it might be great.

Never mind that now, Claire, get the damn ski on before you look like a drowned rat. He's watching.

She fumbled with the rubber footguard. It slipped maddeningly out of her hand. Damn! Well, screw him! What if I do look like a clumsy fool, it's getting dark and I'm no athlete!

But she wrestled tenaciously with the ski—and not without some sense of pride: she'd done well on the water this morning, despite the fact she hadn't skied in years. It had pleased Dias. And that, in turn, had pleased her.

She adjusted the ski, settled back, waved to the ChrisCraft that she was ready. The boat surged forward slowly, a ripple forming at the bow, gaining speed. Claire felt the drag of the lake, the tension along back and shoulders, the sickly wobbling in her legs. She gritted her teeth.

This was the tough part, the wavering edge just prior to lifting her rump above the surface. Done incorrectly, she would either spill over backward or shoot ungracefully over her skis onto her pretty face.

Serve you right. You're a married woman. Bitch.

Shut up. He hasn't touched me yet.

No. Not yet.

Dias hit the throttle expertly, watching over his shoulder her every trembling move, guiding her encouragingly, smiling in triumph as her fanny cleared the mirrored surface, her back straightened, and she leaned back, leg muscles finding their rhythm, skis bouncing in tandem across the frothy wake. The evening air was a chilly blast along her suddenly exposed torso, but she grinned excitedly: she was up!

Claire put her head back, closed her eyes a moment: he was right, night skiing *is* pretty terrific.

They headed for midlake, Dias easing the launch into a wide U. Claire followed gracefully, helplessly, leaning into the turn, knees bent, hair flying, watching the droplets jump from the tight umbilical cord of nylon connecting them. Dias was really pouring it on, giving her the ride of her life, bouncing her across the ebony surface like a skipped stone, the wake a trail of phosphorescence. She shuddered from the chill, from the thought of spilling at this speed, but she couldn't deny the thrill of adrenalin racing through her vitals. This was living. Being with Dias was being alive. She knew it, he knew it. And in that breathless, windswept instant she suddenly knew something else: this was his plan all along, to get her excited, get her heart pumping . . . then make her come to him. Then, under his conditions, he would fuck her. Until she screamed.

The boat leapt forward. Faster. She gasped, breath torn from her by the shrieking wind, legs trembling weakly beneath her, skin tingling as if on fire. And it was working. She found herself abruptly wanting him.

And found herself just as quickly resenting the fact.

She pulled back on the tow line, hunkered, leaned and skipped rebelliously over his churning wake, bouncing high, hanging in dizzy terror, slapping down perfectly again. She was in control again. Free as the exultant wind.

She never saw the other powerboat charging across her path.

Dias did.

He slammed the ChrisCraft into a stall, began waving frantically to her from behind the wheel. Her arms pinwheeled at the sudden loss of power, desperately seeking balance, rope abruptly slack in her hands. Inertia propelled her forward, face a mask of questions, skis bumping over the floating, serpentine length of rope. She caught the first part of what Dias was anxiously shouting before the new boat's motor buried all sound under a frenzied roar. Face white, she saw the invading prow, a towering wedge that would surely disembowel her. Instinct threw her weight to the left, skis skidding out from under her, striking the locomotive blur of fiberglass and steel. A quick view of oblivious adolescent faces, hands clutching aluminum cans, the awful proximity of churning outboard, a phantom vision of kneeless legs, bloody foam, then a sudden, airless heat, green and darker green, and the terrible certainty she was passing out in all that roiling warmth. She heard the thrum of distant engines and what sounded like a voice calling her name, down there in the darkness. . . .

Mitch Spencer, sitting in his rowboat, saw it all. The other boat, the collision, the woman's plunging form, Dias laboring over the ignition button of the stalled ChrisCraft.

Now all he had to do was get there in time.

He thought he might actually do it, if the woman's lungs didn't immediately fill and drag her to the muddy bottom. He braced his feet against the gunwales and bent his back to the oars.

The wriggle of tow line traced his path. But only for a while; it abruptly vanished downward. When he reached a still churning froth of bubbles beyond it, he kicked off his shoes, dragged in a breath, porpoised high and dove.

Mitch knifed through warm gloom, seeing nothing at first, trusting to luck, colliding finally with a ghostly cable, which guided him down; the nylon cord had entangled her ankle. He found her twenty feet below, a pale doll beckoning. Adrenalin carried him into her arms, supplied the necessary manpower for the weighted return trip, the wide-eyed clawing for the surface, one arm about her slim waist. Just yards from the top, it suddenly all became an effortless dream . . . he might have been Superman soaring in a void. He would pay the price tomorrow with racking limbs and tender muscles—but for now he was indomitable. He wondered distantly if he was on the edge of narcosis.

And then he was up, chill night air searing his lungs, the hero of all his childhood dreams, lovely damsel at his side, the sense that he'd just done something terribly right illuminating his soul. He got her head back, cleared seaweed hair from her mouth, and was struggling with the idea of mouth-to-mouth when Dias bumped along side. "Hand her to me!"

Mitch turned gratefully, treading, adrenalin used up, hoisting under her arms with the last of his strength. Dias plucked her from the lake with ease. A sinewy bronzed arm followed a moment later and hauled Mitch over the dripping gunwale.

Mitch sat dizzily on plastic cushions, finally feeling his exhaustion, while Dias bent over her, his mouth pressed to hers. Seconds later, the woman convulsed, coughed lake water and vomit, and they were home free. He watched the gentle rise of her breasts, the sticky tangle of hair glued to her pale cheek, as Dias arrowed the ChrisCraft back to his yacht. Mitch's own arms felt like lead weights. He couldn't have lifted a kitten just then.

Dias said nothing in the rushing wind, merely reached over once and gripped Mitch's wobbly leg with a strong right hand. It spoke volumes.

Many of the guests had departed by launch, but there were enough stragglers yet on deck to generate a gratifying buzz of excitement. Mitch was given a warm towel and a hot cup of coffee. A lot of slaps on the back. A kiss from one dark-haired beauty. Someone informed him that someone else had gone to retrieve his dinghy. The woman he had saved had been spirited away below deck. After a time, he was mostly alone with the coffee and blanket and a few milling strangers who kept telling him what a brave thing he did and thank God he was there and was he sure he was all right?

Dias came on deck awhile later.

He spoke to the few stragglers, who moved off quietly, then he came over to Mitch and sat down.

"Some more coffee, *señor?*"

"This is fine."

"Let me get you some brandy."

"No, I'm fine, thanks."

Dias nodding appraisingly.

He was indeed handsome, Santiago Dias, tall and well-built, lean and muscular despite his close approximation to Mitch's own age. He looked like he worked out, or maybe swam. His skin was like rich, lightly creamed coffee, hair thick and black. The mustache, small and trimmed, was perfect, the perfect touch. His smile was incandescent. Mitch wondered if he could take him.

"You saved the lady's life. We are all much in your debt." Even the almost imperceptible Spanish accent was endearing.

Mitch had the sudden premonition he was going to like the man.

"I'm just glad I happened to be in the neighborhood."

Dias's dark eyes brimmed with veneration. "It is not enough to merely be in a place—one must act. You did this, my friend. Without fear."

"Not without that, I'm afraid."

"All the more commendable, then. I am Santiago Dias. My boat is yours." He extended a hand.

Mitch took it, returning a squeeze that was surprisingly gentle, probably overcompensating for the strength behind it. One sensed a refinement still in the practice stages. But Dias's indebtedness needed no rehearsal: it was genuine.

"Mitch Spencer." He wasn't sure what to add, so he simply said: "Happy to be of service."

Dias clapped Mitch's shoulder, a brotherly gesture of affection. "And now you must let the young lady thank you herself." He led the way below deck.

It was a considerable distance across a considerable boat. They descended beneath immaculate coaming down varnished teakwood steps, turned at a narrow corridor, and headed straight to the fo'c'sle. Aft of the forward cabin there was a roomy head-compartment harboring two bunks, one occupied by the woman. Mitch stepped through the hatchway to wine-colored transom seats and richly polished brass, the smell of real leather. A single kerosene lamp swung from the bulkheads, bathing the woman's blanketed form in soft amber.

Dias took the woman's hand in his, pale moon enveloped by fingers of night. "*Señora* Greely, your benefactor is here. May I present Mr. Mitch Spencer. Mr. Spencer, *Señora* Claire Greely."

Mitch accepted tapered fingers cool as plaster. "Hello."

"I want to thank you for saving my life. That was a very brave thing. I'm afraid there's no adequate way to repay you except to thank you again from the bottom of my heart."

"That's all the payment required. Besides, Mr. Dias delivered the kiss of life."

Dias, behind him, clapped Mitch's shoulder again. "A worthless gesture without your speedy actions, *señor*."

"Are you feeling all right?" Mitch inquired. He instantly understood Dias's preoccupation with her; she was a knockout, even pale and shaken.

"Considering I swallowed half the lake." She looked to Dias. "Forgive me, Santiago, but believe it or not, I'm famished again."

Dias smiled, relieved. "Not surprising, considering you gave most of your dinner to the lake. I'll have Sanchez prepare something for us. You'll join us of course, Mr Spencer."

"Yes, please!" Claire added.

Eyes like blue crystal, Mitch was thinking.

"No, I couldn't, really."

"But I insist!" Dias urged.

"Please, Mr. Spencer," the woman enjoined, "it will give me the chance to thank you again properly. With my hair combed, I'm somewhat less forbidding than a sea hag."

"I can see that already. No, thank you, I really can't. I just wanted to stop down and see the face of the person who allowed me to play hero for a few moments."

She took his hand again. "There was nothing theatrical in it, Mr. Spencer. Again, my deepest thanks."

Dias led the way through the winding boat.

"A beautiful woman, is she not?"

Mitch nodded. "Mr. Greely is a lucky man," he answered without looking to see Dias's expression.

On the foredeck, Dias turned to him.

"I insist on a raincheck for that dinner. Where may I reach you?"

Mitch thumbed a business card out of his wallet. A no longer valid business card, but no one knew that yet. Boy, some day this had been.

"Ah, you live in Los Angeles! I have many acquaintances there. You are in insurance?"

"Yes," Mitch lied. *Was.*

Dias grinned. "I have a great admiration for American businesses. They epitomize capitalism at its finest. 'Epitomize,' is that a word?"

"A very appropriate word. Your English is excellent. Have you been in the States long, Mr. Dias?"

"Off and on. Currently on. And please drop the 'Mister.' My full name is Santiago Rodrigues Dias, but my friends, and not a few of my enemies, call me simply Dias. I would be honored if you would allow me to call you Mitch."

"The honor is mine."

This was fun thought Mitch. Sort of like a 1940s Gilbert Roland movie. You didn't often get to talk like this. Or be with a man this charming. He was liking Dias more all the time, sensing the feeling was mutual.

"Do you have enemies yourself, Mitch?"

He thought of John Stillman. "Only my share."

Dias chuckled heartily, slapping Mitch's arm. "You can judge a man by his enemies."

"I think I've heard that one, yes."

Dias smiled. "Another of your country's marvelous sayings. An enviable place, America. A great place, I think. I would give much to have been born an American."

"Not a prerequisite for gaining status. Simply be a good boy for two years and sign some papers, happens all the time."

Dias's smile was iridescent. Something had just been exchanged between the two men, a mutual understanding. Perhaps even a trust?

"I think you are a most interesting man, Mitch. I hope we can make that dinner engagement soon."

They shook hands.

"Is our guest leaving so soon, Santiago?"

A stout, handsome woman in a loose-flowing dress approached them, martini glass in hand. She smiled demure admiration at Mitch beneath a mane of silver hair, her face powerful, confident. She offered him her hand.

"Allow me to introduce Mr. Mitch Spencer, the man of the hour."

The dark-eyed woman bowed her head as Mitch took

the hand. "I heard all about your heroics, Mr. Spencer. You have our deepest gratitude for your act of bravery."

Dias beamed as Mitch shook the strong, tanned arm.

"Mr. Spencer—Mitch—I'm pleased to present my dear mother . . ."

Mitch moored the dinghy to a dock cleat and stepped gingerly up to the weathered planks.

He was halfway up the narrow jetty, dragging his rattling gear with him, when the voice wafted clear and crisp from the cabin.

"Buggers aren't biting, are they?"

Mitch looked up in surprise, squinting in the darkness.

A portly figure under a glowing-white panama sat on the porch swing puffing a cigar stump. The silhouette was Winston Churchill familiar, the pudgy cheeks ruddy, the smile, lit from rosy puffs, disarming. "Never a very good lake for fishing, despite its reputation. Of course, it depends on what you're fishing for. It appears you caught a rather large specimen today!"

The man raised his bulk painfully from the swing and stepped down from the porch toward Mitch. "Forgive me. Introductions are in order! The name's Greely, Franklyn Greely." A scrim of sweat dampened his temple, despite the evening breeze.

The name struck a chord. "Greely . . . Claire Greely's husband?"

"The self-same personage, dear boy, and most decidedly your humble servant. I was watching from shore when you saved my dear Claire's life—an impotent whale to your Herculean bravery. You may place me at the top of your list of most egregious debtors. Please"—he extended spongy fingers—"accept my most humble and heartfelt gratitude, Mister ah . . ."

Mitch stopped gaping and stepped forward. "Spencer. Mitch Spencer." He shook Greely's soft hand. How could so beautiful a woman be married to this—this massive cherub? "Sorry if I'm a little slow on the uptake—it's been a big day."

"A monumental day, dear fellow, a pivotal day, a day like all days, filled with those events that alter and illuminate our time!"

Mitch blinked into the cherry face. Greely smiled. "Walter Cronkite, 'You Are There.'" He smiled inscrutably at Mitch for a moment longer, then reached into his pocket suddenly and took out a white envelope. He handed it to Mitch.

Mitch looked at it. "What's this?"

"A reward. For saving the dearest part of my life—my lovely Claire."

Mitch reached inside and drew out five thousand dollar bills. He hastily shoved it back into the envelope. "I didn't rescue her for money."

"Of course not, dear boy, I never said you did. It was a pure and selfless act, a rare commodity on today's market."

"But five thousand dollars! I can't—"

Greely's eyes were moist.

"I was hoping you might accept it as an act of friendship."

Mitch hesitated, considering. Mortgage . . . bills . . . the car . . .

A warning bell went off. You don't get something for nothing.

He pushed the thought back as the fat man extended his hand again, trembling.

What could Mitch do but take it?

CHAPTER 6

MITCH

*T*HE CLOSER HE GOT TO HOME, THE WORSE IT WAS.

Mitch kept stopping for coffee at little roadside dives, topping off the gas tank unnecessarily, constantly checking the oil, stalling, lagging, anything to avoid getting to Los Angeles, to his home, to Joanne.

What to do.

He sat stone-faced behind the wheel of his expensive car trying to form some plan, trying not to think about having to sell that expensive car. Knowing he would anyway.

What do do.

Okay. He'd be clearheaded about this. It isn't the end of the world. He'd find work somewhere, at something. What if he did have to sell the house, the car? What if Joanne did have to postpone her education? They'd survive. Things would level out. They always did. They'd been down before, not in years maybe, but they'd been there and they'd always landed on their feet.

Well . . . sort of.

He thought about all the money he'd borrowed from his brother, his parents. Thousands were still owed to the latter when Dad died. Not that Dad had cared, really, but Mitch would have given the world if he'd been able to pay back the old man in his lifetime. All his life he'd sought approval in his father's eyes, the acknowledgment that he—Mitch—was a man, a responsible human being, a useful contributor to society. Yet all his life he'd flitted from one half-baked career to the next, all—until All-American—a string of failures. Especially that first one . . .

Oh, yeah, that first one . . .

Mitch squeezed his eyes shut a moment, trying not to conjure up unwanted memories.

Being a cop didn't count . . . didn't count.

Didn't count.

He opened his eyes and found himself drifting slowly over the center divider. He righted the wheel. Too late for that. The time for that was at the lake. They'd need the car for resale.

All right, stop this now, nobody's committing suicide here today, m' boy. Get a goddamn grip on yourself. You're not a worthless human being. You tried your best to pay your father back. If he hadn't died, if the job at All-American had held, you *would* have paid him back. In any case, there's nothing you can do about that now. Now is the time to think of your own family. *Their* future.

All right, so you and Joanne haven't exactly been on the best terms of late. You've been distracted, she's been finding herself. Maybe you should take the time now to work on that. Maybe a marriage and children are more important than a frigging career anyway. When you were first married, everybody told you she was the best thing that ever happened to you. Maybe they were right.

You've got the five thousand from Greely. A windfall, under the circumstances. Something to bank. Certainly an indication that not all of your luck has gone sour. At least it will give you a few days to think. At least it will soften the blow to Joanne.

Yes, but how did you earn it?

All right then, lie if you have to, tell her you found it. No, no. Tell her . . . tell her you won it from Stillman in a card game. You both got drunk, the game got carried away . . .

No. Better tell her it was just part of the severance pay from the job. If you tell her at all—

And what about the job?

Maybe it's worth confronting Carlson about that. Maybe there's still a chance. Stillman hated your guts anyway, maybe he made it sound worse than it really was. March up there to Carlson on Monday, let him know you don't appreciate being screwed out of a job. Be a man. It might even work.

Mitch didn't believe this, really, but it made him feel a little better fantasizing about it.

That was it, then: go home, walk into the house, kiss Joanne, hold her a moment, even tell her you love her, take her out to dinner—a final dinner—and give her the news. Don't try to cover up. Hell, you don't know, she might even jump at the idea of finding a job. She's been at odds with herself lately anyway, this might be just the ticket. Think of it as an adventure, you're young again, just married, starting out on the road to life together. Nellie's almost five, not that much of a burden anymore. There are babysitters, preschool. It will work. If you make it work, it will work.

She was waiting for him at the door.

And right away he knew something was different.

For one thing, she was smiling. Coming up the front walk, lugging his fishing gear under both arms, he had, for one moment of brief madness, the ridiculous idea that she was having an affair, that she had finally found herself another man, had come smiling to the door to tell him so.

"Hi! You look tanned! How was the fishing?"

"Hi. Terrible. You look nice, though."

He didn't have to press for the kiss and the hug, she came immediately into his arms.

When their lips parted he pulled back and looked at her carefully. Joanne was radiant, really lovely.

"Everything okay here at the fort?"

She wasn't moving out of the doorway. She couldn't seem to take her eyes off his, and her own were brimming just slightly. He had never seen such happy contentment in the lovely face.

"Hey, miss me that much, did you?"

She bit her lip, wiped away a joyful tear.

"Jo? Hey—? Tell me. What is it?"

She couldn't contain herself, rushed in close again, hugging his neck painfully.

"Mitch! Oh, Mitch! I'm pregnant!"

Monday morning.

Welcome home.

TULLY

*T*ULLY WAS PISSED.

Things weren't resolving themselves and he didn't like it when things didn't resolve themselves. It was sort of like hunkering down to watch your favorite show on a Tuesday night and finding out the damn cable was on the blink. It was irritating, acid-inducing.

He sat now in his beige Chevy Nova across the street from Suspect One and reflected on the past week.

The case on Mrs. Charlotte Cunningham, rape, homicide, and mutilation victim, was about as embarrassingly open as a local homicide can get. The best chance any homicide has of being solved is in the first forty-eight hours after the victim's death. If a decent lead is not established within that time, it becomes increasingly harder as the hours tick by. Within a week the case is considered cool. Within a month, cold. This one was cooling rapidly, as Tully was all too aware. The papers were getting ready to have a field day with it. Tully's ulcer was getting ready to go into overdrive.

The facts up to now were mostly academic: Mr. Cunningham had viewed his wife's remains, confirmed she was who she was, something Tully already knew. Wanamaker's postmortem had showed that, aside from a few light upper arm and shoulder bruises, there were no other wounds or abrasions, no ligature marks about the neck. The genital wounds alone had killed her.

The investigation had come to an inauspicious halt after that. The latent prints on the sunglasses had come up worthless: one of them was Mrs. Cunningham's, the other might have been or might not, but was too smudged to get more than a couple of traceable lines. The blood-soaked beach towel yielded no foreign fibers, no pubic hairs. She probably was not killed on it. There were indeed traces of semen in the vaginal cavity, which did not match Mr. Cunningham's blood type but, according to Wanamaker, were several days older than the estimated time of the victim's death. This didn't mean the semen didn't belong to the killer, it just didn't mean it did. Mrs. Cunningham could have been getting some on the side—Mr. Cunningham was.

Detective Tully had interviewed four of Charlotte Cunningham's closest friends: Did they know anything about a recent affair, a possible boyfriend outside the marriage? One of the friends was outraged, one was shocked, another was surprised, the last one giggled. The giggler spilled it. She'd promised Charlotte she wouldn't, but now that she was dead, well . . . only one problem. She didn't know who.

The spent flashbulb had been dusted and come up a smooth blank. Gloves? Maybe. Maybe just a windy beach and scouring sand. Or maybe it had been lying around there in the kelp for the past sixteen years, who knew? Probably a dead end in any case. But they had pursued it, gone to every camera store in town with the thing, stuck it under the nose of every clerk. No one had anything to say about it. No one carried old flashbulbs like that anymore. As far as anyone knew, no one *made* flashbulbs like that anymore. Great. Tully had kept it anyway.

They weren't getting much further with the killer's modus operandi. The genital wounds gave no clues as to the kind of weapon used, except that it was long (probably ten to twelve inches), at least three inches in circumference, and sharp. It could have been practically anything. But, aside from providing the department men's room with a raft of unfunny jokes about Kong-sized French ticklers, it yielded nothing.

Frustration built.

Tully sat in his bachelor apartment and munched Doritos and stared at the flashbulb. Time dragged. Every minute he expected to get a call about the next one.

He juggled the flashbulb.

On impulse he reached for the phone book, turned to the yellow pages, began flipping toward the Photography section again. Maybe he'd missing one. As the pages whipped by he caught nearly subliminally the words "Flea Market." Again on impulse, he flipped back to the page.

Conway's Flea Market and Nostalgia Store, Area's Largest, 1412 Paseo Street.

Tully dialed.

"Conway's . . ."

"Yes, I wonder if you can help me. I'm looking for a camera I used to have but lost. The thing is, I can't remember the name of it. It was an older style, and I still have one of the spent flashbulbs."

"Hmm. Flashbulb, huh? Can you bring it in?"

Tully was there in ten minutes.

The proprietor was young, still in his mid-twenties, but he knew his stuff. He studied the little bulb through Coke-bottle glasses, nodding.

"Um-hum. Westinghouse number 5. She's a bayonet."

"A 'bayonet'?"

"See the base here? They made two kinds in the old days, ones that screwed in like a lightbulb and ones that popped in like yours here. Both Sylvania and Westing-house made them but only Westinghouse made the number 5. Got any idea where you purchased the camera?"

"No."

"Long time ago, huh? Well, most people shopped at Monkey Ward's or Sears in the old days. Sears sold a Westinghouse number 5 for both their German imported Tower cameras and their Ansco outfits. I'd try one of those two."

"Any way you can tell the age of the camera, how long ago it was I might have bought it?"

The Coke bottles rode down on his nose as the young man shrugged. "Not to the month, but I'd say—bulb that old, pre-cube style—probably early fifties. Take a guess at '53. Don't hold me to it. Sorry."

"Sorry?"

"Don't have any cameras that old here."

Tully smiled. "Never mind, you've been a big help. '53, you say?"

"Just a guess."

"Sometimes that's enough."

Well, finally something, however fuzzy.

And then, within the hour, another possible break. He was heading back to his apartment when his pager beeped. When he got home he phoned the office.

Ted Sears told him someone at the VA where Charlotte Cunningham was employed had seen her leave the week before with a consultant who occasionally worked for the department. There had been rumors about a relationship. Sears ran a check on him and came up with a record still on file in Narcotics: Raymond C. Hartley, 1421 Sagamore Circle, Montecito, California. Busted 2/24/86 for possession of illegal drugs. And his blood type, AB negative, matched the blood type of the semen found in the corpse.

Talk about luck. Captain Sparrs, Tully's next in command, was happy. The department eased back a notch. At least they for chrissake had something.

Tully was less elated. Fifteen years ago a Narc file make might have meant something—today we live in a drug-ridden society.

Raymond Hartley was thirty-six, good-looking, if his police file photo was any indication, a stockbroker for L. M. LeBrae. He cleared two hundred G's a year, according to his superior. Tully knew the type. Hartley probably ran with a fast-lane crowd that used recreational drugs like others use water. He was a bachelor, no doubt an avowed womanizer. He drove a Corvette, a restored fifties convertible. Sure, he could have been a psychotic killer, too, but Tully didn't like the way it smelled.

He took the information from Records without making out a report, drove to Montecito and parked across the street from Hartley's expensive tile-roofed, palm-flanked house.

He strode to the front door and knocked, waited.

Nothing.

Tully went back to his car and sat and watched the house across the street. It was a Sunday. Hartley may have been at the beach, may have been out of town. It was five or six P.M.; if Hartley had to be at work on Monday, he might be heading home soon to rest up. Or he might be out for the night balling his secretary somewhere. Tully would wait. It was what you did in Homicide, what you were used to doing: waiting and hoping. You did it a lot. Detective Tully had grown up watching Sergeant Joe Friday do it in black and white every Wednesday night on his parents' Motorola. It had looked romantic back then. Especially with that great theme song.

An hour passed.

Tully was staring absently at the brown plastic barrels in front of Hartley's driveway. Trash day. Tomorrow morning a big noisy truck would come and empty the weekly garbage, leaving all the neatly manicured lawns with the empty shells of brown and green plastic barrels.

On impulse, Tully got out of the car and strode back

to the house, dragging the barrels with him. He walked around to the back of the house; there was a low wooden gate but it was unlocked, Tully gave the neighborhood a cursory glance for prying neighbors and pushed the metal latch. He dragged the barrels into the flagstoned backyard. Hartley had a newly trimmed lawn and a barbecue pit. Tully set the barrels down and walked up a short flight of cement stairs to the screened-in porch. He tried the door, found it locked. He looked about the house for other exits, side entrances, found none. He retreated down the stairs again, turned and plastic barrels over on their sides gently, and placed them below the last step, one beside the other. He returned to his car.

Hartley came home at six fifty-eight. It was beginning to grow dark. Perfect.

The suspect skipped up the front steps without noticing either Detective Tully or the missing trash barrels. It wasn't something you thought about.

Once inside, he closed the door behind him, and Tully saw a light go on. Tully got out of the car.

He walked rapidly across the street and knocked sharply at the door. After a moment, Hartley opened it, shirt half unbuttoned. "Yes?"

"Raymond Hartley?"

"Yeah?"

"Santa Barbara Sheriff's Department, Mr. Har—"

The door started to slam in Tully's face.

Tully caught it with his toe, shoved inward.

Hartley was already halfway down the hall.

"Halt or I'll shoot!"

Hartley looked as if he wanted to go right, changed his mind at the last second, and veered confusedly toward the back door. Tully didn't even bother to pull his piece.

Hartley got the screen door open, plowed through, hit the plastic barrels full tilt. Banana peels, beer cans, old newspapers blossomed skyward. Cursing, somersaulting, he slammed down hard on the flagstones and lay groaning softly under a rain of coffee grounds. Tully had him rolled and cuffed without even breathing hard.

"Don't tell me—you were just coming back here to start the barbecue . . ."

"I don't have to let you in, you don't have a warrant!"

"Yeah? How do you know I don't?"

Tully hauled him to his feet, shoved him against a stucco wall, kicked his legs apart, made the frisk while reciting the Miranda.

"Looking a little nervous there, Hartley. Something to hide?"

"I don't have to say anything without my lawyer present."

"Is that a fact?" Tully's practiced fingers slid over a flattish bulge in Hartley's shirt pocket.

Christ. Hartley thought he was a narc.

Tully smiled, pressing Hartley's face into the rough stucco façade. "You look like a man who needs to go to the john. Needs to go real bad."

He spun the suspect around, pushed himself up to the sweating face. "Is that right, Mr. Hartley, do you need to get rid of some crap?"

Hartley, drenched in perspiration, said nothing.

Tully grabbed the man's shirt collar and shoved him through the back door. He dragged him down the expensively paneled hall. "Where's the john, asshole?"

Hartley motioned with his head.

Tully pushed him through the bathroom door, uncuffing him in the process. "Take care of business, hotshot, and get out here on the double. Any funny stuff and you're meat." Tully pulled the door closed.

After a moment he heard the expected flush.

Hartley came back through and Tully grabbed him, shoved him unresisting against the wall. His trailing fingers found no flat bulge this time. He spun Hartley around again.

"Okay, Mr. Big Shot Broker, I did you a favor; now

you're going to do me one. Tell me everything you know about Mrs. Charlotte Cunningham in less than sixty seconds."

"My attorney—"

Tully slammed him against the wall again. "Your attorney my ass, dickhead. This is Murder One we're talking about. You're going to need Clarence Darrow to get you off this time!"

This was the moment. Tully watched the face.

It was always in the eyes. If you were good, you could spot it. Proving it was another thing.

But Hartley wasn't looking scared—not the deep, trapped fear. Just confused.

A bad sign.

"What're you—has something happened to Charlotte?"

Shit.

"You know something has, asshole!"

But he didn't, goddamnit. It was all there in his handsome face: he was genuinely nonplussed.

"What—is she hurt?"

"Somebody tried to get into her pussy with a can opener."

Watch the face.

"What . . .? W-where is she?"

"City morgue. What happened, Hartley—her husband leave too big a path to follow? You get frustrated, was that it? Big car, little dick?"

Hartley was alabaster. He swallowed hugely. "Charlotte. Oh, Jesus—"

He threw up on Tully's shoe.

And threw away an airtight case.

On the way downtown, Hartley sat cuffed in the front seat, staring mesmerized out the window. The front of his shirt still stank; his face was drained of color.

After nearly five minutes he turned to Detective Tully with sudden fear etched in his face, as though the full ramifications had just slammed home.

"I didn't kill her! Jesus Christ! I had a few drinks with her! I screwed her! But I didn't kill her! Where are you taking me?"

"You're going to jerk off into a paper cup for us, Mr. Hartley."

"I swear to God, I never hurt her!"

"Tell that to the judge, Mr. Hartley."

But Tully knew it would never get that far.

There was still a killer running around out there.

He was back to square one.

At the station, in the process of having Hartley booked, Tully looked up to find Brumeister converging on him, stench-radiating cigar clenched in his mouth like a dark turd.

"How goes the floater case, Eustes?"

Brumeister's patronizing smile said it all; he knew precisely how the case was going, the whole department knew how the case was going, which was to say it was going nowhere at all. Brumeister puffed reeking smoke with smug satisfaction.

"Swell, William. How's the numbers racket?"

Brumeister grinned, showing yellow teeth. Everyone knew interdepartmental betting was against station rules. "Won me eighty bucks on the Celtics game. Those niggers never miss a shot. Put you down for Saturday's playoff?"

Tully was fishing for his Tums, remembering now they were still somewhere on the floor of the car. "Don't think so, haven't got the spare change."

Brumeister leaned against the watercooler, looking Tully up and down appraisingly. "A bachelor and you ain't got the change? Where you been banking all your quarters, Eustes, in the stroke shop booths down the street?"

Tully shouldered past, heading for his office.

Brumeister chuckled his piggy chuckle. "By the way, Wanamaker's been looking for you."

Tully turned.

He had to wait for Brumeister to stop grinning. "Think he might have something, Eustes? Like a—what do they call those things?—a 'clue'?"

"Why didn't you give him my pager number?"

"Clean slipped my mind. Let me know if you change your mind about Saturday's game—my door is always open."

"Next time the county coroner is trying to get hold of me, Brumeister, give him my goddamn number!"

He'd shouted this and two duty officers looked up from the front desk.

Tully and Brumeister regarded each other coldly across twenty feet of station house linoleum. Then Brumeister grinned.

It was perfect: everyone was looking at Tully. Everyone had been looking at Tully for days. Waiting.

Waiting for answers he couldn't give them.

He'd played right into Brumeister's hands.

Tully turned away and gave the stares his back.

He took his time getting to the morgue, thinking: I'm tired, this thing's wearing at me, otherwise that wouldn't have happened. Bringing in Hartley was just a lot of show, and everyone, including Captain Sparrs, knows it. I need a break, a goddamn *break!*

Praying that Wanamaker would supply it.

Fred Wanamaker was slicing brains when Tully walked in; he was standing over the humming metal machine, like a contented Safeway butcher, oblivious to the continual cold blast from the air-conditioning vents, gloves and apron pink with viscera, squinting through his glasses, wincing back cigarette smoke.

Tully shook his head.

He always shook his head down here. He loved Fred Wanamaker like a brother, but he couldn't imagine why anyone would want to spend his daylight hours in this freezing death pit surrounded by inanimate, pale-skinned husks and the reek of embalming fluid.

Wanamaker snapped off his gloves and nodded at Tully's approach, holding up the back of one of his slim-fingered hands. "You're a hard man to find. Take a look at this."

Tully studied the man's upheld hand.

"What am I looking at?"

"The nails. What do you see?"

Tully squinted at Wanamaker's fingers. "Nothing. Yellow stuff?"

Wanamaker nodded. "Know what that is?"

"Tell me."

"Human skin. From the cadavers. Flakes off and gets under the nails when you don't wear gloves. I don't like the gloves for the really delicate work."

Tully wrinkled his face. "Jesus, Fred."

Wanamaker grinned. "Drives the medical students nuts. You can't get rid of the stuff no matter how hard you scrub. Just has to wear off. Try explaining it over a candlelight dinner sometime."

"No thanks."

"Brumeister give you my message?"

"After a fashion."

"Asshole. Come take a look at this."

Wanamaker led the way past a stiff with a missing skullcap and a stacked female corpse with a slit throat to a wooden workbench and an electron microscope. He switched on the microscope light, racked down with a twist of knobs, and stepped aside for Detective Tully. "Take a peep."

Tully squinted through aluminum tube and ground glass at a dark, fibrous smudge.

"What is it?"

"Paint chip. Two-sixteenths centimeter square." Wanamaker lit a Lucky, blew smoke at a dental chart. "I took another vaginal swab before they shipped Mrs. Cunningham home, like you suggested. Came up with that."

Tully squinted harder, elated. "Bless your little heart, Fred. Any ideas?"

Wanamaker shook his head. "Only that it's a foreign substance that doesn't normally belong up there."

Tully straightened, peered again at the mounted slide, which showed an object so small he could hardly detect it. "Part of a weapon?"

Wanamaker shrugged. "Don't get too excited yet. I've yet to find a black tampon in my days down here, but if they can come out with edible panties anything is possible. It could be from the instrument that ruptured her, or it could be anything—flaking paint from a worn chair, anything."

Tully gave him a skeptical look. "Chair? And it got up her . . . inside her?"

Wanamaker puffed patiently. "I've seen worse. A woman's sex organs are a lot more exposed than a man's, more prone to infection, disease, foreign material. Found a toy airplane inside one corpse. Rubber snake up another. Once pulled seven inches of plastic fishing worm out of a fifty-year-old man's nasal passage. If it's an open cavity, it's vulnerable. The one place God fucked up— giving us openings. I sent the other half of that chip over to the lab in your absence."

"Good for you."

"Ted Sears says they'll have an answer for you by Tuesday. If we can trace the paint manufacturer—"

"—we can narrow its application, maybe find our weapon. You're a gem, Fred, thanks."

Wanamaker smiled. "Figured you could use a little good news."

He reached over to a squat medical jar, milky with serpentine lower colon, and retrieved a styrofoam cup, taking a sip. "Coffee?"

Tully turned away, pale. "Some other time."

Tully stood at the edge of the dock, looking out at the marina. He often came down here when things were slow, or when he'd gotten a piece of good news like on the flashbulb or the paint chip. It helped him think, down here in the ocean breeze. He liked to watch the gulls spat, liked to throw them popcorn.

Liked to dream.

It was in the form of a little red ketch, his dream, moored securely to the dock in front of him, with the same FOR SALE sign tacked to its dodger that had been there for months. The ketch was real, the dream wasn't.

Tully gazed longingly at the trim craft, allowed the dream to expand. He was at the helm, wind in his face, rolling steadily outward from the wharf toward the orange glow of the sun-kissed horizon. Usually he was alone—Mother, the department, all his cares and woes far, far behind. Sometimes, on his more adventurous fantasies, he was with a woman. She was always faceless, and she was always at his side, arm hooked about his waist, hand clasped in his. Together they faced the endless sea, the beckoning future. . . .

Tully blinked, came back to reality.

A two-masted yawl, anchored dangerously close to the ketch, threatened to bump it, mar its beautiful red hull. Tully winced impotently. He wanted that little ketch. He wanted to put her to sea, get her out of this crowded marina. He wanted to stroke her mahogany decks and talk to her staysail and make her his own.

But that would take money.

He had it. Or, rather, Mother had it. It was in the house. The house he'd grown up in, she'd grown old in. Selling it would pay for the little boat and leave plenty over for a lengthy, leisurely ocean voyage.

But that would mean putting mother in the Home.

It was a perfectly nice Home. A lovely Home, really. He had been in it several times, talked with the polite staff. And God knew it was the best thing for her. She could no longer manage the house, it was too large. She couldn't keep it dusted and refused to hire a maid. It was like a huge mausoleum through which she rambled, alone and bitter. The Home was the best answer.

He could do it. He had the legal right.

But it was the way she looked at him. The way her mouth set every time he mentioned it. The tension-filled silence that inevitably followed.

Tully watched the gently rocking little red ketch.

One thing was for sure: someday the FOR SALE sign would be gone. So would the little red ketch. And his dream.

He walked back to his car and made himself concentrate on the case.

CHAPTER 8

CLAIRE

CLAIRE GREELY PULLED INTO THE DRIVEWAY OF HER husband's mansion and cut the Bentley's powerful engine. She sat behind the leather-wrapped wheel a moment looking up at the ivy-traced stone façade of the enormous house. She was debating with herself whether or not to pretend.

She usually did.

No. She always did.

And not just about the weekend. She pretended about everything these days, everything that had anything to do with her marriage to Franklyn.

She pretended she enjoyed it.

Which was mostly unnecessary, really, since he probably already knew she didn't enjoy it. She just pretended. Because she didn't know what else to do.

Not that the pretense of living with him was that difficult.

Franklyn never bothered her. She had the run of the house, the pool, the butlers and maids, her own car. The

run of her own life, really. He never questioned her com-
ings and goings, even if most of them really were innocent shopping outings. He never pried, never complained,
always had a smile for her return. All he seemed to
require was her infrequent companionship, someone to
look good on his arm at a dinner party. They maintained
separate bedrooms.

During the entire course of their seven-year marriage
he had attempted to sleep with her exactly once: on their
wedding night. An unmitigated disaster.

He was impotent.

Somehow the fact that he'd never tried to make love
to her during their courtship had appealed to her romantic sense; he was an older man, a knight in shining
armor, and she'd been charmed. Even though she was
warned against marrying so hastily, he had been attractive and rich, and she was a spoiled young girl intent
on being spoiled the rest of her life. But after that first
embarrassing try, she lay naked and cold and staring up
at the gilt-etched parabolas and gamboling cupids and
wondering how on earth she had ever gotten into this
and if she could bear another such humiliating—no,
degrading—attempt.

She never had to.

From that moment on, her relationship with her husband had remained platonic. He had avoided her physically after that, had aged before her eyes, gaining weight
and losing hair until she couldn't believe he was the
same man she'd married.

She'd urged him to seek therapy, but he'd refused. A
man in his position? What if it should get out?

What about a woman in her position? He didn't seem
to care about that. "Love" was not a word that entered
into the vocabulary of their lives anymore. Nor, in the
deepest sense, did "respect." What they had could best
be termed "an understanding."

In its own way it worked quite well.

Until Santiago Dias.

She'd met him at a party in her own house; he'd

come with another guest. She'd been immediately attracted, and soon his invitation had come to spend the weekend on his yacht. Not Franklyn; just her. She knew what that meant. The attraction, apparently, had been mutual. . . .

Claire pushed away from the leather upholstery of the Bentley and strode up the flagstone walk to the main entrance. Yes, she would pretend today. And it wouldn't even be that hard. For, even given the undeniable sexual attraction between her and the handsome Colombian, there was something missing, something off-center there.

She couldn't quite put her finger on it, but she'd been secretly glad when the skiing accident had given her the excuse not to sleep with Dias that night. Not just because of the guilt she'd feel later over Franklyn, but because she wasn't sure she was really ready for it. Oh, she wanted it. But that's not the same as being ready for it, feeling right about it. Something askew. Something bothering her.

Then, swinging open the heavy oak double doors and stepping into the mansion's air-conditioned depths, she suddenly knew what.

It wasn't Dias at all that was bothering her.

It was his mother.

"Welcome back! Did you have a good time with Jayce?"

Franklyn Greely was seated in the library before heavy velvet brocades and a burled wood writing desk, nursing a pipe and reading one of his Agatha Christie mysteries. He looked up with his usual warm smile. For an instant she was terribly glad Santiago Dias had not made love to her. She saw the shadow of the man she had fallen in love with, and it touched her.

"Hi, darling, yes. Jayce is fine, sends her love."

A lie. The first of the day. She hadn't seen Jayce Peterson in three years. "How are things here?"

"How are things with *you*, Buttercup?"

Claire wheeled at the familiar voice, squealed her surprise and delight. "Uncle Joe!"

He was behind her, in the big red leather chair opposite her husband's desk; she hadn't seen him. She rushed into his arms, squeezing him tight, kissing his cheek. "Where have you been, you bad uncle? I'm out of town one lousy weekend and that's the time you decide to pay a visit? I shouldn't even be talking to you! Give me another hug!"

Joe Wallace, eyes crinkling, laughed and hugged back, delighting in the fresh smell of her. "How have you been, Buttercup? It's been too long."

"It certainly has. Why do you sit clear across town in that stuffy house all by yourself when you could be seeing more of us? Taking me to the movies while this boring old husband of mine buries his nose in his books. Taking me shopping. Taking me to the circus. Taking me—"

"—to the soda shop next to McGonigle's deli for a double-decker tutti-frutti!" they both chimed in tandem, breaking into peals of laughter.

Uncle Joe patted her cheek. "That was a long time ago, Buttercup! How you used to love your tutti-frutti ice cream! God, I must have bought you gallons of it!"

Claire smiled down at him beatifically, face aglow. "Does it show, Uncle Joe?"

His smile was pure love. "Not on you, sweetheart. Not on you."

Claire hugged him again, then stood back and contentedly appraised him. "Say, whatever happened to tutti-frutti? You never see it around anymore."

"Gone the way of the Edsel and the mimeograph machine, probably," Franklyn Greely put in from behind his orderly desk.

Uncle Joe nodded. "Your husband's right, I'm afraid. Progress. Inexorable progress." An edge of sadness etched the jolly crinkles. "Whenever you gain something, Buttercup, you lose something. Progress isn't always such a good thing." The smile returned. "You look wonderful. My big girl."

She kissed the top of his head and swept toward the door, pointing a finger at Franklyn. "You will not let him

get away while I take my bath. That is an order." She
turned and pointed the finger at Uncle Joe. "You will
stay to dinner and mounds of dessert, that is my second
order. I will scour the town for tutti-frutti ice cream!"

Uncle Joe raised his hand. "I'll stay, scout's honor."

Claire winked and left the room.

Uncle Joe turned to Greely, beaming. "You're a lucky
man, Franklyn, but I needn't tell you that, need I?"

Franklyn Greely watched the empty doorway, ex-
pressionless.

Dinner was disappointing.

She had hoped to sit next to Uncle Joe, chat about
the old days when he used to take her for ice cream or
down to Sutter's Lake to that old dinghy and teach her
to fish. They'd never caught anything but sunburn, but
Claire wouldn't trade those childhood memories for anything. He wasn't even her real uncle, just a neighbor who
loved children, but he had spoiled her after her mother
died—he had money and he wasn't afraid to use it. Her
own father was cold, demanding; he'd finally moved back
east when she was sixteen, leaving Claire to fend for herself. If it hadn't been for Uncle Joe—generous, unselfish
Uncle Joe—she might have ended up on the streets, or
worse. She was one of his orphans, one of the children
he took in and protected as if they were his own, and she
knew she was the best-loved of the lot. He loved her, in
fact, far more than she deserved.

But she hadn't sat next to Uncle Joe at dinner because Franklyn's business cronies had been invited, and
most of the evening's conversation drifted to stocks and
bonds and the machinations of Wall Street. Claire had
sat apart from the men, playing desultorily with her but-
terscotch parfait, wishing it were tutti-frutti, wishing she
were eleven again.

After dinner, Uncle Joe repaired with the rest of the
men to Franklyn's oak-paneled den to cloud the air with
foul-smelling cigars and continue the business meeting.
Claire endured politely five or six suffocating minutes

of it, then excused herself and went for a walk in the garden.

It was a typically cool, dry California night, and the mansion's back terrace was pungent with the myriad roses, jonquils, and other blossoms growing in profusion along the neatly aligned flagstones. Claire walked down to the stone-ringed koi pond and threw in her requisite bread crumbs, ever delighted in the way the big orange, yellow, and white Japanese carp fought over them. Franklyn had stocked the small pond below the waterfall with the large exotic fish at her request. Some of them reached two feet and more in length; some were so tame she could pet them as they fed.

It was quiet in the garden, relaxed and fragrant and refreshing. It was usually her favorite spot, day or night.

But not tonight. Tonight she was confused, out-of-sorts, maybe even a little sad. The Santiago Dias thing was fast reaching a point of no return, a point at which it would become a genuine affair, or nothing at all. It would have reached that point last night but for the skiing accident and the arrival of the stranger. That had given her a convenient grace period.

But Dias was a forceful, if patient, man. He wouldn't tolerate demure handshakes, over-dinner flirting, and vague promises forever. He was playing it cool because he was a gentleman—or wanted her to think of him that way—and because the situation was superficially delicate: she was a married woman. But a man like that had doubtless bedded dozens of married women. Protocol was one thing, hot Latino blood another. She couldn't expect to string him along indefinitely.

And, truthfully, she didn't want to string him along at all. One part of her wanted nothing more than to take him below in that fancy yacht of his, rip his clothes off, pull him down on that gently rocking bunk, and show him how American women make love. It was the other, indefinable part of her that was preventing the play from reaching a climax. The part of her neither Dias nor her-

CLAIRE

self could quite reach. The confused part. The indecisive part. The part that wanted—corny as it was—true love.

She watched the koi.

Maybe the truth was she was nothing but a spoiled brat rich girl, too bored to stay home but too frightened to take real chances. She enjoyed his company, his hard good looks, his foreign accent and manner. She enjoyed, thrilled to the chase—*needed* the chase—it was what might follow she couldn't seem to deal with.

Maybe she was crazy.

It was just a piece of ass, that's all it had to be. What are you saving it for, Claire? You're not getting any at home.

I'm not a whore!

You're not getting any younger, either.

Franklyn believes in me! I'm a married woman.

It's the nineties, Claire, wake up and smell the coffee.

Yes, and die of AIDS!

AIDS or boredom—we all die sooner or later. You've already got all the money in the world, what's left?

What's left.

She sat down on a stone bench flanked by a cactus garden, and gazed quietly at the lazily circling koi. Lucky, lucky fish ... all you have to do is swim about all day and make little fish and wait for your mistress to come feed you.

She rubbed her arms against the chill, feeling suddenly very old.

"Hi, Buttercup."

Claire turned unexpectantly, then smiled warmly. "Uncle Joe. You didn't have to."

Uncle Joe shrugged, returning the smile, patting her goose-pimpled arm as he joined her on the stone bench. "Bunch of iguanas already up to their asses in too much money and figuring how to get more. Now me, I prefer the moon and the garden and a lovely girl by my side."

65

She nestled against his warmth, rested her head on his shoulder. "Can you ever forgive me about dessert?"

He squeezed her hand. "Couldn't find it, eh? Probably doesn't taste as good as it did in your childhood anyway. Nothing is ever quite as rosy as it once seemed."

Claire heard herself sigh, heavier than she'd intended. "Some times I wish we could go back to it, though ..."

Uncle Joe looked down at her with concern. "Want to tell me about it?"

Claire squeezed his hand and allowed herself another sigh. "It's nothing. I'll work it out."

"Helps to have another ear sometimes."

Claire closed her eyes. She pushed away, swept a hand through her hair. She walked over to the koi pond and gazed down into the moving shadows. "You'd think me awful, Uncle Joe."

"Never. No matter what."

She smiled wistfully. "Yes. Oh, yes. You would. I think myself pretty awful sometimes."

Uncle Joe pulled out a pipe, began to stack it. He didn't say anything until he'd found a match, then: "I can't give you money, Buttercup, you've already too much of that. I can't give you back your childhood."

Claire grinned, her back to him.

"All I can give you is advice. And friendship. If you're in trouble, I wish you'd let me do that, at least."

Inexplicably, Claire found herself crying.

"Buttercup. Come here. Come to Uncle Joe."

She let herself be gathered into his arms.

"Shh. There, there."

"I'm sorry."

"No. Shh. You tell me now—has someone been hurting my angel?"

"I can't tell you."

"Is it so terrible?"

"Having you think so would be terrible."

"You'll always be little Buttercup to me."

He arranged a handkerchief for her, held it to her nose. She blew a short tweet, thanked him, dabbed at her eyes. "God. I'm such a jerk, I must look terrible."

"Prettiest girl at Sutter's Lake."

She coughed a laugh.

He rubbed her back. Let her take her time. When she was ready, it would come.

Claire sat up, shoulders slumped, looking absently into her lap where her hands folded and unfolded the handkerchief. After a time she shook her head slowly. "I'm tired, Uncle Joe. Too much of the time. And I'm too young to be so tired."

He gave her a moment, relighting his pipe. "With the marriage, you mean?"

She nodded at the handkerchief. "With the marriage. With myself. My life. What I've . . . become."

He puffed smoke. "What have you become, Buttercup?"

Her delicate shoulders slumped. "Not much."

He gave it time to breathe, settle. "Is there another man?"

Claire sighed, looked up at the stars. "Not yet."

He watched her. "But there could be?"

"There could."

He nodded. Pulled out his pipe, examined it. "Well. That isn't the end of the world."

She turned to him, surprised. "Uncle Joe! You aren't telling me you'd approve!"

He wasn't smiling, but neither was there judgment in his eyes. "I didn't say that. Look, Buttercup, let's put our cards on the table. I was against your marrying a man Franklyn's age. Not that I don't like Franklyn—after all, I introduced the two of you. But we're nearly the same age, he and I, and I know what an old fart I am. It just wasn't my place to say anything at the time."

"I knew how you felt . . . I was so stupid! I wouldn't listen to anybody!"

He waved his hand dismissively. "You were young, just a child, you had your reasons. Probably money. I could hardly blame you for that. Now you're discovering that money isn't all there is. The point is, I knew there'd be trouble; frankly I'm surprised the marriage has lasted this long. I just can't bear the thought of you being . . . used. Do you mind my talking to you like this, honey?"

She shook her head gratefully, sniffing. "No. I wish you had long ago."

"I've seen my share of May-December romances and they all—most, anyway—suffer the same problems. On the other hand, you'd be surprised how many work out."

She turned to him on the bench. "What are you saying, Uncle Joe?"

He put the pipe back in his mouth and hoped he looked the wise old sage. "I'm trying to say that nobody—perhaps even Franklyn himself—is going to deny you an occasional flirtation. You're a healthy, attractive woman, a beautiful woman. But that doesn't mean it all has to come crumbling down."

"You mean have an affair, just don't be serious about it? I don't know if I can do that, Uncle Joe. I don't know if that's all I want. I thought money meant a lot to me at one time. Now . . ."

"Is it really just the money, Buttercup? Frankyln's a good man, he loves you."

"And I love him! I just don't know if I'm in love with him anymore! Our marriage hasn't exactly been a hotbed of passion . . ."

His smile was patient, uncondescending. "I've lived a long life. Been in love many times. What you're talking about—looking for—is romance. And young or old, romance is a transitory thing. It has its purpose, to bring boys and girls together. But believe me, sweetheart, the love you feel for Franklyn now—that good, solid love of him and family, and yes, even wealth and security if you must—that love is worth a hundred short-term romances. Take it from an old bachelor who knows . . . who wishes he had what you and Franklyn have."

Claire sat back, folded her arms against the night's chill, tomorrow's terrors. "I don't know. Maybe you're right. I just don't know anymore. I shouldn't have burdened you with this."

He laughed his relaxed, comforting laugh. "Buttercup, I've nothing better to do, believe me. I'm as weary of making money as you are of seeking romance." He patted her hand. "Just be careful, my dear. Go have your fling if you must, but choose a good man who will treat you well. Put your heart and soul into it, skate on the edge with the wind in your hair and your heart on your sleeve, until you're thoroughly, gloriously *flung*. Then come back to this garden and feed your fish and look back at this house and ask yourself what it is you really want. You'll know the right answer. Just do your old Uncle Joe one little favor, though?"

"What, dear?"

"Don't go running off somewhere with some dashing sheik without saying good-bye."

She put her arms around him, looked up at the stars, letting the warmth and safety of him settle over her. "Not at least until we've found some tutti-frutti, right?"

He laughed, kissed her cheek. "Right!"

CHAPTER 9

ELEANOR

ELEANOR RANKIN HAD NEVER ASKED MUCH OF LIFE and, as a consequence, had been given quite a lot: good looks, an intelligent husband, a stunningly beautiful son, good health. She would have asked for little more in light of so much bounty, but she would certainly have asked for some rational explanation the day that Harold, her husband of ten years, walked out of her life for good.

She got, instead, a lengthy letter from Harold's attorney. It outlined, in infuriating detail, exactly what it was Harold now requested of her—namely the house and the car. Also, if she didn't want them, the barbecue grill and croquet set in the garage. She could keep the kid.

She endured crushing heartbreak for exactly eighteen and one-half seconds, then turned it forever into vile, deep-seated hatred. Maybe that was Harold's intent, because she went immediately to the wall phone in the kitchen, dialed the attorney's number, and shrieked at him that if that's what her bastard husband wanted, he could damn well have it. Her fury lasted long enough for the attorney to get her to sign a paper to that effect and mail it back to him first class. When the smoke cleared, Eleanor sat in the kitchen over her cold morning coffee and examined the remains of her life: she was broke, unskilled, and left with the care of a six-year-old child. It was beyond infuriating. It was unconscionable. It was grotesque. But it was all true.

If not for Robbie, their six-year-old, she would have seriously contemplated suicide.

Robbie. So innocent. So adorable. So beautiful.

Everyone thought so. Only the other day her neighbor Cynthia Cuttle had remarked how Little Robbie looked like one of those child TV actors you saw in the commercials. Mr. Franks the mailman was forever calling Robbie his "little star."

Eleanor's own mother had used the word "glamour boy" when the child was only four.

"You ought to put him in the movies," the girl at the bank had said.

Eleanor was lying in bed leafing through the family album—tearing out all the photos of Harold—when the notion really struck home. She was holding up a picture of Robbie at the beach, playing with his little pail and shovel, adorable chin tilted up at the camera, afternoon sun playing delicately along the fine cheekbones, the almond eyes, the lustrous hair. The smile you could die for.

He isn't a burden of love at all, a distant voice echoed in Eleanor's brain, he's your *salvation!*

She bought two rolls of Kodak 35-mm Tri-X at the drugstore the next day. She didn't know much about photography, but she knew that model resumés were always in black and white and usually included several poses with different backgrounds. She couldn't afford a professional photographer or professional lights, so she'd just have to fake it. She decided on the beach, using the shot with the pail and shovel as inspiration; the lighting had looked so good, she realized, because the late afternoon sun was going down—the same kind of soft, ethereal lighting they used in those country lemonade commercials.

If she used that kind of lighting for the resumé shots she might get away with it. Robbie's natural beauty and vitality would mask her amateur approach.

She chose Laredo Beach because it was usually less crowded.

Halfway through the first roll she began to believe she might really be on to something. It didn't matter how you posed Robbie, or what he was doing, he was always gorgeous. Couples passing him beside the surf would smile at him there on the sand with his little pail and shovel while the proud mama ran around snapping and clicking. And not just the women; the men smiled, too. A sure sign of her son's irresistibility.

By the end of the roll Eleanor was convinced she had a gold mine. Harold could take his house and croquet set and stuff them. She and Robbie were going places.

"Is he a model?"

She was sitting on the sand, trying to shield the open camera with her body while she reloaded. The tall stranger stood behind her, sun over his left shoulder, smiling down at Robbie.

"Well, I hope so." Eleanor smiled shyly. "Someday."

She squinted up long enough to see that the man had a good physique and was strikingly handsome himself with his little mustache.

"He's really adorable."

"Thank you."

"How old?"

"Six and a half."

"Hi there!"

Robbie waved "hi" with his shovel.

"What a smile!"

"Thanks," said Eleanor. She hadn't really considered the idea of a new father for Robbie—not seriously, anyway. She found her eyes flicking to the man's ring hand, her body shifting to a more alluring pose on the sand. Why hadn't she worn the new suit?

"Well, good luck!"

"Bye now!"

The stranger moved on with a graceful, muscular gait. Eleanor watched a moment, then got up and shot the second roll of film.

She saw him again a couple of hours later at Ralph's supermarket.

She had dropped the film at the One-Hour PhotoMax, dropped Robbie at her mother's for the afternoon, showered and changed, then gone shopping for dinner. Her intention was to put Robbie to bed earlier tonight (the excitement of the beach would ensure an easy bedtime) and finish her new romance novel. It was her favorite part of the day, being alone with her novels. Harold had always wanted her to rub his feet.

She was going toward her car, pushing her cart, which was not as full as she'd have liked it to be. The man had his back to her, loading groceries into his trunk; his car was parked right next to hers. He was chewing on something, eyeing it speculatively. He turned as she rolled her cart by, eyes brightening, smiling. "Hello again!"

He was good-looking, even out of the swimsuit. "Oh. Hi!"

"Where's the little model?"

"At his grandma's. For the afternoon. Until I pick him up." How did she say she wasn't married? She wasn't good at this anymore. But he was shopping alone, that was a hopeful sign. Should she ask him to help her unload her cart? No, that was stupid. Think of something, Eleanor!

"Do me a favor"—*Anything!*—"does this taste spoiled to you?"

He held out a tentatively bitten orange half.

She took it without hesitation, bit. Wrinkled her nose, chewing. "Tastes bitter!"

He nodded. "That's what I thought. Should I ask for my money back?"

She was about to answer when he stepped in front of her. "Let me help you with that!"

She unlocked the door gratefully and opened it for him. He was flirting! Thank God!

She watched the muscular back through his tight-fitting Izod. She had always loved those pretty-colored alligator shirts. This one fit him well. Harold would never wear them because of his pot.

Should I ask him to dinner? she was thinking, suddenly glad Mama had volunteered to watch Robbie tonight if she wanted to catch a movie.

She hadn't noticed how thick her tongue had become until she opened her mouth to speak. "I feel sick . . ." she heard herself saying, as from a far, echoing distance.

"It will pass," he offered, taking her hand, maneuvering her toward the opened door. "Where are the keys?"

She was thinking the word "purse" and might have even told him. It was hard to be sure down there in the darkness. . . .

Fit to be tied.

It was in her dream. Something about Indians and pine cones and being tied between two spruce trees that smelled amazingly like salt air. A tall white man who rode an alligator was coming to save her, she was sure of it, no matter how many times the Indian who looked maddeningly like Harold told her in that accusatory way of his that she was fit to be tied.

She awakened bound. Arms and lower limbs tingling. For want of blood flow, her sluggish mind informed her. Your limbs are asleep, move them. But how can I do that if they're tied? her other mind wanted to know.

The Indian stood before her with a terrific black erection. It was thrilling in the way the best dreams were thrilling. Except that somewhere beyond him another figure lurked in shadow, eyes gleaming, white hair glowing, and now the Indian had the face of the handsome stranger, the one who thought Robbie was so cute, and the salt air smell was overpowering. It reminded her of that time on her brother-in-law's boat.

74

ELEANOR

I should at least know your name, she thought as he knelt before her, put the big black thing to her tender flesh, and shouldn't we be alone? Who—?

He seemed to read her mind. "Mother," he smiled softly.

But that isn't right—is it? Well, never mind, don't let him get away, now you've got him. What in the world was it that we were drinking? Had it been a nice evening? She couldn't for the life of her remember.

You must love Robbie, too, she was thinking as he put it inside her, that's very important. . . .

She wanted to smile for him, but now there was pain.

It's hurting.

The words were formed but were belched aside with her scream.

He's allowing, she noticed through a dimming reality, the pain to go on for far too long. . . .

TULLY

DETECTIVE SERGEANT EUSTES TULLY BIT INTO HIS Egg McMuffin and wondered what part of his job as a cop was the most tedious.

Probably it was talking on the phone.

He did a lot of phone work. Every cop did. Oh, there were the chases, the rare shoot-outs, there was danger. Even, to an outsider perhaps, a modicum of glamour, though only in the most superficial, uneducated sense of the word. Mostly the job was filling out reports. Hoofing it. Waiting. And talking on the phone.

He consoled himself with the fact that once he had thought a Hollywood agent's life must be very glamorous and exciting, until he'd investigated that strangled starlet case and interviewed a series of jaded, chain-smoking agents and found out that those guys spend more time on the phone than cops do.

Today, though, it didn't seem that way. Today his right ear was red and itchy with phone-itis.

Ted Sears had called from the lab to confirm that

the chip from Mrs. Cunningham's vaginal swab was indeed black paint and that its various components included titanium dioxide, vinyl acetate, hydrous aluminum silicate, and polystyrene resin. This information was fed into the department computer, which revealed that the above compounds were used in the manufacture of four major brands of paint: Dutch Boy, Sears Latex, Olympic, and Glidden.

Tully had then gone to the Santa Barbara yellow pages and made a list of all the local stores that carried those brands. He found Dutch Boy, Olympic, and Glidden. That narrowed the brands to three, unless the killer used an out-of-town paint brand to fashion his weapon, in which case Tully had a whole other problem.

Tully then traced down the home office of each brand of paint with the idea of phoning each and trying to secure some kind of information on the most common manufacturing use of that particular brand. It *might* narrow things down to the type of weapon used, though Tully recognized this as a bit of a long shot: theoretically one could use any kind of paint to cover any kind of job. But it was all the lead he had at the moment.

He phoned the Glidden offices in Bangor, Maine. He talked to the sales manager, a Mr. Kirkley, who was very polite and very patient and gave Tully a list of names of all the manufacturers his office was aware of that used Glidden products, particularly that specific type of black latex paint. Of course, there was no way the list could be absolutely complete, since most companies ordered directly from the distributor and the distributor had offices all over the continental United States and sometimes those invoices made their way back to the home office in Bangor and sometimes they didn't. Also, some companies exercised their right to switch brands at will and with little provocation. Mr. Kirkley felt sure, however, that he could supply the Santa Barbara Sheriff's Department with the major businesses that used their product.

One was a file cabinet manufacturer in Ohio.

Another was a lawn chair company in Florida.

Another was a manufacturer of lawn mowers.

And on and on.

Tully thought it improbable that Mrs. Cunningham had been attacked with any of these items, though a lawn mower provoked some interesting if bizarre mental images.

He dialed the Olympic Paint Company. Their sales manager was out to lunch but a Miss Hawthorne with a syrupy Southern accent and a zealous approach to life was glad to accommodate Detective Tully. Miss Hawthorne was absolutely enthralled with police work and the idea that her humble paint company might somehow be involved in a homicide. She dragged this last bit of information out of a reluctant Tully, who usually tried to keep things on a more superficial level. Miss Hawthorne, though, would clearly be of more assistance if she thought her job could somehow be connected with a major crime, the ghastlier the better apparently.

"I had a girlfriend who was murdered in college! They never caught the man! Carved her up like a shank of beef! Is it terribly exciting being a policeman, Mr. Tully?"

"It can be very rewarding, at times. Especially when we find polite, cooperative people like yourself, Miss Hawthorne. Now, about your company's products . . ."

But Olympic paints covered nothing that seemed even remotely a potential murder weapon—unless you considered the concept of clobbering someone with a Big Boy barbecue grill.

All the same, Tully had taken down the name of every manufacturer Miss Hawthorne gave him and dutifully phoned and pumped their respective sales reps, who in turn scoured each of their individual departments for anything that might resemble an implement of violence. And they came up with pretty much nothing.

This isn't a long shot, Tully thought now, hanging up wearily, it's stratospheric.

His back ached. His Egg McMuffin was cold and getting colder. And he was still hungry.

He sat and looked at the wall calendar.

It didn't help his mood in the least, so he turned and found himself looking at the department clock above Brumeister's desk.

That helped even less.

His ass hurt.

He kept having the sniffles, but it wouldn't turn into a real cold.

Tired of that, he got up, grabbed his jacket, informed the clerk at the front desk that he was going to get a bite, and drove down to the marina.

On the way he passed a dozen places to stop off and eat, but he couldn't seem to work up an appetite for any of them today.

What he really wanted was one of those big fat glazed doughnuts that squatted behind the front window of Foster's Pastry, but he was beginning to look even more lumpy than usual, so he fought that one.

Still, he felt truculent. If he couldn't by God eat what he wanted to eat, he goddamn wouldn't eat at all!

It was childish, but he indulged himself. It was one of those days. Phone-call days were always one of those days. That was why he was getting fat: he ate shit food to combat depression. Which raised his blood sugar, made him more depressed, wanting yet more shit food. A vicious cycle. The life of a cop. That would make a good name for a book, he told himself as he pulled into the harbor area: *Vicious Circle—The Life of a Santa Barbara Cop.*

On second though, it stunk.

He parked the car and wandered toward his favorite haunt and bought a bag of buttered popcorn. Black paint chip . . . what kind of murder weapon would be covered with black latex paint? It was probably the most obvious thing in the world. He knew he'd kick himself when he finally discovered it. *If* he finally discovered it.

He stood on the jetty staring out to sea.

It was a nice enough day. Southern California days mostly were, if you could get past the smog.

He watched the gulls. Filthy birds. Scavengers. Picturesque, though. He liked to watch them scramble for his popcorn. Greedy little buggers.

Yeah, nice day . . .

It actually took him a minute to miss it.

Then his heart leapt into his throat.

The little red ketch was gone.

His shoulders lumped involuntarily. Then he gritted his teeth and threw the remainder of the popcorn at the gulls, who tore into the sack.

Shit!

Well, that figures! That just pretty much caps the whole goddman worthless fucking week!

Fine! Fine! Somebody bought it! Somebody bought his dream! Somebody was having their own dream now! Sailing away into the sunset! Great! Why not? Why should it be him? Why should he have any fun? It was a much fuller life taking care of his mother in that crypt of a house that she wouldn't let him sell! Fine! Great!

He was quitting. This was it. He'd had enough of this shit. He was marching back to Sparrs' office and slamming his shield on the desk and announcing his early retirement. They could take his promotion and shove it! He was through!

Sure he was.

He didn't get five yards.

Really getting to you, isn't it, Eustes? Biggest case in Santa Barbara County in years and you can't get to square fucking one with it.

He turned back wearily, resolve vanishing, to give the sparkling horizon a final look.

And was rewarded. Here it came.

Tully smiled. The little red ketch was just tacking the edge of the jetty, smooth and pretty as a picture.

He squinted, holding his breath, and sure enough, the FOR SALE sign was still there.

He turned quickly after that, feeling a bit better. He didn't want to see who was steering her. If he saw, if he put a face to the owner, he might be tempted to go down and talk. Might be tempted to make an offer. Might end up buying a boat today.

And that would end the dream.

Instead he drove to Foster's Pastry and selected the largest glazed doughnut he could find.

Back at the station he dialed the Dutch Boy offices and talked to a Mr. Brentwood, who was getting ready to close up shop.

"This won't take a minute, Mr. Brentwood. I'm working on a police case here in Santa Barbara that might entail the use of one of your paints. I was wondering if you could supply me with a list of known companies who use your Dutch Boy black latex?"

"Well, that's apt to be quite a list. I was just on my way out the door."

"I know. Look, I could call tomorrow . . ."

Mr. Brentwood sighed. "Naw, that's all right. Thursday is spaghetti night. Thick and red and juicy—that the way you like your spaghetti, Detective Tully?"

"That's the way I like it."

"Me, too. Maybe you could get my wife to fix it like that. Hers just sort of lies there looking at you. Got the list here somewhere. Hold on . . ."

Tully waited.

He happened to look up.

Stacey, the department clerk, was looking at him. Was he wrong or had she been doing that a lot lately? Was she flirting? With *him*? Seemed unlikely. Still, he wouldn't exactly mind even if she was young enough to be his—

"Okay, let's see. We got Bailey and Sons, manufacturers in Texas. They do farm implements, stuff like that."

"Farm implements. Like sharp tools, you mean?"

"Naw, mostly heavy equipment, I think. Big stuff. While we're at it, we also contract to the John Deere outfit, you heard of them?"

"Yes, more heavy equipment. What else?"

"Let's see ... says here, Dolphin Swimming Pool Supply, San Diego, California. Out your way. Any help?"

"Swimming pools. I doubt it. What else?"

"Okay, how about the Blaine Lathing and Tool Company, Rhode Island?"

"What do they make?"

"Uh, let's see ... fencing material, dowling, nightsticks, home decorating—"

He nearly missed it. "Hold it. Did you say 'nightsticks'? Like police nightsticks?"

"Says so here. That a help?"

Nightsticks.

Shit.

It was the best and worst piece of news he could have gotten. The weapon may have just dropped right into his lap, but good Christ, it couldn't have been worse news if a plague had suddenly swept the department.

A nightstick.

Yes, it fit; figuratively and otherwise.

Or seemed to.

Fred Wanamaker would know.

On his way to the morgue, randomly selected a nightstick from supply, took it with him to the morgue.

Fred Wanamaker, cigarette dangling from his lip, right eye squinted nearly shut, held up the length of dark wood, examining the heft of it, touching, rubbing, shaking his head.

"Jesus Christ, Tully," he whispered.

"Yeah, that's what I said."

Tully watched the other man's eyes and could tell that, for a moment, the county cornoner wasn't seeing the wooden stick held beneath the soft lights before him; he was seeing the same thing Tully himself had seen the moment the idea of the nightstick as weapon had entered his brain. He was seeing the faces of all the patrol officers he knew in the department. It was a thought better not contemplated.

Except that it had to be contemplated.

"It's possible, then?" Tully queried.

Wanamaker set the stick on a lab table, nodded. "It would certainly fit into a woman's vagina, though how far would depend somewhat on the woman. But a lubricated female could take it with no particular trouble, take a lot more than that, in fact. If he used a cop's billy to kill her he used it with help."

"What sort of help?"

"The labia was shredded, the vaginal wall torn, uteral area punctured, all with an instrument sharper than the blunt end of a billy. Unless it was a billy studded with something sharp."

"Like a nail?"

"Or nails." Wanamaker picked up the stick again, caressed it. Nodded. "Yeah. Goddamnit it to hell, I hate to say it, but this could be what the bastard used. Jesus, Tully . . ."

"It still doesn't mean it was a cop."

"But the implications."

"Yeah." Tully hung his head. "It isn't going to help our local PR much."

Both men stared at the stick a moment.

Then Tully took it and headed for the stairs. "I'm going to tell Captain Sparrs your nail theory, okay?"

"Tully?"

Tully turned at the coroner's tone.

"Brumeister was here."

Tully waited. "Was he?"

"He got wind of the paint chip."

"Okay. We're on the same team."

Wanamaker looked doubtful. "He pumped me. I had to tell him."

That was okay, too. "So? I'm not grandstanding this one."

"He looks . . . smug, Tully."

Tully smiled. "Brumeister always looks smug, Fred."

Wanamaker shrugged. "Watch yourself. I don't like that asshole, and I don't trust him."

"Thanks, Fred, that makes two of us."

He could feel the cool breeze the moment he opened Captain Sparrs' door, and it wasn't from the captain's air conditioner.

"I think we might have a break on the Cunningham woman, Captain, if you could call it a break. It has some pretty dire implications."

It took Sparrs a moment to look up from his paperwork. Longer than it should have.

"What have you got, Tully? Sit down."

This was a big moment. The captain, along with everyone else in the department, had been waitng for him to come up with something, *anything*, for weeks. It was too bad the first really solid lead they had simultaneously blemished the department.

"Fred Wanamaker took an additional vaginal swab, found a minute foreign object—a paint chip. I traced it down. It's the same black paint they use on our patrol billys. Wanamaker feels, with the addition of a nail or several nails, the billy could be our weapon."

He waited for the startled expression on Sparrs' face. When it didn't come, Tully felt the acid hit his stomach. Then he knew. Brumeister had been here first. Stacey . . . Brumeister had bribed her to monitor his phone calls. Bastard.

"You don't look surprised, Captain."

"Bill Brumeister just left here with the same theory. I didn't like it ten minutes ago and I don't like it now, though I suppose we'll have to consider it, won't we?"

"Detective Brumeister's on his toes these days."

"He has a big family to feed." Sparrs looked away.

What the hell was that suppose to mean? That he, Tully, had no family other than his mother, so he could afford to be less on his toes? All of a sudden he didn't like the air in this office.

Sparrs was busying himself lighting a pipe, avoiding Tully's eyes. "Jim Shingleton was in here this morning, Tully."

Here it came, whatever it was. "Oh? How is Jim? Haven't seen him for a while."

"He's fine, speaks very highly of you."

"Jim's a sweet guy."

Sparrs blew smoke. "Nothing sweet about it. You're one of the best narcotics men his department ever had."

" 'Had' being the operant word. I like it in Homicide, thanks."

Sparrs wasn't blinking and this was looking worse by the minute.

"Tully, have you ever heard of a man called Santiago Dias?"

"No." A lie. Tully had heard of the man, some squib in *Time* magazine, but he found himself not wanting to know anything about him all of a sudden.

"He's a South American drug runner, usually throwing big snow parties over there, or bigger ones in Miami. Right now he's in Santa Barbara. Shingleton's people want to know why."

"Maybe he likes the tofu here."

"His nickname is 'The Butcher.' He's got his hand in every filthy pot from here to Florida—drugs, gambling, pornography. Miami police consider him one of the most dangerous men alive. He's got a big white yacht up at Big Piney and a bigger one moored downtown at the harbor. They say you need a snow shovel to get through one of his parties. Not to mention a special invitation."

"Sounds like fun. Where do I get one?"

"That's what Jim Shingleton wants to talk to you about."

"Forget it, Captain."

"Only a couple month's work—"

"Forget it."

"Jim says you're the best—"

"The Cunningham case will be *ice* by then!"

"Tully . . . I'm taking you off it."

Well. There it was. That was that. You don't argue

with the captain. And why, with all his premonitions, was he still surprised? Still sick to his stomach?

Brumeister. Motherfucker.

"Do I get an explanation?"

Sparrs leaned back, sucking hard on a pipe he didn't realize had gone out. "You don't need one, Tully, you know what I think of you, of your record. If Jim Shingleton thinks highly of you, well, I double that."

"But not on this case."

"It isn't that . . ."

"What then?"

Sparrs leaned forward, taking the pipe from his mouth—he seemed to be having trouble finding a comfortable position. "To tell you the truth, I owe Shingleton one, and I can't justify two homicide detectives on the same case."

" 'Same case'? Captain, this is *the* case! The biggest case to hit Santa Barbara in decades!"

"That doesn't make us any less understaffed."

"Christ, Harry, I thought we were friends. Quit making me chase my tail."

Sparrs fumbled with his lighter. "Brumeister can handle it alone."

Tully watched him. "Maybe. But so could I. Why take me off it now, just when things are heating up?"

"I told you, Narcotics needs you."

"Harry—"

Sparrs threw down the lighter with a disgusted sound. "Jesus Christ, Tully! I don't owe you a fucking explanation! You'll do as you're told!"

Tully nodded. Started to get up.

Sparrs ran a hand through his hair. "You bastard. Sit down."

Tully sat.

Sparrs battled the pipe again. Finally he looked Tully in the eye. "Why the fuck didn't you ever get married, Eustes?"

"Is that why you're taking me off the case?"

He expected Sparrs to grin, but when he didn't, Tully felt himself swallowing thickly. Jesus! That is why he's taking me off! He felt the room expand suddenly. Or was it merely that he was shrinking?

"You're both up for grade—you and Brumeister. Solving this case will get it for one of you. I can afford to have another lieutenant in this department, but not two more. Not just now. I know you're a better detective than Brumeister. Everybody knows it. Fuck, Brumeister knows it. But he's got something you haven't, Eustes."

"A wife and kids."

"Remember Billy Shumacher? No, you weren't with us then. Billy Schumacher was a loner, too. Nice guy. Good cop. Everybody liked him. Everybody wondered why he opened the window of his apartment one fine June night and jumped out. And then there was Jerry Burlington. You wouldn't remember him either. Terrific at undercover stuff. Made it all the way to retirement. Blew his brains out."

"Lots of married cops commit suicide, too, Captain. It goes with the territory."

"You know it, and I know it. But the Chief doesn't like the way it looks. The fact is, married men stay with the job longer, try harder, get more commendations. The fact is . . . you've gone just about as high as you can go as a bachelor. There. I've said it. And don't come off frog-eyed, like it's a big revelation you hadn't considered before."

No. He'd considered it before. He considered it every day. Why hadn't he ever married?

And the answer, of course, was simple:

"I have a mother to take care of, Harry."

Sparrs gave an inch. "All right, Tully. And it's none of my business. But there are homes . . ."

Tully slowly shook his head, staring listlessly at the edge of the captain's desk. "No, that wouldn't do."

Sparrs watched him for a moment. Silence.

Then: "I'm sorry, Tully. If it were up to me . . . Look,

87

a promotion's still not out of the question. Go get something on this swine, Dias, you'll be a goddamn national hero."

"As long as I stay away from the Cunningham case. Maybe I can arrange to get married over the weekend."

"You know how much I hate this prejudiced shit."

"There must be a rule somewhere—"

"Probably. Which is why you and I never had this conversation; you're just a good cop doing what he's told to do by his superior."

Tully smiled wanly. "Like you, Harry?"

"Yes, like me."

Tully stared at the desk corner. Then he got up.

"What does Jim want me to do?"

"Get on the boat, for starters. See what you can find to incriminate Dias. Or at least see what the fuck he's doing in our humble city. Jim will brief you. I told him you'd call this afternoon."

"I'll call right now."

"Right now, why don't you take the afternoon off, have a few drinks, and hate me for a while?"

"Oh, that wouldn't do any good, Harry. I've hated you for years."

Sparrs grinned. "All right, asshole, get out of here."

Tully reached for the doorknob.

"Oh . . . Tully?"

"Yeah?"

Sparrs shifted uncomfortably again. "Anything you've got in your files . . . anything you think Brumeister could use . . ."

Tully snorted. "I wish I could say I did have something. My big score was the paint chip, and it looks like Detective Brumeister's scooped me there. I'll be in touch."

And he left.

He headed for his mother's house.

It was a good opportunity, and he thought he'd make

the most of it. Now that he was off the case (Christ, he still couldn't believe it) and he could clear his mind of dead women on the beach, torn genitalia, black nightsticks, and the thing that still stalked the night out there, he could afford to give some of his normally harried attention to his mother.

He didn't realize until now, driving to the home of his childhood, how much he'd used his job as an excuse not to spend more time with her. How much the pain in his already beleaguered stomach increased the closer to her street he got.

It wasn't the biggest house on Flores Street, but it was by no means the smallest. Dad had left it to them. Dad, who had been a sailing enthusiast, an expert marlin fisherman, an even more expert stockbroker, and so many other expert things that he, Tully, had never had the talent nor ambition to be. Dad had sailed all over the world, been good at everything he tried. Tully preferred the safety, simplicity, and order of the cop's life, something that filled all your time, devoured it. So you didn't have to think about things like ambition and expertise and taking care of an aging mother.

Tully, parked the car, locked it, strode up the familiar front walk. Johnny Benson had beat him up on this walk in 1956. A year later, he had grown taller than Johnny Benson and beat *him* up. A week after that they'd become best friends.

The old neighborhood, the old street. It still looked pretty much the same. And yet so different.

A few months ago, on one of his rare visits, he had arrived to find Mother not at home, off on a grocery errand. He hated that. He insisted she have the groceries delivered, it didn't cost much. But she was stubborn.

He had rambled about the old house, shaking his head at the dusty furniture, reliving childhood memories. Finally bored, he had wandered up to the attic, a place he hadn't visited in years.

It was like a museum, the attic, a museum of his life.

Mother never threw anything away. Anything. Even when it became old, broken, or useless. She merely moved it from down there to up here.

That wasn't strictly true. She'd thrown away his EC comics. And his Lionel train set. The things that meant the most to him when he was a kid.

Let's face it. She only kept the junk.

It smelled in the attic. Not badly. Just agedly. It smelled of his past.

Tully stepped around stacks of dusty books, a rusted birdcage, cardboard boxes piled to the roof—with what, he couldn't imagine. Something skittered beneath his shoe, found a dark corner; he ignored it.

He found the old photo album atop an antique end table, blew off the patina of dust, and turned the padded cover. That was when he realized just how much the house, the old neighborhood, had in fact changed. The sprawling maple out front was a willowy sapling in the scalloped-bordered black and white photos. The stone wall Dad had built in the sixties was still a white picket fence; he had almost forgotten it. And look, there was the sailboat and trailor parked in the drive! Dad had loved that little boat.

Mother came home then, and he'd gone downstairs to greet her, leaving the old photo album where it belonged with his past. You can't go home again.

One thing, though, he was now sure of: if Mother ever died, he'd sell the place in a minute.

No, not *if* Mother ever died . . . *when* Mother died.

Tully stood on the weathered porch now, rang the front bell.

She kept him waiting. It was one of the games they played.

And when at last the wooden door swept aside reavealing her as it did now, he was struck once more by how old she looked. Even in the short space of time since he'd last seen her. How old she looked. How frail. How bitter.

"Hi!"

She never returned the greeting. Not once. She merely stepped aside for him, closed the door behind them.

"Nice day for a drive! How about it?"

"Maybe later."

Another game they played. He always said it was a nice day and they never went out. Unless it was to get groceries, she never left the house.

"What's the matter?" she asked at last, turning to him as he found the green easy chair, the one he'd sat in for as long as he could remember.

There was no fooling her. He was here in the middle of the day and they didn't have a date. And—knowing her—she could read frustration in his tone.

But he went into battle anyway. "What do you mean?"

She gave him a tired, come-off-it look.

"It's a nice day," he began innocently. "I thought I'd spend some time with my mother."

Mae turned giving him her broad back; if he wasn't going to cooperate, very well then.

He let his eyes drift around the room, coming to rest on the gold-framed high school portrait of him. He sighed. "I got taken off the case."

"Brumeister?"

"Captain Sparrs relieved me. He couldn't spare the personnel, needs me for another assignment."

"But Brumeister replaced you? I told you he was trouble."

"Can we talk about something else? How are you feeling?"

"How am I ever feeling? I'm feeling old. I'm feeling lonely."

"Mae, I'm here now."

"Because you got fired."

"I didn't get *fired*!"

"Otherwise, you wouldn't have bothered."

"Are we going to start? I thought maybe you'd like lunch."

"I would have, at lunchtime. I already ate."

"It's only twelve-thirty, for chrissake!"

"Is it always necessary for you to curse? I already ate. You might have phoned. But then, you didn't know you were getting fired, did you?"

"Dammit, Mae, would you prefer I didn't come at all?"

"I'd prefer it not to be an afterthought."

"I think about you all the time! I'm a cop! I lead a busy life!"

"Too busy for your own mother, apparently."

"Too busy for anyone! Even friends! Even a . . . family."

Now she looked at him.

He turned away.

"Are you trying to say I've stood in the way of your getting married, Eustes—is that it?"

"The job, Mae, not you." He would *not* let her win this one!

"You could have followed into your father's business. He always had plenty of time for his family."

"I'm a cop, Mae. That's what I am. And we've been through all this before."

"It's not my fault you don't have ladyfriends, Eustes."

"I never said it was."

He had to get away from here. It had been a mistake to come. He should have stopped at a bar, like Sparrs suggested.

"I've never objected to your bringing ladyfriends around. I only ask that you introduce me before you . . . decide on anything."

His hands were trembling now, he had to stick them in his pockets to stop. "I just thought you might like to have a little lunch."

"I've eaten, thank you."

"I thought we could spend the afternoon together."

"I have a telephone, Eustes."

He turned to leave. "S'long, Mae."

She gave him a moment. "What will you do now?"

"What do you mean? I told you—I have another assignment."

"But you won't get the promotion."

His head was beginning to throb, a dull ache way in the back. "Probably not as soon as I'd hoped."

"You're spending too much time in that apartment, Eustes—"

Oh Christ! "S'long, Mae."

"It's a waste of money, son!" She came toward him as he moved toward the door.

"I gotta get back to it! I'll call you!"

"You could move in here with me! There's plenty of space! You can have your old room! Eustes?"

It was an act of will not to run.

Mae collapsed in mock defeat on the sofa, sending up motes of dust. She then dealt her ace: her hurt pout. "You're leaving now? You just got here and you're already leaving?"

He wrestled with himself. Her ace always worked. She was right—he *was* always running away. Why bother to come at all if you're going to run away the second you step through the door?

Yet he couldn't bring himself to sit again.

He walked to the picture window, gazed out at the front lawn, the rust-stained sidewalk. It needed sweeping.

Johnny Benson's ghost played Wiffle Ball with his own ghost out thee.

"I don't suppose . . . you still have my Schwinn?"

"Your what?"

"My old red Schwinn racer. I loved that bike. Went everywhere with it."

"Is that what you want to do, Eustes, get on your little red bicycle and ride away from here, like you used to do? I was always worried about you on that bike."

"I know."

"You knew then, but you did it anyway. You'd be gone for hours."

"Yes. I was free."

She made a derisive sound. "Free of your own family."

"No. Just free. Outward bound. You could really move on that thing. I thought I was Tom Corbett."

"I don't recall him, one of the neighbor children?"

"Tom Corbett, Space Cadet."

"Oh. Where did you go?"

"Anywhere. Everywhere. I usually ended up down at the library. The science fiction books. Bradbury. Burroughs."

"Who?"

"Never mind. Did you sell it?"

"The bicycle? No."

"Where, then?"

"If you left it here, it's in the attic."

He found it sandwiched between an ancient Singer sewing machine and a rusty attic fan. The bike was so much smaller than he remembered. The metal horn didn't work anymore. The tires were flat, the leather seat worn and shredded. Still, he fought back the sudden desire to sit on it, knock back the kickstand, ride it away, past the movie house, on and on forever . . .

But no. You couldn't do that on a child's bike. You'd need a bigger toy for that, Detective Tully. The red ketch down at the marina, maybe. . . .

He started to leave, remembered the photo album, paused to leaf through it.

Here was the old Pontiac, looking fat and heavy as a Sherman tank, the bright front grill ready to gobble you.

Here was Grandma Tully's kitchen, the oil cloth-covered table heaped with Thanksgiving pies.

Here was the family at the beach.

How young they all looked. How distant. How so much from another world.

He bent, peered closer. A smiling ten-year-old Tully squinted back at him from the bright sand, his mother's

94

hand on his skinny little shoulder. His mother, he realized with a jolt, had been a lovely woman. And he, for
that matter, a handsome little boy.

All gone. All blown away and scattered with the
wind. The only thing that remained the same was the
beach.

"Eustes! Are you going to spend the whole day up
there?"

As a matter of fact, he'd like to; he was enjoying this,
looking at his old self, his young self, his happier self. It
was nice.

"Eustes!"

He closed the album, wanting suddenly to kill her,
and tramped back down the stairs to the present.

CHAPTER 11

TULLY

*H*E DROVE, NOT REALLY KNOWING WHERE HE WAS going, not wanting to go back to his apartment and not yet in the mood to call Jim Shingleton and get briefed on the Santiago Dias thing.

He drove into town, down State Street, past the elaborate, old movie houses that still existed there, even though some had been sliced and diced into tri- and quadri-plexes. While other cities were closing down their big movie houses and restaurants as residents migrated to the suburbs, Santa Barbara was refurbishing and touching up, turning stately old architecture and sturdy auditoriums into tourist attractions. Sure it was greed, but it kept the old days alive. He liked that. Eventually the streets would become too crowded, the traffic too congested, the tourists too thick, turning the tables on this current bounty. But for now, it was just fine to see a downtown that looked alive. Like the downtown of his youth. The truth was, Tully loved this town. The truth was, he couldn't imagine any other place he could call home.

The decision about where to go next was answered for him by the pager beeping at his waist. He stopped at a pay phone.

"Detective Tully."

"Fred Wanamaker. Tully, you busy?"

"Not since this morning."

"I heard, I'm sorry. With asshole Brumeister on the job we can expect to have this thing solved by the turn of the century. Sparrs is out of his mind."

"Well, it's done, Fred. What can I do for you?"

"Nothing. I'm down here at Laredo Beach again, we've got the next one—same sunglasses, same savaged organs, everything. Lifeguard found her around noon. I know you're off the case, but thought you might be curious. Brumeister isn't here yet."

"That's good of you, Fred. Maybe I will drop by."

"Don't be long, the cavalry's on the way."

"Thanks, see you in a minute."

But by the time he arrived, Brumeister was already there.

Tully scooted under the yellow police tape anyway. Brumeister, scribbling notes on a pad, didn't bother to look up, but then, Tully was used to that kind of treatment.

"Haven't you talked to Sparrs, Eustes?"

"I've talked to him, William. I'm on my lunch break."

Brumesiter grinned. "Came down here to munch burritos and stare at dead pussy, did you?"

Tully was staring at the body on the beach. Young, well-built, sunglasses, bloody crotch; it could have been Mrs. Cunningham. "Who is she?"

"Why? You wanna date?"

"Are you going to tell me or do I have to talk to Fred Wanamaker?"

Brumeister turned, lowering his pad. For once he wasn't grinning. He didn't have to anymore. "I don't have to tell you anything, asshole, except to get the fuck off this beach and my back. You're suppose to be blowing snow up your nose on that spic's yacht, not fucking off down here with a case you botched."

Tully felt his knuckles fisting. He had never really conceived of the idea of physical combat with Brumeister, but he felt close to it now. He'd taken about all the shit he wanted today. Never mind the fact that Brumeister outweighed and out-youthed him by several miles. It would be so nice to mash that smug puss just once. "I didn't botch a goddamn thing, you fat prima donna. I was the one who found the fucking paint chip, not you."

"Fred Wanamaker found it, dickhead."

"Through my insistence that he do another swab."

"Yeah? Well, why don't you go suck his dick for a while, then, and leave me to solve this case?"

Good idea.

Tully turned, trudged through the sand and found Wanamaker scribbling his own notes.

"Maybe this wasn't such a good idea, Tully. Sorry."

"I can handle that asshole, Fred. What have you got?"

"What did we have before? Could be a carbon copy. Ted will dust the glasses, but my guess is you won't find anything. Her name is Eleanor Rankin, she bears a physical and facial resemblance to the Cunningham woman. Good shape—dancer or swimmer, I'd say. You can get the details from the ex-husband."

Tully was combing the area around the bloody beach towel with his eyes. "Fred, did you see—"

"The flashbulb? No. But I didn't look all that well, busy with the body. Ted Sears got here late. Brumeister was futzing around with the towel. He might have picked one up, I can't be sure. Sorry."

"Quit apologizing, Fred, it's not your job, and I'm off the case anyway."

"I wish you weren't."

Something in the coroner's tone made Tully turn to him.

"What, Fred?"

Wanamaker looked out to sea, at two gulls wheeling above the breakers. It was a hazy day, smoggy down in L.A., probably. He pulled off his wire-rimmed glasses with a roundabout gesture, pinched the bridge of his nose. "This one gives me the creeps. And I don't get the creeps easily."

That was the truth.

"Go on."

Wanamaker shrugged. "That's all. I'm not saying it's someone in the department, I'm not saying anything. I just don't like it, that's all. I wish it were over. And I wish anyone but that asshole was on it. Sparrs is nuts. I'd swear he doesn't want to solve this case at all."

Tully smiled. "That must be it. He's our killer."

"It's not funny, Tully. I don't like it."

"Sparrs is trying to keep his job like the rest of us."

"I guess. Can I keep you abreast of this one, Tully? I'd feel better."

"Yes, I was going to ask you to."

Wanamaker nodded. "Good, then." And went back to his notes.

He kept Tully abreast by calling him at one o'clock the following morning.

Tully fumbled for the receiver, wrenched from a deep sleep. "Yeah, Tully here . . ."

"It's Fred. I'm sorry—Christ, I just looked at the clock."

"Are you at work? What's up?"

"No, I'm home. I just thought of something I forgot to tell you earlier, maybe it isn't even that important. Did you have a chance to talk to the husband at all?"

"Some, yeah."

"Mrs. Rankin was on the beach yesterday with her son, did you know that? Not far from where her body was found."

"Yeah, I heard."

"I just thought—it's just like the Cunningham woman. Probably doesn't mean anything. I shouldn't have called."

"Don't be silly. Listen, I don't suppose you've had time—"

"I'll let you know if there are any more paint chips. But do we need them, really, at this point?"

"No. It's the same guy. Is there anything else you want to tell me, Fred?"

"No. Do I sound like it?"

"You sound upset, a little."

A metallic sigh. "I don't know. This one's got me spooked. Maybe I need a vacation. I'm due one."

"Maybe that's it."

"Been thinking of Hawaii."

"I hear that's nice."

"I wish the motherfucker would turn himself in."

"So do a lot of people. Get some rest."

"I will. Tully?"

"Yeah?"

"Is it getting to you, too?"

"Yeah, it is. Goodnight, Fred."

CHAPTER 12

MITCH

*H*E'D SPENT THE ENTIRE MORNING AND PART OF THE afternoon on job interviews. It was hopeless, of course, but what else could he do? The money he had grudgingly accepted from Mr. Greely at the lake was nearly gone. Bills were mounting. The house payment alone was colossal. Not to mention the credit cards—all sixteen of them. Not to mention the zillion other daily bills.

Not to mention Joanne was pregnant.

Damn. And they'd been so careful. *He* at least had been careful. Could she have . . . is it possible she did this . . . no, surely not on purpose! Deliberately left her diaphragm out? Deliberately tried to get pregnant, without telling?

But why?

Was her life that empty? Were they such strangers? Did she live in such a vacuum she needed a baby to give her life meaning?

But not tell him? Even ask him? Even discuss the damn thing with him?

Mitch tightened his grip on the Porsche's steering wheel, squeezing until his knuckles went white. A line of sweat was working its way down his right cheek. It was suffocating in the sports car's interior; the electrical system was on the blink, and the windows had frozen in the place the last time he'd used them, leaving a breathing space of only an inch near the top. Of course it was the dead of summer.

Six job interviews, six zeros. The guy at Grayson-Morris was honest, at least: "The truth is, Mr. Spencer, you've a bit of a blot on your record just now. Not that we don't understand these things or believe your side of it, but we have a reputation to uphold. Now, maybe in a few months, when this thing cools down . . ."

A "few months" meant a few years and he didn't need a frigging job in a few years—he needed it now! Now, goddamnit! Why in Christ's name couldn't he get a break?

Well, insurance positions were out, that was clear enough. Which left freelance work, *if* he could find it, and even if he did that would never cover their nut. Joanne would simply have to go to work, if only for a few months. Boy, he could hardly wait to deliver *that* piece of news! But he'd better do something quick—he wasn't getting anywhere on his own and he'd put off telling her he'd been fired until their finances had reached rock bottom.

He slapped at the sweat on his cheek, gritting his teeth as bus fumes crept through the narrow window opening. He was sitting at a red light, one of those red lights that seem to go on forever. Was the goddamn thing broken? What the hell was going on? Should he start honking?

He forced himself to relinquish his death grip on the wheel, willed the tightness from his shoulders. Calm down, calm down, flying apart isn't going to help anything.

He pushed his mind elsewhere, found himself thinking of the woman at the lake, the one he'd rescued.

Greely's wife. What was her name? Clarie. That was it. Pretty name.

Pretty, faithless Clarie.

There had been something about her, even in her semiconscious state. Something even more memorable than her pretty face, pretty name. What was it? A vulnerability? No. Not quite. What then? A sadness? A loneliness? Something about the way she'd looked at him. Something more than just gratitude. A reaching out . . . ?

This was ridiculous!

Here he was, out of work, totally broke, on the edge of financial ruin and thinking about some poor bimbo he'd—

The Porsche jolted.

Mitch froze, held his breath. *Not now!*

The engine coughed, jolted again, rumbled threateningly. *Not now, bastard!*

Cursing the sudden trembling in his knees, Mitch eased off the gas pedal and moved into a slower lane, the rivulet of sweat on his cheek a sudden river.

Another jolt. The car bucked, made a metallic, grating sound, bucked again. Lunged.

And died.

He just managed to coast onto the shoulder. In a vain attempt at hope his eyes leapt to the dash, but the gas needle read full.

It wasn't the gas. It wasn't even the transmission or the fuel line or the celanoid in the ignition. . . .

It was the goddamn fates out to screw him good!

It was his whole pathetic, worthless piece of shit life going up in ten-foot flames!

It was the end, brother . . . the living fucking end!

He sat at the roadside staring stupidly at the dusty hood, thinking absently that it needed a wash, unable to stop the spastic tremors now racking his entire frame.

Great! Now you don't even have a fucking car! Now you can't even get to the fucking interviewers who won't fucking hire you in the first fucking place! Now you don't even have wheels to drive home and tell that woman with the burgeoning belly that you got fired last month and you don't have ten cents to buy a piss at the local pancake house!

Why don't you just get out of the car, drop your drawers, and let God shove the whole fucking world straight up your ass?

No! Better idea!

Why don't you go home and get into that closet of yours and pull down that cardboard box and unwrap that infamous .38 Police Special you never learned to fire worth a shit during your aborted career as a cop, then fit it into your left ear and blow what little brains you've got left out your right? Good idea? You like it? Yeah? I like it, too!

Only trouble is, it's fifteen fucking miles back to that swank neighborhood where you live in that swank house you can't fucking afford!

He began to laugh then.

And to pound the wheel and slap the smooth leather dash. Kick the smooth leather dash. The soft, smooth, sweet-smelling leather dash he would no longer see once he finally sold the car.

But you can't sell the car until you get the frigging thing running, can you?

He laughed even harder at that.

Threw back his head and howled his strangled mirth at the roof. Laughed and laughed. Until his sides ached, and his throat was raw.

And finally, after all his laughter was spent, he began to cry.

He sat in the empty house. Joanne was off to god-knows-where. One of her fund-raiser meetings, maybe. Or maybe she was off having an affair. Who the hell cared.

The Porsche was in the shop. He'd put the towing bill on his credit card, despite the fact that card was probably invalid because he hadn't paid last month's bill. But the tow truck guy didn't know that.

Too bad he wasn't much of drinking man. He'd love to tie a good one on about now.

Too bad you're not much of a man, period. You wouldn't be in this mess.

He got up after thirty minutes of vacuously staring out the living room window at the fireplug across the street and strode deliberately to the closet. He opened the door without hesitation and dragged a chair in front of the coats and jackets and brought down the box. He took off its dusty lid.

The nightstick was on top

blood . . .

and he stared at it

screams . . .

and even held it in his hand before putting it aside and getting to the real weapon, the real firepower, and this he hefted for a moment, too, staring down at the black oily length of it, which wasn't much for a weapon that could deliver so much kick, so much sudden, painful death, well not all that painful if you hit the right organ at the right angle, pretty quick death when you thought about it, bullet in the old brain pan, and he didn't even bother to put it to his head because he knew that even if he had the conviction for such an act he sure as hell didn't have the courage, which was pretty funny, he didn't have the courage to live and didn't have the courage to die, it would make a good movie, or a book, somebody should think about that, he was once going to be a writer in high school, remember . . . remember, yeah, going to be a cop, too, just like your dad only that didn't work out so swell, did it, hotshot, that worked out about as swell as the private eye license and the door-to-door shit and that really colossal job with All-American that was the best thing that ever happened to you best thing that ever *will* happen to you and you totally completely blew it because you didn't have the gray matter to figure out that you might talk a good game, you might have this half-ass facility to second-guess the other guy, but when it comes to what really counts you don't know jackshit!

Hey!

Maybe you really *do* have the nerve to pull the trigger!

Let's find out, shall we?

Only not now, asshole, because the phone is ringing and it might be Ed McMahon with ten million dollars from Publishers Sweepstakes.

"Yeah?"

"Mr. Mitch Spencer, please."

"Here."

"Ah! Mr. Spencer! This is Franklyn Greely, how are you, sir?"

The rich fat man at the lake, Claire's husband. Five thousand dollars. . . .

"Mr. Greely, how are you?"

"Fine, dear boy, exceptional. That is, I think I'm fine. Max, my trusty chauffeur, says I'm a bit overweight. It's the strawberry daiquiris, he says. Very probably he's right. However, I put it to you, sir—have you ever had the common will to refuse a Café Frank's strawberry daiquiri out of hand?"

"I'm sorry, Mr. Greely, I don't believe I'm acquainted with the establishment."

There was an astonished gasp. "Not heard of Café Frank's? My dear fellow, where have you been all your life?"

"Hiding out in a Brentwood home I can't afford, I'm afraid."

"Well! We simply must make amends for that immediately. I insist you join me there this minute. Uh, do you know the Santa Barbara area, sir?"

"Mr. Greely—"

"Or why don't I simply send Max around to collect you? Would five o'clock be convenient?"

Mitch found himself smiling, a not unpleasant sensation considering the current state of his life. "Mr. Greely,

I'd love nothing more than to share a drink with you, but it's been an extremely trying afternoon—"

"I should love to hear all about it, dear boy!"

"—and I'm afraid I'm a family man and my wife—"

"I was going to ask you about that. You see, I've been, shall we say, checking up on you a bit. I wanted to see what kind of man risks his life for a stranger. You've had a run of bad luck recently, have you not? I understand you lost your job through no fault of your own."

Pause.

"What do you want, Mr. Greely?"

"Mr. Spencer, it's Friday. Would you happen to have the weekend free?"

That was a laugh. He had all his weekends free.

"Mr. Greely—"

"The truth is, I seem to be having marital problems. The good wife's scampered off on a rendezvous with our friend Dias. Right here in Santa Barbara. Another yacht party. Man seems to collect yachts. I was wondering if you might be interested in a little reconnaissance job. You are an investigator, are you not?"

"Insurance investigator. I haven't done divorce work since—"

Mr. Greely chuckled. "My dear boy, no one said anything about divorce! I merely need someone to, shall we say, keep an eye on Claire, just to make sure she remains safe and sound. You seem just the man for the job, Mr. Spencer—reliable, trustworthy, selfless—"

"I don't know, Mr. Greely, my wife—"

"Thought we might take the opportunity to talk about your position at All-American as well. I believe your employer, Stanley Carlson, owes some friends of mine a few favors. Cash favors, as I recall. Would you be interested, sir?"

Mitch swallowed thickly.

"Mr. Spencer? Have we been disconnected?"

"Uh . . . what exactly is it you're trying to say, Mr. Greely?"

"That you have not truly lived until you have sampled the strawberry daiquiris at Café Frank's, my good sir, which coincidentally happens to be located just a short way from the marina that harbors Mr. Dias's yacht. I believe my dear Claire plans to spend the entire weekend on it. Shall I have Max collect you, then?"

Mitch's chest was hammering painfully now. "Are you implying that you might be able to reinstate me at All-American, Mr. Greely? Is that what you're saying?"

"All things are possible under heaven, Mr. Spencer. You'll need an excuse, of course—for Mrs. Spencer, I mean. Does she know of your recent dismissal?"

"No."

"How convenient. I suggest you fabricate something, then, a last-minute convention in Santa Barbara, perhaps. You can phone her later tonight. Max can collect you in ten minutes."

"Ten minutes?"

"He's in the L.A. area now. Are we agreed then, Mr. Spencer—you scratch my back, I scratch yours, as they say?"

"You really think it's possible—"

"My influences are far-reaching, dear sir, on this coast and the other. I'm quite sure some equitable arrangement can be reached with your Mr. Carlson. You will help me, won't you, Mr. Spencer? Claire means the absolute world to me. I'd be devastated should I lose her. Perhaps you can empathize with the feeling . . ."

Mitch was staring absently at the shiny .38 nestled against the nightstick in the carboard box.

Amen to that.

Mr. Greely was one hundred percent correct: the strawberry daiquiris were delicious.

In this fine old coastal saloon—replete with teakwood booths, polished brass trim, rigging and nets that draped the ceiling, and a plethora of other authentic nautical decor—Mitch felt himself slowly unwind, for the first time in days. Maybe it was the distance between

himself and all his Los Angeles problems, maybe it was
the second strawberry daiquiri, but more probably it was
the benevolent smile on the red-cheeked Falstaff across
from him. Greely definitely had an air about him—for
Mitch, it was a soothing air. Maybe all rich people were
like that: they never had to worry about money so they
became fatalistic about everything else.

Greely smiled like a naughty kid beneath the fifteen-
foot glossy varnished marlin mounted over his head, sip-
ping his drink delicately. "Max took care of your needs
on the way up, I trust?"

"Max was the perfect chauffeur."

Greely nodded, consoled. "Dear Max. One in a million, what would I do without him? The only true friend
I ever had, I'm afraid." The big man's eyes seemed to
drift for a moment. "You may not think it possible that
two individuals from entirely different walks of life could
ever be as close as brothers, Mr. Spencer, yet Max and I
are—in our own ways, we are. I think it can truly be said
that in the best sense of the word, we love each other. I
want you to quit fretting about money, Mr. Spencer, it
does not become a man like yourself."

Mitch lifted his drink. "And what is, in your estima-
tion, a man like me?"

Greely considered. "Strong, I think. Resourceful.
Reliable. Yet independent, courageous even, under the
right circumstances. In other words, all the things I am
not. Which is doubtless why I enjoy your company so
much."

Mitch was touched. It was the nicest thing anyone
had said to him in a long while. And the way Greely said
it, Mitch could almost believe it was all true. He certainly wanted to believe it was all true.

"Well, thank you for the generous evaluation, Mr.
Greely. I hope I can live up to it."

"You already live up to it, dear boy, when you're not
concerning yourself with money. You're not terribly good
with money; making it, at any rate."

Mitch stiffened a fraction.

"Your problem," Greely continued, "is believing the making of money to be a virtue. Or that anything even vaguely connected with money is a virtue. It is, I assure you, not the case. As I explained before, I started with nothing myself, yet amassed a fortune before my thirtieth birthday. I am quite ingenious at making money, and you can see the extent to which it has comforted me. Not a whit. The only thing I care for in this life is the love of one rather flighty individual, yet it is the one thing that eludes me completely. I would give much, nay all, to be in your shoes, sir—a wife, child, the love of those dearest to you. Compared to that, money is a paltry thing indeed."

Greely sighed heavily, shifting his considerable bulk in the saloon's hard-backed chair. "But of course you won't realize that until you have it. Pity." He drank.

Mitch didn't know what to say. Greely said it for him.

"It is my advice, dear fellow, that you content yourself with what it is you are good at, such as loving your family, friends, and using that rapier mind of yours. The rest God will furnish—in this case, God being me. I'll talk with Carlson on Monday. For now, put the thought out of your mind. Concentrate on other things."

"Such as getting on the Dias yacht?"

Greely smiled. Grunting with the effort, he reached inside his jacket, produced a small pastel envelope from his vest pocket and handed it to Mitch. "That has already been attended to."

It was an invitation.

Mitch started to ask how he got it. "Dias sends dozens of them; this one is addressed to you. I had Max intercept it; I hope you won't think me presumptuous. I wanted to make certain I spoke with you before you received it. From what you told me before, Dias shouldn't be at all averse to entertaining you again."

Mitch thumbed open the invitation, a simple but elegant missive in cursive giving time and place. "And what is it you expect me to accomplish, Mr. Greely?"

"Very simple, my boy. Information on my wife and Dias, how serious they are, what it might be leading to, if possible, what her intentions are. The modus operandi I leave to you. I would suggest concentrating on Claire, not Dias, since the latter could lead to possible danger. But, again, that is up to you. You might try to gain Claire's confidence, even ask her for a date. With luck she'll accept."

Mitch looked incredulous.

Greely smiled. "If she accepts a date with you, Mr. Spencer, then she's unlikely to be serious about Dias. It's not a summer fling that concerns me at this point, it's my wife sailing off to the other side of the world with a coke-dealing killer. Do you understand?"

"I think so. When do I begin?"

"Right now. Dias's boat is docked less than a mile from this restaurant. The party has already begun. There will be ten thousand dollars awaiting your return. A fair price, I believe. Oh"—he reached into his wallet, handed Mitch a sheaf of bills—"here's an additional thousand operating capital. Dias loves to gamble. Call the restaurant when you want to be picked up. Max will be there promptly. Any questions?"

"I guess not."

Greely smiled contentedly. "Then good luck."

CLAIRE

W ELL, THIS WAS IT.

She sat in her cabin gazing at her reflection in the expensive gilt-framed antique mirror above the equally elegant and expensive antique Chinese vanity, and she knew it to be the truth.

And it was, indeed, *her* cabin. Though Dias had never actually confirmed the fact when showing her below deck, he had bypassed the main head and brought her here, to this beautifully trimmed boudoir with its private facilities and its one very large bunk. Whether it was hers alone or his alone he didn't say, but it was clear he intended them both to bed here tonight.

The social foreplay had gone on long enough.

Claire Greely took another drink of champagne, watching herself in the mirror.

Not so young anymore. Still pretty. Maybe, to some, even beautiful. But hardly the ingenue of years gone by. Which was okay. She had absolutely no desire to be an ingenue anymore. It was just that by now she assumed she would have reached some form of equilibrium in her life, some kind of long-rehearsed-for solidity. Some kind of mature happiness. In fact, *any* kind of happiness. A loving husband, children of her own. Wasn't that the way it was supposed to happen?

But of course, that was out of the question with Franklyn.

Why else would she be here on this strange boat with—let's face facts—someone who was essentially still a stranger, seeking that happiness? Or seeking a night of good sex? Or were those the same thing? Don't ask. She wouldn't know. All she had was money. And a fat husband.

A loving husband, in his way. But no children. And no chance of them.

She suddenly got very tired of looking at herself and looked away.

And saw the bed.

She turned away from that just as suddenly, not wanting to think about it, not wanting to make a decision about it, even though the time to put bed off was rapidly running out. Dias *might* let her go tonight, but by Saturday night, tomorrow, he would definitely expect some form of reciprocation for all this life among the beautiful people and carloads of cocaine she had spent the last few weeks demurely but tactfully refusing.

She looked in the mirror. Who the hell are you, Claire Greely? What in the name of God are you doing here? With your life?

A knock sounded at the cabin door.

Claire turned. "Yes?"

"It's Maria Dias, Mrs. Greely. May I have a word with you?"

Claire tightened. The mother. Oh God, not now! She wasn't in the mood. Besides, the old lady gave her the creeps even when she was in the mood.

"Of course. Please come in."

Dias's silver-haired mother moved into the cabin with a gracious smile, colorful caftan flowing, strong tanned arm shutting the door behind her with a click.

Claire brushed absently at her hair, nervous.

Mrs. Dias watched her for a moment. "Are you comfortable, Claire? You don't mind if I call you Claire?"

"No, of course not." Claire tried a smile. "I guess"—should she do this?—"it's easier than calling me Mrs. Greely."

What the hell and why not? Surely Dias had had lots of married women, and his mother must have known about some of them. Besides, there was no reason to be coy yet—nothing had happened. Claire was just a ladyfriend attending a yacht party.

Mrs. Dias was looking at the bed.

But maybe that was because there was little other furniture. "Please, sit down," Claire offered, remembering herself. She felt a little funny: it wasn't her yacht, or her cabin, and her invitation to sit on the bed only pointed up the idea of something more than friendship between her and Dias.

"Thank you. I won't stay long."

"I'm glad to have the company."

Mrs. Dias sat, watched with what might have been envious eyes as the brush worked at Claire's thick curls, the deft graceful moves of the younger woman's slim arm.

"You're a lovely girl," she said simply, perhaps sincerely.

"Thank you. But hardly a 'girl' anymore."

Mrs. Dias's smile seemed genuine. "Depends upon your point of view. From my distant age, the fact of your youth is quite undeniable." The accent was strong, but so was the confidence behind the words.

"Well," said Claire politely, plucking a hair from the brush, "you're a woman who can speak of beauty with some authority."

The older woman took the compliment with silent grace. There was no denying the competition, the cabin

was rife with it. But there was no denying the keen intel-
ligence behind it, either—and with some degree of
respect from both sides. Under different circumstances,
the two women might even have been friends. Except . . .

What was there about Mrs. Dias that bothered her
so? It was more than just the matriarchal clinging of a
forceful parent. Something . . . darker. Something almost
angry. She wasn't afraid of losing her boy . . . it was
deeper than that. There was an underlying frustration, a
suppressed fury. With Claire? Or Santiago himself?
Claire couldn't tell.

Silence. Was it her turn to talk? She was trying to
remember the last thing that was said.

What am I doing here? How did I come to this? Who
is this strange woman and her handsome, deadly son?
Why aren't I home in bed watching Johnny Carson and
getting fat on macadamia nuts with Franklyn?

It was time to say *something*.

"You have a lovely boat, Mrs. Dias."

"Thank you."

Silence.

God! This was torturous! There was nothing to talk
about! Claire cleared her throat.

"Forgive me," the older woman intoned. She stood.
"I just wanted to see you close up, in the light. It's hard
sometimes, on deck. You're really a lovely girl."

She held out her hand then and Claire took it lightly.
Mrs. Dias quietly watched her for another moment.
Then: "A lovely girl. I hope you enjoy the party. Has
Sonny invited you to stay the night?"

Here it came. God, was the mother staying on board,
too? Claire swallowed. "Yes." There, she'd said it. Wasn't
so hard.

Mrs. Dias squeezed her hand once, then let it go.
"How nice. I do hope you enjoy the party, Claire. And I
hope that we shall become friends."

"Thank you, so do I."

The silver head smiled. "I'll see you above, then."

"Yes."

Mrs. Dias lingered at the door.

Then spoke again. "It's best," she began in the most offhanded of ways, "not to make him angry. Not to make him jealous. It's really best not to do that."

Claire stared.

"Are you surprised that I know what he is? We can't always make our children into what we would like them to be. But they are still our children ... you have children, Claire?"

Claire was suddenly frightened. "No. I'm not that lucky."

"Ah. Then you wouldn't know what I'm talking about. Take care, my dear."

Mrs. Dias smiled and shut the door behind her.

Leaving Claire alone again with her champagne and the reproachful eyes of her pale, reflected self.

She came on deck some time later, but Dias was busy with some friends. Business contacts, she guessed. Probably figuring out the next big drug deal, the next competitor to kill off.

She had, of course, no proof of these half-serious thoughts, but it was not secret among her friends and the other partygoers that Dias's reputation was less than spotless, that his company often employed *exotic* ways of dealing with the competition.

Let's face it, he was a dangerous man. Mrs. Dias's said as much.

But then, that was part of the attraction, wasn't it Claire, old girl?

She turned away from the laughing dancing couples in sudden disgust. She didn't like herself very much tonight, didn't like this whole tawdry nouveau riche scene, in fact.

Then why are you here?

Shut up. You've had too much to drink.

She moved to the rail, stumbling—*way too much to drink*—and stared down at the dark water. The noise from the live band was annoying, bringing the beginnings of a headache to her temples. She could feel the bass thumping through her feet. This wasn't the kind of romantic moonlit night at sea she'd hoped for—or read about in those trashy romance thrillers she dismissed so handily. She'd hoped to be alone with Dias tonight, to go for a quiet walk with him, or maybe just stand here at the rail and gaze at the cloud-filtered moon, look into his eyes, perhaps find something there that would make her want to kiss his cruel mouth, hold his hard muscled body, spread her legs for him, maybe even fall in love with him a little. . . .

Instead, she'd gotten noise, headaches, and enigmatic mothers. And a date who was off on his own, consumed by some tiresome business affair. Too busy for her. Not unlike her own husband . . .

Too bad, old girl, that's the way make-believe dreams go sometimes.

I said, *Shut up*!

She sighed, squinted her eyes against the building throb in her head. No, she really didn't like herself very much tonight.

"Mrs. Greely?"

She turned, found a face at once familiar and strange. And then, in a moment, she had it.

"Mr. Spencer! Hello! How good to see you again. I didn't know you were attending our little ball."

Mitch proffered a gin-and-tonic, held on to one of his own. "I didn't either, exactly. Sort of a last-minute thing. How are you feeling?"

Claire took the drink. "Well, I haven't had the opportunity lately to drown myself again. You?"

Mitch shrugged, watching her pretty blue eyes. "Okay. Business as usual."

She watched him. Remembering the face. Liking it. Liking the sound of his voice. "Which was—forgive me?"

"Insurance."

"Ah. Sounds . . . exciting."

"Does it?"

He looked her over appraisingly. "And what do you

do, Mrs. Greely, when you're not attending expensive yacht parties?"

Claire took a long drink, suddenly very thirsty, both for the gin and the talk. She lifted her chin. "Well now, let's see. I ride, when I get the chance, at my husband's ranch. I sit, when I get the chance, on the beach and read cheap romance paperbacks. I gamble, when I get the chance, as much of my husband's money as I can get as often as I can get to Vegas, and"—she took another long drink, emptying the glass—"I waste my life." She handed him the empty glass, looking him straight, challengingly, in the eye. "When I get the chance."

Mitch took the glass, looked down at his own un-touched drink.

"Sounds exciting," he said lightly, finding her eyes again.

Her expression was solemn, maybe a little sad. "Does it?"

He sat her glass on the rail, turned, combed the merry-makers again? "I haven't seen our host this evening."

Claire leaned out over the water, delicate shoulders hunched against the cool breeze. "He's conferring with his cronies. Business. He has a lot of friends. Which one is yours, Mr. Spencer?"

"Mitch. Pardon me?"

She motioned with her head at the swaying crowd. "Which friend is yours?"

Mitch hesitated. "I'm ... solo tonight, I'm afraid." She was drunk. Charming, but drunk.

"Why?"

"Why am I alone?"

"Why are you afraid?"

Drunk but smart. "Just a figure of speech. My wife's in Los Angeles. Our kind friend extended an invitation, and since I was up here in Santa Barbara on business anyway I thought I'd drop in and say hello."

"What about me?"

"Well of course I hoped you'd be here, too."

She took his drink from him, sipped at it. "That's

nice. You really should see me when I'm not comatose or drunk. I'm a knockout."

"You're a knockout now, Mrs. Greely."

She did not attempt to hide her surprise and pleasure at his candor. She cocked her head, closed one eye histrionically, mocking her own intoxication. "Are you flirting with me, Mitch?"

"I don't know. Are you flirting with *me*, Mrs. Greely?"

"Claire." She took another sip, looked him up and down. "No, if you were really flirting you wouldn't have said 'Mrs. Greely.' Probably just as well. He can be extremely jealous, or so I understand."

"Your husband?"

"Dias, of course. Do you like rock and roll, Mr. Spencer?"

"Mitch. Depends, why?"

"Do you like this rock and roll?"

"Not really."

"Would you like to go below and have another drink, then, and listen to me be embarrassingly unabashed? I really get going with a few drinks in me."

Mitch found himself looking around nervously.

"Are you afraid?"

"Well, not of Mr. Dias, anyway."

She smiled broadly, and Mitch was startled at how beautiful it made her under the soft Chinese lanterns and what the smile did to him.

"I like you, Mitch. You're okay. You can rescue me from drowning anytime."

"The pleasure is mine," Mitch said graciously, and stepped aside as she led the way below deck.

Claire poured them drinks from the half-empty champagne bottle, handed Mitch his, and flopped on the bed with her own, unwittingly spilling some on her chest.

She took a sip, kicked off her high heels, and lay back. "Ah! Now, isn't that better? Blessed silence!"

Mitch took a sip of champagne, glanced about the neatly trimmed and paneled cabin.

"It cost a fortune, in case you're wondering," Claire supplied between sips.

"I can imagine."

She rested her glass on her bosom. "You tell me your life story and I'll tell you mine." She waggled a finger. "But only if it's unscrupulously honest and full of lurid detail. I refuse to be *bored* anymore this evening!" She emptied the glass, set it back on her bosom, where it instantly fell over. She eyed him critically.

Mitch smiled, set down his drink. "Okay. I already told you I was in insurance, Mrs. Greely—"

"Why do you keep calling me Mrs. Greely? I hate that name. It's Claire. Why do you keep calling me that? Are you flirting with me or not, goddamnit?"

"Sure."

"Well then, quit calling me *Greely*, for chrissake! Sounds like *greedy*! Is there any more champagne?"

Mitch smiled. "It isn't working out so hot, huh, Claire?"

"What?"

"Your affair with Dias."

She watched him a moment, then went back to her glass. "If you're going to flirt, *Mr.* Mitch, I really wish you'd stop bringing up the other men in my life."

"Sorry."

Remembering the glass was empty she flung it. "No, it is not working out the least 'hot.' It is not, in fact, if it is any of your business and I am herewith making it your business, it is not even luke. Warm, that is. It has yet, in fact, to be begun, in the official sense, that is. Do you think you could get us another bottle?"

"Who's fault is it, yours or Dias's?"

He was taking advantage of her drunkness, but he didn't feel as guilty about it as he'd thought he would. Maybe, he told himself, it's because you don't have to relay the information to Greely even if you get it. Maybe you can just keep it to yourself. Maybe that's why you're

interested anyway. She's a beautiful woman. Charming
and intelligent. Here, take my money and my wife,
please.

Claire closed her eyes and for a moment Mitch
thought she was going to pass out. But when she spoke
she was not slurring. "I am not, Mr. Mitchell Spencer,
as inebriated as you think I am. However, my present
condition is, I admit, somewhat the result of my own
angst about sleeping with the aforementioned Mr. Dias,
and the fact that the aforementioned expects me to make
up my mind about that this evening, very most probably
on the very bed on which you see me now reposing. It
occurs to me that I may have subconsciously gotten precisely this smashed to further avoid such an eventuality,
the fact of which will not, I fear, lessen to any degree the
wrath and scorn of the aforementioned. He has, to put it
succinctly, *waited long enough*. The truth of the matter
is, that no matter how loose I may appear at the present,
I not only have never slept with Mr. Dias, I have never
slept with anyone but my husband! How's that for shel-
tered? Is this sufficently unabashed for you, Mr. Spencer?"

Mitch laughed silently at how much Claire sounded
like her eloquent husband, but he managed to keep a
straight face.

"Quite."

"Good. I believe it is your turn now. I suggest we get
back to the real truth about your affair."

He grinned. "I'm afraid that *was* the truth. I'm here
alone. No friend, no affair."

Claire sighed, reached mechanically for the champagne glass again, remembered she'd thrown it, and
flopped back. "How utterly unchivalrous of you, Mr.
Spencer. I delve into the darkest corners of my life and
you give back not so much as a morsel. How can you call
yourself a gentleman?"

He considered. Was there any reason he shouldn't
talk about himself to her? He felt, peculiarly enough, a
desire to do so with this strange, lovely, intoxicated
woman. He sensed a sad kind of kinship between them

that was growing by the moment, a similarity he couldn't yet define.

Claire sat up. She swayed a bit, but actually appeared less drunk than before. Her face was flushed, body tense with anticipation. Eyes soft with sudden vulnerability. "Mitch . . . ?

"Yes?"

"Will you kiss me, please?"

He watched her. "Yes."

She was visibly trembling. "Like you mean it?"

"Yes."

He came to her.

Sat. Embraced her, pressed then crushed his lips to hers. She groaned and gave him her tongue. She wouldn't let go, gripping his neck with lacquered nails, breath whistling through flared nostrils.

When he finally pulled back her face was slack, but her eyes said it all.

"Mitch."

He bent to her lips again, left hand seeking her breast, when there was a clanking sound behind them.

Through a crack in the cabin door, Mitch saw movement.

"It's Dias," he whispered.

With a strength that surprised him, she shoved him aside, pushed up, stumbled across the room. She opened another door, a seamless one he hadn't noticed before, and darted inside, pulling it closed.

In another instant, the cabin door opened and there stood Dias.

He was not pleased.

Mitch thought he had never seen such unbridled hatred and humiliation in a man's eyes.

Before either could speak, there was a gagging sound from behind the hidden door. Then movement, then a flushing noise.

Dias moved to the toilet door and pulled it open. Claire was just turning, hair in disarray, bodice of her gown soiled, face ashen. Jesus, thought Mitch, she really did throw up.

She stumbled toward Dias, "Santiago . . ." and collapsed in his arms.

Dias carried her to the bed, stretched her out. She had passed out. Mitch turned to see a silver-haired woman coming through the door, looking first at Dias then, concerned, at Claire. There was a frozen moment during which everyone looked at everyone else.

"Too much to drink, I'm afraid," Mitch offered at last.

The woman moved to the toilet, secured a wet washcloth, knelt beside the sleeping woman. "I'll take care of her. You two attend to the party."

Dias showed Mitch to the door. On the way through the narrow corridor to the deck, Dias turned to him, smiling warmly, clapping Mitch on the back. "You always show up just in time to rescue my guests! Did you have to carry her to her cabin, my friend?"

Mitch shrugged. "Not quite."

Dias shook his head with distaste. "She drinks too much, I knew it from the first. But do you know, she will not touch cocaine? A very strange woman." He smiled at Mitch. "But that is what makes them fascinating, no?"

Mitch returned his smile.

On deck, in the crisp night air, Dias grabbed two drinks from a passing tray and handed one to Mitch. "I'm delighted to see you again, Mr. Spencer. It appears as though Manuel was able to secure your address—you received the invitation?"

"Yes, thank you."

"Good." Dias looked briefly at the noisey crowd. "I'm afraid I have been a poor host this evening to Mrs. Greely. Business affairs, you understand." He looked back at Mitch, clapped his shoulder in rugged, manly fashion. "I want to thank you for assisting her. You know what it is to be a gentleman."

"I'm just glad she didn't get hurt."

"Thanks to you. *Again* thanks to you."

Mitch waved a hand at the yacht. "Please let me compliment you on another spectacular vessel."

Dias grinned, pleased. "Thank you. My downfall, I'm afraid. I collect them." They walked to the rail, looked out at the winking lights of the marina.

"I was hoping to meet your lovely wife tonight, Mr. Spencer. She could not attend?"

"Joanne's a bit under the weather," Mitch said. Then added, "We've just learned she's going to have a baby."

Dias beamed. "Ah! Congratulations! You are alone then this evening?"

"Yes."

Dias clapped him on the shoulder again. "Then this time we will not let you get away so fast! You must spend the night, I insist!"

"Well, I—"

"No, I will entertain no excuses! There is plenty of room aboard, and I think you will find the accommodations more than comfortable."

"I'm sure of that."

Dias grinned ear to ear. "Then it's settled! Tomorrow we will have breakfast together, the four of us!"

Mitch turned. "Four?"

"You, Mrs. Greely, myself, and Mother!"

CHAPTER 1 4

TULLY

DETECTIVE SERGEANT EUSTES TULLY MET JIM SHIN-
gleton at Tully's favorite Jack-in-the-Box on Anacapa for
the briefing about the Dias operation.

Shingleton, a lieutenant in Narcotics, was techni-
cally Tully's superior, but it was no secret to anyone how
hard Tully had worked on the Laredo Beach homicide and
how deflating it was to be jerked off the case, even in the
course of official business. So, instead of making Tully
come to him, Shingleton had come to Tully, at Tully's
favorite fast-food restaurant. They were old friends—they
were old, period. Too old to worry about rank and protocol.

Shingleton softened the dismissal blow by pointing
out how uniquely invaluable Tully was for the Dias job.

"It isn't just the fact that we're old friends who've
worked together before, and it isn't just my high opinion
of your talents as a cop, Tully. The really important thing
is that you're a homicide dick with a background in Narcotics. The latter makes you invaluable to us, the former
makes you an unknown to Dias."

Tully glanced up over his cheeseburger. "Dias gets around that much?"

Shingleton snorted wryly, roamed the restaurant's interior with frustrated eyes. "Son of a bitch knows every narc between here and Hoboken, all their wives and their kids' first names. And if he doesn't, somebody in that Colombian entourage of his does. This is a very sophisticated man we're talking about, an intelligent, well-read man from good stock. The aristocratic Dias family was not always in the drug game, you know. Their legitimate dealings in the international export business go way back, to cleaner, more prestigious times. Only then it was coffee and orchids instead of coke. Dias hails from a little Colombian town called Medellín."

Tully stuffed in fries, nodded. "Rough town."

"Since the late seventies, five homicides a day. You think we got it bad here in Southern California? Only in Medellín they don't waste time in back alleys, they pop them off right on the busiest street corners. Think of it as Chicago during Prohibition, with Dias one of the top leaders of his own little South American brand of Cosa Nostra. Only there they call it *la mafia cirolla*. Every year at least forty-five tons of coke are channeled through Medellín to the U.S. Another ten tons get siphoned off to Europe, usually inferior stuff. Dias controls a good portion of it. Up to now he's stayed on his own turf, run the show from there. Lately he's been hanging around the West Coast. Maybe he likes the shopping malls and the Valley girls. Maybe he's got something else in mind. We want to find out."

"But you can't get close enough."

"We can with you."

"How do we go about it?"

"Put you on the yacht. Get you invited to one of his famous parties."

"I repeat the question."

"Well, you can't pose as a phony drug dealer, that's for sure. Dias is too smart for that; he really *will* check you out. No, we've got to come in from another angle, give him something else he wants."

"Like what?"

Shingleton sat back with a weary grunt. "That's what we have to figure out."

Tully grunted. "Let me finish my fries first, huh? I'm not quite through digesting my last case."

Shingleton smiled sympathetically. "I'm sorry, Tully. I think you got screwed. Everyone thinks you got screwed. I know what solving that case would have meant to you, gotten you, but you've still got a shot at that promotion with this Dias thing."

"I've also got a shot at being shot. And, unlike Brumeister or anyone else at the station but a rookie, I don't have a wife and kids."

"Bad luck for you, maybe, but damn good luck for me. I wouldn't want to work with anyone else on this, especially not that shit Brumeister. He'd get himself killed and set us back six months. You're the right man—the best man—for the job, Tully, like it or not."

Tully accepted the flattery stonefaced, wiped at his mouth, crumpled the napkin with the rest of his waste paper, spotted a refuse container, and aimed.

"Besides," Shingleton continued, "you've got another leg up on this thing—you know something about boats. Your old man owned one, didn't he?"

Tully tensed, thinking of the little red ketch, spoiling his aim. The wastepaper ball missed its mark, bounced across the restaurant floor.

After the meeting with Shingleton he drove around for a while.

He ended up down at the marina adjacent to Stearn's Wharf, where he'd been told Dias's yacht was moored. No little red ketch here—this is where the big fish swam. The sharks.

He parked, sat a moment memorizing the snapshot of the big white vessel Shingleton had given him, then

got out and moseyed along the rock-bound seawall to
the edge of the marina until he spotted it. It was late
afternoon—pelicans skimming before a smoggy, blood-
red sunset, people going home to dinner—there was little
activity aboard Dias's yacht, at least on deck. Tully
couldn't see too well from his vantage point, but he
didn't want to get closer yet, didn't want to appear as
anything more than a sightseer or potential boat buyer
until he had a more concrete plan. The best way to get
on board, he'd decided on the way down, was to be a
partygoer. Depending on how well Dias scrutinized his
myriad guests that could be easy or dangerous. Best if
he knew someone, though Tully didn't exactly run with
the beautiful people.

If Dias was supplying some of the locals with drugs,
that might be an avenue, assuming it was a local Tully
had befriended sometime over the years. Unlikely but not
impossible. On the other hand, if it was someone with a
record, and Tully's true identity was uncovered, he could
always use the excuse that he'd been tailing the other
guest, had no interest in Dias himself. It would probably
blow the case, but it might come in handy toward saving
his life.

The more he thought about it, the more it sounded
like a good idea. He decided to go downtown, look
through the mug book and see if he could refresh his
mind, find any users who might seek out Dias. But before
he did that, he'd stop off at that bar he'd passed on the
way down and knock back a couple on company time.
Fuck 'em, they owed it to him for switching cases on him
like this.

The bar was called Navy Bob's, a greasy little dive
not too far from the marina, near State Street. State was
enjoying a major urban renewal plan, putting in new
sidewalks for the tourists, tearing down questionable
structures, which were either fire hazards or fudging
with the county on zoning laws, making the line between
the commercially viable Stearn's Wharf and the hub of

downtown Santa Barbara a clean and unbroken one. Navy Bob's, hardly a beauty spot, cringed deep in the shadow of the wrecking ball, its ancient wooden facade badly in need of paint, its Budweiser sign in the dust-grimed front window too stained and outdated to be paying any current rent. Navy Bob's looked like a good place not to be seen.

Tully had three drinks, more than he should have and less than he wanted, and was thinking about a fourth when he glanced up.

Detective Sergeant William Brumeister was seated six booths over, grinning and leering at a blonde floozy across from him who wore a grab-me sweater and an inch of pancake. Tully groaned inwardly. He was just beginning to forget about work; one more drink would have done it.

Hidden from view by a deep shadow coming off the bar, Tully watched the grinning, giggling couple. He sat silently gripping his drink, studying them with a kind of masochistic verve. There was something almost hypnotically perverse about spying on Brumeister, listening to his piggy laugh, watching his loutish gestures; something wonderfully repellent about the way the stupid little blonde ate it up.

Brumeister glanced over once and for an instant Tully thought he'd been made, but it was a false alarm. Not that it mattered; if Brumeister wanted to get some on the side that was his business. Far from being embarrassed about being caught, Brumeister would probably use the incident to rub it in Tully's face. Tully could hear him:

"Come on over, Eustes, join us for a drink! Give you a chance to be around a woman for a change—other than your mother, that is! Is it true what everybody says about her apron strings? Say, why is it you never married, huh?"

Tully sank lower into the shadows. He ordered another drink. And then another.

He watched them. Watched the supercilious grin on

Brumeister's face, watched the way his fat lips flapped
when he laughed his disgusting laugh, watched the way
he ogled the blonde's tight sweater, the way the blonde's
pale fingered hand kept reaching under the table and
squeezing the detective's knobby knee. The way she giggled every time he made one of his stupid, unfunny, no
doubt racist jokes.

He watched and drank and grew angry. Angry
enough to punch someone. Angry at the injustice of it. At
the injustice of the world. Of life. His life.

With his mother.

His, doting, clinging, unbearably omnipresent mother.
His—

They were leaving. Brumeister was throwing down
a bill, pinching the blonde's fat bottom as they moved
toward the door, getting a yelp of feigned indignation
from her, a grunt of piggy pleasure from himself. She
was still giggling when the door shut behind her and the
night swallowed them. Tully got up to follow.

It wasn't hard. Brumeister was pretty drunk himself.
He'd be lucky if he could find whatever urine-stained
roach motel he was taking the blonde to. Probably the
one out on 101 past Montecito. Why the hell was he following them anyway, what the fuck did he expect to
accomplish?

Go home, Tully. Mother's probably been calling.
Wants to make a date. Or did they already have a date
tonight? He was too stoned to remember. Fuck it.

He followed a judicious six car-lengths behind them.
It was later than he'd thought, well past rush hour traffic.
Good thing, he was weaving a bit. Brumeister passed the
motel on 101 and headed for the suburbs. What the hell
was he doing that for?

Tully followed, head bobbing occasionally, white line
blurring. This was stupid, stupid and dangerous and
unprofessional. It was all he needed on his record right
now, a drunk driving cite. They would practically *hand*
him a promotion! Jerk. Keep your head up! Christ. Go

home, Tully. Detective Eustes Eugene Tully. What kind of fucking name was that anyway? Go home. Sleep it off.

He followed until the passing lights burned his eyes and the highway melted into suburban streets and manicured lawns. And then with a revelation that nearly sobered him, Tully knew where they were: in Brumeister's neighborhood.

He'd been there only once, years ago, when the other detective's car had broken down and Tully had been elected to go pick him up. It was an average house in an average neighborhood that an average cop's pay could buy in the early seventies. Ruth Brumeister was an average woman with an average cat and four average fat kids. Nothing remarkable about that morning had stayed with Tully; he was simply cursed with a good memory.

He stayed a discreet distance behind Brumeister's Volvo, backing off even more now in these less trafficked neighborhood streets. He passed by at medium speed as Brumeister pulled in front of his house and cut the engine. Tully circled the block and came by again in time to see the lights go on inside and the front door shut. Mrs. Brumeister and the kids must be on vacation. Christ, what a slime the guy was, bringing his girlfriend to his own home!

Tully parked down the street several houses away and sat watching the house, still completely oblivious to why he was here or what he was doing.

All he really knew was that he wanted to kill them both.

After a time, he got out of the car and walked casually down the sidewalk toward the dimly lit home. It was past nine, the street was pretty empty; a woman walked a white poodle on the other side, but she soon disappeared around the corner, her heels clicking distantly.

Tully found himself walking between Brumeister's ranch and the neighboring house adjacent to the bedroom. If car lights found him now . . .

But none did, and he crept into deep shadow, pressing himself against a balding trellis, praying for no dogs, pretty sure Brumeister didn't have one, inching by degrees toward the softly illuminated bedroom window. It looked as though the blind was down.

It was, but not all the way, and Tully could see the couple inside plainly enough. The woman sat topless on the neatly made bed next to a nightstand, upon which sat a framed photo of Mrs. Brumeister. Brumeister stood wobble-legged above the half-dressed woman, holding his pecker in one hand, dipping it into a glass of champagne, alternating the the purple crown between the lip of the glass and the lips of the blonde, alternating his piggy eyes between the woman's engorged mouth and the prim mouth of his framed wife. He grinned as he did this.

Tully leaned against the clapboard siding staring into the glowing interior and wondered how many years he could get for this.

When Brumeister tired of the champagne, he forced the blonde to drain the glass, most of it spilling down her heavy bosom. Apparently tickled by this, Brumeister squatted over her thighs, thrust his sagging member between her cleavage and aped a drunken bump-and-grind. The blonde scrunched the cleavage tighter, making a pillowy passage, licking the rosy head, trying not to laugh, collapsing at last in a fit of giggles as the fat cop lost his balance and tumbled across her. Afterwards he sat on her chest and tried to get her to blow him, but he was too limp to produce much result and keeled over after a time, big chest working like a bellows, face running with sweat. He looked asleep, face almost childlike, no matter how gamely the blonde squeezed and tugged at him.

Tully turned to go, feeling a drop on his ear. It had been threatening to rain all evening.

But now Brumeister was up again, lumbering around the bedroom, talking animatedly to the woman sprawled across the bed, gesturing wildly with his hands. The woman watched him, calmly nodding now and then at certain gestures, yawning a few times, looking at her watch.

The rain began in earnest, pelting Tully's hair, drumming across the tiled roof. He pulled his collar up, tensed, body telling him to go, something else warning him he might miss out.

Brumeister continued to wave his arms about, nearly shouting now; were it not for the drumming rain, Tully could have almost made out the words. The blonde sat up on her elbows, watching, nodding, face impassive.

Abruptly, Brumeister seized a nearby drawer, yanked it open, pulled something out. Tully pressed closer, water in his eyes, gelling the rippling pane, squinting into the blurry bedroom.

The woman was trying to get off the bed, eyes wide with terror, mouth trying to scream above the storm. Brumeister grabbed her by the neck, slammed her on the mattress, knelt above her, holding her tight. He was forcing her legs apart with his knees, shoving down hard against her writhing form, teeth bared, wielding something in his free hand. Just before it pressed downward between her legs and was lost to view behind the big cop's torso, Tully saw the length of black nightstick.

He tore away from the window and skidded around the corner of the house, slipping in the muddy lawn, tripping over a drowned hedge. Cursing, he regained his footing, sprinted across the short length of lawn, hopped up on the doorstep, trying the knob with one hand, fumbling for his wallet with the other. He had the credit card out and run expertly between door and jamb in less than ten seconds. He pushed into dry darkness.

The screams echoed from the bedroom.

He was down the hall and crashing through the door in time to a tremendous rocking thud of thunder; it shook the frame of the house. It also shook the slippery gun from Tully's surprised hand.

I'll never drink again.

Brumeister turned with a start of surprise that echoed the shock on the blonde's white face; Tully could see the big nightstick deep inside her. He leapt on Brumeister like an animal, not taking the time to look for the gun in the gloom.

But his wet soles slipped on the throw rug and he fell short, nails raking Brumeister's chest, face slamming into his wilted crotch. He caught a quick whiff of musk and felt Bruemister's knee slam his chin as the detective pinwheeled backward across the bed. Tully was on his feet and after him, not wanting to lose the already half-blown element of surprise. They hit the bed beside the screaming blonde and bounced, once, twice, locked together grimly, naked skin against his sodden suit, bounced a third time, and crashed sideways to the hard-wood floor, between bed and wall.

Tully really thought he had him, his one hand at the fat throat, the other fumbling for his cuffs, when Brumeister shot his legs up under him and pushed him backward through the air in a half-somersault. Tully crashed down, flattening a fragile French table with an explosion of glass.

When he got up, Brumeister had found his own gun.

He had the hammer back before he recognized his fellow cop. "Tully? The fuck you doing here?"

Tully fought for breath, pointed mutely to the length of nightstick still jutting from between the startled blonde's legs.

Brumeister looked blank, nonplussed. "What? She a friend of yours? You been following me or what? The fuck's going on?"

All of a sudden it started to dawn: something wasn't right, or quite what it seemed.

Tully pointed to the stick again. "Is that the murder weapon?" he said lamely, no longer believing it himself.

Brumeister made a face. "It's my old nightstick, ass-hole, is what it is!"

"What the hell were you doing with it?"

"Whatever I damned well pleased! She's a whore, dickhead!"

Now he could see, of course, that she was. She hadn't yet even bothered to remove it.

Tully tried valiantly for some ground. "Is that how you get your jollies, William?"

Brumeister shoved the gun back in his holster, tossed it on the dresser. "No, jerk-off, that's how I test a theory, to see if it fits!" He was using his shirt to towel off Tully's rainwater with short, indignant strokes.

"She was screaming, goddamnit!"

"It was an act, dickhead! She's a whore! She gets paid to do what I say, and I said scream! Get it?" He whirled on the blonde. "Tell him!"

The whore nodded innocent compliance.

Tully knew he'd been had. "Yeah? Well, you're one sick fuck, you know that?"

The big cop looked up, unharried, smugly in control. "And I could burn your ass on a B and E, Eustes." He shook his head in disgust. "Breaking into a man's bedroom like a fucking animal, the hell you think you are, a freakin' football player?"

"I had probable cause—"

"You had shit, asshole! A man can do any goddamn thing he wants in the privacy of his own bedroom in the state of California. It's on the books! I can drive a goddamn semi up her cunt as long as it's not hurting anybody. So take your probable cause and go pull your pud with it!"

The maddening thing was, Brumeister wasn't even really steaming: he had Tully, had him good, had made a fool of him, or more pointedly, stood and watched him make a fool of himself. It had all worked out fine for Brumeister. There're good ones and there're bad ones, Eustes, but this just ain't your day.

The blonde, nightstick still in place, was signaling from the bed. "Are you going to need me anymore, sugar? 'Cause I need cab fare . . ."

Brumeister collected his pants, began fishing in his wallet.

The blonde found Tully's eyes, struck a suggestive pose, with a lip-biting grin. "Sure you don't want to stay, honey? I do doubles. Put on a real good show for you boys." She began to manipulate the stick.

Tully turned toward the door, found himself halted by a glint atop the chest of drawers. It lay there amid a pile of loose change and an aftershave bottle shaped like a Corvette. Tully picked it up. "From your camera, William?"

Brumeister was pulling on his trousers. His face grew truly angry for the first time when he saw the little flashbulb between Tully's fingers. "Hey, keep the hell away from my stuff, huh?"

He reached for it and Tully snatched it. "Is it *your* stuff??"

The bigger cop grabbed Tully's hand and dragged the bulb away without resistance. "Get the fuck out of my house! Now!"

Tully leaned against the dresser. "So tell me, did it match the one I found?"

"Leave now, or so help me Christ I'll nail you on a breaking-and-entering."

"You fucking creep, the goddman thing wouldn't even have caught your eye if I hadn't found the first one."

"You goin' or am I callin'?"

Tully pushed away, headed for the door. "Where was it, in the sand beside the corpse, just like with the Cunningham woman? I can check with Fred Wanamaker."

"Piss off."

Tully found his way to the front door, walked out into the rain.

Halfway down the block he heard Brumeister's raspy cry behind. "Stay the hell away from this case, Tully! Stay the goddamn hell way from it!"

C H A P T E R   1 5

MITCH

*H*E AWOKE WITH THE UTTER CERTAINTY SOMETHING was not right.

It was more than the obvious fact that he was in a strange bed, aboard a strange boat, the guest of someone who was, essentially, a stranger, a dangerous stranger. It was something deep in the pit of his gut sending up little warning waves of queasy unease. Telling him that, all things being equal, things were not equal at all.

And then he knew what it was. Or thought he did.

He slid off the soft bunk, grabbed his pants, ran a hand through his rumpled hair, and pushed through the cabin door to stairs that would take him above deck to the answer. Buckling and zipping as he went, he stepped over the coaming to topside.

The sea air was marvelous. He was all alone on deck, the yacht seeming to gleam with a painful whiteness that was nearly iridescent. The breeze was morning cool, rich with the mysterious smell of the deep, the sky nearly cloudness, the big sails bowing gently.

They were moving ... *underway*—wasn't that the correct nautical expression?

Mitch sagged, hand clutching a halyard, dry breath caught, heart pressed tightly against empty morning ribs. The harbor was a pencil line in the distance, the great blue Pacific an endless lolling plane that stretched forever with no hope, no forgiveness. He was, in essence, a prisoner.

They were *moving*.

He couldn't accept it, couldn't quit shaping the word in his mind. Where in Christ's name were they going?

He caught you with his woman, kissing his woman, and now he's exacting his revenge.

The notion was so absurd it almost brought a smile, and did, in fact, bring a calming wave of relief. Dias might indeed be a killer in his own country, perhaps even in this country, but he would hardly abduct innocent American citizens and drown them at sea over an incident as innocuous as last night's. At least Mitch didn't think he would.

Untightening a notch, he absently rubbed morning chill from his shoulders and tried to make the fact of their motion work rationally. A morning fishing trip, perhaps? Or merely a short jaunt to the three-mile limit and back before breakfast, clear the head with clean ocean air? Or was Dias in some sort of trouble with the local law, heading out to sea for temporary retreat? If so, he apparently forgot he had local passengers.

Mitch looked about, scanning the immaculate deck and rigging. He was still alone. Had anyone besides him and Claire spent the night? We'll have breakfast in the morning, Dias had said—you, Mrs. Greely, myself, and Mother. And, of course, there must be some kind of crew aboard, too, running all this. The thing to do was to go to wheelhouse and ask whoever was in charge what was going on.

He turned, caught the line of sail. It reminded him of his mother's clothesline and her spanking clean sheets in the warm San Diego sun and his carefree youth. That made him think of his own daughter's youth and that, in turn, made him think of Joanne.

What was she doing now, his faithful wife, what was she thinking? Was she awake yet, having her morning coffee? What time was it? He should be there with her. Not here spying for this strange fat man Greely, lying to her about his whereabouts. Putting his neck in a noose. Scrambling to hang on to an insurance job he didn't really want.

He hesitated, shocked.

Well! That was a revelation!

He didn't *want* the damn job! That was the plain simple truth of it! Or the house in the suburbs or the damn Porsche! He didn't want any of it!

Well, what do you know.

He stood blinking in the warm sun feeling light-headed. Light, period. Unburdened. Frightened, but finally clean.

It had taken this long, coming this far, to here on the deck of this yacht heading out to sea, to realize it. He just didn't want any of it anymore. The stupid job least of all.

He shook his head slowly. Incredible.

And what about Joanne? The new baby?

Yes, what about them?

"Ahoy there!"

He turned and found Claire smiling at him. She was dressed all in white: white shorts, white blouse, white headband, white deck shoes, with a slash of nautical blue at the belt. It caught the blue in her eyes and emphasized the swirl of windblown blonde curls and made her look like a sophisticated water nymph. She flashed a hundred-kilowatt smile at him. "Sleep well, Mr. Spencer?"

Mitch unconsciously ran a hand through his tousled hair, suddenly aware of his thick stubble, morning puffiness. "Fine, thank you. And you?"

"With all that bubbly dancing in my tummy? Like a

log. One thing about champagne, it never gives me a hangover. I'm glad I found you alone, it gives me the chance to apologize."

"No apologies necessary."

"Not for the sloppy drunk. I wasn't that smashed, I told you. For the pass, I mean."

"Definitely no need for apology there."

She watched him a moment. Then looked out to sea. "Yes, there is. I've been told—by his mother, if you can believe that—that our Mr. Dias is very jealous. I assume that's to imply he has some kind of claim or other on me, all of which is news to me." She looked back at him, curls caressing her cheek. "Anyway, it might not pay to rile him. He has something of a dangerous reputation, did you know?"

"I've heard." He felt his heart skip a little beat of fear, but he was damned if he'd let her know it.

"It was thoughtless of me to jeopardize you like that. Beyond that, it was just thoughtless, period. Ergo, my apologies, to you and your wife."

"It was a nice kiss, though," he heard himself saying.

Her smile sent his stomach buzzing lightly. "Yes. It was that."

They watched each other.

"Maybe another time, another place," he said.

She was gazing at his lips when Dias came on a deck with a tromping of feet and a terrific yawn. He wore a monogrammed silk robe, silk pajamas, deerskin slippers. He stretched mightily at the sun, grinned, spread his arms wide to greet them. "Ah, my dear friends! You are already up, up with the sun, eh?"

He kissed Claire on the forehead, clapped Mitch on the shoulders, yanked at the sash of his robe. "A beautiful day, no? There is nothing like the sea breeze! You have been at sea before, Mitch?"

"A few times," Mitch admitted.

"*Bueno!*" He put an arm around Claire, drew her to him, kissed her hair again.

He seemed effusively familiar this morning. Was he trying to show Mitch something? This is my property?

"And how is my most beautiful guest this morning? Feeling better?"

"I'm fine thank you, Santiago."

He hugged her, biceps swelling, grinned at Mitch. "I hope you like a big breakfast! I always eat a big breakfast every morning! It is the best meal of the day! And the most important meal of the day, according to nu . . . nu . . ."

"Nutritionists," Mitch supplied.

"Thank you, yes! You slept well, Mitch? You look— forgive me for saying—somewhat distressed."

Mitch looked out to sea. "I slept wonderfully. I was just wondering where we're bound for."

Dias laughed. "Did I not tell you?" He laughed his big laugh again. "To Poquito! To dive!"

"Poquito?"

Dias pointed over the lazaret. "A tiny island—a jut of rock, really—near the tip of the Channel Islands. We call it 'Poquito.' There is good diving there, clear water. You have skin-dived before, Mitch?"

"A little."

"Ah, *bueno*! You must join us then! I have promised the Garcias a short dive after breakfast!" He slapped Mitch on the shoulder. "Never fear, Mitch, I will return you to port safe and sound!" He turned his radiant smile on Claire. "And you, my dear, will you share the charms of the underwater world with us?"

Claire smiled back, rubbed at her arms. "You bet! I'll try anything once."

Dias laughed.

Mitch watched the horizon, vaguely uneasy.

Breakfast was fabulous, the best Mitch could recall eating in years: fresh guava juice, macadamia nut pancakes, Italian sausage, three-cheese omelets, an enormous plate of bright, fat fruit, rich Kona coffee, as fresh-tasting as if it had been brewed on the Big Island of Hawaii. All of it was served by a serious-looking waiter in a freshly starched uniform whose attention to detail and his guests' needs was almost embarrassing.

Mitch, Claire, and Dias were joined by Dias's mother and by three other guests, a darkly handsome couple, the Garcias, and a svelte ingenue with black flowing hair and almond eyes, introduced simply as Olin. She sat quietly throughout the meal in leggy shorts and straining halter top, nodding politely, smiling, and peering over the rim of her cup at Mitch. Apparently she spoke no English.

The Garcias did speak English, if haltingly. An attractive couple in their early forties, Mrs. Garcia was Olin twenty years later, still well-proportioned, stately, graceful. Like her husband, she carried herself well. Though obviously wealthy, the couple had an air of simplicity. Mr. Garcia's knotted arms and callused palms bespoke hands-on experience in whatever it was he did for a living. It was in some way connected to Dias, from the incessant and somewhat intense way he and Garcia conversed mostly in Spanish. Always the gracious host, and prompted by occasional glares from his silver-haired mother, Dias didn't allow these conversations to intrude unduly on an otherwise pleasant breakfast. Still, Mitch couldn't help noticing their import to the Garcias, both of whom appeared solemn, if not outwardly troubled. Whatever was going on between the Dias and Garcia families, it was not equitable.

"You must forgive Sonny," Mrs. Dias explained to Mitch at one point, "he does not mean to be rude." She waved her hand at their opulent surroundings. "I keep reminding him that all this extravagance is wasted if one's eyes are blinded by business and commerce. Olin has promised to set my hair; perhaps you and Mrs. Greely would care to take a stroll around the deck until all this boring business chatter has ended?"

"I'd appreciate that, Mitch," Dias said, overhearing. "We'll reach the dive area in about an hour."

Mitch pushed back his plate. "Fine with me. Mrs. Greely?"

They rose together, Mitch taking Claire's arm. Dias had already turned back to his business guests.

"Garrulous this morning, isn't he?" Claire offered, leaning against the rail watching the bow wave, wind lifting her pretty blonde curls.

Mitch was gazing out past the transom, trying to envision a marina and city that were no longer there. "He's a businessman. The best of them are a talkative lot, I suppose."

"You suppose? Weren't you among them?"

"No. Not really."

"I thought you were in insurance or something."

"Not in my heart."

She looked at him, thinking he was quite naturally handsome in the warm morning light, remembering thinking it was nice to kiss him, wondering if maybe he were wishing they were anyplace else but here and he could kiss her again.

"What is in your heart, Mr. Mitch Spencer? Not your wife, certainly."

He watched her.

She turned away. "Sorry. That was crass." She colored. "Something about you . . . I keep having this compulsion to state the absolute brutal truth. Were you a Boy Scout?"

"No, but I'll take that as a compliment."

"You should. I'm truthful with practically no one. Here's another—you kiss well, did you know that? Not that I'm an expert, by any means, but I know what feels good, and it felt wonderful . . . However, since that way lies madness, how about if we compromise? Confidants instead of lovers. How does that sound?"

"Is there a distinction?"

She looked at him, tilted her head, curious. "I always thought so . . . but in your case, I don't know, perhaps not. Perhaps they could be the same thing. Gee ... that would be novel." She turned back to the rail. "Anyway— Mr. Confidant—what about it? Should I have an affair with him or no?"

He watched the sea ahead, looking for the island, hoping it wasn't a lie. "I'm afraid I'm rather biased there. You kiss well, too. I might get jealous. Stranger things have happened."

Claire reached over and squeezed his arm. "How sweet. My sweet, charming rescuer. Are you really jealous or just trying to wiggle out of an answer?"

"Both."

She laughed. "Oh, Mitch, Mitch. Let's be absolutely crazy and leap overboard and swim away together to a tiny atoll with a sleepy lagoon, shall we? You can make me coconut juice and I'll dance in a grass skirt for you, what do you say?"

"I'm married, remember?"

She nodded conciliation. "Yes, that's true ... but then again, maybe that's why we'd have great sex together."

"Why is that?"

"No risk. You're unavailable, I'm unavailable. It's a Freudian thing, I think, a subliminal desire to start all over again, fresh. 'Like a virgin,' you know? I'm practically a virgin myself, would you believe that?"

"Really? How does one become 'practically' a virgin?" Her girlish candor was charming him, just as he knew she knew it would, but he couldn't help being delighted by it, glad it didn't depend entirely on alcohol.

"By hardly ever having sex, and never enjoying it. And all this time you thought it had something to do with physicality, didn't you?"

"Live and learn. What about Dias?"

"Well ... Dias is attractive *and* single."

"Isn't that a contradiction in Freudian terms?"

"I haven't slept with him, have I?"

He leaned against the rail beside her and watched her fluttering curls. "You're okay, Claire. I like you."

She grinned. "Same to you, Mitchell. You haven't answered my question, though—what's in your heart? What makes you happy, if not the insurance business?"

He watched the waves awhile, wondering if he should tell her, feeling the same lack of guile between them that she felt. Why not? Why not match her candor with his own.

"I was a cop once. Long ago. That made me happy."

"Why?" She was interested.

"I was good at it."

She nodded. "That's a good reason. What happened? Meet a girl like me who demanded big money?"

He turned and looked at her searchingly. Could he trust her? He wasn't sure. Under this intense scrutiny, she blushed.

"Sorry, did I cross the line again?"

He took a breath. "No, you didn't cross the line. I met a girl, yes. My first year as a cop. Unfortunately she was a prostitute. It was a pretty routine bust; I was with my partner. I'd had a good year, I was good at my job. This girl . . ." He hesitated.

"What, Mitch?"

"She couldn't have been more than twenty, really pretty, dark hair, dark eyes . . . but she was vicious. She started calling me names when I tried to take her in. Stupid things, like loser, dumb cop—I dunno. Nothing really, but it got to me. I decided that enough was enough, and I started to put the cuffs on her, and from out of nowhere she brought out this shiv and started slicing me with it and screaming at me. 'Fucking loser! You're a worse whore than I am!' I just . . . lost it, I guess. Lost it."

Claire watched him, his face was slack with the memory.

He shook it off. "I took out my nightstick and I hit her—I couldn't seem to stop hitting her . . ."

He gazed off into space, pain on his features. Claire spoke softly.

"Did you . . . kill her?"

145

Mitch shook his head. "No, but I wanted to." He was silent for a moment. "She was in a coma for three weeks, finally came out of it. She sued the police department for brutality, sued me personally. Of course she lost—it was obviously self-defense, but that was enough for me. I quit shortly thereafter. Resigned."

"Why?"

He turned and gave her a wry smile. "Because she was right."

He stared at the waves, remembering.

Then, he looked at her. She was pale. "Up to then, I was happy. Up to then, I thought I was a good cop. But I wasn't, really. I thought I was too good to be a cop. I resented it. The truth was, I wasn't good enough."

Claire swallowed. "What happened . . . I mean—"

"It was time to do something else. Only ..." He sighed and looked back behind them, the city vanished. "There wasn't anything else I was any good at. I got a private investigator's license and went into business for myself. Trouble was, I'm good at investigating and lousy at business. I went bankrupt. Then, when this insurance investigator thing came up, I jumped at it. Unfortunately I was fired last week."

He felt her warm hand on his forearm. "I'm sorry, I didn't know."

He shrugged, cleared his throat of sudden phlegm. "Okay, your turn, Mrs. Greely."

"What—?"

"Sorry. Claire."

"Oh. My turn. Yes." She faced the breeze, raked tapered fingers through her hair, let the wind have it. "Well. When was I most happy? Let me see. I don't know. Nothing stands out. Before the marriage, I guess. College? No, grade school. I was pretty happy then. I used to love the summers."

"Where?"

"Here. Santa Barbara. The summers seemed to last forever. My parents were always fighting, but I'd go swimming with my girlfriends, biking. Every kid had a bicycle in those days, boys and girls. We rode them everywhere, everywhere. And there was Uncle Joe. My favorite uncle. He isn't even really my uncle, just a neighbor, but he kind of adopted me. He was always bringing me presents, always taking me to get ice cream." She smiled, eyes filming slightly. "Tutti-frutti. God, I must have eaten a ton of it. Do you remember tutti-frutti, Mitch?"

"Never tried it."

"That's too bad, it was wonderful." She bit her lip. "Uncle Joe was wonderful. Like a father. Much more than my real father. When my mom was killed and my dad started drinking, Uncle Joe just kind of took me over. He really became my father and my mother. He was so soft-hearted; he must have felt sorry for me. Poor lonely little Claire ... I guess those were the happiest days of my life, going to get ice cream at the local sweet shop with Uncle Joe. I always felt so safe, so warm, so loved. Maybe ... maybe that was the only time in my life I ever felt truly loved." She turned to give him a smile.

"Let's do it, Mitch, let's really do it—let's jump overboard and swim away together and find that little atoll. The hell with Dias and the hell with money. You can start over again as a private eye. I can help you run your business—I've got a head for it! I can keep the books like a good little wife. I can—oh, that's right, you have a wife already.

"Sorry," she continued, "I forgot. Oh, well. Maybe I can find my own island, all alone. I'm used to being alone ... look at this! Why am I crying? Isn't this silly? Such a lovely day, too. Jesus, what a bore, forgive me—"

"Claire ..."

"Does she kiss well, your wife?"

"Listen—"

"As well as me?"

"Claire—"

She turned to him, tears trailing down her cheeks, a valiant smile on her lips. "Why *did* you kiss me, Mitch? Not that I'm complaining. But I was the one who was drunk. Do I look awful? Of course I do, mascara's running. Was it nice, the kiss? Do you think you'll be wanting to do it again? Soon? Come on, Mitch, jump in and rescue me, I'm drowning here . . ."

He stared to say something, started to reach for her, when he saw Dias approaching.

Claire caught his expression and turned away, pressing her cheek with the heel of her hand.

The tall, muscular Colombian was smiling broadly, clapping his big hands together.

"Ready for a little scuba diving, you two?"

CHAPTER 16

TULLY

D ETECTIVE SERGEANT EUSTES TULLY STOOD ON THE sun-baked dock beside the empty wooden slip the Dias yacht had occupied, and stared out at the glinting ocean horizon.

He thought he'd seen a whale once, but now he wasn't so sure. They migrated this way, the big Pacific grays, but he could never remember the season.

It was Sunday. The boat might be out for a short pleasure jaunt, or it might be sailing back to Colombian waters. Part of Tully's sullied brain hoped for the latter and part just didn't care anymore. He was tired—and a little depressed. Make that a *lot* depressed.

Shit. Sunday. Other men were coming home from church with the wife and kids or stoking up the barbecue or heading out for frozen yogurt or walking the malls or sunning at the beach. He was standing alone on this miserable dock, no longer officially involved with the case he wanted, not sufficiently motivated to pursue the case he'd been assigned, staring down at the oil-filmed surface of the empty slip and thinking it was just about as empty and meaningless as his life was right now. He thought of calling Captain Sparrs, telling him where he could stick his Colombian drug-runner case, then shuck the job, the promotion, his pension, the whole nine yards.

He shook his weary head.

Thinking yet again: Sure, Eustes. And go where?

Back to your apartment, your glorious bachelor pad? Back to your mother's house? Sit there nursing an iced tea, watching her crochet another in an endless string of grotesquely colored afghans while reminding you just how hard it is for a man your age to find a suitable young female companion, how hard it is to find suitable employment, remind you just how ridiculously vapid and sterile your whole unsuitable life is?

Or you could mosey over to the south dock and stand around mooning over that little red ketch that you'll never buy and never sail off in with the girlfriend and lover you'll never have. . . .

Oh Christ. You really should stop this.

Wallowing here, at this lovely Santa Barbara marina, in morbid self-pity? If the boys on the shooting range could only see crack shot Tully now. Get a grip on yourself, boy. Go *do* something, something useful. Go eat some junk food. Have new tires put on your car. Find a hobby. Find a girlfriend. Go up to the attic and trip down memory lane with that dusty old photo album your nagging mother won't let you finish looking at—

Tully blinked. Chewed ice slowly . . .

Something happening. Something falling together.

"nagging mother—

"album—

"pictures of the beach—"

Something . . .

He looked up at the sun-swept ocean horizon as if seeking confirmation.

A series of seemingly unrelated, essentially abstract thoughts, circling, circling . . . conjoining in a single concept: Mother. Anger. Beach. Body.

There was something there.

He could almost taste it.

He tossed his half-finished snow cone into the water and hurried up the dock to his car, feeling real excitement again for the first time in weeks.

He paused at the car door, snapping fingers in frustration. It was Sunday, Wanamaker wouldn't be at the station, was probably at home with his kids.

He turned, hurried across the street, and entered the run-down saloon he'd gotten drunk in the night of the Brumeister fiasco. Just thinking about that made him wince.

But he let it go, there were bigger fish to fry. Fish he intended to land before Brumeister even got his line wet.

He headed straight to the johns in the back and the grimy pay phone beside them.

"Ellen? Hi, it's Tully. Fred around? Thanks."

He could hear TV racket in the background, kids screaming. What could he say? He didn't really have anything, nothing substantial, just a gut feeling. Sometimes that was a lot, though, and he needed to talk to someone, someone he could trust, bounce ideas off.

"Yeah, what's up, Tully?"

"Probably nothing."

"You're up to something, I can tell. Been doing some lateral thinking again?"

"What's that?"

"Never mind. Tell me."

"Want to take a walk on the beach?"

"Christ yes—get me out of this madhouse. When?"

"Ten minutes. No, make it twenty. Have to stop somewhere first."

"Bless your heart, an official excuse. Which beach?"

"Laredo, where else?"

They walked down to where the two women had been found. The yellow police tape had long since been removed. It looked like just another beach, not even crowded for a warm day. There was a game on the tube, a Spielberg movie at the Granada. One or two young mothers were plopped down on the sand trying to run rein on their pre-schoolers.

"What have you got, Tully?"

"Don't get excited, just a feeling."

Fred nodded, grinned. "That's why I like you, Tully— you're a lateral thinker."

"You said that before."

"It's true. You make leaps of logic not necessarily based on available evidence. It's a lost art. One I envy. I started out trying to be a cop, you know."

"Fred, you're kidding!"

"Didn't have it, didn't have the instinct like you. Like I said, a lost art. Most of these young pups today are helpless without their computers. What the department needs is a course in abstract thinking. Anyway, what have you got?"

Tully cleared his throat. "Lateral thinker or not, you may find this a stretch. I think our man is killing his mother."

He waited for a response, got none and looked over at Fred.

"I'm listening."

Tully continued cautiously. "Okay, let's look at what we got. For one, the same beach, the same *area* of the same beach. For another, the weapon, a policeman's truncheon fitted with spikes or nails so that the victim is savaged, mutilated. In the vagina, the canal that gave him birth. These are acts of sexual ferocity."

"And?"

"The type of victim, physically always the same— strong, athletic, perhaps overbearing. Women with young children. Not only that, but women with children who coincidentally were seen with their children on Laredo Beach the day before the killing! And the sunglasses. He's killing the same woman over and over."

"What about the fact that both women were either divorced or in the process? Wouldn't that point up an adulterous wife, a two-timing girlfriend?"

"That's what's been holding the investigation up,

we're searching for the wrong motive, a jilted lover. This guy doesn't want to obliterate the living, he wants to obliterate the dead. His mother, his overbearing, sunglass-wearing, beach-loving mother. This is where she brought him, years ago, when he was a boy. He hated her then, he hates her now. And he's still trying to get rid of her . . . What do you think?"

Wanamaker was thoughtful. "Maybe. Could be. But it's no more concrete a theory than the jealous lover concept."

"Yes it is, Fred, and for one very important factor—the flashbulbs. The one I found, the one Brumeister found. Sure, they were left behind deliberately, we already know that. The guy wants to be caught. But there's more to it than that; he knows the bodies will be found, he's counting on it, and he wants them found a certain way, in a certain, precisely arranged setting. The kind of setting you might have found thirty years ago or so. Back in the fifties, when you might have tripped over a lot of discarded flashbulbs lying on the beach. He *wants* these travesties discovered, it's part of his punishment, his revenge on her. He wants the world to know."

Wanamaker was nodding slowly, digesting it.

"Can't you see, Fred? He's re-creating part of his childhood, a very painful part. Right down to the old-fashioned sunglasses, the old-fashioned flashbulb, the . . ."

He fished in his pocket, found a scalloped-edged photo he'd pryed from the attic album, handed it to Fred, who studied the picture of ten-year-old Eustes Tully and his pretty mother. His pretty mother in her fifties beach attire.

"The swimsuits!"

Tully nodded, adrenalin flowing. "What kind were they, Fred? Were they old-fashioned, like this one?"

Wanamaker slapped his forehead. "I didn't even notice, nobody did! Nobody thought it was important, just a one-piece swimsuit—they're back in style, I think."

Tully groaned. "Christ, we need more women detectives in Homicide! Where are the suits now?"

"Still in the evidence box if we're lucky."

"Come on! If we can find a tag, trace it to a used clothing store that sells fifties swimwear— Christ! We should have done this long ago!"

"No one thought of it till now, Tully!"

They ran up the beach.

Though not identical, both suits were black in color, of the one-piece variety, and *looked* oldish, at least to Tully and Wanamaker's untrained eyes. But that wasn't good enough. Tully signed both suits out at the desk, folded them neatly into a paper bag and drove over to show them to Fred Wanamaker's wife.

"What do you think, honey?" Fred urged.

They stood in the Wanamakers' kitchen, Ellen Wanamaker holding up the Cunningham woman's garment, tilting her head speculatively. After a moment, she picked up the one worn by Eleanor Rankin, nodding. "They're old, all right. I'd say early to mid-fifties. Like the Jantzens my mother used to wear. Sort of an Esther Williams look. Look how the material pleats here in the front, forms a straight line at the crotch instead of the less discreet V. Very demure by today's standards. These are definitely pre-Bardot."

Tully could hardly contain himself. "Any ideas who might sell this kind of thing, Ellen?"

A piercing shriek from the living room, higher even than the cacophony of the TV. Ellen Wanamaker pushed through the two men. "Stephan! What did I tell you, young man? You heard me! Do *not* hit your little sister! Stephan? Answer your mother!"

There was no answer.

Apparently anticipating this, Ellen came back to the men and picked up the material again. "There's a little place on Anacapa called Wear It Again, Sam's that sells vintage clothing, thirties and forties stuff, maybe fifties, too." She folded the suits, handed them back to Tully. "Of course, these could have come out of somebody's attic. I guess you thought of that."

Tully conceded this solemnly. Fred had not married a fool. "Yes, we thought of that; we didn't want to, but we did."

She smiled. "Sorry. I know it would make it easier if you could trace it to a sales slip. How about some coffee, Tully?"

There was a tremendous crash from the living room.

Fred Wanamaker groaned; his wife hardly seemed to notice. "My turn," Fred relented, and exited the kitchen.

Ellen began pouring coffee without waiting for an answer from Tully. "Probably just my ancient Ming Dynasty tea set that's been in the family for six generations . . . I can't remember, do you take cream?"

"And sugar. Lots."

"Ah, yes, the junk food junkie. When are you going to come by for a real dinner, Tully?"

"When I get my engraved invitation."

"Cut the bull." She came to the table with their coffee, sat across from him.

"I don't know, just been too busy, I guess."

"Doing what?"

Tully shrugged. "You know."

"No, I don't. Tell me."

He sipped coffee. "The usual, you know."

"I don't know *anything* yet."

He looked up. "What is this, the third degree?"

"That's your department. How's your mother, Tully?"

"Okay."

"Still at the house?"

"Yeah."

"Kind of expensive, isn't it, with property taxes and all?"

"Expensive enough."

"Ever think about selling it?"

He put down his coffee with a resigned clink. "Where are we going with this, Ellen?"

She didn't bother looking innocent. Like her husband, Ellen Wanamaker never pretended. That's why he loved them. "So who've you been dating lately?"

He groaned, looked toward the living room for Fred. "I gotta go."

"Finish your coffee, I just brewed it. So. Any prospects?"

Tully looked about, appraising. "I really like what you've done to this kitchen, did I ever tell you?"

"Francine says you never called back."

"I called back! Once."

"Not to make a date, you didn't."

"I told you, I've been busy."

"Yeah, the 'usual,' I know. Why don't you call her, Tully, you got something against my sister-in-law?"

"Of course not."

"Something against divorced ladies?"

"No."

"Great cook, Tully. Great pair of tits."

"Jesus, Ellen."

"Why don't you give her a ring? I have it on the best authority she'd love to hear from you."

"Sure. I will. Soon."

"*Love* to hear from you, Tully. Love to cook you something. How long since you had any, Tully?"

"Any what?"

"You tell me."

"I'll call her. Soon."

"Tully, are you queer?"

"Of course."

"No, you can tell me. Fred and I love you."

"Well, okay, the truth is I've been porking Fred pretty regular, didn't want to hurt your feelings."

"What about the girls at the office? Fred tells me there's a new girl in ballistics with terrific legs. Not as good as mine, of course, but pretty terrific."

Tully sighed, fingered his saucer. "That's just the trouble, honey, they're all *girls* these days. And I, handsome and irrestible as I am, am no longer a boy."

"Oh, bullshit, that doesn't mean anything."

"The hell it doesn't."

"Plenty of women in their twenties and thirties go

for the older type, especially your older type. I'd have had your pants down in ten seconds."

"Yeah, but you're a shameless hussy."

"And the girls today aren't? Hah!"

"They're all afraid of AIDS."

"Which makes you a perfect candidate. Sell the house, Tully. It's killing you. Put her in a home. You have a life to lead, too. Get out. Circulate. Get laid. What are you doing, giving it all to the sink?"

"You're gross."

"Yeah, but I wake up with a smile. Come on. Talk to me."

Tully threw up his hands. "What can I say? I'm a confirmed bachelor."

"Uh-huh. Come on, Tully."

He puffed out his cheeks, pushed back a foot from the table, rapped a knuckle absently on Ellen's table top. "The truth, as they say, is stranger than fiction."

"I'm listening."

He looked toward the living room. "Where's Fred?"

"Beating the kids. Give."

"You'd think ill of me."

"I already think ill of you. Talk."

He sighed, rubbed at his forehead, trapped.

"I don't know. It just all seems to slip away after a while. You become . . . complacent. Ritualized."

"Dead."

"Maybe. But there's a weird kind of peace about that. I have my favorite places to eat, junk food places, my favorite times to shop, my favorite kinds of movies, TV shows. I have my routine. I don't know if I could change now."

"You could change for a decent piece of ass."

He rolled his eyes. "Jesus, Ellen, I *do* get laid now and then! Once in a while anyway. Occasionally."

"With who?"

"Nice girls! I just . . . don't seem to get around to the commitment part. It goes along and then . . . it just doesn't seem to go along anymore."

"When was the last time?"

"My last date?"

"The last time you got laid! Come on!"

He hesitated. "I don't know . . . awhile."

"Hookers and barflies. Christ, Tully."

"It isn't so goddamn easy!"

"Join a service."

"Christ."

"Don't the guys at the office have any sisters?"

"Where the hell is Fred? Did you two set this up?"

"Why will I 'think ill of you,' why'd you say that before?"

He hesitated, looked down at his coffee.

"I'm waiting."

He cleared his throat. "A long time ago, right after the Academy, I walked a beat in San Francisco for a year. They brought in a girl one night, a Latino type, the most incredibly beautiful girl you can imagine. Body like . . . like a goddess. Face—well, she was just beautiful, that's all. She was lying there naked on the morgue gurney, little purple hole above her breast, these incredible breasts. It could have been a mole, that little hole, she could have been asleep. I kept staring down at her, waiting for her to wake up. I got the strangest feeling. I know it sounds crazy, but I almost believed that if I bent down and kissed her, she would wake up. And smile, ask me what it was all about. And maybe I would put my coat over her so the others wouldn't stare anymore and take her out of there and we'd go somewhere for coffee or something. I used to dream about her, that she wasn't really dead, that she and I would walk around the city, go to the movies, take the Golden Gate to Sausalito. She was dead, see, but I was in love with her."

"Tully, is this going to get sick?"

"Shut up. Anyway, I quit dreaming about her after awhile. I still thought about her, though. And at all the wrong times. Like after a date. I'd go out with some girl, have a good time, maybe even get to like her after awhile, bring her home to meet Mom. Start getting pretty serious. Then I'd be lying there alone in bed at night and start thinking about that slab and actually comparing this current girl with the dead one and— Look, I know it sounds crazy, it probably is crazy, but she just couldn't measure up, couldn't compare with the beautiful dark-haired girl on the slab. And after a while, I'd, you know . . . lose interest. And after a *long* while, I guess I just sort of stopped trying, stopped in earnest, anyway. Just sort of lost interest in the whole thing. The years went by"— he looked up at Ellen— "and here I am."

He took a drink of coffee.

Ellen watched him silently.

"Sell the house, Tully."

"Huh?"

"Get rid of it. Put your mother in a home. Get out. Get laid."

"Have you been listening to any of this, Ellen?"

"Tell me something. When did you usually start to lose interest in these girls?"

Tully scratched his chin. "I don't know, after awhile."

"After you brought them home to meet Mother?"

He looked at her.

"Sell the house, Tully."

"Are you trying to say—"

"It wasn't that the other girls didn't compare, it wasn't that you were really in *love* with this dead girl, Tully. Can't you see that?"

"See what?"

"You didn't have to worry about her measuring up because she was dead, you *couldn't* bring her home. She was safe. Safe from Mother."

Tully stared at her.

Fred came back into the kitchen. "We may need a new TV, unless you don't mind the people looking real skinny like that. Are we going to try that place, Play It Again, Sam's?"

"*Wear* It Again," Ellen corrected. "They're probably closed on Sundays."

"Let's try anyway." Tully jumped up, pushing in his chair.

"Coward," Ellen shot at him.

"What's going on between you two?" Fred asked.

"As if you didn't know," Tully said. "Let's go before I drink any more of this bitter, tasteless coffee."

Ellen stuck her tongue out at him. "Have you still got Francine's number, Tully? I have it right here."

"Good-bye, Ellen."

He hit the back door, Fred hurrying to catch up, carrying the paper bag of swimsuits.

"Slow down!"

"I love you, Tully!" Ellen called.

"You hear something?" Tully asked Fred as he hurried down the sidewalk.

"You really should call Francine sometime, Tully. Great tits on that woman. Even if she is my sister."

"Fred, shut up."

Wear It Again, Sam's was open, as it turned out.

Tully pulled up before the clapboard storefront and braked. He leaned forward, read past Fred's shoulder. " 'When Men Were Men and the Clothes Made Them.' That's pretty bad."

Fred hit the door handle. "Let's hope they're better at keeping records."

They weren't. The shop had a lot of old clothing, all right, even a few casually put together dress dummies, but mostly the place was all heaped boxes and loaded down sale counters. A machete would have been handy for getting to the girl behind the cash register.

She wore a draped, forties-style dress, dark blue with tiny white dots, the kind you saw on women in old WW II newsreels, pearl necklace, bright Bakelite earrings in the shape of clustered fruit, multicolored Bakelite bracelets. Her hair was done up in a forties roll at the bangs, parted and cinched with a Bakelite comb. The girl wore glasses and didn't look up until the two men approached the counter, then she mostly looked at Tully. She'd been a

fan of forties movies all her young life and especially a
fan of Humphrey Bogart, and although this older guy
didn't exactly look like Humphrey Bogart, there was
something world-weary yet vulnerable about him that
made him immediately attractive. She had been chewing
gum, but she stopped.

"May I help you?"

Tully flashed his shield, showed her the two suits in
the paper bag.

The girl, who had pale, nearly luminescent skin and
smelled of Beech-nut, fingered the material. "Yes, they
could have come from here. We had a whole slew of them
from an old warehouse down on El Alhambra. You don't
have the receipt?"

"No. We were wondering if we could check your
records."

The girl, probably in her early twenties, small-
breasted, even skinny, gave Tully an odd look. It was
hard to say if it was a smile or if she always looked that
way. She had a funny mouth.

"Records." A soft, musical laugh. "Alice doesn't
exactly keep the greatest records in the world."

"Who's Alice?"

"The owner. I just help out on weekends while she's
with her kids. I'm Kim Dillinger. Like the crook. Though
I've been told I look a bit like Lauren Bacall ..." She
stopped for a moment, staring at Tully, waiting for his
response. He looked at her briefly but said nothing. Still,
the girl thought, he might be the strong silent type, you
never knew. "What's your name?"

"Detective Sergeant Tully."

The girl looked him up and down. "I didn't ask for
your *rank*."

Tully didn't know what to say.

"Would you have a record book, receipts or something?" Fred asked.

The girl turned, one smooth movement, flopped a
cardboard shoe box on the counter, shoved it at Fred. It
was overflowing with slips of pink paper. "There you go.

Good luck." She looked back at Tully. "What'd she do,
this girl in the swimsuit?"

"She died."

"Yeah? Murdered?"

"That's right."

"Gee."

She turned to Fred, who was laboriously digging
through the stack. "How we doing?" Fred grunted. She
turned back to Tully.

"I've got some similar suits in the back, wanna see?"

"I doubt it would help, thanks."

"Never can tell, might give you a clue. I mean, if
there's lots more styles like this, that just increases the
chance this is the place she got them, right?"

"Maybe."

"So, come on, I'll show you."

Tully looked at Fred, who was looking at the pile of
sales slips. "All right."

"Just yell if anyone comes in," she instructed Fred
over her shoulder.

She led the way through a maze of boxes smelling
of mildew, through a dingy gray curtain to a back room
of cement walls and poor lighting. "You get used to the
smell after awhile, some of these duds are pretty old.
We've got some that go clear back to the 1800s. Does
your wife like old clothes?"

"I'm not married."

"Yeah?"

She led him to a long bamboo pole studded with
wire hangers from which hung swimwear of every shape,
size, and description. She yanked one down and turned
to him. "This look like the right kind?"

Tully nodded limply. "Might be the same."

She held it up to her breasts, pressed it to her, looked
up at him.

"Maybe."

There was an immaculate thirties Fada radio with a
deep yellow chassis and a lipstick-red dial on a shelf
behind her. Tully wondered if it still worked.

"Kind of hard to see the lines on the hanger. Here, I'll model it for you." She stepped behind a screen of towering boxes.

"That's okay, Miss—"

"Kim. It's okay, part of the job. We don't have a regular dressing room. But I guess a guy like you won't mind, right?" Another musical laugh.

Tully wasn't sure what her last remark meant. Hands in his pockets, feeling slightly foolish, he stood and waited, looking around the cement room at the stacks of smelly boxes, heaped clothing, racks of hats, ties.

The girl behind the boxes began to whistle softly, then said, "So what's your first name, Sergeant—you got a first name?"

"I do."

"So, what is it?"

"Eustes."

"Eustes, huh? Huh. Don't believe I've ever met a Eustes before. How do you like being a cop, Eustes?"

"I like it fine. This really isn't necessary."

She stepped out from behind the boxes wearing the suit. She really was a shade too thin, but nicely put together. Tully thought of a line in a Spencer Tracy movie: "Not much meat on her—but what there is, is cherce!"

"What do you think?"

"Could be the same model, I guess."

He cleared his throat. This was ridiculous.

She put her hands on her hips, looked down at herself. She turned around and showed him her ass. "How about this side?"

Tully didn't know what else to do so he nodded.

"Hand me that one on the far left end of the rack."

"Look, I appreciate this, but it probably isn't really necessary . . ."

She shrugged. "You got something better to do? Your partner's still digging through our shoe box." She snapped her fingers at the clothes rack. Tully pulled down the suit, handed it to her. She disappeared behind the boxes.

She began whistling again.

Then: "So, Eustes, you live around here, or what?"

"Pretty close."

"I'm thinking of leaving, myself. Leaving town."

"Why's that?"

"Too expensive. Rich girl's town. Can't make any money in Santa Barbara running a used clothing store on weekends. I'd like to go back to school, get my degree, teach. Can't seem to hold on to the tuition fee, though, know what I mean?"

"Yeah."

"You make much as a cop?"

"Not enough."

"Yeah . . . what do you think?"

She'd stepped out wearing a two-piece, the halter top cut full, leaving little room for cleavage, which she didn't have anyway, neck straps and back straps keeping things sensible, the briefs hardly brief at all, waistband covering her navel.

"This one's a little more daring." She laughed. "For those days, anyway."

"Very nice. Our victims had a one-piece, though."

She shrugged. "I know, just thought you might like to see it." She turned around for him. She really did have a nice figure, despite the lack of pounds. She should try some of the places he ate, though obviously she was proud of her skinniness. Maybe she should be, most people would kill for her problem.

She moved back behind the boxes again. Tully shifted his weight impatiently, eyes roving the room again, wondering how Fred was doing.

"I seem to be having a problem here."

He turned toward the wall of boxes. "Oh?"

"Zipper's stuck."

He watched the boxes, hands in his pockets.

"Well? Are you going to help me or what?"

He took his hands out of his pockets and stood looking at the pasteboard box screen. "What do you want me to do? Phone someone?"

She snorted behind the boxes. "No, Eustes, no. I want you to help me with this zipper."

He hesitated, then crept around the edge of stacked boxes. She was standing with her bare back to him, straps down, arms tucked, holding the unfastened suit top in place, bathed in the dirty glow of the single dangling bulb. The moment seared indelibly into his cortex, stored away safely for future playback. She was twisted at an angle, tugging at the zipper pleat at her left hip, something innocently boyish about her, woodland fresh; the corrugated line of ribs poking at pink, porcelain flesh; the soft corona of flaxen down against her neck; the translucent shell of finely carved ear, glowing as if lit from within, an ear to touch and taste with the tip of your tongue—he could imagine the tart lingerings of bath soap there—the sweep of vertebral trough dividing her body like ripe fruit. The terrible, aching, *actuality* of her.

She'd already gotten it halfway down, that zipper, exposing a partial, milky swell of buttock, unblemished and clean as turn-of-the-century crockery. She looked up at him imploringly.

Tully cleared his throat and approached uncertainly, hands as confident and sure as rubber Halloween gloves.

"Give it a try, huh?"

He nodded, licked his lips.

His fingers, suddenly slick with sweat, kept slipping off the little metal tab. He set his teeth, gripped, yanked, hoping he wouldn't drip perspiration on her; it was so close in the room.

"You're attacking it from the wrong angle, here . . ." She took his wrist, pulled his arm around her waist, positioned his fingers on the zipper, leaning into him. "Now try." She nestled spongy buttocks snugly into his crotch.

Tully swallowed, yanked. Dripped.

He could smell lilac shampoo in her hair, feel the strands tickle his nose.

His fingers kept slipping.

———

165

"Take it easy, we've got time." She pressed into him.

Fred Wanamaker called from the other side of dingy curtain. "Let's go, Tully! It's a blank!"

Tully started to let go but Kim gripped his wrist. "Just a little more, you've almost got it."

Tully pressed his lips into a determined line, yanked downward.

"Come on, Tully!" Fred called impatiently.

"Just a friggin' second!" she yelled in Tully's ear.

She twisted about, Beech-nut breath against his cheek. Then, softly: "Come on, one more time." Her flat stomach was a heat-tightened drum against his wrist, a marvel; he could feel a delicate pulse there, radiating from the core of her; this too seemed impossibly marvelous, quite beyond his comprehension: cosmic dust had created this, and wasn't it fine?

He gripped the edge of the material and pulled and the zipper descended in one smooth motion. "Atta boy . . ."

He pulled away, feeling sick and dizzy, and watched in light-headed confusion her next act: she ducked farther behind the boxes, trying to be modest, but he was still close enough to watch as she slid the briefs down matter-of-factly, like a man tipping his hat—down and down, past the knot of tailbone, over the full, pale moons, showing him the dark, perfect, secret cleft of her, a wonder of shadows and promises. When she bent over to step out of the briefs, it was all too blindingly much: he turned away, banged into the edge of the boxes nearly toppling them, floundered out. It might have been her musical laugh behind him.

Fred was waiting at the curtain, lighting a cigarette. "What the hell were you doing back there?"

Tully was grateful for the dim lighting, masking the sweat, his flushed cheeks. "Nothing. Looking at suits. You get anything?"

Fred shook his head, blew smoke. "Records are a mess. I couldn't find any bills of sale for a black, fifties-style swimming suit, or any swimming suit for that matter."

They hit the door and the ocean breeze was like a gift from heaven.

Fred looked up and down the street, crestfallen. "So I guess we're back to square one, huh?"

Tully shook his head, watching the sky. "Not entirely. My theory's correct, I can feel it. If he didn't get the suits here, he got them somewhere. Or kept them when his mother . . . well, kept her suits."

He wiped the back of his neck, which was cool and clammy. "Something happened on that beach, thirty-five, forty years ago. If we could figure out what, we might begin to get a profile of this guy. That might tell us more about his previous victims." He stopped. Neither one of them wanted to think about the possibility of future victims.

Fred sighed. "Sounds pretty nebulous."

"It is. But it's all we've got."

"And neither one of us has the time or the jurisdiction to do it. A burnt-out pathologist and a disgruntled dick. Shit."

Tully smiled, slapped his friend on the back. "Come on, buy you the best cheeseburger in town."

They started for the car, Fred tossing the storefront behind them a final glance. "Cute kid, all done up in those forties duds. Too skinny though. And bossy! You hear the way she snapped at me? Hate to get in a clinch with that babe."

Tully opened the car door, said nothing.

MITCH

*T*HE DIVE WAS REFRESHING, EVEN EXHILARATING.
The group spiraled lazily into emerald depths lanced with shards of golden sunlight, circled a towering column of dancing kelp, played tag with a grouper.

Here in the airless void, Mitch found the first true peace, the first sense of total relaxation he'd known for days. The only vaguely disconcerting note was the way the lithesome Olin managed gracefully to collide with him time and again, trailing her endless legs across his chest like a cat, smiling innocently at him through her faceplate. Mitch watched her tanned bouncing buttocks with interest, if not lust. Olin was a magnificent swimmer, but here in the mysterious depths, Claire was a living mermaid. A golden vision. His breath rasped noisily through his regulator, sure to give him away.

After the dive, Dias accompanied Mitch to his cabin. The Colombian snapped open a chrome lighter, held it to the tip off Mitch's cigar while he puffed. Dias lit his own Havana, snapped the lighter shut.

"I am hoping you will agree to help me with a small problem I have," he began. "The thing is, I am a very busy man. Some extremely important business matters are about to transpire both here in Santa Barbara and in my native town of Medellin, matters that require my utmost attention, matters that—if mishandled, imbalanced—could cost certain parties millions, tens of millions, amounts of currency it is hard to comprehend. The point, my friend, is that I cannot devote as much time to the charming Mrs. Greely as I might like, as may be necessary to keep her sufficently interested in my companionship. It does no good to offer recreational drugs, she is not interested. It is difficult, in fact, to ascertain exactly what it is she *is* interested in. She seems to relish and deplore money at the same time, did you know that?"

"Interesting."

"*Si.* An interesting woman. And an elusive woman. An easily bored one, I think. A woman who needs . . . scin—scintillating company. This is a word?"

"That is a word."

"Company like yours, my friend."

Mitch stared at him.

"Excuse me?"

"You were once a private eye, is that not the term? It is important to me for many reasons that Claire is, ah, accounted for at all times," Dias continued. "She enjoys your companionship, perhaps because you are a happily married man and, sensing this, she feels no threat in your presence. I saw the way you responded to Olin. A man who resists her must be very much in love with his wife."

Or someone's wife, anyway, Mitch thought.

"Whatever the case, when Claire is with you I know two things—she is never bored and she is safe. That means a great deal to me, Mitch, a great deal."

Mitch cleared his throat. "Well, I—"

Dias held up his hands. "Please. I realize the extent of my imposition. You, too, are a busy man. And you have a family. Here is what I am proposing. If you would be willing to make arrangements with your company—take sick leave, vacation time, something like that—I would more than make up the lost time monetarily. Call it moonlighting, if you like. Some pocket change, perhaps?"

Dias drew a leather wallet from his jacket. He withdrew several packets of thousand-dollar bills, handed them to the speechless Mitch.

"My business deals should—if all goes well—conclude within the next few weeks. Part of that time I will need to be in the Los Angeles area. If you would consent to look after Mrs. Greely during that time, be her escort as it were, entertain her, dine her, dance with her, take her to the cinema; see, in other words, that she wanders no farther than her husband's mansion; if you will do this for me, my friend, you will earn my everlasting gratitude. And I am not a man who takes the word gratitude lightly."

Mitch stared numbly at the bills: fifty thousand dollars.

Dias nodded at the currency. "If it is not enough, just say so."

Mitch started to object, but Dias interrupted. "Please do not be offended by the offer of cash, it is merely payment for your time away from your regular job. I know that you would be pleased to do this favor for me out of friendship alone, were that possible."

Mitch stared at the money. "Where do you propose—where would I stay?"

"Here, if you wish, on my yacht. You can have the run of the place. All of the servants, my aides, will be instructed to take orders from you, just as if I were here. It is an excellent place to entertain, to keep Mrs. Greely from prying Santa Barbara eyes. You will not run into her husband's social acquaintances here. What do you say?"

Mitch fingered the bills.

"You could return home to L.A. tonight—I will pay for the flight—inform your wife that you have business in another city—a convention, perhaps—take care of any personal matters, and be back on the yacht by next weekend. How does that strike you?"

Mitch couldn't seem to get his breath.

Dias smiled, clapped him heartily on the shoulder. "At least consider my proposal. Think about it." He stabbed out his cigar and moved to the door. "In the meantime, may I have your promise that you will not mention our little conversation to Claire?"

Mitch nodded. "All right. I'll keep your secret."

Dias smiled. "*Bueno!* And now, please get some rest, my friend. Dinner is at six bells. We'll reach the marina in Santa Barbara by then."

Dias shut the door behind him.

Mitch realized he was still holding the stack of bills. He put them on the table beside him.

After a few minutes, he got up and placed the bills inside his jacket pocket.

Dinner was above reproach.

For Mitch, the scene bordered on the surrealistic, as so much of his life did these days. He sat at a table of crisp white linen, crystal champagne glasses, and opulent cuisine, surrounded by a group of people who, if not personally drug dealers or pornographers or worse, were no doubt privy to Dias's operation. He was reminded of the Howard Pyle pirate stories of his youth. He could almost see the Jolly Roger flying above the dinner table—on deck with a crew of pirates! All save one.

And that one, golden hair shimmering in the moonlight, innocent blue eyes wavering toward his own, that one was becoming more breathlessly beautiful each time he saw her, more and more impossibly entangled with his own life. What made the situation all the more absurd was that every time their eccentric host caught Mitch gazing at her, he winked!

It was beginning to approach burlesque.

He would have laughed aloud but for the grotesque circumstances surrounding the farce.

And the warm weight of bills in his pocket. There
was nothing facetious about those.

After dinner, he and Claire took a moonlit stroll
around the deck. Dias, in fact, suggested it.

"If I didn't know better," she said lightly to the cool
evening breeze, "I'd think he was throwing me at you."

Mitch had to force a smile. "He's a busy man, he just
wants to see that you're entertained."

"And the burden falls on you."

"Hardly a burden."

She turned to him at the rail. She was radiant under
the soft deck lights. "I suppose you'll be going back to
L.A. tonight."

"Yes. And you'll be going home."

She looked outward toward winking harbor lights.
"Yes."

Neither spoke for a time.

Then Claire put out her hand, a bit stiffly, he
thought. "Well, it's been nice, Mr. Mitchell Spencer. Will
we see you again?"

He took her hand, not shaking it. "Do you want to
see me again?"

She watched him.

"No."

He nodded. "Me either." He rubbed the back of her
hand with his thumb.

"It might be dangerous," she added, a little less
officiously.

"In what sense?" he asked.

She turned away, cool again. "In every sense."

"I thought you liked danger."

"Not that kind."

"What kind?"

"Mitch. I've already wrecked my own marriage."

"Not yet you haven't."

"Oh yes, I wrecked it the day I married him; I just
didn't know it. Can you say the same of your marriage?"

He turned to watch the lights with her.

"I want to see you again, Claire."

"No."

"I have a . . . job prospect here in Santa Barbara next week. Dias has graciously invited me to save hotel bills by staying on the yacht."

"I can't be around the two of you anymore, Mitch, it's too—"

"Dias won't be here."

She looked sharply at him. "Won't be here?"

"He has business in L.A."

"Are you crazy? That's—"

"He asked if I'd take you to dinner while I'm in town, chaperone you while he's away."

Her expression was one of incredulity. "*Chaperone* me? I have a husband! God, this is ludicrous! And you agreed?"

"I haven't told him anything yet. I wanted to talk to you first."

She shook her head, eyes closed, clutching her temples as if dizzy. "This is becoming *baroque!* He wants you to see me here on the yacht, without his presence?" She looked at him. "What exactly did you do to arrive at this dizzying pinnacle of esteem?"

"He likes me."

Her eyes softened. "Well, one can hardly fault him there."

"So what's it to be, Claire?"

"It's suicidal."

"It's perfectly safe, aboveboard. We're staying on the yacht of a mutual friend."

"You know what I mean."

"What do you mean?"

"That you're falling in love with me, you idiot."

"And what about you?"

She looked out to sea. "I fell already. After that first drunken kiss."

He wanted so much to embrace her, pull her up close, smell her hair, taste her, crush her. "Is that a yes?" his voice nearly cracking.

Claire sighed, hugging her slim shoulders. "And if we

do, Mitch, what next? Swim away together to that lonely little atoll?" There was a great wistfulness in her voice and he found himself loving even that.

"We'll never know if we don't try."

She turned to him, face strangely impassive.

"All right then, my sweet Mitchell ... let's dance with the devil ..."

Two hours later, he sat in a dumpy little seaside bar over a glass of bourbon, counting the lies of his life.

There were many.

First, Joanne: he had certainly lied to his wife.

Dias: he had lied to him since the offer from Greely.

Claire: he had not told her about the money Dias had given him. That was, he vainly attempted to justify, not perhaps a lie as such, but simply not the entire truth. Yes, but it amounted to as much.

And now he was about to do the same with Greely, the very benefactor who had gotten him into all this.

No, Mitch, don't pass the buck, old pal. You got into it all by yourself. You could have given the money back.

Yeah, and ended up dead.

Did he really believe that?

Hard to say. Dias was a killer; Greely had probably not misconstrued there. Otherwise why was he known as "The Butcher"? Yet there was something undeniably straightforward about the man, almost innocent in its way, a core of veracity that was seductive. An old-world gentility. Back when men were men and all that. Almost corny these days, yet Mitch believed the Colombian's affection for him was genuine.

Not that that justified things. But maybe you *could* like a man without liking his business.

He drank up and went to the back and found the grimy wall phone beside the johns. He dialed the number Greely had given him.

"Yes?"

A voice he didn't recognize.

"Mr. Greely, please?"

"And this is?"

"Mr. Spencer. Mitch Spencer."

"One moment."

Had that been Max, the chauffeur?

"Mr. Spencer, how good to hear from you. You are well, I trust?"

For the moment, anyway. "I'm fine. I spent the weekend with the Diases."

"Yes, took a jaunt, I noticed. His cubby at the marina was empty."

"He sailed out to the Channel Islands to dive this afternoon."

"I see. Go on."

Mitch shifted his weight. "Well, we ate a lot, the food was excellent. We swam. Played cards—"

"Please, Mr. Spencer . . ."

Mitch abruptly found himself impatient with this routine, this running back to report to daddy. "Claire slept alone, as nearly as I can tell. She was pretty drunk Friday night. She mentioned she would be home, with you, tonight. I don't think anything inappropriate transpired with Dias; not to my knowledge, at least."

"You talked with her?"

"Well, sure, somewhat."

"What about?"

"Oh . . . this and that. Nothing memorable. Santa Barbara versus L.A., that sort of thing."

"Small talk."

"Small talk, right."

"And how did she seem?"

"Seem? Well, gracious, friendly—"

"Happy? Was she enjoying herself?"

"She seemed to be."

"Mr. Spencer, are you being deliberately vague?"

Mitch sighed into the mouthpiece, a tinny, rushing sound. "Look, Mr. Greely, this is not exactly my usual line of work. I did the best I could. She seems fine. Not joyously happy, not inordinately unhappy. She seemed like a woman having a weekend on a yacht with friends.

But let's face it, once the lights go down, it's impossible for me to speak with any real authority."

He found himself strangely riled at this last truth, as if he had just unearthed ugly possibilities. His life seemed labyrinthine, a thousand indistinct avenues leading nowhere. And he couldn't seem to stop this feeling of resentment toward Greely. He could see the pink, chubby cheeks, the cupid's mouth pressed to the other receiver. It filled him with revulsion.

"You're telling me the truth, Mr. Spencer? You're not concealing things from me, attempting to protect me?"

"Of course not! Why would you say that?"

"You seem agitated. Are you sure nothing happened?"

Mitch licked his lips, wished he had another drink. Calm down. Everything's okay. "Look, I told you everything that happened, everything I saw, anyway. It was just a weekend boat ride. Pretty boring, really. I don't think you have any reason to be concerned at this point."

"At this point?"

"Excuse me?"

"You said, 'at this point.' Is there a point at which I might need to become concerned, is that what you're intimating?"

Mitch rubbed the film of sweat across his forehead. It was a goddamn furnace in this crummy bar! "Look, I'm not 'intimating' anything. It's been a long weekend, I'm a little tired. Worried about my wife and kid. I need to get back home. Everything's fine, Mr. Greely, I wish you'd believe that."

There was silence on the other end.

Then: "Do you think she wishes to see him again, Mr. Spencer?"

"Do you want to know what I honestly think, Mr. Greely?"

"Most assuredly."

"I think your wife is just a very gregarious person who doesn't get out quite as often as she'd like to enjoy the companionship of others. That's all. I really don't think there's anything out of line going on aboard Dias's yacht."

Another silence.

"I am very much in your debt, my boy." The voice was softer now, less anxious. "You have done an excellent job. I know you are weary. I will instruct my bank to transfer ten thousand dollars to your account on Monday. I know you're anxious to see your family. Again, my deepest gratitude. Goodnight."

"Goodnight."

Mitch hung up. Stood staring at the receiver for a moment.

Ten thousand dollars. In one weekend he had earned sixty thousand dollars.

Earned? Is that what you call it, old pal?

He turned away, went back to his table, and ordered another drink. He ought to be going soon, Joanne and the baby . . .

"You're falling in love with me, you idiot."

He knocked back a gulp, wincing at the burning liquid. *Don't drink too much, you've got a long drive.* Then he remembered—he was catching a plane, courtesy Mr. Greely. His car was in the shop . . .

Sixty thousand dollars.

He snapped his fingers, ordered a drink.

Joanne's face swam up from the bottom of the glass. *"Mitch! I'm pregnant!"*

He drank, hand trembling.

A lonely little atoll . . . dancing palms . . .

He drank.

Burned. Winced.

Mitch looked up. Froze.

Someone down the bar was watching him.

Mitch set down his glass carefully, looked away, pretended not to notice. He smoothed back his hair. Glanced nonchalantly around. Took another look. The man was still watching him.

Mitch swallowed, took another drink.

177

Now he remembered; the man had been sitting there when he'd first come in, first sat down at the bar. He'd passed the man, in fact, on his way to the phone. Even then he'd felt the man's eyes on him, but he hadn't thought about it. Maybe that was why he'd been so nervous during the phone call.

It was dark in the bar, too dark to discern the man. Did he know him? One of the guys from work? An old college friend? Why was he staring like that? A crazy thought formed in his whirling mind: Joanne had hired a tail, was checking up on him. She knew all about the woman on the yacht.

All about what? Nothing had happened. Yet.

Mitch stiffened. The man was getting up, coming his way.

Mitch took another drink, tried to look relaxed, unaware.

"Am I nuts, or are you Mitch Spencer?"

Mitch looked up into a broad, chiseled face; big hawk's nose, friendly eyes. A cop's topcoat. Some things don't change.

Mitch squinted. The face was almost familiar . . .

"Tully. Eustes Tully from San Francisco? We went to the Academy together, remember? Back in seventy."

Mitch's mouth dropped open. "Chrissake!"

Tully cracked a wide smile, cheeks coloring. He stuck out a hand, grabbed Mitch's, grabbed a stool with the other. "Never forget a face! How you been, Spencer?" Tully sat.

Mitch could only shake his head slowly. "Jesus. I haven't seen anybody from the old days since . . . well, since the old days! What are you now, chief of police? You live here in Santa Barbara?"

Tully nodded, signaling for a drink. "Don't start with the embarrassing questions first. I'm still just a sergeant. Detective, homicide."

"Nothing wrong with that. You look great!"

"You're the one who looks great. You live here in

town?" The bartender, set a drink down in front of Tully, who took a sip, watching Mitch. "Or just visiting?"

Mitch smiled. "I'm in L.A. now."

"Whoa! Big time cop! Get your ass shot off down there! What're you, busting dopeheads and dodging gangs?"

Mitch's smile faded a notch. "I'm an insurance investigator, Tully. Have been for a couple of years now."

Tully's glass froze in mid-air. "Insurance? You? Christ! At the academy you were so gung-ho—all you ever talked about was being a cop! Why? I mean, if it's any of my business."

Mitch looked down at his glass. Tipped back the last jolt. "After the academy I walked a beat in L.A. for a year. There was an ... incident. Gal almost got killed. Long story. Anyway, I lost my taste for cops and robbers. More money in insurance anyway."

Tully watched him soberly.

Then he smiled warmly. "Yeah, I'll bet. You look like you're doing all right. Wife and kids?"

"One of each." And one in the oven.

"Atta boy."

"You?"

Tully held the smile. Took a drink. " 'Fraid not. Not yet." He winked. "Working on it, though."

Mitch smiled. "Good to see you, Tully. Christ. The years do go by, don't they?"

"They do indeed, my friend. They do indeed."

An uncomfortable silence ensued. They drank. All at once Mitch could feel something coming. Just before it happened, he knew what it was.

"So. What brings you to my beat? Business?"

"Just seeing some friends."

"Ah. Fellow investigators?"

There it was. The circuitous cross-examination. Tully's nose pinked a bit from the drink, a bloodhound on the trail. Mitch stiffened, remembering the routine.

"Nah, not really." Rule one: volunteer nothing in an interrogation.

Tully nodded. Almost let it go. "Sailing buddies, huh?"

"Pardon?"

"Thought I saw you coming out of the marina on the way here. Maybe it was someone else."

Bingo.

Homicide my ass. Tully was a narc. Dias was the quarry.

And Mitchell Spencer was caught right in the middle. Fine. Way to go, Mitch. Well, let's see you get out of this one. Come on, you were a cop once.

"That was me." Mitch lowered his eyes, made a show of feeling uncomfortable, which hardly required acting under the circumstances. "Look, Tully, you're an old friend and a cop, no use fooling you. The truth is, I've got a girlfriend on that boat."

Tully didn't wink and smile soon enough. Yeah, he was after Dias all right. "Naughty, naughty."

"Just keep your trap shut when you come visit my family in L.A., huh?"

"Anybody I'd know?"

"Somebody I might not even know if things keep going the way they are. Something screwy about that tub—awful lot of drugs at the parties."

Tully wore his best poker face. The humor had left his eyes. "Shall we cut the shit, old buddy? How deep are you in?"

Mitch stiffened, though not, he hoped, visibly. "What do you mean?"

"You tell me."

Mitch sighed. Shit. Should have come clean right from the start. Tully was good. Had been good at the Academy. Have to make it look as real as he could now. Start by turning the tables. "How deep are *you* in, Mr. *Homicide* Detective?"

Tully grinned now and it was good to see. "That wasn't a complete lie. I was in Homicide up until last week. They bumped me over to Narcotics until we figure out what it is your pal Dias is up to. What is he up to, Mitch?"

"Dias?" Mitch shook his head. "I have no idea, Tully, and that's the truth, though I guess it's no secret he has something to do with drugs, something big. I wasn't lying about the girlfriend either. There's just one sticky little problem—she's Dias's girlfriend, too."

"Jesus! Do you know about this guy?"

"I've heard."

"How'd you meet him? You into coke?"

"Christ, no! It was purely accidental. I was fishing over at Big Piney a few weeks ago. Dias has another boat anchored there. The girl was involved in a skiing accident and I intervened, that's all. Dias took a shine to me. I didn't know at the time he was the goddamn drug king of South America."

That was mostly the truth. Mitch saw no reason to mention Greely's part in it. He felt a little better. Honesty really was the best policy.

"What about the girl?"

Mitch shrugged. "Local lady. Married. Some fat millionaire."

"And you're screwing her under Dias's nose? Mitch, you're crazy. This guy eats gringos like you."

Mitch shifted in his chair, uncomfortable again. "It's not exactly a full-fledged affair yet."

"But you're friendly with Dias."

"Oh yes. Practically like brothers. I don't doubt that he's a bloodthirsty S.O.B., but honestly, Tully, there's something likable about the guy. I honestly think he'd go to bat for me."

"Yeah. With a real bat!"

"I can watch after myself. Remember the Academy?"

"I'm thinking about it right now."

Mitch frowned. "What do you mean?"

"I'm taking a big risk talking to you like this, Mitch. Okay, we used to be friends, you were a cop, but it's been a lot of years. I have to know if I can trust you."

"Trust me for what?"

Tully knocked back his drink. "I need to get on that boat, Mitch. Only there's just about no way I can and not be found out. Dias has eyes everywhere." He glanced about the bar and leaned forward. "But maybe I don't have to get on the boat, personally anyway ..." He watched Mitch's eyes.

"You're the one who's crazy."

"Think about it—you used to be a cop, you probably still even remember a little about Narcotics. Only as far as anyone knows or can find out, you're in the insurance business, right? It's an undercover man's dream."

"It's an insurance investigator's nightmare is what it is. I start looking like anything more than a pencil pusher and Dias will have me dangling by the yardarm."

"They're called 'spreaders' on yachts."

"Fine. You're the nautical expert, you snoop around Dias's ass."

"We both know how long that would last. He'd make me in two shakes and sail off into the sunset, find another port to pillage."

"Fine. You'd be off the hook."

"And out of a promotion. A promotion I need, Mitch. Badly."

Mitch could see by the look on the cop's wide face that it was true. He knew what it was like to want a promotion. He shook his head no anyway. "Forget it, Tully. I'd like to help, but—"

"How much do they pay you where you work?"

"Why?"

"I might be able to squeeze some operational pay out of the department for this, plus some personal money I could kick in."

Mitch looked at him. "*You* could kick in? Jesus, Tully, you got a vendetta against this guy?"

"Yeah, he took me away from a case I was close to solving. He took me away from a promotion that would have gotten me transferred out of my department and into another life. I want the bastard nailed. Or sent back to Medellín with a clean nose, whichever comes first. You can help me do that."

Mitch looked down at his drink. Just a few weeks ago he was packing for a fishing trip with one of the boys from the office and everything was normal and happy and made perfect sense.

"You want me to spy on Dias."

"That's right. Listen, what's the big deal? You're chasing after his girlfriend anyway, right?"

"And you want to pay me."

"As much as I can. May not be that much. But one thing's for sure, it'd be like being a cop again."

Mitch looked up sharply.

Christ. How had Tully known? Did it show that readily, how much he missed being a cop?

"What do you say, Mitch?"

Mitch finished his drink, sat thinking a moment. Then he lifted his wrist and glanced at his watch. "It's late. I have to fly back to L.A. tonight."

He pushed back, stood, extended a hand to his old friend.

"Let me sleep on it, Tully."

Later, on the way home to yet more lies, he wondered how it ever could have gotten this crazy this fast.

RENE

SHE'D PUT THE CHERRY TOP TO SPINNING, THE SIREN to whooping, and had driven recklessly for twenty straight miles up 101, past gorgeous Southern California coastline, mascara running, throat constricted, passing cars as though they were standing still until, approaching Montecito, she'd finally realized just how much she was jeopardizing others and forced herself to slow.

Herself she'd already jeopardized; herself, her job, possibly even the department. Stupid. Stupid! *Stupid!*

She slowed the black-and-white, but she did not stop, could not stop, not yet, not for maybe a long time—and certainly she could not yet go back. Dear God. That was unthinkable.

Stupid!

She eased through Montecito behind rush hour traffic, headed blindly toward the darkening skies, not really knowing where she was going, not really caring, just going, going, letting the miles take her, letting the miles erase the awful pain, the unbearable humiliation, the nascent fear, building in her middle. Letting the flashing lane markers put a breathable distance between her and her incredible, unforgivable stupidity.

At the outskirts of Santa Barbara, Rene began to forgive herself just a little.

Come on, let's face it, the woman was beautiful: young, and slim, with those pale blue eyes that went right through you, that soft crop of rusty hair, cut so wispily and inviting at the nape, the deep, husky voice, that fluttery way she walked. And sweet. So goddamned overpoweringly, endearingly, maddeningly sweet. Christ, you couldn't rile her, couldn't insult her if you tried.

Her real name was Laverne Scottisi, but the men had all taken to calling her "Scotti" by the end of the first week. All right then, Scotti it was. Scotti was all right, even cute in its way. It fit well enough. But for Rene, for quiet, reticent Rene who had never gotten in anyone's way, always done what she was told, endured the lecherous murmurs, the surreptitious grab-ass in the hall, to demure little Sergeant Rene Draper of the Ventura police force, the new arrival with the wonderful husky voice and the impossible eyes and the lovely nape would always be a butterfly.

Kiss me, Scotti.

Not that she hadn't played it cool.

If there was one thing Rene was good at, considered herself an expert at, it was playing it cool. Hadn't she married Brad right out of the Academy, let her own urges languish as she attempted a life her parents, her friends, the department would approve? Sweet little Brad, so helpless, so lonely, so . . . nonthreatening. And when Susie was born, it almost seemed right for a time. She was precious and tiny and pink and she belonged to Rene in a way that no human being had ever belonged to her—belonged to her and to Brad. It should have been enough.

But of course it wasn't.

After awhile she just couldn't bring herself to make

love to him. She loved him, in her way, but the act
was repulsive to her, unnatural. Then one day, after he
pleaded with her to tell him what he could do, how he
could please her, why it was she seemed to push him
away while she was holding him near, she had told
him.

She'd never dreamed he'd take her daughter away
from her.

But he'd hated her for it, for fooling him, for making
him love her. He somehow got himself transferred to
Santa Barbara and managed to convince the courts that
her sexual preference made her an unfit mother.

She'd tried to commit suicide after Susie was gone,
but that hadn't worked out—the doctors told her she was
just too tough to die from a few sleeping pills. So she
worked. Brad let her see Susie every other Sunday. It
wasn't enough, but it was something. She'd gotten herself transferred to Ventura, for two-thirds the pay, just
to be close to Susie. Last Sunday they had gone to the
beach, she in her modest one-piece, Susie in a miniature
bikini, a five-year-old dynamo investigating the sand as
if needing to memorize every grain. Rene took pictures
with her Polaroid, stuck them on her bulletin board at
work.

It was the picture of Susie with the blue spiral shell
that had attracted Scotti in the first place.

Kiss me, Scotti.

"Your daughter?" Rene had nodded, too thunder-
struck to speak. "You're lucky. She's a doll!" Scotti had
looked at the picture wistfully, then walked on down the
hall. Rene watched her go, knowing she'd missed an
opportunity and glad of it, knowing that it was impossible, that she was a fool to even consider it. . . .

If she just hadn't found Scotti crying.

It had been at the health club on Tulip. Rene had
been slipping into her swimsuit, turned to find Scotti
stepping out of her clothes, smoothing back those rusty-
colored locks, breasts jutting as she arched her delicate
back. Rene followed the newcomer, at a discreet dis-

tance, to the pool, then spent a full hour in the water, shamelessly cavorting like a lovesick dolphin, trying to impress with her best backstroke. Rene was good. Certainly the best swimmer on the force, maybe the best swimmer on the Coast. She looked lovely in the water, strong but sensuous. The other woman watched her with casual interest, then headed for the Jacuzzi without attempting to strike up conversation. Shy? Rene sagged panting against the side of the pool, feeling the fool. She headed back to the locker room, threw herself into the shower.

Afterwards she came around a cement divider and found Scotti wrapped in a towel, still wet, head in her hands, body shuddering on the long wooden bench. Her locker door stood open.

"Is there anything I can do?"

The shuddering stopped. But the burnished head did not look up, did not leave the hands, merely shook no. Rene watched for a moment, then turned away. She went back to her locker, gave herself a final look in the mirror, and closed up. She was winding her watch when she heard the movement behind her.

Scotti was clutching the towel to her breast. "I'm sorry."

For the first time, looking directly into the other womans' pale eyes, Rene felt amazingly calm. "What for?"

"For the scene. I thought everyone had gone."

"Hey, no problem. Blubber away. I do it like clockwork every month, two days before my period."

Scotti smiled. A wonderful smile.

Rene smiled back. "Just going for coffee. Want to join me?"

Mistake! Too soon!

But no. Scotti brightened. "Oh, I'd love to! Just give me a second!"

Rene's underarms had been soaked then from the tension, but not as soaked as they were now.

A light pattern of rain dirtied the windshield. She let

it gather momentum, then turned the knob, watched the wipers smear it clean. It never rains in Southern California, but it rains tonight. How fitting.

She took the first exit that promised some sign of civilization, a chance for coffee. Or should it be bourbon? Sure, that's it, get soused, wrack up the squad car—that will really earn you points back home. She thought about stopping by to see Susie, suddenly missed her desperately, but Brad had a new fiancée and probably wouldn't take kindly to her showing up uninvited.

It was raining in earnest by the time Rene found some neon, nosed the car to the curb. She didn't like this area of town, but she was hardly in the mood to be picky. This place was either a restaurant or a saloon from what she could tell by the gelatinous blur of neon. It would do.

Rene got out, locked up, tortoised under her collar and trundled toward the worn awning.

It stank of beer inside, but it was dry. She found a private, lumpy plastic booth and ordered a drink. Screw the coffee. The air conditioning was on despite the change of weather, and the cool air hitting her wet skin sent a violent shiver through her. When the drink came she downed it fast and ordered another. Then she sat clutching herself in the darkness, smothering the shivers with her arms until the glow in her belly expanded enough to chase them altogether.

She couldn't quit thinking about it. Damn!

They had ended up at her apartment. Something about records. They found they shared an interest in old-time female ballad singers and Rene had mentioned Blossom Dearie and Scotti had flipped, hadn't heard Blossom Dearie in years. Rene had some albums, would she like to come over and listen?

If she were beautiful just standing there normally, Scotti was heartbreaking when her eyes lit up that way. Rene mistakenly assumed at least some of that light was meant for her. Rule number one: Never assume. Never

take chances. Know where you're headed. If there's the
least bit doubt, cut it off. wait. There will be other times,
other opportunities.

So much for the rules.

They listened to the records until the sun disappeared behind the buildings, until the room was swathed
in friendly darkness. When the last record ended, retracting
with a click, Rene looked over at the lovely creature
draped gracefully across her couch and wondered if she
had fallen asleep. She didn't want to break the trance
with the ugly intrustion of flaring lights, so she stood
quietly and moved slowly to the couch, sat down gently
beside her.

Scotti didn't stir, eyes closed, pouty mouth slightly
parted, gentle breath fluttering delicately. Rene touched
the soft cheek. The wonderful eyes fluttered open.

"Scotti . . ."

Scotti smiled up her submission.

"Kiss me, Scotti . . ."

Rene burped.

Took another drink.

Yeah, sure. Kiss me, Scotti.

You bet.

How about kick me, Scotti? How about gasp at me,
Scotti? How about shrink from me, push away from me,
open your pretty mouth to scream at me, Scotti?

She burped again, hiccupped loudly, not bothering
to look around, ordering herself another drink. Sure, go
ahead and drink. Wrack up the squad car. Wrack up your
life. Wrack up another stupid, lovesick lesbo, boys! Dumb
bitch.

Oh, she could take rejection. She'd been rejected
before. But that look!

That amazed, frightened, accusatory, but most of all
mortified look of unadulterated revulsion!

Like she was a leper. Like she'd just scuttled out
from under a rock. Like no woman on earth ever kissed
another woman in the entire annals of human kind!

Like she was diseased.

No Sappho in this kid, uh-uh, not a drop! Sorry! Hate to eat and run but gotta get up early tomorrow, be on duty! I'll just stop by that construction site on the way home and have that cheek sandblasted where you touched me!

Rene jammed her eyes shut, squeezed out a tear.

Stupid stupid stupid.

"It hurts, doesn't it?"

She looked up into sadness. A sadness not unlike her own. A sadness not at all unlike Scotti's. That was the thing about Scotti that had got her, really got her . . . that little girl sadness. . . .

Where was she? Jesus, she was really drunk! Who was this guy, this sad guy staring down with his cute little mustache and his natty attire and his sadness and his drink. Do I know this guy? Some one from the force, one of the boys?

"Here's how we can do it," he was saying with his sad voice. "One. I can leave you alone and go home, which is certainly what I should do and not at all what I want to do. Two. I can sit down, promise to behave myself, buy us another round and convince you that no matter how significant your tears may seem to be, mine are by far the more tragic."

Rene watched him. The self-assurance was a front. False bravado. He was a frightened little boy inside. Like Brad. She could spot them every time. There was something almost heartbreakingly sad about them. She had a thing for sad. She indicated the seat opposite.

The tall gentleman with the cute little mustache sat. He raised his glass in a salute. "To men, the pricks."

Rene watched him dazedly for a moment, found comprehension and raised her glass. "To women, the pricks."

They chuckled softly and drank.

"So tell me about it."

Rene watched him dreamily. "Not much to tell. My life is wrecked, isn't that how it goes?"

"So they say. Boyfriend or husband?"

She looked at him, almost laughing. Oh, you are innocent, aren't you, sugar? You poor innocent little boy. "Does it matter? It's the same old story no matter how you tell it. Unrequited love. Boring, huh?"

The man shrugged.

"Best I could do. Your turn."

The man watched her. "It's a bit different in my case."

"How so?"

"I can't seem to hang on to a woman for more than a short time."

"That's hard to believe."

He smiled shyly. "Oh, they like me well enough at first. We go out, have a good time. Sometimes I even get to kiss them. Then I bring them home."

"And?"

"Mother."

"They don't like her?"

"She doesn't like them. Doesn't approve. Never overtly, mind you, but she makes them feel not at home. Uncomfortable. She has her ways. She can be quite . . . pervasive, my mother."

"That's a shame."

"Oh, she's a good woman, my mother. She'd protect me with her life. She's the best mother a boy could ever have . . ."

Rene swallowed her drink. "But you're not exactly a boy, are you?"

The man smiled, unoffended. "It doesn't help that everyone is beginning to look young enough to be my daughter. Christ, I detest bars."

Rene smiled, warming even more to him. "Amen to that."

They saluted, drank.

"So, if Mama is the problem, why take them home?"

"What do you mean?"

"Well, you know, go someplace else, to their home or whatever."

"Whatever."

He stared at her silently for a moment.

"But it's a matter of principle, you see. I want her to like them. I mean, she *is* my mother. She's sacrificed herself caring for me. I can't simply *dismiss* her."

"But you can't let her—I mean, she shouldn't rule your life, either. Right?"

He nodded. "Of course. You're absolutely right. But . . . well, you haven't met my mother."

Rene felt a sudden, overwhelming empathy for him, this beautiful, defeated mama's boy, another orphan from the storm. She had the most absurd desire to cradle him in her arms, press him to her breast the way she'd done with Brad. That's why she could never get it on with men, the only ones she was attracted to were all so pathetic, so sad. She had no respect for them. They all needed a surrogate mother, and she didn't want to be that. The problem was, she fit the role so well. It was too bad that she couldn't practice on her own daughter. She was a good mother. Isn't that what Scotti had said, horror-filled eyes staring at her? *"But you're a mother!"* Shit. Life was so goddamn complicated.

He was smiling at her. "I like you," he said softly, almost wistfully.

She smiled back.

"No, I mean it. I—there's something about you, something trustworthy. I knew it the minute I saw you. What's your name?"

"Scotti," she lied.

"Pretty name. I'm Sonny."

"Hi."

"I've never told anyone that before, Scotti, about Mother. I've never told any of the others much of anything. We usually just have a few drinks, maybe go to dinner, a movie, then home to Mother. We don't talk all that much. But I like talking with you."

"I like talking with you."

"Can I tell you another truth?"

"Of course."

"The other women, they all share a common ... factor, I guess you'd call it."

She watched him curiously.

"They all have children."

"How coincidental."

"Oh, it isn't coincidental. I see them with their children somewhere. It's why I ask them out. It's ... what attracts me."

Rene sat back in the booth, perplexed. "Oh? Aren't they usually married?"

He nodded. "Sometimes. But not always. And it's not as difficult as you might think, even if they are. You'd be surprised how many women cheat on their husbands, and vice versa. The bars are full of them." He looked up sharply. "You aren't—I haven't offended you?"

"No. Not at all. I'm touched by your honesty." It was true.

"But you think it's strange, right?"

She shrugged. "We all have our idiosyncracies. Why do you think you're attracted to women with children?"

Now he sat back, stared at his glass, false bravado gone. He looked younger, sweetly innocent. "I'm not sure. I think maybe it has something to do with my own mother. I guess I'm looking for something that's missing. Unconditional love, perhaps."

He looked up suddenly. "Oh, I didn't mean you!"

Rene smiled, took another drink. "You didn't ask me if I had a child. Would you like to see a picture of her?" Impulsively she pulled her wallet out of her purse and showed him a Polaroid of Susie at the beach, one she'd taken last Sunday.

He looked at it solemnly. His face seemed to soften. "She's beautiful ... do you love her?"

Tears came into Rene's eyes. "More than anything."

He looked at her searchingly. After a moment he frowned and said, "I believe you."

Rene peered at him in the dim light of the bar. He looked relieved. So endearing. She wanted more than ever to cradle him.

"Anyway, that seems to be my hang-up," he said softly. The problem is, my mother senses it, too. I bring them home and she seems threatened by them. Sees what they are . . . or what she *thinks* they are. I tell her that they're good women, that they love their children." He shook his head. "But it's always the same. She gives them that look—that condemning look—and they just seem to evaporate. I never see them again." He shook his head. "I can't believe I'm telling you all this. I swear, I've never—"

"Maybe you're trying to gain my confidence."

He looked up. "I'd like that. You have mine. I'd like to have yours, Scotti. I mean it."

Rene considered this silently. "Maybe I should meet her," she heard herself saying.

The handsome man looked up—"Mother?"—then down. "I don't think so. I don't think I'd want to do that to you. Put you through that. I like you too much."

"You don't even know me, Sonny."

"Yes, I do. And I have too much respect for you."

She looked away. "Well, you shouldn't. You shouldn't have respect for me. And you don't know me, not at all."

He was almost angry. "Don't say that! I do know you! You're a good person. A loving person. Anyone can see that. I don't give a damn what your secrets are. I like you. Just for yourself. That's enough."

She knew exactly how ridiculous it all was. But it was what she needed so much to hear tonight. She found her arms aching to hold him, cradle him. Maybe even give him what no mother ever could. She had reached out once tonight and it had nearly shattered her. She needed desperately to reach out again, to try again quickly before it was too late and she would never try again. They were both a pair of bleeding wounds. He was too weak, too terrified. It was up to her to begin the healing.

"I'm awfully tired of this bar, Sonny," she said softly and, she hoped, seductively. "And I really don't want to drive all the way back home tonight. Where's your house?"

"It's not exactly a house."

"An apartment?"

"A yacht."

"Oh?"

"A big yacht. Right down the street at the Marina."

"I've never been on a yacht before. I'd love to see it."

He looked reticent. "I don't know . . ."

"Is it your mother?"

"She's not there tonight, actually."

"Well, then?" She squeezed his hand.

He shifted uncomfortably, tried a little smile. "I think you know too much about me, Scotti."

She reached out and covered his hand. "Listen, call me Rene. That's what my friends call me."

He smiled at her but still seemed uncertain. She tried again. "I'd like to know more. I'd like to tell you some things about me."

He looked into her eyes. "I do like you."

"Shall we go, then?"

She groped for her purse.

When she straightened he had the camera. "Would you mind?"

She frowned curiously. Then smiled "For posterity?"

He smiled back and clicked the shutter, blinding her momentarily with the flashbulb.

She was swimming up from a wonderful dream in which Scotti had come to her apartment late at night, red-eyed from crying, asking for forgiveness, holding her, kissing her, leading her into the living room to the warm couch and the soft Blossom Dearie records. I was just so confused, Scotti was saying, holding her, and Rene was laughing, and crying and caressing her cheek and telling her to shush, that it was all right now, would always be all right now. Then she heard the noise from outside and the Dearie song became another song on another phonograph and the apartment walls became other walls and the blessed dark around her grew heartbreakingly cooler with the knowledge that the naked form beside her was not Scotti but the sad-faced man at the bar. . . .

"Sonny! Honey, wake up! I think someone's come aboard."

He stirred once. Then she saw the glowing arc of his cigarette and realized that he hadn't been asleep at all. She had the certain strange feeling he had never been asleep. Never really enjoyed . . .

"Sonny? Is it your mother?"

"She isn't my mother."

She felt a distant thrill, an impending something growing cancerlike out of the darkness. She tried to push up, but he was embracing her. She sought, in vain, the outline of the door.

"What—?" she croaked. The boat rolled once, a vague stir of nausea gripped her.

"My mother was a whore."

Rene was trying to think of something to say, trying to comprehend why the fear, welling in her so insistently, was there at all. It was such a lovely boat; he'd been so sweet. She'd nearly come. Then she saw, in the dim, uneven glow of the harbor lights, the figure outlined against the bulkhead. She'd been staring at it all along; in the gloom, the muumuu looked like flowered wallpaper.

Again she attempted to rise, again the arm restrained her, gentle but adamant. Now the fear was in her throat.

"Sonny . . . ?"

"It's best if you don't fight."

Even before she saw the length of dark, studded stick in the pale hand, it was falling into place: the half-heard stories circulating the department, the barely glimpsed TV news, the Monday morning edition headline tacked to the office bulletin board: WOMAN—BEACH—BLOOD—SANTA BARB—

The karate came back to her instinctively. She brought her right arm up—the one next to his chest—

hooked it, drove the elbow down hard, guessing in the dark at his solar plexus. She hit high, skidding off the sternum, but taking some breath with her; the arm encircling her broke free.

She was up, naked and exposed, trying to position for a kick at the imposing shape before her. But the shape was gone. And now the room was brilliantly white, now yellow, now deep magenta, and she was kissing the hard floor, something warm running in her ear. She hadn't even seen the blow coming, hadn't even felt the pain. She imagined looking at herself in her brightly lit apartment mirror, a large piece of her temporal lobe missing.

She fought to stay awake, sensing distantly that it was a losing proposition. She felt rather than heard the footsteps coming around to finish her. The other one, the one she'd let fuck her, was thrashing on the bed, moaning. She must get up now—now or never. The idea, clear if not cohesive, extremely reasonable, would not reach down to connect with her limbs.

Now someone was saving her the trouble, lifting her easily under the armpits. She glimpsed silken flowers, a gash of red mouth, luminescent hair, a strength beyond her own. Her toes dragged the floor, floundered for rubbery purchase. She *felt*, did not see, the dark club raised above her. She squeezed her eyes shut and slammed her forehead into the one before her.

She was released with a grunt.

She crashed to her knees, legs still unwilling to cooperate, and stayed upright by clinging to the corner of the bed. Now the pain came with a vengeance, every dark corner of the small room witnessed through a haze of red. There was an even chance she was mortally wounded. She assimilated this with amazing calm, some rational part of her suggesting letting go, ending it here. But a bigger part deeming it improper: these people wanted more than her life—they wanted to defile, savage her. She must make some effort.

She could feel the mattress undulate as the groaning figure began to slide off it, stand. The perpetrator with the club was somewhere before her, blocking the door. In a second they would surround her. If she crawled, used the dark to conceal her movement . . .

"She's getting away!"

It was a hiss, neither male nor female. Directionless. But she must be heading for the door. They'd unwittingly telegraphed it. She could just see the silvery knob, glowing like a beacon, when the second blow crashed on her from behind.

It was poorly aimed, thrown off by the impending dark, the listing vessel, caroming off the back of her cranium, propelling her forward into a small dresser, hands skidding across polished surface, clutching, knocking over clattering, glass things; the sound would pinpoint her like sonar. She was next to the door now, but from the sounds of the thudding steps behind her, she knew she would never make it. She turned drunkenly, waiting, looked down at what she had clutched unconsciously in her palsied hands: the camera.

She found the button as the club raised upward again, and she fired the flashbulb's brilliance into startled, pain-seared eyes. She glimpsed white, enraged face, livid mouth, cadaverous hair. The club, blinded, shattered the dresser behind her, sent shards biting her naked thigh, her arms. Rene spun, yanked, lurched through the door.

She reached the upper deck by sheer luck, not fathoming why they hadn't caught up with her—she'd been so slow, taken so many wrong turns, an easy mark. She stumbled about dizzily and found the answer, guarding the gangplank to the dock. The muumuu had come up another way.

In the mooring lights, Rene could now see the club plainly and was quietly fascinated: a policeman's billy. Like the one she used herself. Only stuck through at the end with something. Nails?

In another moment her recent lover joined his mother and they stood waiting, confidently calm. No one had escaped them yet. No one ever would. Rene tried to imagine how many more after her there would be till somebody smart enough, somebody quick enough . . .

She clutched a dangling rope, trying to keep them in focus, trying to fill her straining chest with great heaving lungsful of air before her captors caught on and cut off her only retreat.

She looked one final time into the sad, handsome face.

Then, amid their startled cries of outrage, she ran the fifteen drunken, serpentine feet to the ship's rail, soared for a giddy moment like a light, sensuous butterfly—like someone she'd known briefly in another lifetime—and spread her arms to the shocking embrace of a cold, indifferent sea.

TULLY

DETECTIVE SERGEANT EUSTES TULLY SPENT MONDAY morning at the library.

He had begun the day in the files of the Sheriff's Department, flipping through dog-eared file dividers and yellowed transcripts, searching for anything connected with Laredo Beach in the early fifties. It hadn't taken long, much of the material for 1951 to 1954 had been lost to a fire that had gutted a large section of the sub-basement and a portion of the filing cabinets therein. The files he could find were sloppily kept and no help at all; the department wasn't big enough or well-staffed enough to keep accurate records dating that far back. He had given up after a frustrating hour and decided to depend on the larger history of Santa Barbara housed in the city's main library.

He kept praying Jim Shingleton's office wouldn't beep him on his pager so they could ask embarrassing questions about how the Dias invesigation was going.

He sat alone in the library basement stacks with

their new microfilm machine, running through front pages of the *Santa Barbara Ledger*. The *Ledger* had folded in the sixties and Tully had had no luck locating their archives from the fifties. The publisher had died long ago, and no one knew or cared what had happened to the records. Tully hadn't the least idea what it was he was looking for anyway; he only had the firm conviction that whatever was causing someone to pile up bodies on Laredo beach, the roots lay in the past, probably on that selfsame beach.

It might lead to something. Or it might lead to nothing at all.

But he had to do something. And if he could get his old academy chum Spencer to do a little light snooping aboard Dias's yacht, it just might give him the needed time to do some extracurricular digging. Sure, it was passing the buck. He could be called on the carpet. He could be suspended. He could be washed up. He didn't care. He didn't seem to care about much of anything anymore except solving this case, preventing another innocent woman from dying—dying so grotesquely.

What else did he have? Not a wife, that's for sure. Not a family by any stretch. Unless you counted Mae and those empty nights sitting on her furniture in the house he grew up in watching her knit. Even he wasn't naïve enough to delude himself into believing that was any kind of life.

Funny thing, he'd always thought of himself as a dedicated cop, putting in long hours because he was conscientious, because he thought he made a difference. Now he realized that was all self-aggrandizement. He put in long hours because he had nowhere else to go, no one to go to. Never would as long as she was in his life. As long as Mother was alive.

He sat alone in the library basement spinning the black plastic knob on the big metal machine, watching the microfilmed news fly past on the illuminated screen, depleting one spool of microfilm and inserting another, rapidly scanning front pages, realizing he was getting only a portion of the past by sticking to page one but not able to justify spending more time, realizing he might very well have missed something in his eagerness to plow through the vast stacks of material, realizing it was all very probably a colossal waste of time.

He had started at nine that morning with January 1, 1950. It was now nine past eleven and he was up to June 3, 1952. He had learned a lot about North Korea, the 38th Parallel, Senator Joseph McCarthy, Eisenhower's golf, the Kefauver hearings, the suburban housing boom, and 3-D movies. He had also read a bit about Santa Barbara crime, which seemed almost surrealistically innocuous by today's drug-redolent standards. But he'd found nothing that stirred his imagination, hinted at suspicious activity on Laredo Beach. He hadn't found anything on Laredo Beach, in fact.

By eleven-thirty it had begun to look like a bad idea and the double meat burritos at Taco Bell were beginning to look like a good one. Then his pager beeped. He phoned the office and was immediately transferred to the morgue.

"Tully here."

"Wanamaker's Charnel House. You stab 'em, we slab 'em!"

"Hi, want to get some lunch?"

"No, and neither will you when you hear this. Another beach victim turned up this morning, only this one was on a different beach—Santa Barbara State, about half a mile from the wharf."

"Oh, shit. That breaks the pattern."

"Hold on, there's more. This one had her private parts intact. All the damage was to the cranial area. Looks like the same weapon, though, from the angle and width of the wounds. No paint chips this time, but the scalp was shredded in the same pattern as the vaginas of the first two victims. Also, she fits their physical description—tall, dark, athletic."

"Who found her?"

"Parks and Recreation Department. She was lying in the surf."

"The surf, huh. Another pattern break. Is she with you now? I'm coming over."

"Not to the morgue you're not."

"Why, is Captain Sparrs hanging around?"

"She's over at County General, Tully."

"What the hell are they doing with her, Fred?"

"Trying to keep her alive, I'd say."

Tully drove by County General after lunch but didn't bother to go in. The place would be swarming with cops and photographers, and it wasn't his case anymore. Besides, the woman had not regained consciousness since she'd been found in the surf.

When Fred had some free time, Tully picked him up and the two went out to Santa Barbara State Beach where the workmen had found the naked woman. There wasn't much to see, it was just a beach.

"Okay," Tully thought aloud, walking on the hard-packed sand next to the breakers, dodging the milky rolls of surf, "the Parks and Recreation guys found her here in the surf at six-thirty A.M. I checked with the weather service, high tide was at six last night, low tide at four this morning. What does that tell us?"

"I give up. What?" Fred wanted to know, trudging after him, hands in his pockets against the cooling late afternoon sea breeze.

"Well, for one thing, we know the other victims were found at least thirty feet from the water. This one might have been left for dead like the others, but why at the edge of the water? The water couldn't have crept up to where she lay because that doesn't coincide with the weather service's tidal forecast. Therefore she would have had to crawl down here to the edge of the sea after her attacker had split."

"What about tracks? There would be drag marks."

Tully shook his head. "Not reliable. If the wind and

water didn't erase them, someone walking through here last night might have. The Parks and Recreation guys smoothed over a lot of the area before they discovered her. Anyway, I don't believe she crawled anywhere. Why head toward the ocean if you're wounded and bleeding?"

'Disorientation? Didn't know which way she was heading?"

"She'd have heard the surf. Also—unless Brumeister spirited them away like he did the last flashbulb—there were no flashbulbs found in the area. Or sunglasses or fifties bathing suits. No, something went wrong here, this is too sloppy. Our boy may be a lot of things, but he isn't sloppy. Not intentionally. If anything, he's methodical."

"Unless he's deliberately trying to throw us off."

Tully watched the slapping waves, shook his head slowly. "He fucked up, Fred. He didn't finish the job. No blanket, no sunglasses, no flashbulb, no ravaged genitals. Just some clumsy blows with a weapon whose puncture marks match those on the other victims."

Fred pondered, aimed a broken piece of shell at an indignant gull. "Maybe we've got us a copycat killer?"

Tully groaned. "Let's not even contemplate that. Goddamn newspapers."

"The people have a right to know, Tully."

"Yeah, until they become the victims."

Fred shivered in the dying sun. "Maybe he dumped her from a boat, a dinghy or something."

Tully grimaced. "Why? Why break this carefully wrought pattern he's worked so meticulously to establish? He's trying to show us something, reenact a crime, or a scene he interprets as a crime. He's telling us a story. Why change it in midstream? I don't think it's his intention to mislead us. He wants us to figure it out, wants us to punish him, or maybe to right some injustice he thinks was done to him."

Fred shrugged, hunched against the wind. "Well, she didn't float ashore, that's for sure. She was still breathing when they found her."

Tully turned to him slowly, eyes widening, his face

suddenly beatific. "No, not washed ... but she could have swum!"

"Swum? Are you kidding? With half her head split open?"

The more he thought about it, the more excited Tully became. "Fred, it's the only way! He didn't finish the job because she got away from him! And it *was* from a boat! It had to be! Fred, you're a genius!"

"I've been telling you that for years. Now, explain why I am."

Tully began pacing in tight little circles. "That's why the graveyard shift hasn't picked anyone up in their black-and-whites! He isn't using a car to haul the bodies, he's using a boat! We've let the fact that the victims' lungs were free of saltwater detour us away from the sea. But it's from the sea they've come! We should have leaned more heavily on the Shore Patrol, the Coast Guard, got them to make random house calls on any suspicious vessels in the area. We should have put more men on the beach itself, instead of the paths leading to it. No wonder no one ever spotted somebody carrying a body down here!"

"Tully, not to throw cold water, but I can't believe anyone with those kind of head injuries could paddle around for long in a cold ocean at night."

Tully began scanning the pinking horizon. "You said yourself she was athletic. Maybe she was a good swimmer. And maybe she didn't have to swim all that far." He pointed. "The struggle could have taken place at the edge of Stearn's Wharf. She falls in, swims to shore"— his eyes slid to the right, to the irregular forest of masts hugging the edge of the bay—"or it could have taken place at the marina."

Fred followed his gaze. After a moment the two men turned and looked at each other.

Tully, flushed with anticipation, started in slowly, building. "This guy, he spots a victim, who knows how, maybe she fits the description of someone he hates, maybe she reminds him of his mother. He follows her, no hurry, finds out where she lives, waits till she's alone, then—well, it depends. Maybe he bonks them and drives away with them in his trunk, maybe he just talks them into going with him. That's more likely—too dangerous the other way. Probably good-looking, or at least a good talker. He takes them to his boat, gets them good and liquored, pulls out the old nightstick, whacko! Afterwards, he wraps the body in a towel, loads it onto a smaller boat, a launch or something, putt-putts over to Laredo Beach, finds a nice deserted area and sets up his gruesome little tableau. It isn't even that risky, because if someone does come along, even spots him, he's back in his motorboat and into the night before anyone can get up the beach to a phone or a cop. Christ, Fred, it's nearly foolproof!"

Fred nodded. "But not this time."

Tully nodded back excitedly. "Right. This time something goes wrong. He waits too long to make his move, or he's caught off guard, or the victim fights back."

"She'd have to be a hell of a fighter."

"Trained maybe. But anyway, she manages to beat back her attacker long enough to get up on deck, get over the side."

"Why doesn't he follow her?"

"Maybe he does. But it's dark, he can't see, and he doesn't want to use lights for fear of being spotted himself. He's bungled it; he's nervous, panicked. He doesn't know which direction she's headed, maybe she goes partway underwater, holding her breath, using the last of her strength to keep herself invisible. He searches, but it's in the wrong direction, up the beach instead of down. By the time he's figured out his mistake, she's long gone. There are people on the beaches, teenagers partying around a bonfire. He can't risk it, and besides those head wounds he gave her will finish the job."

Fred made a wry sound. "They may yet."

Tully grunted. "Let's hope to Christ they don't. She's our only hope for a positive ID. Fred, are you going to be Chief Medical examiner on this one, too?"

"Sure. The DA wants positive proof that there's a link between cases."

"And you'll examine her thoroughly?"

"Tomorrow morning, comatose or not."

Tully nodded, facing the marina. "Ten to one you find traces of semen in this one." He looked back at his old friend. "She got to him, Fred. She got to him before he got to her."

Tully dropped Fred at his home, then went back to the station to finish some paperwork. Shingleton had given him a file to read on Santiago Dias and he still hadn't gotten around to cracking it.

In the big empty office he sat at his desk ringed by overturned styrofoam cups, half-eaten doughnuts, trying to concentrate on the file, uneasy in the mausoleum silence.

Certain he was alone, a sudden movement from behind jarred him. He turned, expecting to find the janitor, and found instead Captain Sparrs, also working late. Why the Christ am I so jumpy?

Sparrs stopped by his desk, coat jacket in hand, sat down on the scarred wooden edge. "Burning the midnight oil, Tully?"

Tully grunted. "Conscientious to the end, that's me."

Sparrs grinned affably, though Tully found little affable about the granite-faced captain, who right now was throwing a shadow across his reading light as he twisted around to look at the file. Sparrs was due to retire next year—just lately Tully had noticed how old he was becoming, old and tired. Sparrs chewed gum loudly—an attempt to quit smoking, Tully guessed. "So, you working on the Dias thing?"

Tully looked up impatiently. He didn't want to read this shit in the first place, he particularly didn't want to read it with his superior standing over his shoulder. "That was the assignment, wasn't it?"

Sparrs grunted. "Any luck getting close to Dias?"

Tully sighed, flipped a page. "What do you think?"

Sparrs grinned. "Stick with it, kid, you'll find a way in."

"Yeah, sure."

Sparrs got up. "Jim Shingleton's a good man," he said at length.

"I know that." What the hell was this about?

"He needs your undivided attention on this thing."

"That was the plan."

Sparrs nodded. Paused. "Spotted Dias hanging around Laredo Beach, by any chance?"

Tully watched the other man. "Not really, why?"

"I understand you've been spending time there."

Tully fought a rising heat. He wondered if he could take Sparrs in a fistfight. Probably not. He was twenty years younger, but Sparrs outweighed him by a good fifty pounds. "I was taking the air. Where does this 'understanding' come from—somebody named Brumeister, maybe?"

"You're supposed to be covering the Dias thing, Tully."

"I *am* on the Dias thing! Jesus Christ! What're you paying Brumeister for, to tail me?"

"I'm paying him to investigate Laredo Beach."

"I told you, I was getting some fresh air. It's a public goddamn beach! Do I have to fill out a report every time I wipe my ass?"

Sparrs held up his hands. "Okay, cool down. I know you think you got a raw deal. Maybe you did. Maybe I'll think of a way to make it up to you later. Let's all try to keep our heads here—there's enough pressure from the DA's office over these murders."

Tully went back to the Dias file.

Sparrs shrugged into his jacket, buttoned it. "Don't forget to turn off the coffee machine . . . Tully?"

"What?"

"It's going to be all right."

"Sure it is."

Captain Sparrs rapped Tully's desk goodnight and

left the room, closing the door behind him. Tully folded up the boring file and leaned back, stretching, eyes closed. When he opened them again they were focused on the closed door. He sighed, shook his head wearily. Prick.

The phone shrilled beside him. Who—this late? "Detective Tully."

"Hi. It's me."

"Sorry—?"

"Kim. Kim Dillinger from Wear It Again, Sam's. Remember?"

"Yes, Miss Dillinger, what can I do for you?"

"Just wondering how you were doing with that case. The woman who was murdered."

"Well, we're working on it, Miss Dillinger."

"Uh-huh. Listen ... Eustes ... I found a bunch more of those old fifties swimsuits. Maybe you'd like to come down and take a look at them."

"Well, that's very thoughtful of you, we'll get back to you on that."

"I'm working an extra shift tonight, if you'd care to drop by. It wouldn't be an inconvenience."

"Actually ... I think we have all the information on swimsuits that's going to do us any good, thanks."

"Uh-huh. So. Getting pretty close on the case, huh?"

"We're doing our best."

"Must be exciting work, police work."

"Well, it can be."

"Ever bring in any really big criminals, Eustes?"

"Not as big as Dillinger, no." He thought he could hear the sound of her gum popping.

"I guess they don't have criminals that famous anymore, huh?"

"Famous in different ways."

"So look maybe you could drop by sometime and tell me how the case is going, huh? We could have coffee or something."

"Miss Dillinger, how old are you?"

Metallic sigh. "Don't you know it's not polite to ask a lady that? I'm twenty."

"Are you? I'm pushing forty-five."

"Yeah, so? I could stand to gain a few pounds, you could stand to lose a few. Together we ought to weigh out pretty good. Have you got a pencil?"

"Yes."

"Here's my number at home. I don't have an answering machine so just keep trying." She gave him the number. "Did you get that?"

"I got it."

"Right, so give me a call sometime. I'm either here or at the store. Eustes?"

"Yes?"

"Okay?"

"I've got the number."

"Right. So I'll wait to hear from you. Goodnight, Eustes, don't work too late."

He hung up.

He sat staring at the scribbled number for a moment, remembering the flaxen color of her hair, the smell of her gum. Her funny lips. Almost a sneer, almost sexy. No, decidedly sexy.

Then he crumpled the paper in his hand and tossed it into the basket at his feet.

CHAPTER 20

DIAS

Santiago Dias had been looking forward to the meeting all day.

He was confident, assured. But then, he was always confident and assured. There was, for him, simply no other sensible approach to life. Either you met the world head-on, with strength and aggressiveness in your corner, or you met it not at all; you sat home on the front porch in your broken-down rocker surrounded by poverty, counting the flies and chickens pecking at your feet, like the poor *cholos* of his native Medellin. If you sat there very long, you would sit there forever. Dias was not a sitter.

Nor was he recklessly ambitious. True, every deal had to be accompanied by a certain amount of risk or it was rarely a deal worth pursuing. He enjoyed risk, but was not—as was the case with so much of his competition these days—a slave to it. He would no sooner be a slave to the risks and thrills of business than he would to anything else: a woman, a drug, or the grouse hunting he loved so. You had to learn to admire and respect a thing without being seduced by it, that was his philosophy.

Unlike most of the men in his line of work, he had no great infatuation with money. Perhaps this was because he was born into it. To generations of it. It had been coffee beans, now it was coca leaf. It was all the same, all a product of the same rich dark Colombian soil. A soil that would, perhaps, someday rule the world. If that was God's will. Santiago did not think himself evil for having supplied a decade of coke anymore than for having served generations of coffee. It was what the people of the world wanted. He simply happened to occupy a corner of the world where this was physically and economically possible and profitable. He felt no great pride in this. Indeed, despite the fact that most of his millions had been made in the export of goods to America, it was not something he gloated about. Choreographing the miltifaceted drug operation was become increasingly more time-consuming, dangerous, and complicated. Dias did not savor a complicated life. He would have been content to keep the operation based in Miami, use freelance runners who paid for their own boats and planes, played cat-and-mouse games with the Dade County Police and their beautiful customs speedboats. Sometimes they won, sometimes he won, but mostly he won. It had been a relatively simple arrangement. It had left plenty of time to stroll the Colombian hills with his rifle, seeking grouse or quail. It had left time for tranquility and self-reflection, time to be a gentleman. A gentleman he respected.

But times were changing. Competition was on the rise. Greed, the great downfall of those American businessmen he'd admired from childhood, had lifted its ugly head in South America. It used to be fun being at the top, now it was becoming a necessity. There was no longer room for second place, and the drop down was a long one. It was impossible now to go back to the safe, peaceful glory days of the coffee business. He was too busy protecting his own back, dodging bullets in his own bedroom. He was beginning to distrust even those who had been with him longest. It would all end badly— perhaps bloodily—someday and he knew it.

He might even find himself envying those poor *cholos* in their broken down rockers. Flies and chickens do not kill. . . .

But for now he was content enough. For now he was about to consummate a business deal that would keep those flies and chickens at arm's length for a good while longer and set the heads of the competition to spinning. And when this current deal was over? Perhaps Santiago Rodrigues Dias would simply vanish from the face of the earth. A feat hopefully of his own making.

He entered the expensive Big Piney restaurant alone. He rarely used bodyguards in the States. He was a strong man, a quick man, he could take care of himself.

He entered the cool, dimly lit interior with its gloriously expansive view of the lake and looked around.

The fat man was waiting for him at the far table in his usual place. Doubtless he had already had dessert, filled his fat belly with it. Dias chuckled softly to himself. How had he ever gotten involved with this miserably self-indulgent American? No matter. A need had been found. He intended to fill it.

Dias moved congenially toward the table.

"*Buenas noches, señor!*"

"Good evening, Mr. Dias! Please join me, sir."

Dias sat, suppressing a sardonic smile. It was impossible for him to look upon the fat man's cherubic cheeks, double chin, wispy hair, without seeing a fat *mamacita* cradling her plump infant, walking Medellin back streets, begging food. The sight always had the same ludicrous effect on him: a rich man perhaps, this soft gringo, but a fat spoiled baby as well. "You are well tonight, my friend?"

"Tolerably," the fat man allowed, "and yourself, good sir?"

Dias raised his hands in a gesture of innocent confidence. "Excellent, as always! Your Southern California weather cannot be bested! No humidity, no fog—it is a lovely night, no? A night for romance!"

"Delightful."

"*Si*. Not a breath of discord in the air! Not a trace of apprehension to mar this beautiful evening! A pity, really, to muddy this lovely serenity with talk of business. But we are, I suppose, victims of our livelihoods, yes? You have thought over my proposal, I trust?"

The waiter appeared. Both men ordered drinks, Dias his favorite Johnny Walker Red.

The fat man put his chubby hands on the table. "I'm afraid I need more time, Mr. Dias."

Dias stared quietly at him. Then he smiled. "My stay in your delightful country is limited, *señor*, as you know . . ."

The fat man cleared his thick throat. "I am aware of that, certainly, but what you are proposing is a monumental undertaking, with monumental consequences. It could, to be blunt, put me in prison forever."

"It could also make you fabulously wealthy."

"I am already wealthy."

"Not compared to this, I think."

"I must have time," the big man insisted. A patina of sweat beaded his baby's forehead; he dabbed at it with his cocktail napkin.

Dias leaned back, lit a cigar comfortably, blew smoke. "Please, it is really very simple. Your American coffee company is failing, or at least stagnating. Mine is a shadow of its former self. Yet both firms are legitimate, ongoing concerns. It makes perfect sense for our companies to merge, for me to control the growing and packing, you the shipping and distribution. It will, in fact, for the most part be a real and viable merchandising enterprise. No one will give it a second glance. No one will have reason to look into it, to open crates containing hundreds of cans of sealed coffee. And even if they did, my people are planted throughout the customs bureaus here in California; there would be ample warning of a raid, ample time to prepare. The scheme is foolproof, and you know it."

The drinks arrived; the fat man gulped his greedily.

"No scheme is foolproof, good sir," he came up breathlessly. He seemed to be sensing something unpleasant in the air, a bigger issue building, something nagging at the edge of conversation.

Dias bowed is head. "Admittedly. But what is life without a few risks, where is the excitement?"

"I'm not sure I am prepared to entertain that kind of excitement. I simply must have more time to prepare."

Dias drank, relaxed, set down the glass carefully. "Take all the time you need, my friend, but I must have a letter of agreement in my hands by the end of the month, stating your participation in the plan along with your signature. Otherwise I sail back to Medellín ... empty-handed in one way, perhaps reciprocated fully in another." He smiled, the lamplight filling his lean face, an amber death's head.

The fat man trembled violently, drink sloshing over his chubby fingers. "You wouldn't dare take Claire! That's kidnapping!"

Dias's chuckle was chillingly calm. "Hardly, my friend. The lady will come, I think, quite willingly. I have yet to find it necessary to coerce."

The fat man appeared to be turning red all over, face bright as a bacchant. "Is she in love with you? Is Claire in love with you? Tell me!" He banged his plump fist on the table, drinks leaping.

Dias smiled laconically, blew tendrils of smoke.

"Why don't you ask your spy, our good friend Mr. Spencer?"

The fat man swallowed.

"Oh yes, I was on to him from the first. A very cordial man, very congenial, if clumsy. I nearly killed him last Saturday—that little trip to the Channel Islands to dive among the kelp beds. I had planned for him to have a little ... diving accident. Then I saw something over dinner that changed my mind. He and the delectable

Mrs. Greely exchanged glances. Only briefly, mind you, even discreetly. But it was enough."

The fat man seemed ready to explode. "What are you saying?"

"I'd caught them before in her cabin, just the two of them. She was apparently inebriated, he there only to help her. Though how he acquired that smudge of lipstick I cannot guess. I suppose there were a lot of beautiful young ladies on board that night."

"Are you trying to tell me Claire is attracted to this man?"

Dias shrugged innocence. "It is not for me to say."

The fat man offered him a jaundiced eye. "You're lying. You're making this last part up to aggravate me."

"Am I? Perhaps. But I do not think the newspapers have been lying, do you, my friend? Have you seen the latest? They discovered a third body on the beach yesterday. A lovely young woman, about Claire's age, I believe . . ."

The fat man's blood drained from his jowls. He looked down supplicatingly, gripped the glass before him until it threatened to shatter. "Please . . . I'm begging you . . . I couldn't live if anything happened to my dear Claire . . . please, Mr. Dias . . . please . . ."

Dias watched him calmly, stubbed out the cigar.

"I cannot protect her every second, my friend. There are times when it is necessary to be elsewhere. This week, for instance, I must spend some time in L.A. I have invited Mr. Mitch Spencer to stay on my boat. He can, of course, invite whomever he chooses to join him. That would leave them alone with only the servants . . . and Mother, of course." He took a drink, holding his smile. "Has Claire plans for the week, by the way?"

The fat man appeared to sink inside himself. The violent tremble had settled into a steady series of teeth-chattering spasms.

"What is it you want from me?" Barely audible.

Dias set down his drink. "The same thing you want from me, *señor*—an equitable agreement. Please, we have come too far, have we not? You know my little secrets, I know yours. We can be of irreparable damage to one another, or invaluable help. Our shared secrets will only act as a bond to better business, a lever to assure mutual cooperation. Rather like two superpowers aiming pistols at each other's heads, is it not so?" He chuckled softly.

The fat man licked his lips. "If I sign this letter of agreement . . . I have your word that you will look after Claire, see that no harm comes to her?"

"You have my guarantee that that arrangement can be made whether I am personally in this country or not."

"It's just that . . . I can't sleep at night knowing . . ." The chuggy fingers twisted the cocktail napkin into tiny shreds. He looked up at the Colombian, eyes brimming. He choked back phlegm as the tear found gravity, traced a plump cheek. "You can't know what life has been like for a man like me, Dias, you can't know. You can't know . . ."

Dias finished his drink, looked at his watch.

"I must get to the airport, *señor*, to my business in L.A. I will be back in one week. It is my sincere hope that we can bring our own business dealings to a close at that time. We wouldn't want to encourage already suspicious minds by overstaying my visa, would we?"

"I'll have the papers prepared," the fat man said to the table. He seemed to have shrunk to the size of a small toad.

Dias stood. "Until next time, then. Have a lovely week. And my best to your charming Claire!"

Dias bowed and left.

The fat man sat alone at the table staring into his half-finished drink.

He was still sitting there three hours later, when the restaurant closed. It was Max who finally came to take him away.

TULLY

*H*E STOOD IN THE AUSTERITY OF THE HOSPITAL ROOM and stared down at the woman on the bed with all the tubes and bottles attached to her, listened to the raspy but steady cadence of her breathing through the plastic air hose. Her mouth and nose were stuffed, her head wrapped tighter than a Sikh's, eyes blackened, one nearly swollen shut, but even with all that, Tully could see the bone structure of a very handsome woman.

Who was she? Where had she been heading that fateful night? How had she ended up naked and half alive in the Santa Barbara surf?

It was after eight. Brumeister and his people had come and gone, the doctors had long since left the room, Fred Wanamaker had run his tests which, as Tully had suspected, came up positive for semen traces. Now they had a blood type; all they needed was a suspect. Which put them about one inch farther than before, but at least it was something.

Everyone had done his poking and prodding and picture taking and gone back to offices to make notes and scribble on clipboards. The hospital halls were quiet now. Uninvited, unwanted, Tully had gotten past the night nurse through the casual flash of a shield; she didn't know one case from another, one cop from another.

He stood gazing solemnly at this latest tribute to insanity.

Comatose.

He hated the word.

More, perhaps, than any other.

He'd seen his share of comas. Car wreck victims, bludgeon victims, falling victims, and mostly helmetless motorcycle victims, some of them somnambulent through it all, never waking up, sleeping the little sleep before the Big Sleep; some of them screeching, sitting up, even thrashing amid the sheets, foaming at the mouth, eyes wide and staring and horrified—but no more awake than the first type. Either way it was awful. Neither conscious, dead, nor truly asleep in the normal sense. Lost in some unfathomable limbo, adrift in the cosmos, trapped in a frightful corridor of their own tortured brains. What did they see in there? What dark paths did they wander? What was it like? Those that came back never seemed to remember very clearly. Yet if it were a benign, even pleasant place, why did some of them thrash about like that? Mere muscle reflex . . . or the clawing retreat from some horrible nightmare—a nightmare of the imagination, in which no horror was impossible, no abomination tethered.

Cancer, heart disease, for all their dread fear, hideous pain, were at least bound to reality; Tully, if he feared anything, feared the bottomless depths of coma.

Spontaneously, he reached out and took the pale hand, tangled in IV tubing, closing his warm fingers around the cool, pliant palm. Maybe it would provide some small comfort during her distant, solitary journey. You never knew.

He heard a sound behind him and turned to find

Brumeister staring at him quizzically. Tully dropped the woman's hand, too late to elude the bigger cop's eye.

Oddly, Brumeister seemed unperturbed by the gesture; if anything, he seemed softened by it. He took the cigar out of his mouth, jabbed it out in a tray, and joined Tully bedside. He looked down at the swollen face.

"Pretty, don't you figure?"

Tully nodded. "Looks like it."

"She's a cop, did you hear?"

Tully turned to him, stunned. "No. Local?"

"AWOL since Friday from Ventura. Found her black-and-white in front of that little greaser bar down near Stearn's Wharf. Name's Rene Draper. Doctors think she has a fifty-fifty chance of coming out of it. Her ex is a cop here in Santa Barbara. Him and their daughter came here after the divorce, he's got custody."

"Rene Draper . . . you mean she's married to Brad Draper? Has he been here yet?"

"Him and the kid, earlier. She was just in town last Sunday, took the kid to the beach . . ." Brumeister shook his head. "Goddamn waste of womanhood."

Tully had to agree with that, but his insides were churning. Brad Draper. A cop, all right. Unfortunately, he was only about twenty-six—too young to fit Tully's theory.

Unless his theory was wrong.

Brumeister unbuttoned his coat, found a chair, grunted into it. "The Dias thing keeping you busy?" There was no sarcasm in his voice.

Tully didn't turn. "Yeah, pretty busy."

Brumeister nodded. "Supposed to be a dangerous character, watch your ass."

Why was Brumeister making nice? They were supposed to hate each other's guts.

Brumeister was watching the woman on the bed again. "Sure make things a hell of a lot simpler if she'd come out of it." Wistfully.

Then Tully knew: Brumeister was worried. He was getting nowhere on this case and the pressure was on.

The limelight was on his ass now, let's see how he liked it. He talked big, threw his weight around, but he knew as well as everyone else he didn't have what it took for hardcore detective work, that necessary sixth sense. What Fred Wanamaker called "lateral thinking." Tully had it. Everyone knew Tully had it. Brumeister knew Tully had it.

And Brumeister was asking for help.

Son of a bitch was asking for help so *he* could claim credit for the collar and *he* could kiss Sparrs's ass and *he* could walk away with the promotion pay. Well, screw him.

"Where you going, Tully?"

"Tully" now, not Eustes. He made for the door. "Got to get my beauty rest, this Dias thing is a real headache."

"Yeah? Well, I was thinking about grabbing a beer, what do you say?"

"Some other time. But good luck with your case. Looks like the evidence is beginning to pile up."

"Yeah, thanks."

If Brumeister caught the sarcasm, he didn't show it. He was too lost in his own frustration. Asshole.

Outside, the night was crisp and clear, free from the constricted air of bumbling cops, the tortured dreams of the comatose.

The library was still open. He went down to the basement again and cranked up the microfilm machine. It was a long, arduous, and probably fruitless procedure, but it was the only way he knew. Certainly Brumeister was finding nothing.

Tully sped through the headlines, shaking his head in sad disbelief. Of all the bumbling oafs to assign to an important case, why had Sparrs chosen Brumeister? Admittedly they were understaffed, but this wasn't exactly a purse snatching they were talking about. If Sparrs had wanted to make sure the case was never solved, he couldn't have made a better choice!

Tully spun the black plastic knob, found himself

smiling with self-satisfaction. Fine. Let Sparrs assign a second-stringer to the job, that would only increase Tully's chances. And he *would* solve this case, goddamnit, he would!

He finished the 1952 microfilm spool with a page one story about chlorophyll. For some time, the 1952 consumer market turned green when housewives snatched up everything from cough drops to toothpaste with the promise that the added plant component, chlorophyll, would sweeten their breath and leave their families daisy fresh. Then the *Journal of the American Medical Association* published a paper pointing out that grazing cows and goats virtually live on chlorophyll and don't smell sweet at all. Wall Street industrials shrank accordingly.

Tully was just about to slide out the exhausted spool when he noticed a small article. It lay innocuously in the lower left corner, buried beneath the bigger headlines:

GOLETA WOMAN ACCUSED OF CHILD ABUSE

SANTA BARBARA—A Goleta woman was arraigned here late Friday afternoon on charges of child abuse and possible child prostitution, according to an officer of the Santa Barbara Sheriff's Department. Names involved in the case are being withheld to protect the child until officials have further studied the matter.

According to sources, the 32-year-old woman is accused of pandering her ten-year-old at designated areas along the county's state beaches, though the official charge is resisting arrest. The woman is being held awaiting five thousand dollars bail at Santa Barbara County jail.

End of spool. End of 1952.

Tully hastily reached upward and grappled in the box on top of the machine for the next spool. He brought down the wrong year, 1954. Puzzled, he stood, examined the box closely. No 1953 spool.

A college-age girl in a tweed skirt was passing behind him, arms loaded with file folders. Tully spotted her. "Excuse me, are you in charge of the microfilm?"

She smiled. "Sort of. Can I be of assistance?"

She was pretty, just short of stunning. Tully thought of the girl at Wear It Again, Sam's and saw a flash of pale buttock. "I hope so—the spool on 1953 seems to be missing."

The girl took the box from him. "So it does."

She smelled faintly of bubble gum. He found himself wondering vaguely if she had a boyfriend. Probably. Probably lots of boyfriends.

"Let me check on that for you. Just a sec."

She marched to a desk, put down her file folders, began digging in a drawer. She produced a large ledger, started leafing through it. "1953, right?"

"Right."

More leafing. Sound of gum popping. What was it like to be that young, that hopeful, that full of promise? Tully couldn't remember, not really.

"Ah, here's the problem. The microfilm boxes were stored in an A-vault in 1966, some of the film was lost in the fire."

He felt a twinge. "What fire?"

The girl stared at him blankly, shrugged, looked back at the ledger. "Says here there was a fire in '66. That's all it says." She looked back at him, smiled brightly. "Little before my time, I'm afraid."

He found himself smiling back. "Of course. What about the original newspapers? I suppose those were all destroyed once the microfilms were made?"

"Oh, yeah. That I'm sure of; not enough space, that's the whole point of reducing the stuff to film."

"So what you're saying is, the library has no accurate record of events centering around the year 1953, right?"

She looked as though she hadn't thought about it before. "Gee, I guess so."

Tully nodded, switched off the machine. "Well, thanks."

She smiled. "Anytime!"

He plucked his coat from the back of the chair. "Oh! You wouldn't know if the Goleta Library is still open, would you?"

She shrugged. "Probably. Most the branches stay open till ten on weeknights."

"Thanks again."

The coincidence was hardly lost on Tully and hardly free of implication. The Sheriff's Department has a fire in '53, the main library has a fire in '66, both of which destroy approximately the same year of records, the same period of history.

Still, it *could* be simple fate.

He needed further proof. No, not proof: *justification*. None of this could ever be considered proof; it happened too long ago. Tracking a possible arsonist after all these years would be foolhardy.

Tully jumped into his car and headed swiftly for the Goleta branch of the Santa Barbara County library system. He couldn't deny his quickening pulse, or the pride he felt at having trusted his instincts, at having taken the long, arduous route. It just might be paying off. His only dread was that he would find Brumeister bending over the Goleta Library microfilm machine. But he didn't think so.

He arrived to find a librarian locking up.

The main interior lights were dark, only the rudimentary burglar lamps glowed dimly. Library staff and a few straggler patrons threaded down the sweeping walk to the parking lot. Something about the scene reminded Tully of the crisp Halloween twilights of his childhood. Southern California nights were always cool, but this one had that earthen edge, that bite of coming fall.

A skeletal young man with a bookish goatee and wire-rimmed glasses was just twisting the lock on the big double doors as Tully hurried up. "Hold it a sec, need a favor." He displayed his shield.

The young man glanced at it, arched an eyebrow to seemingly limitless heights, and inspected the panting detective. The goatee hid a parade of pimples. "What's the trouble, Officer?"

"Can you get me into Microfilm?"

The goatee shook. "Marcie left half an hour ago. We open at ten tomorrow, though."

"Sure you do, but I really need the info tonight. Wouldn't happen to have a spare key on you? I'd make it worth your while."

The young man smiled and Tully could see he was very intelligent, very precise. Tully wished it was the young man who had the key. "Listen," the young man said, "I have no compunctions, I could use the bribe— car's in the shop—but the truth is, Marcie has the only key to the crypt. You could call her at home if it's official, I guess, but let me warn you, she hates breaking routine. Standard librarian matron—tight-lipped, no-titted, bun-in-the-back bluenose. Hear the clank of her chastity belt when she sits down."

Tully settled back on his heels. "No, let's not disturb her."

The young man smiled. "Not that official, huh?"

"What do you do here?"

"Watch the blondes. Hit on them if it looks like I have a chance. Or sometimes even if it doesn't."

Tully grinned. "Nice work if you can get it."

The young man was sizing Tully up. "Tell you what, let me know what you need to look up and I'll run it for you myself first thing tomorrow morning, give you a call. I come in at seven." He started to fish for a notebook and pencil.

"That would be great. Basically I need the microfilm spool for the year 1953."

The young man looked up, lowered his pencil. "Forget it, pal, you're out of luck. Haven't got a thing from that year."

Tully nodded, folded is arms. "The fire, huh?"

The young man replaced his pad and pencil. "Burned one whole corner of the subbasement, couple of shelves of transcripts and some of the newspapers. They never got put on microfilm."

"You're sure of that, right? I mean, even without checking?"

"Mister, you can bank on it. Wiped out all of '52 and '53. Too bad, only records we had of that period. Yeah, I'm sure, I know the inventory top to bottom."

Tully believed him.

"You used to work at the library?" the young man inquired.

"No."

"The fire was over thirty years ago, how'd you remember it?"

"I get around," Tully said.

"It's bullshit," Tully told Fred Wanamaker fifteen minutes later on the phone in a corner drugstore. "The Sheriff's Department, the Santa Barbara County Library, the Goleta Public Library, all three have 'accidental' fires that 'coincidentally' burn identical county property at about the same time, conveniently erasing the local events of 1953 from historical memory. It's bullshit."

"Sure sounds like it."

"Somebody did a little county housecleaning."

"But who?"

Tully took a satisfied breath—he'd been waiting all evening to spill this to someone. "Well, anybody with a library card can get into stacks and use a microfilm machine. But only a cop can get into the sheriff's files. A cop with a nightstick. And a matchbook."

"You're losing me, I'm just the coroner, remember?"

"I keep forgetting. Look, Fred, it all fits! A child— probably a beautiful little child—is born into what probably seems a typically normal family. Mother takes the child to the beach on weekends. She's a nice-looking woman, svelte, athletic, a woman who favors a certain brand of sunglasses. On one particular outing she strikes up a conversation with an attractive young man. But to the mother's dismay, it's not her the man is interested in, it's her offspring. 'What a beautiful child! Really ought to be a model! I just happen to be a photographer!' One thing leads to another. For whatever reason that makes human beings into monsters, the mother agrees to let the man spend time alone with the child, probably in exchange for money. Maybe a lot of money. Maybe the arrangement's as simple as that, or maybe there are many strangers. Who knows? The point is, the kid is pho-tographed, coerced into sexual acts with adults, eventu-ally turned into a child prostitute by his adoring mommy. At first maybe the kid doesn't understand, but as the years go by, the child eventually catches on to how wrong it all is, how abusive. And here's the real clincher—the father, who is off god-knows-where while all this sick drama is going on, that father not only does not intervene to save the child, but makes an already ugly situation tragic by virtue of his occupation!"

"Which is that of a cop."

"Exactly."

"Jesus. And he *allows* this kind of thing to go on right under his own nose? To his own kid?"

"It was thirty or more years ago, Fred, we may never know. Maybe he was a party to it, maybe he didn't find out till after the fact. Maybe he was just in a sick love-hate thing with his wife and couldn't bring himself to stop her for fear she'd leave. It doesn't matter. It doesn't even matter that he snuck into two libraries and a sher-iff's department file system and started his little pyres to erase future disgrace. To the kid—the real object of all this suffering—his old man did nothing. That's why, decades later, the child, grown up now but still seething inside, kills his surrogate mother victims with an instrument of police authority and violence. An instrument, which in his warped mind, his negligent father should have used years ago."

Wanamaker's voice was hushed. "Daddy cop killing Mommy molester. Only not just killing—savaging, defiling. Abusing Mommy to death with his big stick. Just the way he himself was abused with all those other big 'sticks.' Christ, Tully . . ."

The line was silent for a moment.

"Poor little kid," Fred muttered softly, "poor twisted, put-upon little boy."

Tully made a frustrated sound into the receiver, heaved a sigh. "First rule of detective work, Fred—don't assume."

"What do you mean, Tully?"

"Who says our killer is a male?"

CHAPTER 22

MITCH

MITCH HURRIED THROUGH MONTECITO, HOPING HE hadn't held Dias up. Rush hour traffic from L.A. to Santa Barbara had been brutal. Since he was to take over Dias's yacht for the weekend, the least he could do in return for such vast hospitality was be on time.

It wasn't the only thing he had to be on time for.

He'd promised Greely he'd meet him for drinks at six-thirty. Just a short chat, but that was only forty-five minutes from now. Even if he did make that appointment on time, he would have to rush back to the yacht for his rendezvous with Claire at eight.

Dias, Greely, Claire—all in a row, all in one evening. The various illicit components of his life were not only increasing, they were converging on one another. The only thing that could possibly make the evening more complicated was if Tully called up and wanted a slice of his time as well. That's all he'd need, to be lying to a cop about why he was on the yacht while he was lying to

Dias about why he was on the yacht while he was lying to Greely's wife about all of it.

No, it wasn't merely wearying, it was exhausting.

To say nothing of foolish.

It had to end soon, he knew. But for now, he was in deep.

He braked the Porsche near the seaside saloon as usual and locked up. It was a short two blocks to the marina from here.

He began walking briskly down the sidewalk, buttoning his jacket as he went, resisting the urge to break into a trot, hoping he hadn't blown the relationship with Dias. He could see the whitewashed boardwalk ahead and the flotilla of yachts, ketches, and catamarans. Now he could see the prow of Dias's huge vessel. He strained for some sign of the Colombian himself, perhaps leaning on the rail watching for Mitch's approach. In another minute he'd be there. . . .

"Mitch . . ."

She was standing next to her Volvo, wrapped in the fur-trimmed evening coat he'd bought her last winter. She looked drawn in the sodium lamplight.

Joanne. His wife.

He took a faltering step toward her, lips parted, mouth set to say something he couldn't quite seem to form in his mind. Joanne! What in the world—?

Mitch swallowed hard, moved quickly to her, to the pale face, the unblinking eyes. Accusing eyes.

"Joanne? What in the world are you doing here in Santa Barbara?"

Penetrating eyes.

"What's is it? What's wrong?"

And finally she was opening her mouth to speak, thank God for that. "What *is* wrong, Mitch? Why don't you tell me?"

He was lost. "I don't—"

"Marsha Stillman called."

His insides froze. Marsha Stillman was John Stillman's wife. Stillman, the man who fired him. . . .

"She wanted to say how sorry she was about your being let go. She was very sweet. Fortunately she mistook my dumbfounded silence for wifely grief."

"Joanne, listen to me—"

"I didn't drive all the way up here to see the sunset from Stearn's Wharf."

"I didn't want to upset you about the job—"

"So you lied. Jesus, Mitch, it's been weeks! Did you really think you could go on hiding a thing like that? Are you insane?"

"I didn't want you to worry. I—I'm on to something else up here, a new job. I was going to tell you this week."

But it wasn't playing; his throat was too constricted, his eyes too desperate. He'd been caught, in the last place, the last moment he'd have imagined; there was no time to prepare.

"I'm *pregnant*, Mitch! What the hell is going on?"

"I told you—"

"Are you seeing another woman?"

It was like watching some bad movie—he didn't feel a part of it. In a moment he'd throw down his popcorn in disgust and walk out.

"I'm trying to find work, for chrissake!"

Good. His anger had set her back a notch, given him the lead, and the last wasn't a complete lie. It was work, of a sort.

Joanne watched the shoreline intently. "You lied to me, Mitch. You've never lied about anything to me before." Moisture glistened at the rims of her eyes.

"Joanne . . ." He stepped closer, touched her tightly folded arms. She looked as if she were freezing, arms pressed to her breasts as if warding off the world. She hadn't bought his tactic of changing the subject from another woman, but she was too terrified and disgusted to pursue it. Accusing him just that once had drained away her resolve. This was alien terrain for her as well. His heart went out to her with a sudden lurching pain.

"Joanne, it's all going to be fine. . . ."

It sounded so lame she couldn't even look at him. She just closed her eyes, squeezed out that stubborn tear.

He felt a helplessness akin to suffocation. What had he done to her? to them? He stood watching as the breeze lifted her hair idly, hating himself for that familiar weakness he had always hated himself for. Even the fresh salt air seemed acrid and ugly.

"Is she on one of those boats?" she asked softly. "Is that it? Are you going to meet her?"

"Honey, I'm going to meet a man about a job. Please. You're just upsetting everything. Upsetting yourself."

"Can I meet him, too?"

"That wouldn't—it might be awkward."

She smiled wryly at the sea. "Sure."

"Look, why don't you find a motel? We'll have drinks later, I'll explain then."

She was opening the door of the Volvo. "That's not what you want, Mitch." Resignedly.

"Where are you going?"

"Back to Brentwood. Back to my house."

"I don't like you driving like this . . . when you're upset."

She started the engine, rolled down the window. "Are you coming back?"

"Of course! Look, at least stop and get some coffee—"

"I can take care of myself." She put the car in gear, placed a hand atop her barely pregnant tummy. "Thank God for that, huh, Mitch?"

He didn't know what to say. She made it easy for him by pulling away from the curb.

He watched until her red taillights, heading south again, were lost in traffic.

She started weeping uncontrollably just outside of town and had to pull over. But the traffic was whizzing past the shoulder too dangerously close, and she was afraid some cop would happen along and scold her. She pulled away and fought back the tears long enough to find a Marie Callendar's and finish her cry in the parking lot.

Afterwards, Joanne took her husband's advice and bought herself a cup of coffee and a piece of pie. Then— what the hell did it matter now?—another piece of pie.

She left the restaurant just after seven, walked into the darkened lot, and fumbled for the car keys. A motorcycle with a broken muffler was loudly peeling out of the lot so she didn't hear the voice distinctly at first.

"Mrs. Spencer?"

She turned.

She remembered a pleasant smile in the evening breeze. A mustache. Having to look up.

And not much after that . . .

Dias was waiting at the rail, martini in hand, captain's cap cocked back on his crown, a bang of shiny black hair protruding rakishly. He flashed his dazzling smile, embraced Mitch as he came aboard, kissed his cheek. The gesture was too natural to Dias to be embarrassing to Mitch. "Welcome aboard, my friend! How are you this fine evening?"

"Well, Dias, and yourself?"

"*Bueno, bueno!* Come! I have only a few minutes before my plane and I want to show you something."

He handed Mitch the martini, snapped his fingers at Manuel for another, linked his arm with Mitch's, and led his guest below.

In Dias's cabin, Mitch nursed his drink while the Colombian spread wide the mahogany doors of his closest. The interior was lined with a batallion of designer suits and jackets. Dias selected one. He grinned white teeth at Mitch and held it out. "Try this on!"

Mitch set down the drink, pulled off his own jacket, and accepted the other. He stood in front of a full-length mirror and slipped into the jacket, which fit like a dream. He wanted instantly to live in it.

"You like camel hair, I hope?"

"It's beautiful."

"And the fit?"

"Perfect. But look—"

"Ah, *bueno!* I took the liberty of securing the size and length of your own jacket the last time you were on board. I was hoping the tailor would get it right. But then, he should, he's the finest tailor in Paris. Let me see . . . ah, yes, it looks magnificent! You are quite a handsome fellow!"

Mitch turned. "Dias, I can't possibly accept—"

He was looking at his watch. "Please, my friend, do not embarrass me by forcing me to tell you about the drastic discount I received on this beautiful garment. Let us simply say it was one of many favors owed. Wear it in good health! I must leave you now, you will walk me to the rail?"

Topside, the two men strolled to the gangplank, Mitch looking around. "Mrs. Dias isn't aboard tonight?"

Dias handed his empty glass to Manuel. "Mother is in town doing some shopping. She usually gets back late. Mother likes to keep to herself, please consider the boat your own."

The two shook hands.

"And try not to sink her in my absence," Dias grinned, "at least not until I get back to join in the fun!"

Mitch looked down at himself, the jacket. "I'll never be able to repay you . . ."

"Nonsense! It is I who are in your debt for tending to the charming Mrs. Greely!" He clapped Mitch on the shoulder. "*Adios*, my friend, and have a pleasant week!"

Dias snapped his fingers and luggage in tow, his entourage materialized. The dark-haired, olive-eyed Olin was among them. She smiled at Mitch, brushed past closely. The group descended the gangplank to the cab waiting below, Dias's hand on Olin's rounded ass.

"Have a good trip!" Mitch called.

Dias looked over his shoulder, pointed to the steward. "Take good care of our guest, Manuel!"

Mitch waited until the cab was well out of sight,

found Manuel again and told him that he had some business to attend to in town before Mrs. Greely's arrival. If he should somehow be late, please make Mrs. Greely feel at home. The Latino bowed.

It gave Mitch a charge. Wasn't this just a hoot? His very own yacht, his very own mistress, his very own liquor cabinet to raid for an entire weekend! If he ever untangled himself from all this, he must write a book about it.

He went below deck and stood in front of the cabin mirror, admiring the jacket. He felt a little giddy. He couldn't seem to stop smiling at his own foolish face. It would all be so perfect if . . .

If only Joanne hadn't shown up.

He resolutely pushed her pale face from his mind. Not tonight. He'd think about the tangled mess of his life tomorrow, but tonight—tonight might be his last night of true freedom. He was going to enjoy himself.

He came topside again, ordered another martini, ordered another servant to call a cab, and took it to the downtown Santa Barbara Health Club, where Greely had asked he meet him. It was great fun pretending to be rich.

They sat together in the big, frothing Jacuzzi, draining off the sweat from the cedar-walled sauna. Except for Greely and Mitch, this section of the spa was empty, and Mitch had no doubts that his corpulent provider had paid the club's secretary to ensure their privacy. Greely could afford this kind of extravagance.

Mitch watched Greely now, wallowing in surging foam, great bloated body pink as a lobster's, drooping teats large enough to fill a bra. Mitch could imagine the bulbous thighs beneath the cascading water, the great slab of gut, the pink stub of penis all but lost in the burgeoning folds above it. Mitch grimaced. How, even for this man's great wealth, could Claire reconcile herself to this?

But then, she wasn't, was she? She was reconciling herself to Mitch. And anyway, if it came to that, Mitch was as guilty of being a party to Greely as Claire. Cast the first stone. . . .

"I asked to meet you here this evening, Mr. Spencer, because I've found it necessary to terminate our business arrangement."

Mitch started visibly in the hot tub, but Greely didn't see it because his eyes were on the ceiling, head back, resting against the smooth tiled wall.

"I've decided to divorce myself from the dear Mrs. Greely, you see."

Mitch leaned toward him, unable to believe his ears. His heart was hammering and, in the swirling water, sweat running in rivulets, he was suddenly afraid he was going to pass out. "Divorce? Mr. Greely . . . are you sure? I mean, are you sure that's the best thing?"

"Quite sure, my boy. It was not a hasty decision, I assure you. I lost rather a lot of sleep over it. I love Claire more than life itself, you know."

Mitch nodded, stunned. "I thought . . . I mean, I assumed my reports assured you that there was nothing to fear as far as her relationship with Dias."

Greely was silent for a moment. Then he sat up and stared impassively at Mitch. "Yes, I'm aware of that."

Mitch waited, feeling vaguely uncomfortable under the fat man's gaze. "Then, why . . . I mean—"

"I'm convinced—despite your expert undercover work, Mr. Spencer—that Claire can never be happy. She has chosen another path. So. Once a whore, always a whore, as they say."

The word sounded inordinately vulgar when applied to Claire. Mitch lowered his eyes, watched the turbulent bubbles. "You can call anybody a whore, Mr. Greely," he said softly.

Greely grunted, lay his head back. "Please don't worry yourself, my good fellow, I have arranged to have my bank transfer an additional five thousand dollars to your account, and I think I can assure you that the job with All-American is within your grasp again, if you still want it."

Mitch couldn't seem to take his eyes off the swirling water. For the briefest moment he imagined himself being sucked down into it, like a twig in a maelstrom. Sucked down and vanished. Forever. He felt a great, irrevocable emptiness. Sadness.

"Mr. Spencer?" Mitch looked up. "I want to thank you again for your services, for taking time away from your family to perform your task for me. You really can't imagine how comforting it was for me to have you looking after my dear Claire. I shall not forget your participation, your intervention in my life." He held out a chubby hand.

Mitch took it. "I only wish it could have ended on a happier note," he said sincerely.

Greely watched him a moment then smiled cavalierly. "Everything has an end, Mr. Spencer—love, friendships, life. Perhaps it is less important that they begin and end happily, but that some slight instance of contentment was glimpsed along the way. Claire has made me happy in her way. Now it is time for something else. Again, my deepest thanks, dear fellow." Greely squeezed his hand.

A shadow fell over them. Mitch turned to find Max waiting patiently with the fat man's robe.

They were more or less discreet about it.

They weren't, after all, alone on the yacht. There were the servants. A skeleton crew. And Dias's mother, of course.

They waited until supper was over with, until the moon had risen high, and they had engaged in polite conversation at the rail and walked the deck sedately, and the sounds of college kids and partygoers had died down in the marina. They waited until everyone else on the yacht had turned in, and even some time after that. Then, they looked into each other's eyes, kissed each other's cheek, and went to separate beds.

Claire came down to his cabin, not knocking, simply opening the door, stepping in softly. She wore a satin robe.

Mitch sat up in his bunk, started to say something, but was silenced as she raised a slender finger to her lips. She locked the door, came to him, pulled off the robe. She was nude beneath, magnificent in the ethereal light from the single porthole. Mitch reached out breathlessly, but she pushed his hands gently away, kissed him lightly on the forehead. She eased him back on the bunk, kissed his chest once, tugged down his pajama bottoms. She tossed them to the floor and pulled at his naked thighs, nodding sideways.

He didn't know what she wanted. "What—?"

She urged him across the bunk, pulling until he was out of dark shadow, into the perfect shaft of moonlight dividing the bed, the room. She placed his hips directly into it, his skin glowing, and sat back to marvel and smile. After a moment she took hold of him, eyes dancing. "You're beautiful," she whispered, "I knew you would be."

"Claire."

"Shh. Watch me now. I want you to watch."

She brought him to her lips there under the soft yellow eyes of the moon.

He would remember the sight for all the days and all the nights that were left of the rest of his life: her wine-dark lips, bled of all color in the bluish glow; the sunken hollow of her cheeks, like twin, moonlit valleys covered with the finest down; the fattening shaft of him, urgent with reckless need; the etch of her delicate nose, black sweep of eyelash, tangle of tumbled blonde hair.

She looked up at him once, eyes dilated with submission, with pleasure and promise. Can you see?, the eyes seemed to be saying, can you see it all, all that I do? Will you remember it? Now and for always? Does it burn? Burn into your brain? Burn into my mouth? Into our souls? This is my gift, this is how good it can be. This is my tongue, my teeth, my throat . . . this is my warmth, the sacred, searing heart of me. Come for me now, come fill me up, fill me over, fill me through and through . . .

come let me kiss the breath of life from you, suck you into my soul, the furnace of my being. . . .

Mitch gripped the mattress, pushed his head against the bulkhead, and did as he was bid.

Then did the same for her. And more.

Of course, it was the best.

And as assuredly, it had to be the end, the first and last time.

Lying in the musky afterglow of their lovemaking, Mitch knew this with a dreamy certainty that was somehow peaceful.

Something had been lifted away. He seemed to be seeing himself—the two of them—for the very first time, his mind bathed in brilliant clarity. He sensed a vacuous sensation in his stomach, that he had no center, no purchase, no earthly idea what it was he wanted from life. Had never had.

Strangely, it didn't matter.

What he did know—at long, long last—was what he *didn't* want. He didn't want this. Did not want anything this good, this right. No. Anything this right was supposed to be real. This wasn't real enough to last. And if it wasn't going to last, he didn't want another moment of it. Not an instant. It was suddenly terribly, overwhelming important to be honest. Pure. He must hold on to it this time. The whole universe hinged on it. He rolled off her, thinking of his daughter.

Knowing that Claire knew all this, too. They had arrived at more than mutual climax. They had, through the silly twistings of whatever capricious fate that had landed them here, arrived at something at last bigger than themselves.

Wiser than he, even in her youth, Claire was the first to put it to voice: "I love you."

"Claire—"

"No. Don't." She patted his arm. "I know. It's done. Over before it began. I just wanted to be able to remember that I'd said that. I just wanted it to be a part of what we were. Be still. You don't have to say anything. Give me a moment. I'll leave in a moment."

He sat up, sought the porthole with his eyes, saw nothing but the shelf of light, tried to imagine the calming sea beyond. The world beyond that. The cosmos.

Part of what we were.

Then, turning to her, Mitch gave himself to their loss, and told her he loved her, too, by telling her everything.

Afterwards, she sat against the bulkhead, arms wrapped around her nakedness, not really cold, staring into nothing.

For a time, neither spoke.

"So he wants to divorce me," Claire said at length. She said it to walls.

Mitch nodded. "That's what he said."

He shifted uncomfortably, cleared his throat. "You hate me . . . I guess you hate me, right?"

She stared at him.

"I can't tell you how sorry I am, Claire. How sorry I am for everything I've done over the past several weeks. I just wish—"

"Mitch." She reached out and silenced him with a cool hand on his shoulder; in the wonderful light it looked like two pieces of perfectly formed sculpture coming together to form a long sought-after whole. "Please stop," she said. "I don't want to remember us like this. My God, I've mangled everything I've touched. I didn't dwell on it then—when I should have—why dwell on it now?"

She tenderly traced his lips with one finger. "I'm not going to change now because I've suddenly become a good person. I'm going to change because I'm forced to, because he's dumping me."

He touched her cheek. "You are a good person, Claire. A lovely person." She didn't say anything. "Will you be all right?"

She looked at him almost hopefully, then understood. "Oh sure, Franklyn will provide for me. Little Claire will have her money. Jesus . . . I just can't believe he had me followed like that. I never would have guessed it. Shows you really never know someone, no matter what you think."

He sighed. "No, you really never know someone . . . even when that someone is yourself."

She looked at him.

"It's funny," he was saying, with an eerie calm, "one minute you're just loping along through life making the same stupid judgments, same frantic decisions over and over, and then, for seemingly no reason whatsoever, you all of a sudden wake up and everything becomes just impossibly clear. I feel like I'm seeing myself—right here, tonight, this moment—for the first time. I know it sounds corny, like some troubled adolescent suddenly stumbling upon one of the great truths of life, but it's true! That's what I've been doing my whole life, Claire—stumbling. One minute to the next, one job to the next, one decision to the next. Going nowhere. Running after the big house, the big car, the big status. Lying to everyone, lying to myself. Desperate. Getting in deeper and deeper and all for some stupid job, some stupid life I didn't even want. Doing it all for a fancy house in the 'burbs and never once thinking about who was living in that house." He shook his head. "Wondering deep down inside all the while why I wasn't happy. What was missing."

He sighed, smoothed back a lock of her hair. "You know the last time I was really happy, Claire? Walking a beat at two hundred bucks a week. Doing what I was good at. I don't think I ever realized how precious that is, finding something you're good at." He waved his hand at the air. "I'm not good at this. I'm just not."

Claire leaned back, jutted her chin at the ceiling. "Know the last time I was really happy? Having tutti-frutti ice cream with my Uncle Joe. Knowing he loved me more than anything." She smiled wistfully. "Now why couldn't it just have gone on like that?"

Mitch moved closer. "Listen, about Dias—"

"Don't worry."

"I do worry. He's a dangerous man."

"Mitch, he wanted to fuck me, not murder me. I'm nothing to him, but a piece of rich American tail. He likes to stand stud with what he views as the Southern California elite." She supressed a rueful laugh. "He's the only naïve one in this deceitful game."

Mitch looked unconvinced. "Poor Mitch. He finally finds the meaning of life and now he's too gallant to go off and pursue it and leave his mistress to the wolves!" She patted his knee. "Don't worry, I'll be all right." She pecked his lips once. "I have family back east I owe a visit anyway. I'll live. I'm lucky. I have nothing. It's you who's stuck with a future. Are you going to tell Joanne?"

"I don't know . . ."

"Do you love her?"

"I think so."

"Then lie."

He looked up. She was smiling. He smiled back.

"It would have been nice," he said.

She cupped his cheek. "It was nice. Thank you."

"Thank you."

They dressed in silence.

Ten minutes later, he woke Manuel to tell him he'd had a change of plans, had to leave. Then he grabbed his new jacket, his only souvenir of his adventures, hoisted his creaking suitcase, walked down the gangplank, and left her behind on the yacht.

It was a lovely night, free of fog, rife with stars. The stars, he thought distractedly, walking to his faithful Porsche, hadn't changed through any of this. There was something wonderfully comforting in that, both prosaic and profound.

At his car, he paused for just a moment, key in hand, to watch the booming surf lap caressingly at the breast of Laredo Beach.

CHAPTER 23

GAYLORD

O FFICER RANDALL GAYLORD HAD BECOME A COP largely due to his name.

In his youth, at the Montessori School in Burbank, he had loved his name. In those days, the early sixties, the homosexual populace had not yet sufficently insinuated itself on the public's consciousness to displace totally the definition of the word "gay." And, though nothing in his background warranted it, Randall had always thought of himself as aristocratic; hence, the "lord" part fit in just swell. Nothing could be finer, to his young eyes, than to be thought of as a happy lord. Many people with the name King were successful in life, he had read, for that very reason: their name gave them subliminal kind of inner confidence. That was good enough for Randall.

This all changed in high school.

Clearly, among the rougher boys, the more pedestrian setting—his grades were not good enough to prep him—he was in no way a lord. With his slight build, flaxen hair, gentle manner, and pampered demeanor, he might, however, have qualified as gay. At least to the boys at Burbank High.

In horror of this, Randall had begun to hang out with the rougher crowd. He got beat up a lot. In horror of that, he began to hang out with Delbert Shondheim, whose dad was a cop. It was deemed unwise to pick on Delbert or Delbert's friends.

This worked so well that Randall Gaylord decided to simplify matters when he grew up and actually become a cop. To this end, he slugged his way through high school, put up with two grueling years of the navy, moved to Santa Barbara where the rents were high but the crime was manageably low, and joined the local gendarmes.

He wasn't a very good cop, in many ways. Too slight, too falsetto-voiced to be truly commanding, too short-winded to operate successfully outside the limitation of a squad car, and not inordinately bright.

But he persevered, countering his deficiencies by exercising a proper attitude, always being extremely easy to please, obsequiously cooperative, following orders to a T. It didn't get him very far in grade, but on the other hand—with the snappy uniform and that big iron on his hip—it didn't get him picked on either. He was content enough.

Which was why he was so elated when the Big Night finally came along—the long awaited night when he became involved with something so big, so important to his career, that everyone had to sit up and take notice.

It was the opportunity of a lifetime, and Randall Gaylord was there and ready when the call came through.

He had just been thinking about taking another doughnut break. He'd just had one an hour before, but it was late, and there wasn't anything happening, and nothing was open but 7-11s and all-night doughnut shops and he did have a sweet tooth for those caramel long johns at Winchell's. Besides, he had a theory that doughnuts would eventually put weight on him.

When the foreign car swung into view, he made the license number, put in the requisite call to headquarters, flipped on the flashing party hat, and eased in behind.

The fancy car slowed, nosed to the curb, cut its engine.

Officer Randall Gaylord unsnapped the leather holster guard on his .45 service revolver, grabbed his ticket book, and climbed out.

It was a very dark night, you could see all the stars.

Gaylord approached the car on the driver's side, hands at his sides, gun hand free, eyes on the darkened figure inside the vehicle. He was at that moment gifted with supersensory detection, every sensation heightened: the crisp sound of his shoes on the dark pavement, the jingle of the cuffs at his belt, the metallic rattle of his mace can, the distant, booming surf of Laredo Beach . . . the steady thundering chug of his heart.

He approached the driver's window and cleared his throat, down deep for his much practiced command voice. "Good evening, sir."

"Officer. What can I do for you?"

"May I see your driver's license please?"

"Certainly. Is there a problem?"

"Your license, please." He unbuckled his flashlight and let the cone of light play across the piece of pasteboard proffered him. Date: valid.

He handed it back.

"May I ask where you're coming from, sir?"

Pause.

"Well, from the marina, actually."

"Uh-huh. Own a boat there, sir?" I'm doing this very well, Randall Gaylord thought.

Pause.

"Not exactly."

"Sir?"

"I was . . . visiting friends."

"Uh-huh. Would that be the Dias yacht, sir?"

Pause.

"Yes, as a matter of fact."

"Uh-huh. Sir, I wonder if you'd mind stepping out of the car for a moment."

"What's the trouble?"

"No trouble, sir, just step out if you would, please."

Pause.

"All right."

This is it, thought Randall, this is where the gun comes over the edge of window frame and blows out my life. Please don't let there be a gun, not yet. His hand flickered above his own holstered weapon.

The man in the car got out.

"Would you open the trunk, please?"

The man had an obtuse expression. "What on earth for?"

"Sir, I'm afraid we've noticed a lot of drug traffic coming from the Dias yacht. Now, if you have nothing to hide, and if you'll cooperate, everything will be just fine and I'll send you on your way."

Randall gestured toward the trunk. The man hesitated a moment, sighed, walked around, bent and fitted the key. The trunk held nothing suspicious.

"Now the glove compartment, please."

"Really—"

"Please."

The man shrugged resignation, walked to the passenger's side, opened the dash compartment. Randall played his light inside. Maps. Pencils. A coffee cup.

"Almost through, sir. Please empty the contents of your pockets onto the hood of the automobile, pockets first."

"This is fucking ridiculous!" But he did as he was told.

"Fine. Now the jacket pockets, please."

The man laid his wallet on the hood, patted at his chest, seemed to pause, frown slightly.

"Is that all, sir?"

"I believe so, yes."

"You hesitated."

The man said nothing.

Randall Gaylord reached out and pulled back the flap of jacket, exposing the lining, the vague bulge of the inner pocket. "Would you remove that, too, please?"

The man reached inside and produced the small manila envelope. It was blank, front and back. It was sealed.

"May I ask what's inside, sir?"

Pause. "Just . . . some business papers, I guess."

"You guess? Would you open the envelope, please."

I'm really doing this very well indeed, Randall Gaylord thought.

The man seemed to open the envelope without hesitation.

Randall took it from him, shook the contents into his hand, braced for a deluge of white powder, unprepared for the photographs spilling out.

Very unprepared.

"Jesus Mary Mother of God . . ."

Randall Gaylord dropped the envelope, grabbed for the photos, dropped the photos, grabbed for his gun, dropped his gun, grabbed for his cuffs, got the cuffs, picked up his gun, dropped the cuffs, pointed the gun.

"You're under arrest! You're under fucking arrest!" Command voice gone, sounding like a squeaking adolescent.

He picked up the cuffs, dropped the gun again, grabbed it again, grabbed the suspect, and whirled him around, slammed him against the fancy European car with all his might, the suspect apparently too surprised and startled to resist much.

Randall Gaylord kept switching the cuffs and the gun back and forth from one hand to the other, finally frustratedly jammed the revolver into his belt, snapped the cuffs around the suspect's wrists, pulled forth the gun again, fumbled out his Miranda card, and began sputtering the suspect's rights. "Y-You have the r-right to r-remain silent—" thinking all the while, I'm doing this right, I'm really doing this whole thing really well!

Randall sputtered on and on as the suspect, unresisting, blanching with a disbelief, pressed against the shiny wheel well of the sports car, eyes wide with confusion and fear.

On the ground abut their feet, the scattered visages of Mrs. Charlotte Cunningham and Mrs. Eleanor Rankin stared up curiously at them from a tangle of twisted limbs and tattered, bloodied privates.

CHAPTER 24

TULLY

DETECTIVE SERGEANT EUSTES TULLY SAT IN THE Spartan hospital room, sprawled in an uncomfortably cushioned straight-back chair, heavy-lidded eyes staring at the silent figure flattened with tubes and wires.

He was thinking not so much of Sergeant Rene Draper but of a dark-haired girl on a cold white morgue table long ago in San Francisco. The two women were not strikingly similar physically, but something about their situations, their helplessness was congruent.

Detective Sergeant Eustes Tully was thinking these thoughts with a kind of sick hopelessness, because he was realizing for the first time that Fred Wanamaker's wife, Ellen, had been wrong: Tully hadn't been in love with the dark-haired woman in the morgue all these years because he couldn't bring her home to mother . . . he had been in love with her for the same reason he was falling in love with this poor, battered, comatose creature on the sterile sheets . . . because she was safe. Because she couldn't talk back. Couldn't even see him.

Couldn't reject him.

That's why he had never married, would never marry.

He was terrified of the live ones.

And he was terrified to find this out.

But there it was.

It was a sickening revelation. He was like those guys down on Manchester Street who hung around the dirty book stores, brought home their "date" for the evening, and sat in the bathroom with a magazine in one hand and their manhood in the other.

Only he was worse. At least those guys jerked off to a fantasy. There was a realness attached to Detective Tully's dreams ... there was a name for guys like him, for the kind of things he thought about. ...

He squinted, pinched at the bridge of his nose, pinched off the train of thought. Then he opened his eyes and sighed at the ceiling. Maybe he was just tired. Just disgusted with this case, disgusted with himself for it having beaten him. Okay, so he hadn't found the right girl in life yet, so was that a crime? Did that make him a pervert?

At his age it didn't exactly make him normal.

He sat up in the uncomfortable chair—did they deliberately put these chairs in here to shorten visiting hours?—hunched forward and stared down at his shoes, which could stand a shine. He should be home in bed, but he knew he wouldn't sleep. He was close. He was so close. But he couldn't prove a thing and he couldn't quite get the last few pieces to fit.

This was the worst time. This was when the air became rarefied and everything took on rushing urgency and things began to fall together very fast, so fast that if you weren't quick enough, if you took a sudden wrong turn, someone would get there ahead of you, someone else would take the credit. Or—worse yet— someone else would die because you couldn't find the handle quite soon enough. That would be the worst of all: being this close, this near to the end, only to have the killer strike one more time. Tully wasn't sure he could take that.

But hell, he guessed he could.

He looked over at the silent form, the utilitarian hospital bed, the whisper of tubal breathing, the mechanically induced rise of her chest, the network of tubes.

She isn't going to make it, an inner voice warned; she could tell us everything, end the case in an instant, and she isn't going to make it. You got so you could sense these things, better even maybe than the doctors.

So close.

Tully grunted, shook his head.

He had searched through all the back files, of course, now certain, in his own mind, that the killer's father was a cop. It should have been relatively easy to find out which cops had children of the appropriate age during that time period, see if anything out of the ordinary turned up—a sudden retirement, an abrupt move to another city, a divorce; or the more obvious—a suspension, a wife beating, a felony; or better yet, a file, photos and names pointing up the whole heinous case—the cop, his sicko wife, his abused offspring, how the suspects were arraigned and tried.

But he'd found nothing. Hadn't really expected to. If such a file ever existed it would have been spirited away or burned as neatly as a spool of microfilm. But who had done the disposing? The cop in question, or had it gone even higher than that? had the department been trying to protect one of its own? Had they put pressure on the local papers to play down such a potentially disastrous scandal? Were people coerced, paid off? It was, after all, the 1950s, the decade of racial prejudice, Big Dave Beck, and a somnambulent public; such things were easier to accomplish in those pre-Watergate days.

Tully stood, stretched.

Or it could be that his cop theory was all wet and

he was no closer now than he had ever been. It could be that he was getting old and tired and too slow for this shit.

Damn.

You never knew. As long as it was all theory, you never knew. Not until the fat lady sings.

He looked at the window, the black opaqueness of the four blind panes. Where are you, you bastard? What are you doing with your nail-studded dock walloper tonight? Are you going to slip up again? Is the next one going to get away with both her mind and her snatch intact?

His pager trilled. He went to the nurses' station to call.

"Yeah."

"This is Olson, the desk sergeant, you asleep?"

"No, Olson, what's up?"

"Looks like we got our killer is what's up. Officer Gaylord just brought in a collar with a pocketful of Kodaks you don't see in the average family album—four-by-five glossies of the late Mrs. Cunningham and the late Mrs. Rankin. They weren't smiling."

Tully's heart found his throat. "Jesus Christ! He's at the station now?"

"In the flesh, all tucked away and secured in a nice comfy cell."

Tully started to say he'd be right there, then remembered. "Have you called Brumeister? He's heading up the case now."

"Yeah, I know, Tully, I know how you got screwed. Brumeister's on his way down. But this guy keeps asking for you, says he doesn't want a lawyer, doesn't want to talk to anyone, just you."

"Why me? What's his name?"

"Says he knew you from academy days—guy named Mitch Spencer."

Tully blinked.

"Tully, you there?"

"Thanks, Olson, I'll be right down."

"Good. Oh, and Detective—we could use a little

252

sugar around here for the late-night coffee, know what I mean?"

"I hear you. And thanks again, Olson, for the page."

He drove unhurriedly.

There was no point in beating Bruemister to the suspect, the latter had jurisdiction, he'd just shunt Tully aside, cause a scene, and hold things up. No, let Brumeister get in there first, muck around, fuss and fume and get nowhere. Mitch Spencer was a cop—or had been a cop—if he said he'd talk only to Tully that's what he meant.

Mitch Spencer: a chill found Tully's back.

He was thankful, though, that Olson had called him; it showed the department was behind him, not Brumeister, that they understood just how shafted he'd been. It made him feel warm inside, touched nearly to tears.

He parked in the police lot in the slot in front of his name and locked up. Inside, he went straight to Olson.

"Is he here?"

"Brumeister? Yeah, about ten minutes ago. He doesn't look happy"—Olson winked—"I think he was with one of his whores when I phoned. Caught his pecker in his zipper, what there is of it. He won't be there long."

Tully grinned. "What about Captain Sparrs?"

"Tried his home, maid says he's at a party, didn't leave a forwarding message. The way I see it, I tried."

"Right. How about some coffee while I wait?"

Olson beamed. "You bet! You bring any sugar to help it?"

Tully patted his jacket front. "Right here."

The desk sergeant stood up to get the coffee. "Guess you'll want to see these."

He handed Tully the photos.

Brumeister came down the hall half an hour later, face red, shirttail hanging loose, head wreathed in cigar smoke. He looked as though he'd come from bed, all right. Tully lowered his styrofoam cup.

"He wants to see you," Brumeister huffed, eyeing Tully up and down.

"All right," Tully replied calmly.

Brumeister blew rank smoke. "What's this all about? You know this guy? You got information we should know about?"

"Not yet I don't."

Brumeister nodded, suspicious. "Okay, then. He wants to see you alone. Fine. We'll play it his way for now. But know this, Tully—his ass is grass, and I'm the lawnmower now. Me, understand?"

"Whatever you say, William."

Brumeister nodded. "I'll be at my home if you need me. Call if you get anything." He looked up at Olson. "You get ahold of Captain Sparrs yet?"

"Can't reach him, sir."

Brumeister blew smoke. Looked Tully up and down again. Shouldered his way toward the front door.

Tully filled another cup with coffee, sweetened it with the jacket flask, and took both cups down the hall to the lock-up.

The duty officer recognized him immediately and unlocked the cell door. Mitch Spencer was curled against the far wall on his bunk, arms wrapped around his knees, shadows wrapped around that, head down. He looked up at the clank of the key, eyes like a hunted animal's.

Tully walked inside and handed him the coffee.

Mitch took it. "I'll only talk to you . . ."

Tully turned to the duty officer, locked eyes with him, and he left them alone.

Tully leaned against the bars. It didn't look good and both men knew it. The photos would be dusted, but that was purely academic: Mitch had been apprehended in possession. It wasn't exactly a nail in his coffin yet, but it was certainly justification for burial arrangements.

Tully felt relieved and deflated. Some part of him— he'd just discovered—had held out the hope that it wasn't a cop. That it turned out to be a cop he knew was hideous.

"Before you get started, Mitch, I want you to know there's a limit to what I can do. The physical evidence is bad enough, but we've suspected a cop for some time. I can protect your family to some extent, at least spare them the trauma of a treasure hunt in your own living room, but you've got to level with me about the where-abouts of the weapon first—"

"Tully, for chrissake! Do you believe I did it? Are you guys that hard up for a suspect?"

Tully watched him. The face. Okay, this guy was an ex-cop—knew the ropes—but you can often see through an act, especially in the initial stages of interrogation before things got redundant, rehearsed; this face was pale with shock, hollow with fear, but not deceitful. Not in a way that Tully could see, anyway. Still . . . they'd waited so long. And the evidence . . . he had to play this one carefully. He had to be right. For all their sakes. Tully hadn't wanted it to end like this, he'd wanted to make the collar himself, personally. He'd wanted the frig-ging promotion. But he musn't let that fact color his judgment, sway him from the truth. He might be a burnt-out old pervert who dreamed of sexy corpses, but by God he was an honest cop.

"Yes," Tully admitted, "we're that hard up. What have you got to tell me, Mitch?"

Mitch hugged his knees, rocked absently. "I'm being framed," he replied simply. And with what seemed like conviction.

Tully sipped coffee patiently. Take it slow. Listen. Maybe Brumeister isn't a hero yet. "All right. I'm listening."

"It's a long story. It involves your pal Dias."

Tully felt the bourbon-laced coffee freeze in his throat; he showed no sign of it, took another sip. "Go on."

Mitch drew a long breath and told him.

He told him of the fishing trip to Big Piney Lake, of getting the ax at All-American, of his frustration, his fear, his suicidal thoughts; of Greely's wife, Claire, and the skiing accident, of meeting Franklyn Greely on the lake. Of Dias. Of Greely paying him to go on meeting with Dias, spying on Claire.

He told him of his taking money from Greely. He told him of Joanne, her pregnancy, of their little girl Nellie. He told him of his fear of going on, his greater fear of stopping—like an addict who gets in deeper and deeper until he can't see the top anymore. He told about falling in love with Claire, of hating himself, of feeling lost, of being swept away in it all and not knowing what to grasp on to, how to make it stop. He told him all of it, every detail of it, holding back nothing, knowing just exactly how much on the line his ass was. And then he told him about tonight, about Joanne on the dock, about Dias giving him the fancy jacket, a jacket that—according to Mitch—was already loaded with incriminating photos. He told him of leaving the yacht, getting in his car, watching the waves on Laredo Beach, and Officer Randall Gaylord's black-and-white swooping up behind him.

Tully listened. Watched the other's man's face. Drank his coffee and said nothing. He found himself so deep in it, he didn't realize the other man was through, was looking up at him with, sunken, imploring eyes.

"Well?"

Tully smacked his lips, decided to play it straight; there was no rush. "Sounds pretty neat."

Mitch looked up at him. "What does that mean?"

"That means," Tully said, crossing his arms authoritatively, "that it sounds like a terrific alibi. It also sounds pretty goddamn incredible."

Mitch watched him a moment, then nodded and turned away. "Yeah." He leaned back against the cold wall, let his arms hang lifelessly at his sides. "I realized that as I was telling it. Christ, I've realized it for weeks."

Tully set his cup on the upper bunk, began pacing the narrow cell. "That's not necessarily a bad thing . . ."

Mitch looked hopeful.

" . . . not from my standpoint, anyway. I don't think

you'd convince a jury with it, but on the other hand it's pretty far-out. You could have thought of a simpler alibi. It's crazy enough to be the truth."

"It is the truth."

"That's for your attorney to decide."

"It will be too late then, Tully."

"What do you mean?"

"For Joanne, for Nellie. It's bad enough I lied to them, cheated them—and now this!"

"Well, I'm sorry about that."

"And too late for you, Tully." Tully looked surprised. "I'm the wrong guy, Tully. I think you know that in your heart. But only two people know it for sure—me and the right guy. When the right guy finds out about this he'll stop killing, long enough for me to get the chair. Then he'll start in again. Gloating, laughing, making a fool of the Santa Barbara Sheriff's Department. And you'll have missed your chance. An innocent man will be dead, and the guilty one will get away."

Tully shrugged. "Maybe. But we'll still get him. True, it wouldn't help you much, but if Dias is our man, we'd nail him."

"Not in South America, you won't. I'll bet he's made plans to leave already. He knows where I am, who I'm talking to."

Tully leaned against the wall casually, mind racing. "So if that's the case, what can we do? He's gone and your ass is fried."

"Get down to that marina. If Dias planted the photos in that jacket he gave me, then he had no intention of going to L.A. He's probably waiting for a call from one of his protegés informing him of my capture. Then he'll skip back aboard, weigh anchor, and it will be snow parties and sweet whiskey all the way back to Colombia."

Tully thought about it. "Pretty sketchy. Why does Dias give you the yacht for the whole week? Why not figure some less elaborate way to slip you the photos?"

"Easy. He wants to put his own alibi in motion, make sure an entire host of witnesses can give testimony to his absence, including the reputable Mrs. Greely. Can't you see, Tully? He was setting me up from the start. That's why he let me get close to Claire. He had better use for me—as a scapegoat."

Tully grunted. "Maybe. But why now? Why this particular moment in time. Why tonight?"

Mitch made an indifferent gesture. "Who knows? Maybe whatever business he had in Southern California reached its conclusion. Maybe he thought the heat was closing in. Hell, you yourself were trying to get on the yacht!"

Tully snatched up his spiked coffee, shook his head. "It doesn't play, Mitch—why use a scapegoat at all? We weren't close to him. The department has Bruemister chasing his own ass around Laredo Beach. We were weeks, maybe months away from nailing Dias for this."

"Dias doesn't know that! Besides, if you nailed him on a drug charge, one thing might lead to another with a little digging. I'm telling you he got scared. And if you don't nail him now, he'll be off to continue his escapades in some other country."

Tully drank, considered.

"Tully, look, you knew me at the academy—"

Tully held up a stifling hand. "I knew you hardly at all at the academy. Much less thoroughly than I know you now."

Mitch paled.

"Yeah, I ran a profile on you ... why you left the force, that whole incident with the whore, the bludgeoning with the nightstick, which, just coincidentally, happens to be the same weapon we suspect our killer's been using. Hell, by your own admission you're an out-of-work, anxiety-ridden, desperate man. You cheat on your wife, you don't have the balls to be a decent father, you run around with a murderous drug dealer! Christ, man, you're hardly a defense attorney's wet dream."

Mitch buried his face in his hands. "I know that! I know I've made mistakes—" His voice broke.

Tully watched the trembling shoulders, the shadow-cloaked back. "Lie down with dogs, Mitch ..." Tully murmured.

Mitch sobbed, slow wracking spasms that shook his whole frame.

Tully let him do it for a while.

Then he picked up his empty office cup, walked out of the cell, and shut the door behind him with a clank.

He didn't tell Mitch where he was going or why: he was putting the pressure on. It was dirty pool, but he had to be sure.

He walked down the hall to the front desk to refill his cup. Olson looked down at him from behind the scarred oak. "Any luck?"

Tully shrugged. "At least he's talking."

Olson grunted. "They all talk sooner or later." He held out his own cup.

Tully spiked it from the flask. "I could get arrested for this."

"In a police station?" Olson grinned. "Nah!" He gulped greedily.

The two men looked up as a skinny man in uniform came through the swinging doors.

"If it isn't the recently famous Graveyard Gaylord!" Olson exclaimed. "Make another headline arrest, Randall?"

Officer Gaylord was jerking down his tie wearily. He seemed to be walking a little differently tonight; maybe it was a strut. "The only thing I want to get handcuffed to right now is a nice soft bed. I'm punching out, men."

Bemused, Tully leaned against the desk, stuck his hand out to the skinny frame. "Nice work, Gaylord."

Gaylord took it proudly. "Thanks, sir. All in the line of duty."

"Put another stripe on that sleeve, I'll wager."

"Hey, I'll take it! And the money, too!"

Olson and Tully laughed politely.

Gaylord nodded toward the lock-up. "Talked to him yet, sir?"

Tully nodded back.

Gaylord smugly narrowed his eyes, rocked confidently on his heels. "We've had an eye on this monkey for a long time," he drawled in his best tough-cop voice. He hooked a thumb in his Sam Browne belt, effected a stance. "Bastard was running back and forth to the Dias yacht, you know."

"Yeah."

"So when the captain put out the word, I had no trouble spotting his tail."

Tully swallowed coffee. "Sparrs put a pick-up out on Spencer?"

Gaylord grunted affirmation. "Got himself a big fancy red Porsche, this guy Spencer. Fast car. But I got him, all right. He won't be driving it so fast now." He took the coffee out of Olson's hand and downed a jolt, made a pained face. "Jeez, this stuff is bitter! Better brew a fresh pot!" He slapped his holster loudly. "Well, see you fellas in the funny papers, I'm off duty!"

Officer Gaylord swaggered toward the lockers.

Detective Tully watched him for a moment, winked at Olson, then headed back down the hall to the lock-up.

Mitch looked up when the door clanked open again.

Tully tossed him his jacket, sans photos. Mitch caught it with one hand. "What's up?"

"Put it on, we're going for a ride."

Mitch stood, shrugged into the coat. "Quick tour of death row?"

"Quick tour of your pal's yacht. Come on."

The duty officer looked at Tully cryptically as they passed through the bars. "You'll have to sign the prisoner out with the desk sergeant, sir."

"Yeah, I'll do that," Tully muttered, cuffing his wrist to Mitch Spencer's.

In the squad car, Tully cuffed Mitch to the door handle.

"It's early in the game," he said, swinging down darkened streets, light with early morning traffic, "no one will know you've been arrested. When we get to the marina, I'm a friend of yours from school who always wanted to see a real yacht."

Mitch was savoring the rush of wind in his hair, the smell of the night. After the closeness of the cell it was euphoric. "I told the crew I was leaving town."

"You changed your mind."

They arrived at the marina fifteen minutes later.

Tully unsnapped the cuffs. "Stay close. Make a break now and it's my ass," he muttered. "But, innocent or not, it will really be the end of you."

"I'm not a fool," Mitch replied.

"I'm counting on that. This probably means my job."

They walked down the boardwalk. Flanked on both sides by towering masts, gleaming decks, softly winking lights, Tully tried to imagine what lay beyond the silent hulls, the creaking rigging of those vessels whose portholes glowed yellow. Land of the rich, the high rollers, bronzed bodies, and fat wallets. Did one of these sleek crafts harbor a psychopath? Or had the psychopath already been found?

Mitch paused before a floating penthouse. A dark, muscled Hispanic man in a tight, immaculately white tee-shirt stood expansively before the gangplank, massive arms folded. He wore trim white slacks, matching deck shoes, and the impassive face of a bulldog.

When the man made no attempt to move aside, Mitch attempted formal politeness: "I'm a guest of Mr. Dias."

The tiny black eyes looked somewhere beyond them. "No one allowed on board." Heavy with accent and finality.

Mitch exchanged glances with Tully. He cleared his throat, tried again. "I was staying on board tonight. This is Mr. Johnson, a friend of mine. Mr. Dias left instructions that my wishes be obeyed."

"No one allowed on board tonight."

Mitch pulled himself up, started to say something else but Tully tugged him aside. "Forget it. It's all the

English he knows. We're not getting anywhere tonight without a warrant. Let's get out of here."

They walked back to the car.

Tully leaned against it, arms folded. There was a nice breeze and he loved the smell of the ocean. Some people didn't. It was true there was something fishy in it, almost musky. Tully didn't care, it smelled alive to him.

"At least he hasn't taken off yet," Mitch offered.

Tully was watching the waves on Laredo Beach. He was thinking that if he had his one wish in the world right now it would be to get into that big yacht down at the harbor and just sail off away from all this ... sail and sail until he came to the edge of the world and then sail right off that.

"I want you to tell me the truth, Mitch. Were you on that goddamn yacht tonight, or not?"

"Yes! I was going to spend the night there!"

"Then why didn't you?"

"I told you! Claire and I ... we reached a sort of understanding. I wanted to be free of all this. I just wanted to go home to my wife and kid. I ended up getting picked up by the police for my efforts."

Tully watched the sea. "Would Claire corroborate all this?"

Mitch hesitated, nodded. "She would. Of course she would, if she knew I was in trouble."

Tully turned to him. "Even in front of her husband?"

Mitch licked his lips. "Is ... that necessary?"

Tully pushed away from the car. "Look, it's late, but it's getting later. We can wait until tomorrow to get ahold of Mrs. Greely, but by then this is going to be in the papers and out of my hands. Your wife and kid may not be there anymore to go home to. If you want to try clearing yourself, the sooner the better."

Mitch nodded rapidly. "All right, you're right. Let's go see the Greelys."

"Where do they live?"

Mitch thought a minute. "I don't know, all I've got

is a phone number. We'll have to find a phone book, I guess." He looked confused.

Tully grunted irritably, jerked open the door. "For both our sakes," he grumbled, "this damn well better lead to something."

They arrived at the Greely mansion just after one A.M.

Mitch's heart was thundering so violently against his ribs during the long walk up the flagstone path, he thought surely it would shake something loose inside. Detective Tully had uncuffed him again, but he still felt an icy dread dragging at him, turning his legs to rubber.

He wasn't sure who he feared seeing most, Claire or Mr. Greely. Either way it would be terrible. But not as terrible as the alternative.

Tully strode past the big Georgian columns and lifted the huge brass knocker. He let it fall three times.

For one awful moment Mitch entertained the idea that no one was home, that Claire had talked to her husband, that she had moved out this evening, and Greely had taken a plane out of town.

But now interior lights were winking on, and there was movement behind the door. After a moment, it rattled, shushed open with a rush of cool evening air.

"Mr. Greely?" Tully inquired.

"I'm Franklyn Greely." Red-eyed, puffy with sleep, bundled in a silken bathrobe.

"Sorry to disturb you at this hour, sir." Tully flipped open his shield case. "Detective Tully, Santa Barbara Sheriff's Department, may we have a few words with you?"

Greely's face grew tight. He didn't seem to notice Mitch. "Is it Claire? Is something wrong?"

"Nothing like that, sir. May we come in for just a minute?"

Greely's eyes, fully alert now, rocketed between the two men. Then he stepped back. "Of course, come in!"

263

"Thank you."

Tully looked around the expansive foyer: hanging tapestry, gilt-framed oil originals, flanking suits of armor—even more opulent than he would have guessed. A porcelain fountain laughed happily at the center of a sunken, limestone court; plush, eighteenth-century French furniture attended—originals, no doubt.

Tully took it all in.

Mitch gaped blankly at Greely.

"What is it, officers?"

Tully quit ruminating and turned back to him. "Mrs. Greely isn't home this evening, sir?"

"My wife is out. Can I be of assistance?"

Tully indicated Mitch. "You know this man, Mr. Greely?"

Greely, a pot-bellied, but hardly obese, middle-aged man, appraised Mitch carefully. Shook his head. "I don't believe so. Is he a detective, too?"

Tully stared at Mitch. Mitch shook his head. "It isn't him, Tully."

Tully turned back to Greely. "You are Franklyn Greely? Your wife is Claire Greely? This is your home?"

Greely frowned. "Of course!"

Tully nodded. He turned, snapped his fingers at Mitch. Mitch hesitated, puzzled, then got it and fished in his jacket, producing a notebook. He opened it and handed it to Tully. "Is this your phone number, sir?"

Greely looked at the book. "Yes, that's my office number. What's this all about, Detective?"

Tully took back the book. "Maybe you'd better ask Mr. Spencer, here."

Mitch was staring at something across the room.

He walked across the wide courtyard and stopped beneath a large gold-framed oil hanging above them. It was a portrait: sweeping gold hair, pale blue eyes, slender throat embraced by pearls. "This is your wife, Mr. Greely?"

Greely nodded. "That's Claire, yes. Lovely, isn't she?"

Mitch turned to Tully. Nodded.

Tully sighed, then addressed Greely: "Sir, do you know where your wife might be found tonight? I'm afraid it's rather important we ask her some questions."

Greely turned away, his face pinched. "My wife's time is her own. I assume she's having drinks with friends somewhere. I don't keep a leash on her. Would you gentlemen care for some brandy?"

"No, thank you. Would you have some idea when she might return home?"

Franklyn Greely had opened an antique mahogany cabinet, was pouring himself a shot from a cut glass decanter. "Not the slightest. Tonight, perhaps. Next week perhaps. Her time is her own, as I said. This is an excellent vintage, gentlemen."

"You wouldn't have a number we might reach her at?" Mitch put in.

Greely shrugged his back to them. "I might. But I really wouldn't know where to begin. Especially this late at night. My wife has a lot of friends, both male and female. A rather gay group. I seldom find myself able to maintain those kinds of hours. I'm a working man, you see." He knocked back the brandy, faced them again. "I suggest you try again tomorrow morning. She dislikes being awakened early after one of her late-night revels, but—assuming she comes home at all—it might do her good." He stopped, seemed to consider for a moment. "Of course, she could be visiting her Uncle Joe. He's my partner, you know. Joseph Wallace. He . . . introduced us . . ." He wrote down a number on a slip of yellow paper, his face a bitter mask. He handed the paper to Tully. "That's the best I can do . . ."

Tully cleared his throat, finding all this more than a little uncomfortable. "Yes. Well, thank you for your time, Mr. Greely. Sorry to disturb you, sir."

At the door, Greely called after them. "If you do find my wife, gentlemen, try to get some black coffee into her before you send her home, will you?"

They walked in silence down the flagstone path.

At the car, Tully reached for the cuffs.

"You don't believe me, do you, Tully? You don't believe any of this shit."

Tully snapped the cuffs in place. "Look. You can't get back aboard a yacht where you supposedly had carte blanche, you suddenly don't recognize a man you've been accepting money from for weeks, the man's wife's portrait you do recognize but she's conveniently not home tonight. I'm not calling you a liar, Mitch, but I'm about out of ideas and my feet are killing me."

"Someone's running around impersonating Franklyn Greely! Someone who paid a lot of money to have Claire's every move watched! Doesn't that alarm you the least little bit?"

Tully opened the car door for him. "It might, if I could be sure it was the truth. But so far, pal, you've got a lot going against you and not very much going the other way."

He secured Mitch to the handle, shut the door, walked around the car, and slid in behind the wheel, twisting the ignition. He sat for a moment in the softly shuddering vehicle, then turned to the other man. "It's going on two in the morning. I did all I could for you, Mitch. I think it's time you got hold of your lawyer. It's going to get sticky after this. I'm sorry."

Mitch said nothing, turned and studied the black ribbon of road ahead.

CHAPTER 25

MITCH

*H*ALFWAY BACK TO THE STATION, TULLY PULLED THE car to the curb. He sat there quietly a moment with the motor idling.

"What are we doing?" Mitch inquired solemnly.

Tully was staring out the windshield at the lonely, empty streets. He sensed his tiredness, but his mind felt clear, unusually agile. It didn't seem to want to quit yet. "All right, last chance. Tell it to me again, from the top."

Mitch sighed exhaustion. "I already did—everything. Every detail."

"You're sure about that?"

Mitch sat thinking.

A street cleaning truck chugged past, spraying water, rumbling by in a brief wall of a sound.

"Look," Tully announced, "I was at the hospital all evening, didn't get supper. You hungry?"

Mitch shrugged. "I could go for some coffee."

Tully pulled back into the traffic lane, gunned the

engine. "Let's find a Denny's. Maybe we can get ahold of this Uncle Joe character . . ."

After the waitress took their orders and picked up their menus, Tully looked both ways across the restaurant, leaned across, took Mitch's wrist, and cuffed him to a leg of the table.

"Hey! In here?"

"Have to make pee-pee. Sit tight."

"Christ."

Tully left the table, walked back to the johns, put a quarter in the pay phone and dialed a number.

Dead asleep voice: "This better be good . . ."

"It is. Wake yourself up, Fred."

"Wait a sec. Okay. Go."

"I now have in my not-so-legal custody one Mitchell Spencer, former cop and current murder suspect."

"Jesus, not our Laredo Beach boy?"

"Recently confirmed in everyone's eyes but my own. Get a pencil and paper, it gets intriguing."

"What's up?"

"It's inner-departmental, all right, but not in the way we thought, Fred. Are you listening, 'cause this is all still theory."

"I'm listening! Go!"

"I'm not too sure how the rest of the evening's going to turn out, and I need someone I can trust to take this down . . ."

Five minutes later, Tully settled himself beside Mitch Spencer in the booth and removed the man's cuffs.

Mitch rubbed at his wrist. "I wish you wouldn't cuff me."

"Just a precaution. Okay. Shoot, hotshot. From the top." Tully picked up his coffee.

Mitch sat back. "All right, but it's a waste of time."

He started over, from the beginning, talking slowly and precisely, trying to fill in the smallest details, leaving nothing out, putting it together chronologically, trying—

as he spoke—to make sense of why he did what he did. Of how he could ever have been that desperate, that frantic. It was as if he were reflecting on the actions of a different man. A man he felt he no longer knew.

Tully sat listening intently, eyes wavering from the other man's face only when the waitress came by to refill their cups.

Their food came; a full meal of meat loaf and mashed potatoes for Tully, coffee and cheesecake for Mitch.

Mitch finally brought the story up to date, to the events of that evening. Driving up from L.A., meeting with Dias briefly, accepting the jacket, bidding Dias and his entourage good-bye, checking with Manuel, driving over to meet with Greely—

"Wait a second, you met with Greely earlier this evening?"

"Yes, I told you that, remember? It was no big deal, I was only over there for a few minutes."

"Over where?"

"The Santa Barbara Health Club. I guess he—hey! He must have a membership there! We could check names!"

Tully remained collected. "If he is a member. We'll see. Go on, what else happened?"

Mitch picked at his cheesecake. "We sat there talking, Greely told me how he'd decided to call it quits with Claire, how this would be his last payment to me, but not to worry because the All-American job was practically mine again."

"What else?"

"That's about it. It was hot and uncomfortable in there, I wanted to get out."

"Why hot?"

"We were in this Jacuzzi thing, you know, one of those whirlpool baths. I was broiling. Greely looked like a fat lobster." He thought about it. "I guess it wasn't really Greely, but I don't know what else to call him."

"You were naked in the water."

"Sure, what else?"

269

"Where were your clothes?"

"In the lock—" Mitch looked up sharply.

"Anyone have access to the locker besides you?"

Mitch was almost whispering. "I don't know. Max must have had access to Greely's locker. I remember looking up and he was standing there holding Greely's robe . . ."

"Who's Max?"

"The chauffeur."

"So this guy Max was back there fooling around by the lockers while you and this phony Greely had your little bath, right?"

Mitch nodded. "Jesus . . . you mean you think Max might have planted the photos?"

"Was there any other time during the course of the evening you took off that jacket, Mitch?"

"No. Except for later with Claire. And don't worry, I was watching her every second. No, the only time I had the jacket off was at the health club."

Tully sat back. The spicy meat loaf had started a nagging edge of indigestion. "I'll snoop around the health club tomorrow, see what I can dig up on this alleged imposter. Not that many guys around with a chauffeured Rolls. What color was the car, do you remember?"

Mitch thought. "Dark. Gray with black trim, I'd say."

Tully nodded. "Okay, that's a start."

The waitress reappeared.

"You going to have some dessert this evening, Sergeant?"

Tully patted his stomach. "I don't think so, thanks."

"Got some awful good pie!"

Tully smiled patiently. "Not tonight."

"How about some fresh ice cream? Got all the flavors!"

Tully gave her a jaundiced look.

Which did no good at all. "Strawberry," she drawled on, "Chocolate, Butter Brickle, Mocha Fudge, Tutti-Frutti . . ."

Mitch had been staring absently at the fanny of a young waitress across the room. Now he jolted so hard he knocked scalding coffee across the table nearly into Tully's lap.

Tully jumped. "What the hell—?"

Mitch was half out of his seat, eyes wide with revelation, terrifying the startled waitress who staggered backward, dropping her pad. Mitch grabbed Tully by the arm, fingers digging deep.

"Uncle Joe!"

Tully winced in pain at the tightening fingers.

"Jesus Christ, Tully—tutti-frutti! Who loves Claire more than anything in the whole world? *Uncle Joe!*"

CHAPTER 26

CLAIRE

*T*HE QUESTION NOW WAS: WHERE WOULD SHE GO?

Claire leaned against the tile wall of the small stall shower and let the hot steaming water blast over her, breathing in great lungful of roiling vapor. She smiled wryly to herself: go ahead, just try to wash that man right out of your hair. It isn't going to be that easy.

No. But she had to get on with her life, and now was as good a time to start as any.

She twisted off the muscle-soothing barrage of spray and stepped out of the ship's head, patting herself with one of Dias's fluffy towels.

Dias.

Would she ever see him again? Somehow she didn't think so. Somehow, after tonight, it seemed appropriate to put an end to all of it. To start over with a clean slate.

So the answer to where to go was simple: back to the mansion. Back to Franklyn. Back to her life there.

She dressed quickly, trying not to look at the rumpled bed. She could still smell Mitch on it. Still smell both of them, in fact.

She pulled on pantyhose, sighing. This wasn't going to be easy, not at all. Mitch had told her that Franklyn intended to divorce her.

Well, there was still Jayce and her other friends, card parties, good movies, the opera, the museums. Santa Barbara was hardly a cultural wasteland.

There yet remained a pearly ache between her legs. Sweet Mitch . . .

Damn.

She snatched up her purse, retrieved a comb, and began flicking it through her hair with quick, nearly savage strokes. Time to grow up, old kid, time to put it all in perspective. And even though it hurt—hurt like hell—she had to admit part of her was feeling very good about this, especially the part of her that loved Mitch. He had found himself, and she was truly happy for him. If nothing more, she had helped contribute that to a life. At least one of them knew what he was doing. Now it was her turn. Time to get home.

She paused in combing, caught at her reflection in the mirror.

Still young. Still pretty. Still desirable, obviously.

She sighed, put the comb away.

No, she couldn't go home, not right away, not this soon. She needed to be alone for a time, or at least out of the range of Franklyn's presence. She needed to sit down somewhere, have a cup of coffee, sort this thing out. Yet at the same time she had this terrible fear of being alone . . . this fear that being alone now would remind her of being alone for the rest of her life.

God . . . maybe I shouldn't have let him get away.

Enough of this!

She smoothed her dress, put her compact away, opened the cabin door, and climbed to the deck above.

It was better up here in the crisp night air—that wonderful sea breeze. Maybe she really would go somewhere for a little while, an all-night cafe, somewhere just to think.

Or, better yet!—but no, it was late, she shouldn't. He would be angry. And she had no right to burden another with her late night problems.

But then she scoffed at herself. Bother Uncle Joe? Don't be ridiculous! He'd love to see her. Anytime.

Feeling better already, she hurried down the gang-plank into the night.

At first she thought no one was home.

The exterior lights were out, but that didn't necessarily mean anything. A lot of owners doused their mast lights after midnight.

She descended the teak steps to the main cabin and reached out to knock at his door. It stood ajar.

Claire hesitated, caught between fear and obligation. If anyone was hurting Uncle Joe and she did nothing to help—she'd never forgive herself.

She put an unsteady palm to the smooth wood and pressed inward silently.

All darkness within, save the scant light from the undogged aft ports.

Uncle Joe was lying in bed. Asleep?

But no, she could see now that it wasn't Uncle Joe at all. It was . . .

A woman?

Was Uncle Joe involved with a . . .

On the bed . . .

Tied to the bed . . .

She gawked in disbelief, then almost smiled, backing away clumsily so as not to disturb them. Wasn't this a panic? Uncle Joe!

Except . . .

It didn't feel right.

It didn't—she realized now through quickening breath—fit. The whole atmosphere of the place didn't fit.

Dear God, could she have gotten on the wrong boat?

Claire whirled, stumbled over something that rattled, groped outward and found the door frame again, pushing through, heart hammering heavily. *Get out!*

In the closed-in darkness on the stairs she almost didn't see the big shadow, not until it was blocking her way.

She would have screamed at the tall figure looming there if she hadn't recognized the mustache in time.

"Max! Thank God!" She laughed nervously. "You scared me to death!"

She stepped backward involuntarily.

The mustached man wasn't laughing back.

CHAPTER 27

TULLY

THEY DROVE STRAIGHT BACK TO THE GREELY MAN-
sion and again rousted out the man, who, oddly enough,
was still sitting up with his decanter of brandy.

Yes, Greely knew where Joe Wallace lived—it was
the company's yacht, after all, even though he hadn't
been aboard it in ten years. It was at dock in the Laredo
Bay Marina. Did the officers know where that was?

Tully drove quickly, feeling the familiar rising urgency, the prickly tingle at the back of his neck, that
growing, breathless edge that always accompanied times
like these when things were rushing to conclusion, when
he knew with that sixth sense that the long-searched-for
door had been found, was about to open . . .

He lurched to the curb before twinkling marina
lights and cut the throbbing hum of engine. The sound
of slapping waves rushed in immediately to replace it.

He turned to Mitch, reached across him, secured his
cuffed wrist to the door.

"Hey! I can help!"

"You can help by staying right here. I can't swim."

Mitch yanked irritably at the steel cuff. "What's that got to do with anything?"

Tully opened the door, eased out. "It means that if there's a chubby man in one of those boats that matches your description, I'll bring him out to you—otherwise, there are too many places for a desperate suspect to escape. Now, sit tight and cool your heels, you may survive this one yet." He slammed the door.

Mitch watched him move swiftly, silently, down the boardwalk.

When the detective had disappeared from view, Mitch yanked again furiously at the cuff. He only did it once. It left a red welt around his tortured wrist.

Lips pressed into a flat line, he bent down close, examined the upholstery around the door handle where the cuff was linked. He squinted in the gloom, perceived four large round Phillips screws holding the handle tight against the paneling. He looked about.

A twist of the plastic knob opened the glove compartment. Mitch began to fish around inside, digging under maps, pencil stubs, a half-empty bottle of Brut. In a moment his fingers closed over something cold and smooth. He brought it out, held it to the moonlight.

A slim silver nail clipper.

Mother stood before the full-length mirror, slipping the colorful muumuu over chubby breasts and belly. She straightened it daintily with a twist at the shoulders, and stood back to admire it.

"Do you like it, Buttercup? I was saving it for tonight . . . for this moment."

Claire whimpered puppylike, chewing her lip, the florid colors of the muumuu a gelatinous blur through tear-filled eyes. Max had tied her to a chair the minute she got on board, tied her with practiced efficiency, a touch of malice. She gave an obligatory buck against her bonds, then incredulously, then terror-stricken, as Uncle Joe, *her* Uncle Joe, turned himself into a grotesque parody of a female human.

Mother opened the cedar chest beside the mirror, withdrew the silvery wig, set it neatly in place, adjusting it with practiced fingertips. A bulbous clown.

She began to apply lipstick hurriedly. "Can you begin to know," she started wistfully, "what it is like, sweet Buttercup? Can you possibly imagine, in your dear naîveté, what goes through the mind of an impressionable child when subjected to those kinds of horrors? It wasn't just the men, the endless parade of soft greasy bodies, groping hands, hot fetid breaths. It wasn't the photographs, the blinding flashes of humiliation and shame washing over your young body again and again. It was knowing, deep in your heart, that this was wrong, this was evil, that this was not a thing a child should have to endure ... it was knowing this with an awful dragging certainty, yet being helpless to seek aid! Helpless to turn to your own father—a policeman!—because you were so terrified of what he might think, how he might look upon you, where he might go if he ever found out. That if he ever did go away—far away in his disgust and loathing—he would leave you all alone with her ... with them. All alone in that ongoing pit of vipers ..."

Mother touched the last trace of mascara to her dark lashes and turned.

"And that, dearest Buttercup, was more than any child could bear. Any child who ever lived. I saved you from that fate, darling. Remember? I took you in, protected you. Didn't I?"

Claire blinked back tears, nodding. Mother smiled. "I did the same for Sonny here, did you know? Found him on the streets of New York at fourteen, turning tricks with his own mother! His own foul mother! I rescued him, took him in, loved him as his own mother never could!"

She turned to Max lovingly. "Sonny?"

Sonny lifted the camera, depressed the flash. Claire's flesh flared feverishly.

Mother nodded, moved to his side, kissed his cheek lightly. "Some privacy this time, my sweetness, if you please ..."

Sonny bowed and left the room.

Mother smiled, moved gracefully, sensuously to the edge of the bed. She picked up the stick. Stared down at the dark-haired, still unconcious form lying there.

Were those tears in the heavily made-up eyes? Claire felt her stomach churn.

"If you could know what you meant to me, Buttercup ... if you could begin to fathom what you were to me, how I worshiped you, coveted you, built my miserable life around you. You ... my own sweet Buttercup ... my lovely innocent flower, who would never dream of betraying me ..."

The dark eyes darkened further.

"But you did betray me, didn't you, my darling? You insisted on leaving your warm, safe nest ... even after all the months, all the years I labored on your behalf, to protect you, shield you. If you only knew the trouble I've gone to protect you ... from Dias ... from that traitorous Spencer man ... but most of all from ... from Sonny."

Mother turned toward Claire, eyes soft and loving again, nodding to the other woman tied to the bed. "You knew he had a wife, didn't you, Buttercup?" Claire flinched, staring ridgidly at the woman. "Her name's Joanne, I believe."

Mother turned back to the bed. Smiled. The night-stick descended, a black wand of death, touched a rose-colored areola, puckered the nipple taut, tickled downward across the flat belly, paused at the soft rush of pubis.

"So lovely ..."

The tears again—Mother's tears—falling in fat globules across firm, naked thighs.

"We had an agreement, Mr. Spencer and I, a quite

279

equitable agreement. He would watch you, keep you
from harm on Dias's boat until Dias and I had concluded
our business arrangements. It cost me a great deal, this
agreement"—Mother's face contorted—"until certain parties got *ambitious!*"

Claire shrieked as a ragged point of nail bit Joanne's
lower stomach. A single eye of blood welled. The nightstick snatched back hastily.

Mother's face seemed to shift magically, melt, mascara running in blackened scallops, forehead pinched
in rueful dismay, jowls drooping like a basset's. Claire,
even through the corridor of her terror, thought she
had never seen anything so comically grotesque. She
felt the cold surge of nausea, lingered giddily at the
edge of consciousness.

"I love you, Buttercup. Know now—this night of long
awaited nights—know that I love you. And that when
this is over the three of us will go far from here; just my
own little family. You, me, and Sonny."

Mother turned back to the figure on the bed. Raised
the club again.

Claire bucked desperately, eyes bulging. "You—you
aren't going to kill her! Uncle Joe, no!"

Mother smiled. "Our faithless Mr. Spencer must pay.
I can't let Sonny go to prison, that would hardly do. After
all, he was only obeying his mother. So our Mr. Spencer
must go instead. Just close your eyes, Buttercup, and don't
watch. The lady is sedated. She won't feel a thing . . ."

The club pushed forward.

Claire opened wide for her scream.

"Turn around slowly and drop the billy."

Mother froze.

Claire opened her eyes at the unfamiliar voice, saw
a squat figure occupying the cabin doorway, crouched
professionally, a glint of dark metal held before him. Her
heart surged heavily with a painful jolt of hope.

"Do it! Club on the floor. Turn slowly, hands above
your head. Now!"

Mother did as she was told, eyes blank, face impassive; she might have been a robot.

"Now lace the fingers behind your head, come toward me slowly."

The stranger's face was tight with concentration, eyes riveted, attuned to any sudden moves, gun fingers locked. Yes, a professional, a policeman. A guardian angel.

Too late, Claire came to her senses.

"Hey! There's another one—"

Sonny came crashing in from behind and the guardian angel lurched clumsily forward, gun flying. Claire would remember, as though photographed, the expression on his whitened face—the wide-eyed mixture of startlement and self-reproach—as the floor rushed up to smack him.

Tully sprawled toward the foot of the bunk, arms outstretched to brace him, to grasp for the shiny gun slithering out of his grasp.

One second. One little second, that's all he'd need, and he could gather himself up on his knees, push forward a few precious feet and have his hands around the pebbled grip of the .38. One little second.

But, of course, Sonny never gave him that.

One instant Tully was stretching under the bunk, grasping in the shadows, the next he was screaming in agony as the taller man's hard-toed Italian loafers staved in his upper ribs.

Tully rolled, got his head caught beneath the bunk, screamed again as two more ribs gave way on the other side. Through a reddening haze he began lashing out with the only weapons at his disposal, his legs, thrashing and kicking like a berserk schoolgirl. One caught yielding flesh, followed by a soft grunt, and Sonny pulled back for a moment.

Tully—chest on fire, breath wheezing like an aged accordion—shoved up and caught the edge of the bunk for support. Pulling himself to his feet was like squeezing his upper body through a cheese grater. The pain was so monstrously vivid, the room flickered white, red, white, red. He had just gotten balanced on his heels when Sonny came back to smash his face.

It wasn't the smartest thing the taller man could have done, and it was clear to Tully that his opponent was no streetfighter; if he'd had any sense he'd have gone for the ribs again, which would have put the cop down for good. But he didn't. Tully had taken dozens of licks on the chin, the cheekbones, the temple—he knew how to roll with them, where to give, how to move his aging cop's body. The blow hit hard, all right, but not solid, not flush. Tully took it in stride, slammed back against the bulkhead, and stayed on his feet.

Sonny came in again—fast—still ignoring the ribs— dumb shit—hammering away at the face, the teeth. Tully took them all, grunting, getting his breath: teeth can be replaced, punctured lungs are something else. Then, when Sonny reared back for the haymaker, full of confidence at the sight of his bloodied opponent, Tully moved just the slightest degree to his right at the absolute perfectly timed moment—and Sonny's fist slammed full force into solid steel.

The scream was deafening. But cut short by the rabbit punch to the neck from Tully's flattened left hand, the blow to the solar plexus from Tully's good right fist. Mangled ribs or no, Tully knew he had him now: Sonny had no wind left in him, was doubled up and turning purple, eyes bulging like a frog's, trying to find the bit of breath that his flattened lungs simply would not procure.

Tully grabbed him daintily by the chin, pulled back his good right again, and prepared for the coup de grace.

It would have been so beautiful—and right in front of the pretty blonde lady, too—a perfect knight to a perfect rescue. He could see the commendation and promotion papers. What he couldn't see was the .38 slug from his own gun tearing into his chest.

It didn't spin him about like in the movies, it didn't even jolt him much, but it took all the strength out of his triumphant blow to Sonny; he released Sonny in a

heap and turned in stunned confusion to face his new
tormentor. Mother gave him two more shots in the stomach for his trouble.

This time he slammed backward, squirting blood
like a leaky pipe, crashing into the hard bulkhead again
and down on his hard buttocks ... to lie there in thick-
ening confusion as the blood pooled wider and Mother
put another slug into his shoulder for good measure.

Somebody was screaming, over and over, a terrible,
high-pitched soprano dirge, that Tully—in his rapidly
darkening mind—finally pinpointed as the blonde in the
chair. Nice breasts on the blonde, no wonder Mitch had
flipped out ... a lot like the breasts, the waist, on the
dark-haired girl on the San Francisco slab ...

He wondered, Tully did, if he'd meet the dark-haired
girl now, at long last. Probably, from the way the fat
drag queen was coming across the room toward him,
pointing the gun right between his eyes for a *real* coup
de grace.

Tully saw the hammer go back, saw the ebony bore
line right up with his nose, and had time to wish he had
the strength left to move his right arm just enough to
give this chubby faggot the finger before everything went
black.

At first he thought the Big One had arrived, but there
was still a dim light from somewhere, and he could still
detect the awful, raspy sound of his own breathing. He
finally realized that someone had turned the cabin lights
out.

A smart cop would do that.

A smart cop was charging across the darkened room
now, smashing full tilt against the fat faggot, knocking
them both ass over tea kettle, crashing down with a
sound that shook the small cabin, locking together, rolling, thrashing, cursing, screaming. There were two more
shots that went nowhere and then the click of an empty
chamber. Then more grunts and a single long arm with
something metallic attached to the wrist, reaching out
... reaching out ... for something there on the throw

rug, rolled just beneath that end table. Grasping it now, pulling it back, bringing it up—then down . . . down . . . down until the screams of bloody protest from the fat lips below became gurgling whimpers and the black length of nightstick became shiny and wet and red.

There was still—barely—enough of Tully left for him to see the lights come on again, to see Mitch Spencer standing there with the still dripping billy in his hand, to see him touch the beautiful blonde lady lightly, then to bend with concern to the unconscious woman tied to the bed. Satisfied she was alive and breathing, Mitch found the cordless telephone and put in the ambulance call.

And there was still enough of Tully left to see the ex-cop—who should never have been an "ex" at all—cut the young women free, come over, kneel down, and try to mask his expression as he examined the detective's wounds.

Tully couldn't move, but he could still smile. "Get ahold . . . Fred Wanamaker . . . county coroner . . . he'll know . . ."

Mitch nodded obediently, swallowed drily. "Rest easy now. Ambulance on the way."

There were tears in Mitch's eyes. And Tully thought—as the blackness finally descended—that was about the nicest gift anyone had ever given him.

CHAPTER 28

DIAS

Not that it was relevant now, but Santiago Dias had always secretly hated airports, large or small. Secretly, because air travel was such an integral part of his business these days—the illegal side, at least. And not just for the actual exporting of his "merchandise"; nearly half of the flights were for his business meetings with clients all over the globe: it was a drug world.

So it wouldn't do it to let on to his army of employees, henchmen, and hired killers that the kingpin of South American drugs hated airports, distrusted flying. Without air travel, he could hardly maintain his holdings. It was a necessary evil, like the fax machine, the computer chip, and every other technological gadget that had so recently sped up the world, increased his net worth, added to his headaches, and drawn him—and the rest of humanity—further and further from the genteel life of the country gentleman he both relished and revered.

He had killed and not liked it.

He had swindled and cheated and liked it even less.

He had once anally raped a young Filipino girl in front of a throng of drunken, cheering soldiers merely to impress a fat banana republic dictator with his ruthlessness. An act of defilement to gain the trust of a corrupt, poisonous toad. Later he had secretly paid for the girl's hospital bills and seen that her family received a small fortune, but it had done little to assuage his distaste for the crime. His distaste for himself. In the old days such things would not have been asked of him. In the old days one could do many things yet remain at all cost a gentlemen. But the old days had come and gone. It was a brave new world.

To maintain a foothold in that world, he had done what was necessary. It had brought him much wealth and little happiness. He longed, in private, reflective moments, for the old ways. He envied his father's time, envied more his grandfather's time.

Today it was too late even for reflection.

Today he was here at this private Los Angeles airport not out of business need, but physical necessity.

The fat man was dead. Joe Wallace, his partner in crime. Or near partner. After all the trouble Dias had gone to, finding out his secret vice as well as his pretty blonde Achilles heel! All for nothing!

And the chauffeur had talked. Ejaculated. Vomited every detail of the operation, including Dias's part in it. The newspapers had screamed it, the television and wire services had echoed. There is cocaine and there is coffee, Dias thought ruefully, standing on the tarmac, wind riffling his hair, and never the twain shall meet. Never the twain shall meet.

It had been such an ingenuous plan.

Fool!

He should never have involved himself with a psychopath like Joe Wallace. Still . . . madder schemes have succeeded.   Perhaps . . . perhaps, Santiago, old fellow, your time has merely passed. Perhaps it is time you found other fields of endeavor, new vistas to conquer.

In any case, now is not the time for ruminations, the cat is out of the bag, you are persona non grata in Southern California, in the whole of America, in fact. It is time for a hasty if not altogether graceful departure.

Dias looked at his watch, ears thundering, wind stinging his eyes from the twin Pratt-Whitney engines of the little Cessna warming up at the edge of the runway. Ten after eleven. Where was Mother? This was no time to be fussing with lipstick and powder.

He glanced around at the innocuous little airport. It had cost plenty to get the plane, cost even more just to get safely to the tarmac. Many palms were greased, some of them supposedly official. Dias shook his head. If there was one thing twenty-five years in this business had taught him, it was that the old saw was true: every man his his price. It both succored and disgusted him.

He looked over his shoulder at the small brick terminal behind him. What was Mother doing in there?

Keeping the newspaper and television from her was hard enough, concocting the story about an emergency business meeting back in Bogotá difficult in itself. He hadn't planned on having to unglue her from the terminal ladies' room before the whole place was surrounded by olive drab uniforms and wryly smiling American gendarmes, all of whom had been itching for an excuse to get their cuffs on him for months.

He glanced at his watch again: twenty after eleven.
Damn.

He looked to the thrumming fuselage before him. He could not see the pilot's face clearly from here, but he could imagine the impatience and anxiety lining it.

Christ. He'd have to go back and get her. He turned, but now here she came, mane of frosty silver hair in disarray, lugging her heavy purse gallantly if awkwardly.

Dias couldn't suppress a smile. Seventy-two years old and as full of energy as the day she bore him. Dearest Mother. What would life be like without her? He really couldn't imagine.

Something about the way she was walking . . .

Just the slightest inconsistency, but a son knows his mother. Something was amiss . . .

The eyes. Always alight with love for him, that was still there, but clouded now by something else. Something Santiago didn't want to think about.

The weathered, sun-baked face: handsome, strong, carved with self-assurance, the wealth and poverty of the past, the lessons those two extremes can teach if one is willing to listen. Mother was willing. Mother was wise. Wise beyond her years, certainly well beyond his own. Am I about to find out, Dias wondered, just how wise she can really be?

"Mother, are you ready?"

She didn't answer.

Now, on closer inspection of her purse, he saw the rolled end of the *Los Angeles Times* peeking from above the hasp. And now the vein-webbed hand dipping into that purse, withdrawing the bright silvery glare of the little chrome automatic.

"Mother—?" Almost laughing. Not quite, though.

They stood that way for a moment: she with the gun, he with his incredulity.

"Time to go home, Sonny."

There was great sadness in the voice, wrenching sadness, but great confidence, too, the old self-assurance still in place. She could fend off an army if necessary. How big you are, he was thinking, how strong, how magnificently *you!* How terrible and how sublime. Thank you God in heaven for giving this wonderful woman to me.

He was smiling, not really feeling it. "That's what I'm trying to do, Mother, take us home."

The gun hand didn't flinch. "No. Not that home."

He shrugged confusion. "What then? We can't stay here . . ."

She was tapping her chest with the bright barrel. "The home inside here, Santiago, the home inside your soul."

He wanted to look at his watch. The twin engines behind him gunned impatiently.

"Mother. You're tired. It's been exhausting, I'm sorry. May I have the gun, please?"

She looked down at the weapon as if seeing it for the first time. "How many times, Sonny? How many times did you pull the trigger of some similar instrument? How much blood has been spilled in the name of our success— a stream, a river, an ocean? *Jesus Cristo*, where did I fail you? Can you tell me, my darling son, where under God's heaven did I first fail you? Was it after your father died?"

"Mother ..." His throat was irritatingly dry. This was not the time for clumsy emotion; later, perhaps when they were safe, now they must hasten. "Mother, the police will be here soon, any moment. Please get in the plane."

"I'm staying."

He wanted so much to laugh; why couldn't he? Whence came this impending, irrevocable sense that something vast and significant was at an end, that a great gray wall was descending, over which he could never again find the strength, the selfishness to climb?

"Mother ... I've spent a great deal of money toward our escape. There isn't time for talk now. Where did you find the newspaper, discarded in the ladies' room? Mother, we have to go now!"

"I should have insisted you marry that young Cuban girl, she loved you so. She would have been good to you. I should have made you sell the business the moment your father died. I thought you—we—could cut out the cancer your father let invade the business. But no. We have only let it spread. Why was I so stupid, Santiago? Tell your mother, *por favor!*"

"Mother—"

"*Que hora es, Santiago?*"

He glanced at his watch, grateful for the opportunity. "Eleven-thirty, Mama, we must hurry!"

Mrs. Dias nodded solemnly, eyes brimming. "*Bueno.* It ends at this moment." She lifted the gun.

Dias smiled. "Mama. You would not shoot me. Never."

The mixture of love and resolve in her eyes went straight to the heart of him. "I brought you into this world, *chico*. I raised you, taught you . . . now is the time for the final lesson. I closed my eyes to the others because they were already heading toward their own kind of death . . . but with this man Wallace, with this man my son has made a deal with the devil. He sinned against nature, he mutilated innocent women! Mothers, taken away from their children for his own sick pleasure, and you knew! You protected him for your own gain! God will not allow this, nor will I. This is a sin against humanity. I should have stopped you long ago, but I loved you so . . . more than I loved God. Now it is too late. I have already contacted the authorities, Santiago. It is time for the evil to end."

Yes, he thought, she *would* shoot me. And then, perhaps, herself.

He stepped forward, took the gun from her fingers, flung it far across the tarmac. He reached for her, crushed her to him. The world swam gelatinously through his own tears. "Mama."

Behind him he could hear the big engines turning the Cessna into the runway preparatory to takeoff. Ahead of him a wall of green-clad figures were ringing the brick façade of the terminal. Dias held his mother.

She clung to him, dampening his expensive silk shirt. "It is over, *chico*, it is over . . ."

He rocked her gently, looking past her flowered shoulder at the approaching squadron of uniforms, black muzzles glinting in the sun. The plane behind him took off with a dwindling roar.

He was thinking about how much he knew, about how valuable his life was to these men, about one final bargain . . . about how impossible life would seem without the ranch in Colombia—how empty it would be without Mother, how much he had hurt her, disgraced her, disgraced his father, himself. He was thinking how much he'd miss the yacht, his collection of rare paintings, how much he'd miss the business and how glad he was to be done with it.

He was thinking how very light, nearly giddy he suddenly felt, how blue and beautiful the California sky was, and how a man could grow to love such a sky. He was thinking he was as close as he was ever likely to get to something approaching peace.

He was still thinking these thoughts, still clinging tightly to his mother, when the men in green surrounded them.

CHAPTER 29

MITCH

*T*HE TRICK NOW WAS NOT TO THINK.

Thinking led to speculating about his future, speculating led to anxiety, anxiety led to tears, tears led to breaking down. He'd broken down three times already this month. That was enough. Enough to teach him the invaluable lesson that while falling apart provided a certain momentary, heart-wrenching relief, in the long run it offered little more than puffy eyes, dripping nose, and an inconvenient loosening of the bowels.

So Mitch elected not to think. He tried to keep busy. Which wasn't hard in the beginning; the apartment needed work—a lot of work!—and there was all his clothing and books and records to be moved out of the house he shared with Joanne and into this little dump here in Westwood. He stretched that out as long as possible, making far more trips than were absolutely necessary, inconveniencing everyone, delaying the inevitable and, in the end, finally pissing Joanne off even more than she already was. Finally though, the last trip back and forth was completed, the last toothbrush and nail clipper was secured. Westwood was his.

That at least was a break, finding a place he could afford in expensive, trendy Westwood. The apartment itself was horrific—grime-layered floors, rusted-out bathroom, walls webbed with enough cracks to make you believe the Big One had already come and gone, an army of roaches who glowered at him every time he didn't leave enough food on the already gummy counter—but the area itself was good: clean, respectable, close to shopping, theaters, and, most of all, the business section he was so dutifully scouring for some signs, any signs of employment. The truth was, he almost enjoyed walking the Westwood streets at night all alone, ducking in and out of the antiquarian bookstores, the overpriced clothing stores, the umpteen million bistros, delis, and restaurants, the plethora of immaculately maintained, grandiose movie houses where you could sit in wide-screen comfort in a sizeable auditorium and watch the latest 70-millimeter-Dolby-THX Sound extravaganza with your box of real buttered popcorn.

Westwood was Los Angeles's answer to a car dealer's showroom. Someone once described it as a concession stand surrounded by movie houses. It kept Mitch occupied. It kept the tears out of those weary eyes. It kept him from thinking about Joanne, about his daughter, about how totally he'd managed to fuck up his—their—lives.

At least most of the time it did.

The rest of time he sat around stupidly in his shitty little apartment, watched the roaches crawl lazily across the blurry screen of the secondhand black-and-white TV he'd picked up cheap—which delivered mostly snow because the building wasn't equipped for cable—and fought off the periodic urges toward self-pity, tears, and the B-word: breakdown.

So he sat a lot. And thought a lot. And walked a lot.

Curiously, he didn't think about Claire Greely all that much, other than superficial ruminations of their

lovemaking, which, though remembered as galactic, remained strangely elusive to him now, the details evading
real scrutiny, receding daily in clarity. He'd had a post-
card from her, a short note from the East saying that she
and her husband were going to try a reconciliation. He'd
read it once and thrown it in the trash. The whole affair
was becoming dreamlike, a phantom footnote to his life,
stalking the periphery of his mind like an impatient
gazelle anxious to take flight.

Incredible. How could anything so passionately in-
spired become so drearily plebian?

It made you wonder about the meaning of life.

Which might have been an interesting way to wile
away the hours if he weren't so desperately in need of a
job. Of course he'd had to return all the money.

So far, employers weren't beating down his door.
The fact that he was without a phone didn't help. Even
if some potential employer really were interested it was
next to impossible for them to get hold of him. The phone
company had an interesting explanation for that: something about yes, the building had a phone line but the
line needed to be replaced and the pole outside was
infested with termites, which made it dangerous to
climb, which might be okay except that they shared that
line with the utlity company who didn't want a new pole
installed right now, but it was just a matter of time
before they would, so just be patient please and they'd
have a phone for him any day now except that of course
he'd have to buy his own phone, the phone company
didn't furnish that service anymore, was he aware of
that?

He lost weight.

Mitch had never been able to stomach the idea of TV
dinners, and he knew next to nothing about cooking except
boiling hot dogs or fixing popcorn. He didn't have the
money to keep eating out all the time. And did Joanne ever
call once in a lousy while to maybe invite him over for a
real home-cooked meal? Ha! Not on your life.

It had its own kind of inverse effect. The longer he

lived in the little rat trap, the more he felt, okay, he'd done his goddamn penance, it was time to forgive and forget, then the more she totally ignored him. And the more she did this, the more he hated her for it, which at the same time made him curiously horny for her, even desperately so. Sex between them had been average at best. Now, perversely, he found himself masturbating on his lumpy bed with his wallet picture of her before him, uttering words like "bitch" and "whore" as he came. Then lying there in the darkness staining the already stained sheets with his tears.

The simple, deplorable fact was, he still loved her.

The weeks passed.

He sat, he walked, he wept.

Which was how he found himself the night someone rapped on the wood-scarred door and it turned out to be her.

She'd done something to her hair. Of course she looked beautiful. He was sure she was dating someone. He wanted to kill them both.

"You're sitting in the dark?" He hated her lovely voice.

He stood there with one hand on the jamb, blinking through the remnants of his tears, drowning in the dizzying maelstrom of her perfume. "They turned off my lights—late with the bill."

"Are you going to ask me in?"

He stepped back.

She came into darkness and immediately stumbled over a chair, raking her shin. She caught herself and collapsed onto his garage sale sofa. "Jesus, Mitch . . ."

"Sorry. Does it hurt?"

"No, it feels great."

He felt himself stiffen. Same old crap. He missed her when she wasn't around, then when she shows up—

"Would you like something to drink?"

"Can you find the kitchen?"

He sighed, gave up. "Look, Joanne, what is it you want? Child support? I'm just about drained."

She didn't answer for a moment, gazed solemnly around the room, irises adjusting to the gloom.

"How's work?" he offered at last, hoping still for some mythical peace between them. God, would she ever forgive? Ever?

"Good. They want to make me a branch manager."

"That's great, Joanne."

He meant it. His incredible wife, who had done little more than play tennis, overspend his income, and mess up the house for over five years, suddenly applies for a job at the real estate office where she'd worked before they married, gets her license by studying at night, and zing, right up the ladder. She was making nearly as much now as his old job had paid him before he was fired. All this and preggers, too. Ain't life funny?

"I'm due in five months," she said quietly, "in case you've forgotten."

"I haven't forgotten, Joanne."

Silence.

Then, after a time: "I know you haven't," softly, from her.

He had the most imperious desire to kiss her. Some women break out and get sallow-faced during pregnancy; Joanne's was the kind that made her glow with an inner luminescence. Naturally. He could just make out the small curve of her abdomen beneath the soft blue fabric; before long, he knew from experience, it would be billowing.

"Any prospects, Mitch? For a job?"

"Not much. I need a phone."

He saw her head swivel in the dimness as she appraised the room. "You need a lot more than that."

He tightened again. "Did you come up here to humiliate me?"

"Yes." Pointedly.

He looked at her, startled. "You did?"

"You're not half trying, Mitch."

He bridled. "To get a job? The hell I'm not!"

"The hell you are. Look at you, it's been a month. You're just sitting around here in Westwood jerking off."

She meant it figuratively, but she didn't know the half of it.

"What the fuck do you know about it?"

"I know you."

"Meaning what? I'm lazy?"

"Hardly. You're driven. Just in the wrong directions."

"Joanne, what are you talking about?"

"Get off your ass, Mitch."

"I am off my ass!"

"Be something."

"Like you?"

"Yes, like me. Get on with your life."

"Look, why don't you go home?"

"Quit sitting around here blubbering."

"Who's blubbering?"

"You were crying before I got here."

"Fuck you!"

"That's being taken care of, thank you."

The room went white. "You goddamn bitch!"

He was up and on her before he knew it.

He had his fingers around her throat and was pushing her hard into the sofa, shrieking and bawling at the same time. Joanne watched with calm, patient eyes, and when he crushed his mouth to hers she gave him her tongue without hesitation. He tore open her dress front and got to her breasts with a kind of whimpering convulsion. She had to undo the bra snap for him. He kept sobbing and calling her names, but when he reached between her legs she pushed his hand away. "Careful, the baby. Here . . ."

She turned her back to him, knees punching the lousy sofa, and lifted the dress.

He came too quickly, but it was the best he could ever remember. "Oh, Joanne . . . oh Christ . . ."

"Stop crying," she whispered, "and stay there a moment. There. Push now. Yes. Oh."

Afterwards she lay in his arms and he listened to the baby inside her.

"Are you really," he asked, " 'being taken care of?' "

"No. Of course not. I'm pregnant, idiot. Who would want me, besides you?"

He sighed huge relief. "Do you know how much I love you?"

She pondered. "Show me."

"I just did."

She moved a little and he looked up at her; there was something in her expression.

"What?" he asked.

"This sofa sucks."

He pulled back. "Come on, what is it?"

She looked away, a trifle distant again? He felt a pang, they had been so close, so warm, after so long . . .

"I have to quit work for a while, of course, to have the baby . . ."

"Yes?"

She formed her words carefully. "I like my job, Mitch. I want to keep it."

He waited.

"I can't ask my mom to look after the baby all the time and Nellie can't stay at Kinder-Care past six—I often work later than that."

He was still too set in the old ways to even dream of what was coming.

"I think . . . you should move back in, Mitch. Look after the children."

He looked at her, mind blank.

She turned to watch him. "What do you think?"

"Clean the house and stuff, you mean?"

"Yes, part of it. You're better at it than me anyway. Anyone is."

He sat back, staring at the ceiling.

He cleared his throat. "What about us?"

"What about us?"

"We'd live together?"

"Yes."

"Sleep together?"

"Yes."

"And—"

"I'll fuck you, Mitch, yes."

His heart swelled until it hurt. "You've forgiven me, then?"

"No."

"But you will, someday?"

"No."

He turned to her. "Then why—? What will we have?"

She wrapped her arms about herself. "We'll have what we always had, Mitch. And we'll have something else, too. I wish we wouldn't, but we will. We always will. Did you expect it to just go away?"

He closed his eyes. "No."

"Well, then."

After a moment he reached out, put a palm to the tightening balloon of her stomach. "We'll have another something else, too, though. I haven't given you only pain, Joanne."

She ran a hand across her girth, smiled wistfully. "No . . . not only pain."

After a time he said, "Are you crying, Joanne?"

"No."

"I wish you would cry."

"I know, so do I. Maybe some day."

"I cry all the time."

"You're lucky," she said to the darkness.

He moved back home that night.

CHAPTER 30

TULLY

*H*E SAT AT THE HELM, SEA BREEZE IN HIS HAIR—
against the naked, sun-baked skin of his chest—feeling
an ease, a contentment that heretofore would have
eluded him.

It was just about a perfect day. Ocean nearly flat,
just some small whitecaps, enough wind to keep the sails
fat, to keep the little red ketch clipping along south-
southeast at a comfortable, comforting twenty knots.

They were heading for the Marquesas Islands, French
Polynesia. Tully had wanted to try it all his life. Now he
had the vessel, now he had the time.

The sun sat on the horizon, a squashed tangerine,
radiating amber twilight. It had been the right thing to
do. He didn't even have to weigh that anymore. He felt
as free in spirit as he was in locale.

Mother had been surprisingly amenable, as though
she'd been waiting for him to suggest it all along. He
hadn't even had to put her in the Home; the sale of the
house plus his promotion money had bought her a small,

300

comfortable condo, where a maid came once a week and someone tended the grounds. She had made the move willingly.

Tully himself had pulled down the FOR SALE sign on the ketch, handed it to the owner with a grin.

In his heart he knew it was for the better, all around.

Tully popped another top and let the cold beer slip down his throat, drip across his broad chest. He didn't bother to wipe at it; let it drip, he was on vacation. At last.

The skinny blonde came out of the hold and winked at him. She had on a green bikini, the 1950s model from the store, the one she had to keep adjusting at the top because there was barely enough up there to fill it. The bottom half, though, that was something else. Any adjusting there, he'd see to it.

She came toward him, smiling, amber light playing along the endless, delicious legs. You're a dirty old man, he thought, and it was a nice, warm, appropriate thought to think: she was a dirty young woman.

She came beside his chair, bent to kiss the top of his thinning hair, took the cold can from him and took a sip of her own. Her hair stirred like golden wheat.

"It's like a dream," she murmured, gazing out at the endless peace and beauty of it, "like the most wonderful kind of dream . . . "

He squeezed her hand, kissed her tanned wrist.

I just want to sail, he was thinking lazily, to sail on and on till we come to the end of the world . . . and then sail right off it . . .

They held hands that way for a time.

EPILOGUE

FRED WANAMAKER, COUNTY CORNER, FINISHED UP IN his lab late that night. He washed his hands with antiseptic soap, donned his jacket, and switched off the lights in the morgue.

He came upstairs with a deliberate, measured gait, knowing exactly where he was going, passed though the darkened, cemetery-quiet of the offices, passed by Detective Tully's empty desk with hardly a nod toward it, and heading toward the soft yellow glow of the glass-enclosed office down the hall. Fred Wanamaker wasn't the only one working late tonight.

The office door was open so he stepped inside quietly.

Wanamaker's back was to the darkened rooms outside—even the janitor had gone home—so the man at the desk did not see his shadowed sihouette at first.

After a moment, though, the man looked up.

"Fred! Evening. Burning the midnight oil?"

Fred smiled obligingly, remained by the door. "Looks like two of us are, Captain Sparrs."

Sparrs shrugged, jotted at a page before him. "Gotta keep up with this paperwork. Let it go too long and you can't see over the desk."

Fred nodded. "Know what you mean."

After another minute, Sparrs looked up again.

"Something I can do for you, Fred?"

Fred smiled.

Sparrs frowned, put down his pen. "What the hell are you grinning at?"

Fred shifted his weight against the jamb. "It was you, wasn't it, you bastard?" he intoned softly.

Sparrs watched him.

"You set fire to the microfilm spools."

Sparrs leaned back, swivel chair squealing protest. "You feelin' all right, Fred?"

Fred smiled. "Funny thing is, Tully knew. He knew before he went over there that night. He phoned me . . ."

Sparrs folded his arms behind his head. "Just what is it you're trying to say, Fred?"

Wanamaker came a step into the circle of light. "It will be months until the trial, but we pretty much know what's what. We know almost everything about that fat maniac buried down in the public cemetery. It took a lot of doing—he covered his tracks well. Or somebody did, anyway. Somebody whose job meant more to him than his family, somebody who cared more about being shamed than he did about what was happening to his own child."

"You're nuts! Get outta here!" Sparrs's eyes kept flicking to the top drawer of his desk.

Fred took a step closer. "Was he a fat little boy, too, or was he pretty? Pretty enough for that psycho wife of yours to sell his body on the beach? What'd you do about it, Sparrs? Just sit there and watch her buy stuff with the money he earned her, sit there on your impotent ass while she turned your little boy into a murdering psycho? Look people make mistakes; it can happen. You don't always know what's going on under your own roof, do you?" He said this last almost gently and Sparrs looked up, tears in his eyes, eyes that were begging forgiveness.

"I can understand that . . . what I can't understand is how you could let him do it and not stop him. Because you knew who the beach killer was, didn't you? That's why you took Tully off the case, Sparrs, put a dim bulb like Brumeister in his place."

"No—"

"He called you, didn't he? Told you that he would quit slaughtering innocent women if you nailed Mitch Spencer. I guess he thought if he got rid of Spencer's wife, the charge would really stick. What happened to his mother, Sparrs? The real mother?"

Sparrs swallowed thickly. Said nothing for a time. Then: "She died . . . tried to abort herself . . ."

"What'd she use to induce it, Sparrs? Your nightstick?"

Sparrs turned his ravaged face into the light, eyes lifeless. "What are you going to do, Fred? It's over. Joe is dead. The chauffeur only knows so much, otherwise you wouldn't be here jawing, you'd be talking to the prosecutor. You don't have any real proof. You can prove I'm his father, maybe, but you can't prove I protected him. You can't!"

"You're right. I can't prove it." Fred Wanamaker turned back toward the door.

Turned back. "But Tully won't be away forever."

And left Sparrs sitting there.

Fred Wanamaker sat in the Spartan hospital room beside the figure with all the tubes and wires and machinery.

The straight-back chair with the flat cushion was hurting his ass, but he had only a few minutes more anyway, Ellen would be fixing dinner.

He had brought flowers, but he didn't know where

to put them—the bedside table had been full—so he ended up just setting them on the floor next to the wall, hoping it didn't look too stupid. He didn't know what kind of flowers to get a man anyway, that had been Ellen's idea. Anyway, what's a comatose patient going to do with flowers?

Fred leaned forward and studied the swollen, bruised face. It was stuffed with plastic tubes, one of which rattled pneumatically, in and out, in and out . . .

"Thought you might like to know, Tully, the lady cop—what's her name, Rene Draper—finally came out of it. Yeah. So there's hope for you, too, old buddy! I'm going to bring her in here to see you as soon as she's up to it. She wants to meet the man who solved the Laredo Beach Killings!"

Fred licked his lips, leaned closer. "Can you hear me in there?" He lowered his voice to a stage whisper. "Randall Gaylord wants me to tell you he cleaned out all the drawers on the Joe Wallace yacht, got a lot of stuff in writing. You were right all along, Tully—the father was a cop. It was Sparrs. Yeah. If he'd left you on the case, it would have been solved long ago."

Fred smiled proudly. "You were right all along, you smart old son of a bitch, you lateral thinker. And we need you back, partner. The fat man is pushing up daisies, but the chauffeur is talking. And we picked up Dias, he was part of the cover-up from the beginning! We need you up there on the stand now, buddy, so we can put these bastards away for good."

Wanamaker pulled back, swallowed, sniffed.

"So how about it, Tully? Don't make us wait all year, huh? These goddamn hospital chairs are killing my butt."

The plastic tubes rattled and wheezed.

There was a movement at the door. A blonde head peeked in.

Fred turned. "It's okay, Kim, I was just leaving. Come sit down."

He stood, pulled the chair over for Kim Dillinger,

patted her thin back as she sat down. She was wearing one of the old dresses from the store, one with those funny padded shoulders. Why would a pretty girl want to dress like that? Why didn't she put on some weight?

"How is he?" she said sweetly.

Fred grabbed his coat. "He's going to be fine, don't you worry."

The skinny girl turned toward the broad, bruised face on the bed. "I know that," she replied softly.

At the door, Fred turned. She was holding the detective's hand.

"Going to be here all night again?" he asked, pulling on the coat.

"Maybe."

Fred watched them a moment before leaving. He nodded at the two clasped hands, one large and bronzed, one small and pale. "Think that helps?"

She sat watching the still face, squeezed the big hand once.

"You never know," she said.